**Nicola Cornick's novels
have received acclaim the world over**

'Cornick is first-class, queen of her game.'
—*Romance Junkies*

'A rising star of the Regency arena'
—*Publishers Weekly*

**Praise for the
SCANDALOUS WOMEN OF THE TON series**

'A riveting read'
—*New York Times* bestselling author Mary Jo Putney on
Whisper of Scandal

'One of the finest voices in historical romance'
—*Single Titles.com*

'Ethan Ryder (is) a bad boy to die for! A memorable story
of intense emotions, scandals, trust, betrayal and all-
encompassing love. A fresh and engrossing tale.'
—*Romantic Times* on *One Wicked Sin*

'Historical romance at its very best is
written by Nicola Cornick.'
—Mary Gramlich, *The Reading Reviewer*

Acclaim for Nicola's previous books

'Witty banter, lively action and sizzling passion'
—*Library Journal* on *Undoing of a Lady*

'RITA® Award-nominated Cornick deftly steeps her
latest intriguingly complex Regency historical in a
beguiling blend of danger and desire.'
—*Booklist* on *Unmasked*

D0268565

Nicola Cornick

THE LADY AND THE LAIRD

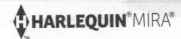

First published in Great Britain 2013
Harlequin MIRA, an imprint of Harlequin (UK) Limited,
Eton House, 18-24 Paradise Road,
Richmond, Surrey, TW9 1SR

© Nicola Cornick 2013

ISBN 978 1 848 45259 6

54-0913

Printed and bound by
CPI Group (UK) Ltd, Croydon, CR0 4YY

To Margaret McPhee, who writes delicious
books and shares delicious cakes

PROLOGUE

Forres Castle, Scotland, June 1803

IT WAS A NIGHT made for magic.

The moon was new that night and the sea was a thread of shining silver. The wind sighed through the pine trees and there was the scent of salt on its edge.

"Lucy! Come and watch!"

Lady Lucy MacMorlan turned over in bed and drew the covers up more closely about her ears. She was warm and cozy and she had no urge to leave the cocoon of the blankets in order to shiver in the draught by the window. Besides, she did not want to join in with her sister Alice in casting a spell. They were foolish and dangerous and would only get the two of them into trouble.

"I'm not getting up," she said, wriggling her toes in the warmth. "I don't want a husband."

"Of course you do." Alice sounded impatient. At sixteen, Lucy's twin was fascinated by balls and gowns and men. Earlier that evening, Alice had run three times around the ancient sundial in the castle grounds, reciting the words of the equally ancient love spell that on the new moon would give her a glimpse of the man she would wed. Lucy had stayed in the library, reading a copy of Hume's *Essays Moral and Political*. Now, after sunset, Alice was awaiting the outcome of her enchantment.

"Of course you will marry," Alice said again. "What else would you do?"

Read, Lucy thought. Read and write and study. It was more fun.

"Everyone marries." Alice sounded grown-up, knowledgeable. "We are to make alliances and have children. It's what the daughters of a duke do. Everyone says so."

Marry. Have children.

Lucy thought about it, considering the idea rationally as she did all ideas. It was true that it was expected of them, and no doubt it was what their mother would have wanted. She had died when Lucy and Alice were no more than a few years old, but everyone said she had been the diamond of her generation, the elegant daughter of the Earl of Stratharnon who had made a dazzling match and produced a perfect brood of children. Lucy and Alice's elder sister Mairi was eighteen and already wed. Lucy was not averse to the idea, but she thought she would have to meet a man who was more interesting than a book, and that was more difficult than it sounded.

"Lucy!" Alice's voice had turned sharp. "Look! Oh look, some of the gentlemen are coming out onto the terrace with their brandy! Which one will I see first? He will be my true love."

"You have windmills in your head," Lucy said, "to believe such nonsense."

Alice was not crushed. She never listened when she was excited. Their father was hosting a dinner that evening, but both his younger daughters were still in the schoolroom and had not been invited. There was a pause. Through the open window, Lucy could hear the sound of voices from below now, masculine laughter. A trace of cigar smoke tickled her nose. There was the clink of glass on stone.

"Oh!" Alice sounded intrigued. "Who is that? I can't see his face clearly—"

"That will be because he has his back to you," Lucy said crossly. She was trying to sleep, but it was impossible while Alice kept talking. "Remember the spell. If he has his back to you, that means he will be a false love, not a true one."

Alice made a dismissive sound. "It's one of Lord Purnell's sons, but which?"

"They are all too old for you," Lucy said. She hunched a shoulder against her sister's chatter. "Don't let anyone see you," she added. "Papa will be furious to hear of one of his daughters hanging out of the window in her nightgown. You'll be ruined before you are even out."

Alice was still not listening. She never listened if she did not want to hear. She was like a butterfly, bright and inconsequential, flitting off, paying no attention. "It is Hamish Purnell," she said. She sounded disappointed. "He is already wed."

"I told you it was nonsense," Lucy said.

"Oh, they are arguing!" Excitement leaped into Alice's voice again. She was as changeable as a weather vane, all disappointment forgotten in a moment. She threw Lucy a glance and then pushed the window open higher, leaning out of the stone embrasure. "Lucy!" she hissed. "Come and see!"

Lucy had heard the change in the voices from the terrace. One moment everything had been smooth and civilized, and the next there was an edge of anger, violence, even, that rippled across her skin, making the hairs stand on end. She slid from the bed and padded across the floor to where Alice was kneeling on the window seat, her body tense as a strung bow, to witness the scene below.

Two men were confronting each other on the terrace directly beneath them. They stood sideways to Lucy, so she could see neither of their faces. She recognized her cousin Wilfred's voice though, smooth, patrician, holding the slightest sneer.

"Why are you here tonight, Methven? You're no one, a younger son. I cannot believe my uncle invited you."

His tone was full of contempt and deliberate provocation. Someone laughed. The men pressed closer, almost encircling the pair like a pack of dogs closing in, sensing a fight.

"Oh!" Alice said. "How rude and horrible Wilfred is! I hate him!"

Lucy had always hated her cousin Wilfred too. He was eighteen, heir to the earldom of Cardross, and he reveled in his status and his family connection to the Duke of Forres. He had spent the past year in London, where rumor said he had spent all his substance on drink and cards and women. Wilfred was snobbish, conceited and boorish, and here, surrounded by his kinsmen and followers, he thought he was brave.

"Perhaps the duke invited me because he has more manners than his nephew," the other man said. His voice had rougher overtones than Wilfred's drawl and a hint of Scots burr. He did not step back before Wilfred's intimidation. He turned and Lucy suddenly saw his face in the light of the new moon. It was strong, the cheekbones, brow and jaw uncompromisingly hard. He was broad, too, wide in the shoulder and tall. Yet studying him, Lucy could see he was still young, no more than nineteen or twenty perhaps.

A whisper went through the men on the terrace. The atmosphere changed. It was more openly antagonistic now, but there was something else there, too, a hint of uncertainty, almost of fear.

Alice evidently felt it too. She had withdrawn into the shelter of the thick velvet curtains that cloaked the window.

"It's Robert Methven," she whispered. "What is *he* doing here?"

"Papa invited him," Lucy whispered back. "He says he has no time for feuds. He considers them uncivilized."

The Forres and the Methven clans had traditionally been enemies. The Forreses and their kinsmen the earls of Cardross had held for the Scottish crown since time immemorial. The Methvens had been brigands from the far north, descended from the Viking earls of Orkney, a law unto themselves. Lucy knew little about the Methvens other than that they were reputed to be as fierce and elemental as their ancestors. She looked down on Robert Methven's face, etched so clear and sharp in the moonlight, and felt a shiver of something primitive echo down her spine.

Enemies for generations... It was in the blood, in the stories she had been told from the cradle. Clan warfare might be a thing of the past, but it was not long gone and old enmities died hard.

"One day," Wilfred was saying, "I'll take back the land your family stole from our clan, Methven, and I'll make you pay. I swear it."

"I'll look forward to that." Robert Methven sounded amused. "Until then, shall we partake of some more of the duke's excellent brandy?"

He walked straight past Wilfred as though the conversation no longer interested him. Wilfred, looking foolish, barged past him to assert his precedence and go through the drawing room door first. Methven shrugged his broad shoulders, uncaring.

Alice let the curtain fall back into place. "I'm cold," she grumbled. "I'm going to bed."

Lucy struggled to reach up and pull the casement window closed. It was just like Alice to leave her to tidy up. That was the trouble with Alice; she was careless and thoughtless and Lucy was always having to smooth matters over for her.

"Hamish Purnell…" she heard Alice murmuring as she slipped beneath the covers of the bed. "Well, I suppose he is quite handsome."

"He's *married*," Lucy reminded her. "Besides, he had his back to you when you first saw him."

"He turned round," Alice argued. "Face to me, back to the sea. True love. Perhaps his wife will die. Be sure to close the window properly, Lucy," she added, "so no one knows we were watching."

Lucy sighed, still struggling to shift the window, which remained obstinately stuck. The heavy velvet hem of the curtain knocked over the blue-and-white china vase on the shelf by her elbow. She watched as in slow motion the vase teetered on the edge, escaped her grasping fingers and tumbled through the open window to smash on the terrace below. Transfixed, she stared down into the darkness. Nothing moved. No one came. She could see the broken shards gleaming in the moonlight as they lay scattered on the stones.

"You've got to go and pick it up." Alice's voice reached her in an urgent whisper. "Otherwise they'll find it and know we were watching."

"You go down," Lucy said crossly. "I didn't knock the vase over," Alice argued.

"Neither did I!" For all their age, there was a danger of this degenerating into a nursery quarrel. "You go," Lucy said. "It was your idea to hang out of the window like a strumpet."

"If I get caught I'll be in trouble again," Alice said. Suddenly her bright face looked young and anxious and Lucy felt a pang of something that felt oddly like pity. "You know how Papa is always telling me how Mama would have been ashamed of how naughty I am."

Lucy sighed. She could feel herself weakening. She would never get Alice into trouble. It was part of the pact between them, binding them closer than close, sisters and best friends forever. Lucy sighed again and reached for her robe and slippers.

"If you go down the steps in the Black Tower, you will be there quickly and no one will see you," Alice said.

"I know!" Lucy snapped. Nevertheless she felt a frisson of disquiet as she grabbed her candle and opened the door a bare few inches, enough to slide out. She stole silently along the corridor to the tower stair. It was not that Forres Castle frightened her. She had grown up here and she knew every nook and cranny of the ancient building, all its secrets and all its ghosts. It was flesh and blood she feared, not the supernatural. She could not afford to get caught. She never got into trouble, never did anything wrong. Alice was the impetuous one, tumbling from one scrape into another. Lucy was good.

Nevertheless when she had drawn the bolt on the heavy door at the base of the stairs and pushed it gently open, she allowed herself a moment to enjoy the night. The breeze was soft on her face, laced with the scents of the sea and the soapy smell of the gorse. The sound of the distant waves mingled with the sighing of the pines. The moon was sickle-sharp and golden in a sky of deep velvet. For a moment Lucy had the mad idea to go running across the lawns and down to the sea, to feel the cool sand between her toes and the lap of the cold water on her bare legs.

Of course she would never do it. She was far too well behaved.

With a little sigh she bent to collect the shattered pieces of the blue-and-white pot. The maids would notice the loss and would no doubt report it. Her father would be upset, for it had been one of the late duchess's favorite pieces. There would be questions and explanations; lies. She and Alice would have to admit that they had broken it, just not that it had happened when they had been leaning out of the window to ogle young men. She hoped her papa would not be too disappointed in her.

"Can I help you with that?"

Lucy jumped and spun around, the shards falling for a second time from her fingers. Robert Methven was standing facing her, his back to the sea. Up close he was as tall, as broad as he had seemed from her vantage point above.

"I didn't know anyone was there," Lucy blurted out.

She saw him smile. "I'm sorry," he said. "I didn't mean to scare you." He bent down and picked up the pieces, handing them to her gravely.

"Why don't you put them down on the balustrade," he suggested, "before you drop them again?"

"Oh no," Lucy said. "I have to go. I mean…" But she made no move to scuttle back to the tower door. "What are you doing out here in the dark?" she asked, after a moment.

He shrugged, a quick, dismissive movement. "The company isn't really to my taste."

"Wilfred, I suppose," Lucy said. "I'm sorry, he's quite horrible."

"I don't particularly mind," Robert Methven said. "But I would not choose to spend time with him."

"Neither would I," Lucy said, "and he's my cousin."

"Oh, bad luck," Methven said. "That means you must be—"

"Lucy," Lucy said. "Lucy MacMorlan."

"A pleasure to meet you, Lady Lucy."

"And you are Robert Methven," Lucy said.

He bowed.

"You're nice," Lucy said.

He smiled at the note of surprise in her voice. "Thank you."

"Aren't we supposed to be enemies?" Lucy said.

His smile broadened. "Do you want us to be?"

"Oh no," Lucy said. "It's old history."

"Old history has a tight grip sometimes," Robert Methven said. "Our families have hated each other for generations."

"Papa thinks feuds are foolish," Lucy said. She watched the play of moonlight across his face, the way it accentuated the planes and hollows, emphasizing some features and hiding others. It was oddly compelling. She felt a strange tug of emotion deep inside.

"That's why I am here tonight," Robert Methven said. "To put history behind us." He nodded toward the pot in her hands. "How did that happen?"

"Oh…" Lucy blushed. "The window was open and the curtain caught it and knocked it over."

Methven laughed. "My brother, Gregor, and I are always getting into trouble for stuff like that."

"I don't believe you," Lucy said. She looked up at his tall silhouette against the deep blue of the night sky. "You are far too grown-up to get into trouble."

Robert Methven laughed. "You might think so, but my grandfather is a tyrant. We are always falling foul of his rules."

Lucy became aware that the sharp corners of the broken pottery were digging into her palms and that her bare toes were beginning to chill within her thin silk slippers. She wondered what on earth she was doing standing here in her nightclothes talking to Robert Methven, of all people.

"I must go," she said again.

He made no effort to detain her. But he did smile. "Good night, then, Lady Lucy," he said.

At the door Lucy paused and turned. "You won't give me away, will you?" she asked carefully. "I don't want to get into trouble."

He laughed. "I'd never give you away."

"Promise?" Lucy said.

He came right up to her. She could smell the smoke

and fresh air on him and see the white slash of his teeth as he smiled. It made her feel a little bit dizzy and she had no notion why.

"I promise," he said.

He bent and kissed her. It was light and brief, but still it left her so breathless and shaken that for a moment she stayed quite motionless with the surprise, the shards of the pot forgotten in her hands.

"Was that your first kiss?" Robert asked. She could hear a smile in his voice.

"Yes." She spoke without thinking, too honest and innocent for artifice.

"Did you like it?"

Lucy frowned. The sensations inside her were too new and confusing to be easily described, but she did know that what she felt was very different from simple liking.

"I don't know," she said.

He laughed. "Would you like to do it again so you can decide?"

Sudden, wicked excitement curled inside Lucy, giving her the answer. "Yes," she whispered.

He took the pieces of the pot very carefully from her hands and laid them down on the stone balustrade. He put his arms around her and drew her closer to him so that her hands were resting against his chest. The texture of his jacket felt smooth under her palms. She felt extraordinarily shy all of a sudden and might have pulled away, but then he kissed her and the shyness fled, lost in a sensation of sweetness and a warmth that made her tingle with excitement. Her head spinning, she dug her fingers into his jacket to steady herself. Her heart was beating a fierce drumbeat. She felt fragile and could not stop herself from trembling.

Then, too soon, it was over and he stepped back, releasing her gently. For a second the moonlight illuminated his expression, surprise, puzzlement perhaps, the flicker of something she could not read or understand in his eyes. Yet when he spoke he sounded exactly the same.

"Thank you," he said.

Lucy did not know what you were supposed to do after you had kissed someone, and now she felt very shy all over again, so she grabbed the pieces of the pot, mumbled a good-night and hurried away so quickly that she almost tripped over the hem of her robe. She sped up the dark spiral of the stair without really noticing the stone steps beneath her flying feet. Her mind was too full of Robert Methven's kiss for her to be able to think of anything else.

Alice was asleep when she got back to their bedroom. Looking at her serene face, Lucy could not help smiling. She could not feel cross with her twin for long. She loved her too much, the sister who was different from her in so many ways and yet closer to her than the other half of the apple.

She placed the pieces of pot carefully back on the shelf and slipped into bed, burrowing into the warmth and falling asleep. She dreamed of the sickle moon shining over the sea and of strong magic and of Robert Methven's kisses. She knew he would not give her away. They were bound together now.

CHAPTER ONE

Forres Castle, Scotland, February 1812

"LUCY, I NEED you to do me a favor."

Lady Lucy MacMorlan's quill stuttered on the paper, leaving a large blob of ink. She had been in the middle of a particularly complex mathematical calculation when her brother Lachlan burst into the library. A gust of bitter winter air accompanied him, lifting the tapestries from the walls and sending the dust scurrying along the stone floor. The fire crackled and hissed as more sleet tumbled down the chimney. Lucy's precious calculations flew from the desk to skate along the floor.

"Please close the door, Lachlan," Lucy said politely.

Her brother did as he was bid, cutting off the vicious draught up the stone spiral stair. He threw himself down, long and lanky, in one of the ancient armchairs before the fire.

"I need your help," he said again.

Lucy smothered her instinctive irritation. It seemed unfair that Lachlan, two years older than she at six and twenty, always needed her to pull him out of trouble. Lachlan had a careless charm and a conviction that someone else would sort out the trouble he caused. That someone always seemed to be Lucy.

They all had their roles in the family. Angus, the son and heir, was stodgy and dull. Christina, Lucy's eldest sister, was an on-the-shelf spinster who had devoted her life to raising her siblings after their mother had died and now acted as hostess for their father. Mairi, Lucy's other sister, was a widow. Lachlan ran wild. Lucy had always been the good child, the perfect child in fact.

What a perfect baby, people had said, leaning over her crib to admire her. Later she had been called a perfect young lady, then a perfect debutante. She had even made the perfect betrothal, straight from the schoolroom, to an older gentleman who was a nobleman and a scholar. When he had died before they married, she had become perfectly unobtainable.

Once upon a time she had been a perfect sister and friend too. She had had a twin with whom she shared everything. She had thought her life was safe and secure, but she had been wrong. But here Lucy closed her mind, like the slamming shut of an oaken door. It did no good to think about the past.

"Lucy?" Lachlan was impatient for her attention. He looped one booted leg carelessly over the arm of the chair and sat smiling at her. Lucy looked at him suspiciously.

"What are you working on?" he asked, gesturing to the papers that were scattered across the desk.

"I was trying to prove Fermat's Last Theorem," Lucy said.

Lachlan looked baffled. "Why would you do that?"

"Because I enjoy the challenge," Lucy said.

Lachlan shook his head. "I wouldn't choose to do mathematics unless I absolutely had to," he said.

"You wouldn't choose to do anything unless you had to," Lucy pointed out.

Lachlan's smiled widened. He looked as though he thought she had paid him a compliment. "That's true," he said. He fixed her with his bright hazel eyes. "How is your writing progressing?"

"I am working on a lady's guide to finding the perfect gentleman," Lucy said. She spoke with dignity. She knew that Lachlan was laughing at her. He thought her writing was ridiculous, a mystifying hobby. All the Duke of Forres's daughters wrote; it was an interest they had inherited from their mother, who had been a notable bluestocking. The sons, in contrast, were not bookish. Lucy loved her brothers—well, she loved Lachlan even though he exasperated her, and she tried to love stuffy Angus—but intellectual they were not.

As if to prove it, Lachlan gave a hoot of laughter. "A guide to finding the perfect gentleman? What do you know of the subject?"

"I was betrothed to such a man," Lucy said sharply. "Of course I know."

The light died from Lachlan's eyes. "Duncan Mac-Gillivray was hardly the perfect gentleman," he said. "Nor was he the perfect match for you. He was too old."

Lucy experienced a tight, trapped feeling in her chest. "You are so *rude,*" she said crossly.

"No," Lachlan said. "I tell the truth. You only agreed to marry him because Papa wanted you to wed and you were still grieving for Alice and you weren't thinking straight."

Alice...

Another cold draught slid under the door and tickled its way down Lucy's spine. She shivered and drew her shawl more closely about her shoulders. Alice had been dead for eight years, but not a day passed when Lucy did not think of her twin. There was a hollow, Alice-shaped space inside her. She wondered if she would always feel like this, so empty, as though a part of her had been cut out, leaving nothing but darkness in its place. Alice's absence was like a constant ache, a shadow on the heart, and a missed step in the dark. Even after all this time, it hurt so sharply it could sometimes make her catch her breath. Her childhood had ended the day Alice died.

She pushed the thought away, as she always did. She was not going to talk about Alice.

"The point," she said, "is that I know what constitutes gentlemanly behavior, and more importantly—" she looked down her nose at her brother "—what does not."

"You know what constitutes French and Italian pornography, as well," Lachlan said with a grin, "and your erotic writings have been far more successful and profitable than your other writing. I wonder why you do not write more of them."

Lucy frowned at him fiercely. "You know full well

why I do not! We don't talk about that, Lachlan. Remember? It's all in the past and no one is to know. Do you *want* me to be ruined?"

Lachlan scowled back at her, the two of them reduced to their nursery squabbling for a brief moment. "Of course not. And I haven't told a soul."

Lucy sighed. She supposed it was unfair to pin all of the blame on her brother when she had been so recklessly stupid and naive, but there was no doubt that he was untrustworthy. A year ago Lachlan had come to her and begged a favor, much as he was doing now. He needed her help with writing a letter, he had said. It had to be extremely romantic, very sensual, and sufficient to seduce the lady of his dreams into his arms.

Lucy had desperately needed to earn some money, and since she was more articulate than her brother, she had agreed. She had culled some lines from Shakespeare for him and added some poetry of her own. Lachlan had laughed and had said he needed something rather more exciting.

It was then that Lucy had remembered the erotic writings in the castle library. The library had always been a treasure trove for her, and she had scoured its shelves from the time she could read, devouring the vast collection that her grandfather had brought back from the Grand Tour. Then one day, among the weighty tomes of political history and the works of the classical scholars, she had found something a great deal more inflammatory than dry politics: several folios of drawings and sketches of men and women in the most extraordinary erotic poses. Some of the sketches had seemed anatomically impossible to Lucy, but it had been both educational and interesting to see them and she had viewed the pictures with intense intellectual curiosity, even turning the books upside down and sideways at various points to check that she had understood the details correctly.

Alongside the drawing had also been writings, vivid and sensual, equally interesting to the curious academic mind. It was these that Lucy remembered when Lachlan asked for something rather more arousing than Shakespeare. She had used the writings as inspiration. Perhaps she had overdone it. She was not sure. But certainly her brother had had no complaints. He had even told his friends and several of them had come forward to ask for similar assistance in their wooing. Lucy had obliged.

Then it had all gone horribly wrong. The first Lucy had heard of the scandal was at a meeting of the Highland Ladies Bluestocking Society. Everyone was talking about a mysterious letter writer who helped the young bucks of Edinburgh seduce the women of their acquaintance. Lachlan was apparently locked in a torrid affair with an opera dancer while his friends were likewise setting the town alight with their licentious behavior. One had impregnated and abandoned an innkeeper's daughter and another had eloped with the wife of the governor of Edinburgh Castle. In all cases the ladies had been wooed into bed with false promises and erotic prose.

Lucy had felt horribly guilty and dreadfully naive that she had not questioned Lachlan's motives before she had written the letters, nor had she foreseen what the outcome of them might be. Her need for the money had blinded her and she had thought of nothing but that. She could only hope that no one discovered that she had been the letter writer, because if they did, she would be ruined. She had promised herself that there would be no more provocative poetry. It was not the sort of behavior that a well-bred heiress should indulge in, and in the future she would have to make her money from other sources.

Lachlan was watching her. There was a decidedly calculating expression in his hazel eyes. It made Lucy suspicious.

"Anyway," Lachlan said, smiling winningly, "let's forget all about that and talk about me." He ran a hand through his hair, ruffling it. It made him look charmingly rakish. Lucy thought it a pity that none of her friends were there to be impressed. They all thought Lachlan was delightful, despite the fact that the words *selfish* and *lightweight* could have been invented to describe him.

"I've fallen in love," Lachlan said, with the air of someone making a grand announcement.

"Again!" Lucy said. "Who is the fortunate lady this time?"

"It is Dulcibella Brodrie," Lachlan said. "I love her and she loves me and we want to marry."

Lucy paused. Miss Dulcibella Brodrie would not

have been her first choice as a sister-in-law. Dulcibella was beautiful, but she was also utterly helpless in a completely irritating manner. No doubt that was what had attracted Lachlan to her, but since he was fairly helpless himself, the combination of the two of them would be a recipe for disaster.

"Dulcibella is…very sweet natured," Lucy said carefully. She prided herself on being polite and she was glad she could find something positive to say. Dulcibella might be a little spoiled and self-centered, and she was drawn to a mirror as a bee was drawn to clover, but she did have her good qualities if one looked hard enough.

Lachlan's open face suddenly looked as tragic as a rejected spaniel's. "She's not free, though," he said. "She is already contracted to marry Robert Methven. The settlements are all drawn up."

Robert Methven.

The papers slipped from Lucy's hand again. She made a grab for them, then straightened up slowly. "Are you sure?" she said. She could feel an unnerving flutter in the pit of her stomach. Her fingers trembled. Her cheeks felt hot. She smoothed the paper automatically.

Fortunately for her, Lachlan was the most unobservant of men and was far too concerned with his own feelings to notice hers. "Of course I'm sure," he said. "It's a disaster, Lucy. I love Dulcibella. I was going to make her an offer myself. I just hadn't got around to it, and now Methven has got in first."

"Lord Brodrie probably wants more for his only

child than a younger son," Lucy said. She kept her gaze averted from Lachlan's while she steadied herself, while she drew breath.

"But I'm the younger son of a duke!" Lachlan protested.

"And Lord Methven is a marquis," Lucy said. "He is a better catch." Her voice was quite steady now even if her pulse still tripped and her body felt heated and disturbed.

Robert Methven was getting married.

She felt light-headed and shocked, and she had no notion why. It was not as though she knew Lord Methven well. Shortly after the night eight years ago when they had met on the terrace at Forres, he had suffered a terrible rift with his family and had left Scotland. He had gone to Canada and was rumored to have made a fortune trading in timber. It had been shortly before Alice had died and Lucy had not paid much attention. She remembered very little from that time other than the smothering sense of grief and the empty ache of loss.

Then Robert Methven's grandfather had died and he had inherited the title and returned to Scotland. Lucy had seen him a few times recently at the winter assemblies in Edinburgh, but the easy companionship she had found with him that night at Forres had vanished. They had exchanged no more than a few words on the most trivial of topics.

Lucy found Robert Methven physically intimidating, as well. The men in her family were all tall and lean, but Lord Methven was powerfully built as well as tall. His body was hard-muscled, the line of his jaw was hard and the expression in his sapphire-blue eyes was hard. He was overwhelmingly male. That masculinity was so blatant that it was like a slap in the face. Lucy had known nothing like it.

He had changed in other ways too. He was somber and the light had gone from his eyes. All the power and authority Lucy had sensed in him that night was still there, but it felt stronger and darker. Tragedy had a way of draining the light from people. Lucy knew that. She wondered what had happened to Methven to change him.

They had nothing in common now. And yet…Lucy's fingers clenched. She felt the smooth paper crumple beneath her touch. There was something about Robert Methven. Her awareness of him was acute and uncomfortable. She did not want to think about it because doing so made her feel hot and breathless and prickly all over. It was odd, very odd.

She sat down at her desk, smoothing her papers with fingers that were shaking a little. She was aware of an unfamiliar emotion, a curious sensation in the pit of her stomach, a sensation that felt like jealousy.

I am not jealous, Lucy thought crossly. *I cannot be jealous. I am never jealous of anything or anybody. Jealousy is neither appropriate nor ladylike.*

But she was. She was jealous of Dulcibella.

Lucy pressed her fingers to her temples. It made no sense. She could not be jealous of Dulcibella. Dulcibella had nothing she wanted. Lucy did not want to marry, and even if she did, Lord Methven in no way constituted her idea of a perfect husband. He was too intimidating and far too much of a man. He was just too much of everything.

"What am I to do, Lucy?" Lachlan asked, reclaiming her attention, holding up both his hands in a gesture of appeal. "Dulcibella would not dare go against her father's wishes. She is far too delicate to oppose him."

Delicate was not the word that Lucy would have chosen. Dulcibella was feeble. She had no steel in her backbone. In fact, Lucy had sometimes wondered if Dulcibella had a backbone at all.

"There's nothing you can do," she said briskly. "I am sorry, Lachlan." *But you will be in love with another lady in the blink of an eye.*

"I need you to write one of your letters," Lachlan said, sitting forward, suddenly urgent. "I need you to help me persuade her. Please, Lucy."

"Oh no," Lucy said. "No and no and no again. Have you been listening to a word I said, Lachlan?"

"I'm sorry about last time." Lachlan did at least have the grace to look a little shamefaced.

"I don't expect you are," Lucy said.

Lachlan shrugged, admitting the lie. "All right. But my intentions are honorable this time, Lucy. I love Dulcibella and I know you would want us to be happy. I want to marry her, Lucy. Please…" He let his words trail away as though he were brokenhearted. Most artistic, Lucy thought.

"No," she said again. "Apart from anything else, I hardly think that Dulcibella would be persuaded by that sort of letter. She is a very sheltered lady."

"Well," Lachlan said, grinning, "you may need to tone it down just a little."

"No," Lucy said for the sixth time. She was thinking of Robert Methven. "They are betrothed, Lachlan. It would be wrong."

"Please, Lucy," Lachlan repeated, with more pleading in his tone this time. "I really do love Dulcibella." He threw out a hand. "How can she be happy married to Methven? The man's a savage! He's not like me."

"No," Lucy said. "He most certainly is not like you." Robert Methven had none of Lachlan's refinement. He had rough edges, a roughness that had been rubbing against Lucy's senses for the past three months like steel against silk. Once again she felt that shiver of awareness tingle along her nerves.

"I can't help you, Lachlan," she said. "You should leave well enough alone."

Lachlan's face took on the mulish expression Lucy remembered from when he was a small boy who was not getting his own way.

"I don't know why you would refuse," he said. "No one would know."

"Because it's wrong," Lucy said sharply. A little shiver rippled over her skin. She knew she had to refuse even if Lachlan's feelings were genuinely engaged. It was not fair in any way to sabotage Robert Methven's betrothal. Besides, more practically, Methven was not a man to cross. He was hard and dangerous, and she would be foolish to do anything to antagonize him. If he found out, she would be in a very great deal of trouble.

"You need the money," Lachlan said suddenly. "I know you do. I heard you telling your maid the other day that your quarterly allowance was already spent."

Lucy hesitated. It was true that her allowance was already gone, given away to the Greyfriars Orphanage and the Foundling Hospital as soon as it was paid to her. Lachlan did not know, of course. He thought she was as extravagant as he was and saw no shame in that. He had no notion that her remorse over Alice's death prompted her to give every penny she had to try to make up for a guilt that could never be assuaged.

"I'll buy you the bonnet with the green ribbons you were admiring in Princes Street yesterday," Lachlan said, leaning forward.

"I'd rather have the cash, thank you," Lucy said. For a moment she allowed herself to think of all that she might buy: new clothes and shoes for the children, books and toys, as well.

There was a sliding sensation of guilt in her stomach as she realized that she was going to do as Lachlan asked. She tried to ignore the feeling. She told herself that there could be no danger of Lord Methven discovering what she had done because Lachlan's name would be on the letters and as long as he held his tongue, no one would suspect her. She told herself that she would be able to buy more medicines for the children at the hospital, as well. The bronchitis was particularly bad this winter.

"How much?" Lachlan asked. He uncoiled his long length from the chair and stood up.

"Ten shillings per letter," Lucy said briskly.

Lachlan glared. "I'll write them myself," he said.

"Good luck with that," Lucy said, smiling at him.

Lachlan stared at her. She looked directly back and did not waver. She knew Lachlan would cave in. Her will was much stronger than his.

"You could do it out of love," he grumbled.

Lucy turned her face away. Love was not a currency she dealt in. "Hard cash works best for me," she said.

"*Five* shillings, then," Lachlan said. "And for that they had better be good."

"Seven," Lucy said. "And they will be."

While Lachlan went to fetch the money, Lucy opened the desk drawer to extract a new quill, sharpened it expertly and refilled her ink pot. She would tell Lachlan to copy out the letters in green ink, she thought. The writing had to look as romantic as it sounded.

A shower of sleet pelted the window. The frame rattled. The wind howled down the chimney. Lucy shivered. She could not quite banish the sense of trepidation that had settled like a weight inside her. She could see Lord Methven in her mind's eye, his face as hard as rock, the dark blue eyes as chill as a mountain stream.

It was wrong of her to help Lachlan take Dulcibella away from him. She knew that. Not only was it morally wrong, but it would also ratchet up the tension between the two clans, a tension that had never really died. She knew that there was some sort of ongoing lawsuit between the Marquis of Methven and her cousin Wilfred, Earl of Cardross. If Lachlan stole Methven's bride, that would only throw fuel on the fire.

She knew she should throw the quill down and walk away now, but she desperately wanted more money to help the Foundling Hospital. Picking up the quill, she started to write. Everything would be fine, she told herself. She would not get into trouble. She was quite safe. Robert Methven would never find out what she had done.

CHAPTER TWO

Two months later, April 1812

THE BRIDE WAS LATE.

Robert, Marquis of Methven, surreptitiously eased his neck cloth. It felt very tight. So did the pristine white shirt that strained across his broad shoulders. The little Highland church was full and hot, and the heavy fragrance of lilies permeated the air. Robert had thought lilies were a flower of funerals.

Appropriate.

The wedding guests were growing restive. The time had long passed for Dulcibella to be fashionably tardy. The only excuse for such a delay could be a malfunction in her wardrobe or perhaps the sudden and inconvenient death of a family member. Robert doubted that either of those had occurred.

Dulcibella. It was a hell of a name. During the two months of his engagement, Robert had not been sure he could live with it. It looked as though he would not get the chance to try.

He turned. The church was packed with guests, for this was the wedding of the social season. Two hundred members of the Scottish nobility had made the journey

northward to this tiny church on the Brodrie Estate to
see the daughter of the laird married to the man who
had rejoined their ranks as scandalously as he had left
them eight years earlier.

"I think you've been jilted, my friend." His groomsman and cousin Jack Rutherford spoke out of the side
of his mouth. Jack was actually grinning, damn him.
Robert scowled. He was indifferent to the public humiliation, but he had not wanted to lose Dulcibella. She
had been the key to his inheritance.

A lady sitting near the back of the church caught
his eye.

Lady Lucy MacMorlan.

He felt his blood heat and quicken as it always did
when he looked at Lucy. Just the looking made Robert
feel as though he had selected his wedding breeches
two sizes too small, a most inappropriate physical reaction in a church, when he was marrying another lady.

He was not quite sure how this damnably inconvenient attraction to Lady Lucy had happened. He
suspected that, lowering as it was to admit it, he had
developed some sort of *tendre* for her when they were
both in their teens, and he had never quite grown out of
it. When he had kissed her years before at Forres Castle, it had been no more than an impulse. His reaction
to the kiss, to her, had been so strong and unexpected
that he had immediately backed off, knowing that if he
did not, they would both be in deep trouble. Time and
tragedy had then intervened to take him a long way
from Scotland both in mind and spirit, but when he had

returned and seen Lucy at one of the Edinburgh assemblies, it was as though a dormant spark was kindled in him, catching alight, burning into a flame.

He had changed, but she had changed too, he thought. The artless, open girl he had known had become a great deal more guarded. She was still charming, but with the town bronze of the sophisticate now. Robert had been surprised to feel an urgent curiosity to know what was under that facade.

He had other equally urgent impulses toward Lady Lucy, as well. They were destined to be unfulfilled.

Today Lucy was sitting near the back of the church between her elder sisters and her father, the Duke of Forres, and her cousin, the ghastly Wilfred, Earl of Cardross, whom Robert simply could not stand. She looked tiny, exquisite and voluptuous, all defiant red hair and lavender-blue eyes that were bright and alive. It was the hair that had been Robert's final undoing. He wanted to know if it felt as sensual between his fingers as it looked. Lady Lucy also had a heart-shaped face and rosy red lips, porcelain skin and endearing freckles. Robert wanted to know how those lips tasted and how far down those freckles went.

Lucy was perfection. Everyone said so. She was a perfect daughter, a perfect lady and she would one day make a perfect wife. Robert had heard that she had been betrothed straight from the schoolroom to some ancient nobleman who had keeled over before they wed. Since then Lady Lucy had rejected all offers because apparently no one could live up to the perfection of her fiancé. Robert found that odd, but there was no accounting for taste.

He stole another look at Lady Lucy's perfect profile. It was a great pity that he could not make her an offer, but he was completely hamstrung by the terms of his inheritance. Dulcibella Brodrie was one of the few women, if not the only woman, who fit his criteria.

He realized that he was still staring at Lucy. He was not much of a gentleman, but he did know that it was bad form on his wedding day to stare at a lady who was not his bride.

"Eyes front, Methven," barked his grandmother in the tones of a parade ground sergeant major. The Dowager Marchioness of Methven sat alone in the front pew, a small stately figure in red silk and diamonds. When his grandfather had cut him off with no word, she had been the only member of Robert's family to keep the faith with him during his time abroad. She had done it in defiance of her husband and she had sent his cousin Jack to him in Canada when the young man had wanted to see something of the world. Robert adored her, though he would never tell her as much. The two of them, Jack and his grandmother, were all the family he had left.

The door of the church crashed open. The organ swelled into "The Arrival of the Queen of Sheba." Robert could sense the minister's relief. There was an anticipatory creak and shuffle as the congregation craned their necks for their first glimpse of the bride.

The music stuttered to a halt. Lord Brodrie, Dulcibella's father, was striding down the aisle. Alone. There was no bride on his arm.

Robert had previously observed that Lord Brodrie was a man in an almost constant state of anger, and his rage was quite apparent now. His face was bright red with fury, his white hair stood up in livid spikes and his blue eyes flashed with ire. In his hand he was brandishing several sheets of paper. One of them fluttered to the floor at Robert's feet.

"She's run off!" Brodrie announced.

"Congratulations on your perspicacity, Jack," Robert murmured.

The shock that had held the congregation mute splintered into a riot of sound. Everyone seemed to be talking at once, gesticulating, turning to his or her neighbor to dissect the scandalous news.

Robert bent to retrieve the page. It was not, as he had first imagined, a letter of explanation or even an apology. It was part of a love letter.

"I can bear it no longer. I am tormented night and day. I cannot speak. I cannot eat. The thought of you in another man's arms, in another man's bed, is intolerable to me. The thought of Methven making love to you when you are mine… You are the very breath of life to me! Come away with me before it is too late…."

There was a great deal more in the same vein, but Robert skipped over it. He had read quite enough for it to turn his stomach. It seemed, however, that Dulcibella had liked that sort of thing given that the letter writer had persuaded her to elope.

"Who wrote this stuff?" Jack asked. He was trying to read over Robert's shoulder.

"It's signed Lachlan," Robert said.

"That must be Lachlan MacMorlan," Jack said, squinting at the signature. "He was completely besotted with Miss Brodie. I didn't think he would do anything about it, though. Thought he was too lazy."

"I'll string his guts from the castle battlements," Brodie said violently. His face was a mottled red and white now. He looked as though he was about to burst a blood vessel. He was shaking his fist, in which he clutched several more handwritten sheets. "Debauching my daughter with romantic poetry!" he roared. "The craven coward! If he wanted her, why could he not fight for her like a man?"

Robert crumpled the letter in his hand. "Presumably because this approach worked better," he said. "I was not aware that Miss Brodie was of a romantic disposition."

He had not, he realized, known much about Dulcibella at all. It was a little late to realize that now, but he had not been interested in her except as a way to unlock his inheritance. He needed a wife—and an heir—urgently. He had proposed to Dulcibella for that reason alone. He had noticed that she was pretty. He had found her laughter grating and her helplessness irritating. That was the sum total of their relationship.

"Daft girl was always reading," Brodie said. "Took after her mother that way. I never paid it much attention. She liked those soppy novels, *Pamela* and the like."

It was all starting to make a great deal more sense to Robert. He tapped the crumpled letter impatiently against the palm of his hand.

"I don't believe MacMorlan wrote that," Jack said suddenly. "I was at school with him. He's no scholar."

"Perhaps he was too shy to share his poetry with you all," Robert said sarcastically. He scanned a few more lines. "He has quite a talent."

"If Lachlan MacMorlan is shy," Jack said, "I'm the pope."

"Gentlemen…" The minister was hovering, anxiety writ large on his plump face. "Is the service to go ahead?"

"Evidently not," Robert said. "If only Miss Brodrie had confided her feelings in me, she and Lord Lachlan could have had the booking instead."

Both Lord Brodrie and the minister were looking at him in perplexity. Robert realized that they were wondering if he could possibly be as cold and indifferent as he sounded. He had not cared a jot about Dulcibella, but he did care very much about losing his inheritance. The congregation was shifting and shuffling now as everyone tried to overhear what was going on and pass word to his or her neighbor. Their expressions were shocked, scandalized, amused, depending on the guests and their disposition. Wilfred of Cardross was making no attempt to hide his glee. He, more than anyone, would welcome the ruin of Robert's plans and the opportunity it gave him to claim back Methven land.

Robert clenched his fists. He was not going to give

Cardross the chance to take Golden Isle and his northern estates. They were the most ancient part of his patrimony, and he would hold them by force if he had to do so.

His eyes met those of Lucy MacMorlan. She was looking directly at him. She did not look shocked or scandalized or amused.

Lucy looked guilty.

Robert felt a leap of interest. He knew that Lady Lucy was close to her brother. He had observed them together at various social events and knew they had an easy friendship. It seemed Lachlan might have confided in Lucy about the elopement. Certainly she knew something.

For a long moment Robert held her gaze. Faint pink color came into her cheeks. He saw her bite her lip. Then she broke the contact with him very deliberately, turned to pick up the little green-beaded reticule that matched the ribbon on her bonnet and touched her father gently on the arm to indicate that she wanted to leave. The guests were spilling out of the pews now, milling around uncertainly in the aisles while they waited for someone to tell them what was happening.

"Well?" Brodrie demanded. "What's to do? Aren't you going after them, my lord?"

"Sir," Robert drawled, "your daughter has gone to a great deal of trouble to avoid marrying me. It would be churlish of me to go after her and bring her back." He pushed the letter into Jack's hands. "Tell everyone that they are welcome at the wedding breakfast,

Jack," he said. "A pity to waste a good party." It was he who had paid for the celebrations, Brodrie being too strapped for cash.

"Party?" Brodrie was boggling. "You would celebrate my daughter running off with another man, sir?"

"We have already given the gossips more than enough cause for conjecture," Robert said. "I refuse to play the heartbroken jilt." He laughed. "Besides, the wedding is bought and paid for. And you have a daughter married and off your hands. One hopes. Celebrate it." He sketched Lord Brodrie a bow. "Excuse me. I will join you shortly, but first there is something I must do."

"By God, sir, he is a coldhearted bastard," he heard Brodrie say to Jack as he walked away. The man sounded torn between admiration and disbelief.

He did not hear Jack's reply. But he did not disagree with Brodrie's assessment.

LACHLAN HAD RUN off with Dulcibella Brodrie.

The gossip rippled down the pews like the incoming tide. Lucy, sitting at the back of the church between her father and her two sisters, was almost the last to hear it.

"Run away to Gretna Green… Gone this morning… Eloped with Lachlan MacMorlan…"

Lucy felt apprehension tiptoe along her spine. Damn Lachlan. Could he not have sorted this out sooner? It had taken two months and almost twenty love letters to persuade Dulcibella to jilt Robert Methven, and she had to do it now, leaving the man standing alone in front of all his wedding guests.

Lucy felt horribly guilty. She had not really expected to feel so bad. Up until this very moment, she had in fact felt rather pleased with herself. Dulcibella's surprisingly staunch refusal to succumb to Lachlan's wooing had meant a big profit on the letters. Lucy had been able to give so much to her charities: warm blankets and medicines and new clothes for the children. But of course there was always a price to pay. And Lord Methven was paying it now. Lucy felt as though she had let him down in some obscure way, as though she had owed him her loyalty and had betrayed him. Perhaps it was because all those years ago he had kept his word and never revealed that he had seen her on the terrace at Forres that night. She had not thought about that in eight years. Yet now she thought that he had kept faith with her while she had repaid him in deceit.

"Papa." Lucy touched her father's arm, leaned toward Mairi and Christina. "I fear we are about to become as popular as a fox in a hen coop," she whispered. "Lachlan has eloped with the bride."

The Duke of Forres pushed his glasses up the bridge of his nose. He looked perplexed. It was his natural state; he was a scholar and a recluse who always gave the impression that half his mind was still in his books. "Lachlan?" he said vaguely. "Has he? I wondered where he was."

"Halfway to Gretna by now, by the sound of it," Mairi said. "Typical Lachlan. He always wants what belongs to someone else."

Lucy looked up. Over the heads of the congregation,

she could see Robert Methven talking to his grooms-man and to Lord Brodrie. He turned slightly toward her and she saw that there were some sheets of paper in his hand. She felt a clutch of fear ripple through the pit of her stomach. Those sheets looked suspiciously like the letters Lachlan had sent Dulcibella.

Suddenly, without warning, Methven looked up and directly at her. His dark blue gaze was intent. It felt as though there were an invisible thread pulled tight between them. Lucy felt the jolt of that contact down to her toes.

He knows.

Her heart started to batter her bodice, slamming in hard beats. She could feel panic rising in her throat, cutting off her breath. How Robert Methven could possibly know that she had had a hand in this was a mystery, and yet she did not doubt it for a second.

She saw Methven's gaze drop to the letters in his hand and then rise again to pin her very deliberately in its full blue blaze. He made some comment to his groomsman and took a purposeful step in Lucy's direction.

She had to get out of there.

"Papa," she said. "Excuse me. I need some fresh air. I will see you out at the carriage."

"Of course, my dear," the duke murmured. "Dear, oh dear, I am not at all sure what to say to Methven. Such appallingly bad behavior on Lachlan's part."

"Excuse me," Lucy said again, hastily. She started to squeeze out of the pew. Out of the corner of her eye, she could see Robert Methven advancing down the nave of the church toward them. She had a sudden vision of him throwing down his gauntlet on the floor of the church and challenging the duke to combat for the dishonor done to his name and his family. A hundred years before, such an idea might not have been so outrageous. It did not in fact seem that outlandish now, especially as Wilfred Cardross was smiling broadly and making his delight at Methven's humiliation all too plain.

"It could not have happened to a more deserving fellow," Cardross said. "I must stand Lachlan a whisky next time I see him."

"Oh, do be quiet, Wilfred," Lucy said crossly, venting her guilt on someone else. "You always have to crow."

"When it is a case of seeing a Methven brought low," Wilfred said, smoothing his lacy cuffs, "of course I do. Besides..." He beamed again. "If Methven cannot fulfill the terms of his inheritance, then half his estates are forfeit. To me."

Lucy looked at him with deep dislike. Wilfred had been making mysterious pronouncements along these lines over the past few months, ever since he had come back from London. She knew there was some sort of ongoing lawsuit between him and Robert Methven, but since the case was still sub judice, Wilfred could not discuss it. Instead he dropped these irritating and self-satisfied hints. But if Wilfred was right and Methven's inheritance depended on his marriage, then he would be even more furious to be jilted. Suddenly Lucy felt so nervous that she could not draw breath.

She was in big trouble.

She squeezed past her cousin and out into the aisle. It was now packed with wedding guests, all milling around and chattering. "Excuse me," Lucy said rapidly for a third time, trying to carve a path through the congregation toward the nearest door.

She threw a look back over her shoulder. Several people had ambushed Robert Methven on his way down the aisle, presumably to ask him what was going on. He was answering courteously enough, but his eyes were still fixed on her, fierce and focused. As he caught her gaze, Lucy saw a flash of grim amusement light the deep blue depths. He knew she was running from him and he was coming after her.

It was only as she reached the church door, out of breath and with her heart pounding, that she realized her tactical mistake. She should have stayed inside, surrounded by people. Robert Methven could not have interrogated her there. She would have been safe. Except she suspected that he was the sort of man who would simply have picked her up and carried her out of the church had he wanted to speak to her in private. He would not care if he outraged convention.

Galvanized by the thought, Lucy started to hurry down the uneven path toward the lych-gate. The road beyond was blocked with carriages. The little village of Brodrie had seen nothing on the scale of this wedding since the laird had married thirty years before.

"Lady Lucy." There was a step behind her on the path. Lucy froze. She wanted to run, but that would be undignified. It would also end badly. She could not run in her silk slippers and Robert Methven would be faster than she was.

She turned slowly.

"Lord Methven." The moment of confrontation had arrived too soon. She felt completely unprepared. "I am sorry," she said. "Sorry for your…" She paused.

"Loss?" Robert Methven suggested ironically. "Or sorry that your brother is such a blackguard that he elopes with another man's bride?"

His voice was rough edged, rubbing against Lucy's senses like skates on ice. No educated man, no gentleman, spoke with a Scots accent, but there was a trace of something in Robert Methven's voice that was as abrasive as he was. Perhaps it was the time he had spent abroad that had rubbed off the patina of civilization in him. Whatever it was, it made Lucy shiver.

He was blocking the path in front of her and he did not move. As always, his height and the breadth of his shoulders, the sheer solid masculine strength of him, overwhelmed her. This time, though, Lucy knew she could not allow herself to be intimidated.

"Lord Methven." She tried again. She smiled her special smile. It was composed and sympathetic and it gave—she hoped—no indication at all of the way in which her heart thumped and her breath trapped in her chest. "I know that Lachlan has behaved badly—"

"Damn right he has," Robert Methven said. "He is a scoundrel."

Well, that was true, if a little direct from a gentleman to a lady. But then Methven was nothing if not direct. Lucy could feel the hot color stinging her cheeks. Generally she had far too much poise for any gentleman to be able to put her to the blush. Perhaps it was because Robert Methven was so blunt that she felt so ill at ease in his company. On a positive note, however, he was blaming Lachlan for the letters so she was perfectly safe. He had no idea she had been involved.

"You look very guilty," Methven said conversationally. "Why is that?"

Suddenly Lucy felt as though she was on shaky ground after all.

"I apologize for that too," she said shortly. "It is just the way I look."

Methven's firm lips tilted up in a mocking smile. Lucy felt mortified. She never lost her temper and was certainly never rude to anyone. It simply was not good behavior. Yet Robert Methven always seemed able to get under her skin.

"I like the way you look," Methven said, shocking her all the more. He raised one hand and brushed her cheek with the back of his fingers. The constricted feeling in Lucy's chest increased. It felt as though her bodice had been buttoned so tight she was unable to draw in her breath at all. The skin beneath his fingers burned.

"I thought you looked guilty because you knew about the elopement," Methven said. His hand fell to his side. "I thought that you might even have helped the happy couple?"

Lucy felt the breath catch in her throat. Under his gaze she felt exposed, her emotions dangerously unprotected, her reactions impossible to hide.

"I…" She realized that she did not know what she was going to say. Methven's cool blue gaze seemed to pin her to the spot like a butterfly on a slide. She felt helpless.

She took a deep breath and pressed one hand to her ribs to ease the rapid pound of her heart. Her mind steadied. She hated to lie. It was wrong. But she told herself that she had not played any part in the elopement. Not directly.

"I had nothing to do with it," she said. She could feel her blush deepening, guilty flags in her hot cheeks. "That is—" She scrambled for further speech. Methven was watching her silently. His stillness was quite terrifying, like that of a predatory cat.

"I knew that Lachlan was in love with Miss Brodrie," she said. Already it felt as though she had said too much, as though she were on the edge of a slippery slope. "That is all. I didn't know about the elopement, or the love letters—" She stopped, feeling her stomach drop like a stone as she realized what she had said, what she had done. A wave of heat started at her toes and rose upward to engulf her whole body.

"I did not mention any love letters," Robert Methven said. His tone was very gentle but the look in his eyes had sharpened.

Once again there was silence, acute in its intensity. Lucy could hear the soft hush of the breeze in the grass. She could smell the cherry blossom. She was captured by the look in Robert Methven's eyes, pinned beneath that direct blue stare.

"I…" Her mind was a terrifying blank. She could think of no way out.

"I hear your brother is no scholar," Methven said. There was a harder undertone to his voice now. "But you, Lady Lucy…you are a noted authoress, are you not?"

Panic tightened in Lucy's chest. She could hear the anger hot beneath his words.

"I…"

"So very inarticulate all of a sudden," Methven mocked.

"Methven, my dear fellow." The Duke of Forres was hurrying toward them down the path, Lucy's sisters behind him. The rest of the wedding guests were spilling out of the church now. "My dear chap," the duke said again. "I don't know what to say. I do apologize for the incivility of my son in running off with your future wife. Frightful bad manners."

The moment was broken. Lucy drew a sharp breath and drew closer to Mairi's side for comfort and support. She could feel herself shaking.

Robert Methven's gaze remained fixed on her face. "Pray do not give the matter another thought, Your Grace," he said. "I am sure I shall find a way to claim recompense." He bowed to Lucy. "We shall continue our conversation later, madam."

Not if she could help it.

Lucy watched him walk away. His stride was long and he did not look back.

"Very civil," the duke said. He sounded surprised. Evidently, Lucy thought, he had missed the implied threat in Robert Methven's words.

Lucy knew better. There was nothing remotely civil about Robert Methven, nor would there be in his revenge. It was not over.

CHAPTER THREE

LUCY HAD NOT wanted to attend the wedding breakfast, but her father had, for once, been adamant.

"Methven has invited us," he said firmly. "The least that we can do is support him. This way we minimize the scandal of your brother's appalling behavior and ensure that there is no more bad blood between our families."

So that was that. Lucy sat through the banquet fidgeting as though her seat were covered in pine needles. She had no appetite. The food and drink turned to ashes in her mouth. She could barely swallow. She endured the gossip about Lachlan and the stares and the whispers with a bright and entirely artificial smile pinned on her face while inside, her stomach was curling with apprehension. She was seated a long way down the table from Robert Methven, but she could feel him looking at her, feel the heat of his gaze and sense the way he was studying her. Yet when she risked a glance in his direction, he was always looking the other way and paying her no attention at all. It could only be her guilt that was making her feel so on edge.

The meal ended and the dancing began. By now the wedding guests were extremely merry because the wine had circulated lavishly. Dulcibella's elopement with the wrong bridegroom had almost been forgotten.

"Damned fine celebration," Lucy heard one inebriated peer slur to another. "Best wedding of the year."

Lucy sat with her godmother and the other chaperones, awkward and alone on one of the rout chairs at the side of the great hall of Brodrie Castle. Lucy hated the fact that at four and twenty she was still required to have a chaperone simply because she was not married. It was ridiculous. She knew it was society's rule, but nevertheless it made her feel as though she were still a child. And since she had no intention of marrying, she could foresee the dismal prospect of being chaperoned until she was old enough to be a fully fledged spinster of thirty-five years at least.

She was desperate for this interminable party to end, but it seemed she was the only one who felt that way. Everyone else was having a marvelous time. She could see her sister Mairi twirling enthusiastically through the reel. Mairi always danced. She was an extrovert by nature. Some said she was a flifrt. No one said that of Lucy. She was considered too serious, too well behaved, and the tragedy of her dead fiancé had added a touch of melancholy to her reputation.

Her sister Christina was also dancing. Christina was not a flirt. She was firmly on the shelf, companion to their father, housekeeper and hostess, destined never to wed. Yet despite that, she was dancing while Lucy sat alone with the other wallflowers. It was a state of affairs that happened with increasing frequency over the past couple of years. Lucy knew she had a reputation for being fastidious because she had rejected so many suitors. The gentlemen had given up trying, swearing they could not live up to the memory of the late, sainted Lord MacGillivray. If only they knew. If only they knew that no one could measure up because no other bridegroom would accept a marriage in name only.

Intimacy with a man was out of the question for Lucy. She was not going to make the same mistake as Alice. She had to protect herself. That was why Duncan MacGillivray had been her ideal; he had had absolutely no desire to bed her. He had an heir, he had a spare and he had no interest in sex.

Lucy's gaze wandered back to the dance. Mairi was spinning down the set of a country dance, passing from hand to hand, slender, smiling, a bright dazzling figure. Lucy felt a curious ache in her chest. Sometimes Mairi reminded her of Alice, radiant, charming, glowing with happiness. Lucy's twin had had an exasperating habit of hearing only what she wanted to hear, of ignoring trouble with a blithe indifference and of charming her way out of difficulties. But in the end the trouble was so deep there was no way out. Lucy shivered. The stone pillars and baronial grandness of the great hall dissolved into another time, another place, and Alice was clinging to her hands, her face wet with tears:

"Help me, Lucy! I'm so afraid...."

Lucy had wanted to help, but she had not known what to do. She had been sixteen years old, shocked, terrified, helpless. Alice had held her so tightly it had hurt, words pouring from her in a broken whisper:

"I love him so much... I would do anything for him..." At the end she had called out for the man she loved, but he had not been there for her. Instead it had been Lucy who had held Alice as she had slipped away, as she had whispered how she was sorry, how she wished she had confided in Lucy before.

"I never told because I was afraid I would be in trouble. Please don't tell anyone, Lucy! Help me...."

By then it had been far, far too late to help Alice. Lucy had thought that they had had no secrets, but that was not true. On the terrible night that Alice had died, Lucy had found out just how much her twin had kept a secret from her and just how high was the price paid for love.

Lucy gave a violent shiver and the great hall came back into focus and the music was playing and the dancers still dancing and nothing had changed, but in her heart was the cold emptiness that always filled her when she remembered Alice.

Her godmother, Lady Kenton, was addressing her.

"We shall never get you a husband, Lucy, if no one even asks you to dance," Lady Kenton said. "It is most frustrating."

Unfortunately Lady Kenton deemed it her duty as Lucy's godmother and the dearest friend of her late mother to find Lucy a man. Lucy had asked her not to bother, but Lady Kenton was keen, all the keener as the years slipped past.

"I shall speak to your father about your marriage," her godmother was saying. "He has been most remiss in letting matters slide since Lord MacGillivray's death. It is time we found you another suitor."

Lucy took a deep breath. Her father was indulgent toward her and she was certain that he would never force her to wed against her will. Seven years ago he had been so anxious for her to marry, straight from the schoolroom, as though in doing so she might wipe out the horrific memory of Alice's fall from grace, her shame, her death. Now, though, the duke had fallen into a scholastic melancholy and locked himself away most of the time with his books.

Lady Kenton straightened suddenly in her rout chair. She touched Lucy's arm. "I do believe Lord Methven is going to ask you to dance." She sounded excited. "How singular. He has not danced all evening."

"Perhaps he felt it was inappropriate when his bride has run off," Lucy said. Her throat was suddenly dry and her heart felt as though it was about to leap into her throat as Methven's tall figure cut through the crowd toward her. There was something about his approach that definitely suggested unfinished business. He did not want to dance. She was certain of it. He wanted to question her about the love letters just as he had threatened to do.

A man superimposed himself between Lucy and Robert Methven, blocking her view.

"Cousin Lucy."

A shiver of a completely different sort touched

Lucy's spine. She had no desire at all to dance with Wilfred. He was bowing in front of her with what he no doubt fondly hoped was London style, all frothing lace at his neck and cuffs, with diamonds on his fingers and in the folds of his cravat. Lucy thought he looked like an overstuffed turkey. He had evidently been drinking freely, for he smelled of brandy, and he had flakes of snuff dusting the lapels of his jacket.

Wilfred's smile was pure vulpine greeting, showing uneven yellow teeth and with a very predatory gleam in his eye.

"Dearest coz." He took her hand, brushing the back of it with his lips. "Did I tell you how divine you are looking today? Will you honor me with your hand in the strathspey?"

Lucy could think of little she would like less, but everyone was looking at her and Lady Kenton was making little encouraging shooing motions with her hands toward the dance floor. Besides, she could use Wilfred as a shield against Lord Methven. He was definitely the lesser of two evils.

After twenty minutes she was reconsidering her opinion. Throughout the long, slow and stately dance, Wilfred kept up a dismaying flow of chatter that seemed to presume on a closer relationship between them than the one that existed. Yes, they were distant cousins and had known each other since childhood, but there had never been anything remotely romantic in their relationship. Now, however, Wilfred lost no opportunity to whisper in Lucy's ear how divine she was looking—simply divine—over and over again until she could have screamed. He squeezed her fingers meaningfully and allowed his hand to linger on her arm or in the small of her back in a most unpleasant proprietary manner. She was at a loss to explain the extraordinary change in his behavior. He had always been obsequious, but never before had he given the impression that there was some sort of understanding between them.

"Dearest coz," he said when the dance had at last wound its way to the end, "I do hope we may spend so much more time in each other's company from now on."

Lucy could think of little that she would like less, and she was beginning to suspect that it was her fortune Wilfred wanted to spend more time with. The rumor was that his pockets were to let, and her father had commented over breakfast only a few days before that he expected Cardross to make a rich match, and soon, to mollify his creditors. Lucy had not expected that *she* would be that rich match, however.

"It would be no bad thing for you to wed your cousin Wilfred," Lady Kenton said, after Lucy had turned down Wilfred's request for another dance and he had rather sulkily escorted her back to her chaperone. "He is a most suitable match and it would strengthen the ties between your two families. I will mention it to your papa."

"Please do not, Aunt Emily," Lucy said. "I cannot bear Wilfred. In fact, I very nearly hate him."

Lady Kenton did not reply, but Lucy felt a chill in the air, a chill that implied that beggars could not afford to be choosers. No more gentlemen came to ask her to dance. Time ticked by. A reel followed the strathspey, then another set of country dances. After a half hour she could feel the dagger-sharp glances of the other girls and sense the covert triumph of their chaperones. She might be pretty, she might be a duke's daughter and an heiress, but no one wanted to dance with her. Robert Methven had vanished again. Lucy knew she should have felt reassured, but instead she felt tense and tired, desperate to retire to the inn at Glendale where they were staying the night before returning to Edinburgh.

She stood up. "Excuse me for a moment, ma'am," she said to Lady Kenton. "I must have a word with Lord Dalrymple. He will be speaking on the topic of political economy in Edinburgh in a couple of weeks, and I have promised to attend the lecture."

Lady Kenton sighed heavily. "Well, do not let anyone hear you discussing it, my dear, or your reputation may be damaged. You know that I encourage your studies, but not everyone admires a bluestocking."

After Lucy had spoken to Lord Dalrymple, she slipped away to the room set aside for the ladies to withdraw. It was empty but for a maid yawning on an upright chair. Lucy washed her hands and face, frowning at her wan expression in the pier glass. No wonder she frightened the dance partners away.

As she came out of the room, she saw Robert Methven's tall figure striding across the hall, deep in conversation with the handsome man who had stood as his groomsman. Lucy froze, drawing back into the shadows behind a huge medieval suit of armor. Although she was sure she had made no sound, she saw Methven's head come up. His blue gaze swept the hall and came to rest unerringly on the spot where she was hiding. Lucy saw him exchange a quick word with the other man before he started to move toward her as purposefully as he had done in the church.

Panic gripped Lucy. She did not stop to think. She groped behind her for the handle on the first door she came to and tumbled backward through it. It was a service corridor of some sort, stone floored and dimly lit. She was halfway along it and regretting her impulsive attempt to escape when she heard the stealthy sound of the door at the end opening and shutting again. Robert Methven was behind her. She was certain it was he. Now there was no way back.

She scurried along, her slippers pattering on the floor. Behind her she could hear the measured tread of Methven's boots. Her heart raced too, an unsteady beat that only served to fuel her panic. It was too late now to turn and face him. She felt foolish for running away and gripped by hot embarrassment, awkward and nervous. She could have brazened it out before; now it was impossible.

The corridor turned an abrupt corner and for one terrible moment Lucy thought she was trapped down a dead end before she saw the small spiral stair in the corner. She wrenched the door open and shot up the steps like a squirrel up a tree trunk, panting, round and round and up and up, until the stair ended in a studded wooden door. It was locked. Lucy almost sprained her wrist turning the huge heavy iron key and ran out onto the castle battlements.

The wind caught her as soon as she stepped outside, tugging at her hair, setting her shivering in her thin silk gown. Darkness had fallen and the sky was clear, the moon bright. Any heat there had been in the day had gone. It was only April and the brisk breeze had a chill edge.

Lucy hurried along the battlement walk to the door in the opposite turret. She turned the handle. The door remained obstinately closed. She pulled hard. It did not budge. Locked. She realized that the key must be on the inside just as it had been on the door she had come through.

She spun around. She could see Methven's silhouette moving toward her along the battlements. He was not moving quickly, but there was something about him, something about the absolute predatory certainty of a man who had his target in his sights. Lucy pressed her palms hard against the cold oak of the door—and almost fell over as it opened abruptly and she stumbled inside. Down the stairs, along the maze of shadowy corridors with the flickering torchlight, back through the door into the great hall, running, panting now, her heart pounding...

She paused for breath behind the spread of a large arrangement of ferns, leaning one hand against the cold hard flank of the suit of armor for support as her breathing steadied and her heartbeat started to slow down.

Five minutes of chasing around Brodrie Castle, but at least she had shaken off Robert Methven.

"It's a cold night for a stroll on the battlements, Lady Lucy."

Lucy spun around. The suit of armor clattered as she jumped almost out of her skin.

Methven was standing directly behind her, a look of sardonic amusement on his face.

"I'm afraid I don't know what you mean," Lucy said.

In silence he held out his hand. Nestling on his palm were several of her pearl-headed hairpins.

"Oh!" Lucy's hand went to tuck the wayward strands of hair back behind her ears. She had not realized the wind had done quite so much damage. "Thank you," she said. "I… Yes, I…I was out on the battlements. I have always been interested in fifteenth-century architecture."

"A curious time to pursue your hobby," Methven said. "If only I had known, I could have arranged a tour for you. In the daylight." He shifted. "And there was I, thinking you were out there because you were running away from me."

"I wasn't—" Lucy started to deny it, saw the amused cynicism deepen in his eyes as he waited for her to lie and stopped abruptly.

"All right," she said crossly. "I *was* running away from you."

"That's better," Methven said. "Why?"

"Because I don't like you," Lucy said, "and I did not wish to speak with you."

Methven laughed. "Much better," he approved. "Who knew you possessed the gift of such plain speaking?"

"Generally I try to be polite rather than hurtfully blunt," Lucy said.

"Well, don't bother with me," Methven said. "I prefer frankness."

"I cannot imagine that we shall have much opportunity for conversation of any sort," Lucy said frigidly, "frank or otherwise."

"Then you are not as intelligent as you are given credit for," Methven said. "We start now."

He put out a hand as though to take her arm, but in that moment a slightly shambolic figure stumbled toward them, almost upsetting the suit of armor.

"Lady Lucy! How splendid!"

A flicker of annoyance crossed Methven's face at the interruption. Lucy recognized Lord Prestonpans, one of Lachlan's ne'er-do-well friends. Prestonpans looked more than a little the worse for wear; his color was high, his fair hair rumpled and a distinct smell of alcohol hung about his person. He leaned confidingly toward Lucy, and she drew back sharply, trying to edge away.

"Been looking for you the entire evening, ma'am," he said. "Need your help. Need you to write one of your letters for me."

Lucy went very still. She could feel Robert Methven's gaze riveted on her face in polite and amused inquiry.

"One of your letters?" he repeated gently.

Disaster. Lucy felt cold all over. How could she silence Prestonpans or steer him away from danger? How could she keep Methven from overhearing? She could feel cool sweat prickling her back, could feel her whole reputation unraveling.

"Of course, my lord," she said quickly, taking Lord Prestonpans's arm to draw him away. "A letter to the Lord Advocate? I would be delighted to help. Come and see me next week in Edinburgh."

She smiled at him and started to walk away, hoping that Prestonpans would take the hint, but he did not. Instead he followed, nipping at her heels like a terrier. Lucy sped up, heading for the ballroom door. Prestonpans galloped after her, raising his voice with disastrous clarity.

"Not one of your legal letters," Prestonpans bellowed. He was trying to keep up with her, slipping slightly on the highly polished floor. "One of y'r other sorts of letters. Your brother told me you write special letters, emotic—" he slurred "—erotic ones—"

"You must excuse me, my lord." Lucy spoke quickly and loudly, trying to drown him out, desperately hoping that Robert Methven had not heard his last words, despite the fact that they had echoed to the rafters. "My chaperone will be wondering where I am—"

"I'll call on you!" Prestonpans said, waving gaily as he staggered away toward the refreshment room. "I'll pay good money!"

There was a long silence. Lucy was aware of nothing but the thunder of her heartbeat in her ears and the tightening of her nerves as Robert Methven walked slowly toward her. He let the silence between them spin out. And then:

"Erotic letters?" he queried in the same deceptively gentle tone.

"You misheard," Lucy said desperately. "Lord Prestonpans said *exotic* letters. Unusual letters, written in…"

"Green ink?" Methven suggested. "That would be exotic."

Green ink. Lucy remembered recommending to Lachlan that he copy out the letters to Dulcibella in green ink to make them look more romantic.

"Or perhaps," Methven continued, "Lord Prestonpans meant letters written in exotic language? Poetic letters, love letters…" His expression was impassive as he waited politely for the next lie she would spin. Through the half-open door of the ballroom, Lucy could see another set of Scottish country dances forming. The orchestra was tuning up. People brushed past them to take their places on the floor. It felt like another world and one she would not be rejoining anytime soon, especially not since Robert Methven had put out a hand and taken her arm, not too tightly but certainly in a grip she could not have broken without making a scene.

"I think it's about time you and I had a proper talk," Methven said.

"We cannot talk here," Lucy said. She pinned a special smile on her face to ward off the curious looks of passing guests. Beneath the pretense her heart was hammering. There was only one thing worse than Robert Methven knowing of her letter-writing skills and that was everyone knowing. She would be utterly ruined, perfect Lady Lucy MacMorlan who was not so perfect after all.

"Then we'll go somewhere else," Methven said. "At your convenience," he added, and it was not an invitation but a command.

Lucy's throat felt dry. "It would be most improper to be alone with you—" she started to say, but his laughter cut her off.

"You write erotic love poetry, Lady Lucy, and yet you think it would be inappropriate to be alone with me? You have a strange sense of what constitutes proper behavior."

He was steering Lucy toward one of the doors leading from the great hall. Lucy tried to resist, but her slippers slid across the polished wood as though it were ice. She tried to dig her heels in, but there was nothing to dig them into.

"I could carry you," Methven said, on an undertone, "if you prefer." There was a dark, wicked thread of amusement in his voice now.

"No," Lucy said. She grabbed some shreds of composure. She must not let him see how nervous she was. "Thank you," she said, "but I have always considered carrying to be overrated."

Her mind scrambled back and forth over various possibilities. She had to get away. Perhaps she could tell

him she needed to visit the ladies' withdrawing room
and then climb out of the window and take a carriage
back to the inn....

"Don't even think about running away again," Methven said, making her jump by the accuracy with which
he had read her mind. He sounded grim. "We can run
around the battlements as much as you please, but in
the end the outcome will be the same."

Damn. There really was no escape. She was going
to have to confront him, try to explain about the letters
and beg for his silence. Lucy was frankly terrified at
the thought. Robert Methven did not strike her as the
understanding type.

"Take my arm if you do not wish to make a scene,"
Methven said. "We can talk in the library. Lord Brodrie
never goes there. I don't believe he has opened a book
in his life."

Lucy hesitated, her hand hovering an inch above
his sleeve. She did not want to touch him at all. It felt
as though it would be dangerous to do so, but at the
same time she was annoyed with herself for being so
aware of him. Her face burning, she rested her hand
very lightly on his proffered arm, too lightly to feel the
muscle beneath his jacket. She maintained sufficient
distance from him that their bodies did not touch at all.
There was no brushing of her skirts against his leg or
her hair against his shoulder. Yet despite her perfect re-
gard for physical distance, it was as though there were
a current running between them, deep and dark and

turbulent. She wanted to ignore it, but she could not. She could not ignore *him*.

He ushered her into the library. Evidently he knew his way around Brodrie Castle, no doubt from the time of his courtship of Dulcibella—a courtship she had so skillfully sabotaged.

Lucy's heart sank lower than her silk slippers. No, he was not going to be sympathetic. It did not take any great intellectual deduction to work that out. She had helped to ruin his betrothal and with it whatever plans he had had to secure his inheritance. He would not be in a forgiving mood.

Methven closed the door behind them. It shut with the softest of clicks, cutting off the distant sounds of the ball, the voices and the music, and cocooning them in a sudden silence that made Lucy's awareness of him all the more acute. He moved closer to her; she could hear his breath above the hiss and spit of the fire in the grate. She could catch the faint scent of his cologne above the pine from the logs that smoldered in the hearth.

"It was you who wrote the letters your brother used to seduce Miss Brodrie away from me," Methven said. Then, when Lucy did not answer: "Well?"

The sharpness of his tone made Lucy jump.

"I'm sorry," she said. "I was not aware that it was a question." She paused, took a deep breath. "Yes," she said. "I did write them. I wrote Lachlan's letters."

CHAPTER FOUR

LUCY SAW SATISFACTION ease into Methven's eyes at her admission of guilt. Her heart was beating hard and fast now. She wondered if she looked as scared as she felt. She would be the talk of Edinburgh for months. Lucy's stomach clenched. She hated the thought of being a by-word for scandal.

But he would not betray her. Surely he would not. No gentleman would betray a lady's trust.

"Do you know what you have done?" Methven asked. His gaze was fixed on her and she could feel the anger in him, held under the tightest control but nevertheless a hot thread beneath his words. "Do you understand the consequences of your actions, Lady Lucy?" The contempt in his blue eyes was blistering. "You have destroyed my betrothal."

"Well," Lucy corrected, "that is not strictly accurate. Dulcibella destroyed your betrothal in running off with Lachlan. I did not make her elope. It was her choice. Perhaps," she added, "she did not want to wed you."

Methven looked supremely unimpressed by her logic. He brought his hand down so hard on the flat top of the mantel that Lucy flinched.

"Will you accept no responsibility?" he demanded. "Do you consider yourself blameless?"

"I wrote the letters," Lucy said steadily. "I do take responsibility for that." She was aware that her words were hardly conciliatory, that she was hardly going in the right direction to appease him. When she had set out to justify herself, she had not intended to provoke him, but there was something about Robert Methven that got under her skin.

"Why?" He growled the word at her, his eyes impossibly blue, impossibly angry. "Why did you do it?"

"I did it because Lachlan paid me," Lucy said defiantly.

She saw Methven's eyes widen in surprise.

"So you did it for the money?" he said, and the contempt in his tone was like a whip.

"You make me sound like a courtesan," Lucy complained. "It wasn't like that."

Methven smiled suddenly. Lucy noticed the way the smile ran a crease down one of his lean, tanned cheeks and deepened the lines that fanned out from the corners of his eyes. She felt a sudden sweet, sliding feeling in her stomach and trembled a little. "In your own way you are for sale," he pointed out gently. "I beg your pardon, but I think it is exactly like that."

Lucy said nothing. She certainly was not going to tell a man so cynical that the money from the letters had gone to charity. That would come too close, expose too much of what really mattered to her. She could not discuss it, not even to exonerate herself. She never spoke of Alice. It was too painful. Besides, Robert Methven would only laugh at her. And probably disbelieve her.

"I have no money," she said. "I need to earn it."

"You are an heiress," Methven said.

"The definition of an heiress," Lucy said, "is someone who will inherit money, not someone who currently possesses it. An heiress could be penniless."

"A nice justification," Methven conceded, "but still no excuse." He ran a hand through his hair. "I thought you might claim to have helped him because you believe in love."

A chill settled in Lucy's blood. "I have no time for love," she said.

His eyes searched her face. "Then we have something in common." A bitter smile twisted the corner of his mouth. "I loved what Miss Brodrie would have brought me, though." He sighed, straightened. "Did you know that your cousin Wilfred Cardross and I are involved in a legal battle?" His tone was conversational, but the look in his eyes was very acute and suddenly Lucy had the feeling that the answer to this mattered far more than anything that had gone before.

"Yes," she said truthfully, and saw the scorn and dislike sweep back into his eyes.

"So you did it to help your cousin too," Methven said. "You wanted to help him cheat me of my patrimony." He turned away from her. The line of his shoulders and back, his entire stance, was rigid with repressed fury, yet Lucy sensed something else in him: a frustration, a powerful protective spirit that was some-

how thwarted as though there was something he longed
for yet could not gain. She felt it so instinctively that
she reached out a hand to touch him, then realized what
she was doing and let her hand fall.

"You mistake me," she said, and her voice was a little husky. "I did nothing to help my cousin Wilfred. I
would not give him the time of day, let alone my assistance. If what I have done in any way was to his benefit, then I am sorry."

Methven turned sharply and caught her by the shoulders, his touch burning her through the evening gown.
"Is that true?" he demanded. There was a blaze of heat
in his eyes that made her shiver. He felt it and released
her, his hands falling away.

"You were dancing with him earlier," he said, and
his tone was cool now, as though that flash of heat had
never been.

"Not for pleasure," Lucy said. "I cannot bear him.
Ever since we were children—" She stopped. Childhood reminiscences were probably out of place here.

Methven's gaze searched her face as probing as a
physical touch. "So you really do not know," he said.
His voice was flat. "You have done Cardross the greatest service imaginable in breaking my betrothal and
you did not know."

Apprehension slid down Lucy's spine. "I don't understand," she whispered.

Methven did not answer immediately. Instead he
walked over to the table and poured two glasses of wine
from the decanter. He passed her a glass; their fingers

brushed, distracting Lucy momentarily. She realized that he was gesturing her to sit. She took a battered-looking velvet armchair. Methven sat opposite, resting his elbows on his knees, leaning forward, his glass cradled in his hands.

"Wilfred Cardross and I are involved in a dispute over clan lands," he said. "It goes back centuries to the time of King James the Fourth." He lifted his gaze to hers. "You know that the Methvens and the Cardrosses have always been enemies?"

"And the MacMorlans," Lucy said. "We talked about this eight years ago, you and I."

A smile slid briefly into Robert Methven's eyes like sunlight on water. "So we did," he said softly.

Lucy suddenly felt very hot. She broke the contact between them looking down, smoothing her skirts.

"Cardross holds to the old enmities," Robert Methven said. "He and I—" He shrugged. "Suffice it to say, he has been waiting for an opportunity to claim back the lands he believes to be his. When my grandfather died I was in Canada and so was slow to return and claim my inheritance. That gave him the chance he needed."

"I don't quite see how I am involved in this—" Lucy started to say, but Methven cut in, his incisive tone reminding her that his patience with her was wafer thin.

"You will," he said. "Under the terms of the original treaty, the Methvens were given lands carved out from the earldom of Cardross. Those lands constitute half my estate."

There was a hollow feeling in Lucy's stomach now. "I can see why Wilfred might not like that," she said.

Methven's smile held no warmth. "Indeed. The agreement was originally reached because the Methven clan had bested Cardross men in battle. King James the Fourth imposed the ruling on both sides back in the fifteenth century, but it still stands today."

The fire roared and cracked as a sudden gust of wind curled down the chimney.

"The only proviso," Methven said softly, holding Lucy's eyes, "was that if any future marquis took more than twelve months to claim his inheritance, he would have to fulfill certain criteria or forfeit his lands. I took thirteen months."

"Why did it take you so long to return?" Lucy asked. "Why were you, the Methven heir, in Canada at all?"

She saw something flicker in his eyes, something of pain and dark, long-held secrets.

"That does not concern you," he said, and the words were like a door slamming shut in her face. "I was late claiming my lands and title and so Cardross had his chance to invoke the old treaty. Under its terms I am required to wed within a year and produce an heir within two." He paused for a heartbeat. "Now you will see what you have done in disposing of my bride."

Lucy did. She had destroyed everything he had worked to safeguard. She had put the safety of his lands and his clan at risk. For a moment the disastrous consequences of her meddling made her feel quite faint.

"I did not know.... Surely you can find another

bride…" she stammered, then fell silent beneath the searing contempt in his gaze.

"That is the delightful twist," Methven said politely. "King James, in his desire to force sworn enemies to bed down together, made it a requirement that I wed a descendent of the earls of Cardross."

"Oh." Lucy frantically tried to remember Wilfred's family tree. He had no sisters—and would no doubt have forbidden them to marry Robert Methven if he had. Dulcibella had been a distant cousin. So was she, of course, but on the female side. There was no one else she could recall. Wilfred was almost devoid of relatives. Which was bad news for Lord Methven.

"I am sorry," she said. She knew the words were inadequate. She had felt guilty enough before, but now that the full extent of the damage was revealed she felt quite wretched.

"You may imagine," Methven said cuttingly, "how your regret moves me." He got up abruptly and placed his untouched glass of claret on the table.

"There is no need to be so sarcastic," Lucy protested. She could feel the guilty color stinging her cheeks. "I truly am sorry. I did not know—"

"Ignorance is no excuse," Methven said roughly. "It is not as though your letters on behalf of your brother are unprecedented."

Apprehension breathed gooseflesh along Lucy's skin. Wrapped up in the tale of the Methven inheritance, stifled by guilt, she had forgotten for a moment that Lord Prestonpans had dropped her well and truly in trouble with his ill-considered ramblings earlier.

"You do not deny it," Methven said after a moment. "So it must be true. You wrote the erotic letters that scandalized society last year."

He strode across to the fireplace and laid one arm along the mantel. Every action spoke of latent power and authority. Lucy felt completely intimidated and was equally determined not to show the fact. She stood up, because being seated when he was standing made her feel at an acute disadvantage.

Her palms were damp. She rubbed them on her skirts. "I did not realize how Lachlan's friends would use those letters," she said. "I had no notion."

"Ignorance is an excuse you have already tried this evening," Methven said pleasantly. "It wears thin. Your gullibility has been fairly extensive, hasn't it, Lady Lucy? How did you expect people would use erotic letters?"

Lucy's face was burning. "I agree that my naïveté has been extensive," she said, between shut teeth.

Methven stepped away from the fireplace and came toward her. He took her gently by the upper arms, turning her so the candlelight fell on her face. He did not let her go; his hands were warm on her bare skin above the edge of her gloves, and his gaze on her face made her feel mercilessly exposed.

"Are you a virgin?" he asked.

"My lord!" Lucy was genuinely shocked. She could feel even hotter color stinging her cheeks now.

"It's a fair question," Methven said, "under the circumstances." He looked unmoved by her outrage, amused even. "The erotic letters hint at an experience far greater than that of the average debutante. Not—" he appraised her thoughtfully "—that you are average, precisely. Far from it."

"My experience or lack thereof is no business of yours, my lord," Lucy said. "That is a scandalous question. No gentleman would ask it."

Methven inclined his head ironically. "Then I am no gentleman. And I would still like to know the answer. Could one write like that without knowing what it truly felt like to make love? I think not."

"There was no personal experience in my writing," Lucy said. She was feeling strange; her head felt too heavy and too light at the same time, as though she had been drinking champagne. She was suddenly aware that Methven's hands had slid down her arms to hold her lightly by the elbows. She wanted to tell him to let her go because it felt disturbing, far more so than a simple touch should. And then he stroked the tender skin in the hollow of one elbow with his thumb, such a sweet caress that it made her catch her breath and made the blood flow heavy like honey in her veins.

"You must have an extremely vivid imagination," Methven said softly.

"I have no imagination at all," Lucy said, trying to concentrate. "Writing is purely an academic exercise for me."

She saw her words had surprised him. His hands

stilled on her. There was curiosity and speculation in his eyes.

"Pure is not really the right word to describe your writing," he said. His gaze narrowed on her face. "Are you telling the truth? Such provocative words did not affect you in any way?"

"I don't know what you mean," Lucy said impatiently. She gave a little dismissive shrug. "Lachlan wanted love letters, so I researched what a love letter should be and wrote some. I do understand that some people find them stimulating to the senses, but I—" She stopped. She was not going to tell him that she had locked any and all desires away long ago in order to spare herself pain.

"You?" Methven prompted.

"I don't find them remotely arousing," Lucy said truthfully.

Methven nodded slowly. She did not understand the expression in his eyes. "How interesting," he said. "So the letters were not drawn from personal experience at all."

"Certainly not," Lucy said. "They were drawn from my grandfather's library."

That made him smile and in that moment she saw her chance. His attitude seemed to have softened toward her a little. She would have to take a risk.

"Are you going to give me away?" she asked. She thought it was better to be direct than to prevaricate. Or beg. Begging was out of the question. She was not that feeble even if she was desperate.

For once he did not answer her immediately. His face was pensive. After a moment he said, "Perhaps you should have considered the consequences of your actions, Lady Lucy."

He was right, of course. She should have done so. She wondered now if rather than being naive she had been deliberately reckless. In her deepest heart she had known the trouble that would be caused if the truth about the letters came out, and yet she had written them. She had no explanation as to why she would do such a thing. Except that the letters had been a small rebellion, exciting, dangerous. She had challenged all the stifling rules that bound her, and it had been exhilarating.

Besides, she had thought herself safe. She had thought no one would ever unmask her.

"You are right," she admitted grudgingly. "It was stupid of me."

"It was foolhardy and dangerous." He sounded unyielding and unsympathetic. "You have interfered in several people's lives and done a great deal of damage."

Lucy felt like a chastened schoolgirl. "I realize that it was wrong," she offered. She tried her special smile again, the one without guile, the one that generally made men melt like butter. "I have apologized."

It did not work. Methven smiled too. Grimly. "You are trying to manipulate me," he said. "I am not so susceptible, Lady Lucy, I assure you. I think…" He paused. "I think the people you deceived should be told."

"No!" The stark, black panic was on Lucy now,

threatening to swallow her whole. Perhaps begging was not out of the question after all. She struggled to stay calm.

"You could not prove I wrote them," she said defiantly.

His smile deepened. "I could have a damned good go at trying, and it would please me to do so."

Just the hint of impropriety would be sufficient. Lucy knew that.

"Please—" She heard the entreaty in her own voice, and this time there was no guile at all. "I know I deserve—"

"To be punished?"

His words, hot and dark, tugged something deep inside her. It was a sensation Lucy had never felt before and it was so swift and so fierce that she gasped. A shocking bloom of warmth and pleasure spread low through her body. Her eyes jerked up to his face, to meet the turbulent heat in his eyes. He gave a low exclamation and the next moment she was in his arms and he was kissing her.

Lucy had not been kissed since that night at Forres Castle. It was not the sort of thing that she invited gentlemen to do. She had never even thought about what it might feel like to kiss someone again, not even out of intellectual curiosity.

This kiss was not like the one she had shared with Robert Methven years before. It felt fierce, heated and complicated, with no concessions to her inexperience. She felt his tongue tease her lips apart and she opened to him and he took her mouth completely. His tongue swept across hers, tasting her as though she were honey, and a powerful heat washed through her, scalding her, shocking her. Immediately she was lost and out of her depth. There was too much here, too much of dark pleasure, too much carnal promise, overwhelming, impossible to understand. It had happened far too fast and now the shock and the fear caught her equally quickly. She was shocked that after what had happened to Alice she could even feel like this, feel such passion, such desire. Then, a heartbeat later, guilt caught her too, and the familiar terror, and she froze in his arms.

He felt it and drew back from her. She heard him mutter a curse. She wanted to run away, frightened at emotions she could not begin to comprehend, but he held her close, her cheek against his shoulder, his lips on her hair, and gradually the fear faded. Within the circle of his arms she felt safe and protected; she felt sixteen again holding his promise against her heart. It was so unexpected a sensation that she relaxed, her breath leaving her in a sigh and her body softening. Only then did he speak.

"I'm sorry," he said. His tone was rougher than she had heard from him before, but it did not frighten her. She knew his anger was not for her. He released her. She could not look at him, gripped as she was by a sudden shyness that paralyzed her. So he put his hand under her chin and made her meet his eyes.

"I'm sorry," he said again. "I went too far, too fast." There was regret and gentleness in his eyes and Lucy felt the floor shift beneath her feet and felt her stomach slide.

He released her. Confusion swept through Lucy then because she was remembering that no matter how she had felt before, this was now, and she had betrayed him and he did not like her for it. Yet despite that, something had happened between them, something dangerous, something she did not understand.

"I think," she said—and her voice was a thread of sound—"that you should go."

He looked at her for a long, long moment and his eyes were dark, his expression opaque, and she had no idea what he was thinking. Then he nodded abruptly.

He bowed and went out. Lucy heard the library door close.

She sank down onto one of the spindly cherrywood chairs, then got up again straightaway and went over to the sideboard, where she poured herself another glass of Lord Brodrie's best claret. She needed a drink. The burn of the liquid against her throat steadied her. She drained the glass and filled it again.

The fire felt too hot. She moved away to a window seat, pressing her fingers against the cold diamond panes. It was as though her body was too heated, sensitive and on edge, wanting something.

"Lucy?"

She had not heard the library door open, but she saw that Mairi was standing on the edge of the Turkish rug, watching her. The candlelight glittered on the silver thread in her gown. Mairi's gaze went to the glass in Lucy's hand. Her eyebrows shot up.

"I saw Lord Methven leaving," she said.

"We were discussing literature," Lucy said. She drank some more claret and felt it slip through her veins, soothing her.

"Of course you were, Lucy," Mairi said dryly. "I always find literary discussions so exciting they leave me looking as dazed as you do now."

"It's the drink," Lucy said.

"And the kissing," Mairi said. "You should see yourself."

Lucy looked up at her reflection in the big mirror that hung above the fireplace. Her eyes looked a hazy dark blue. Her lips were stung red and slightly swollen. She pressed her fingers to them and felt an echo of sensation through her body. Her hair had come undone from its remaining pins. She had no notion how that had happened. She had no notion how any of it had happened. She was not sure what disturbed her more: the kiss or those sweet moments after in Methven's arms when she had felt protected and safe.

Now you know how Alice felt.

Immediately Lucy felt the cold fear take her. It was impossible. She had never felt physical desire, not when she had read the erotic tales, not even when she had written her own sensual poetry. Yet one minute in Lord Methven's arms had awakened emotions in her that she had never known, feelings that terrified her because she knew where they could lead.

She did not want to feel any of them.

Lucy shrank in on herself, the cold lapping around her again. Alice had given herself up to love and passion, given her heart, given her whole self, body and soul. It had ended in shame and misery and pain, and Lucy would never, ever make the same mistake as her twin had done.

"It mustn't happen again," she said aloud.

There was a mixture of amusement and cynicism in Mairi's eyes.

"How naive you are," she said gently, taking Lucy's arm and steering her toward the door. "Once it has happened once, of course it will happen again. The only real question is when."

CHAPTER FIVE

"ROBERT NEEDS TO find another bride now that his first choice has fled." The Dowager Marchioness of Methven, radiating energy and disapproval, seated herself with orderly care on the upright chair Robert held for her. She had a habit of speaking about people as though they were not present. Certainly it felt to Robert as though his input into the conversation was not required.

It was a week after the wedding and they were in the library at Methven Castle. Mr. Kirkward, the family lawyer, had traveled up from Edinburgh to advise them. He was sitting on a lumpy gilt-and-cream sofa and looking most uncomfortable. Lady Methven was seated opposite and Jack drew up a chair to one side. Robert preferred to stand. He crossed to the window and looked out; a soaking gray haze hung over the far mountains, damping the day down and casting dark shadows across the glen.

This was how he remembered his grandfather's castle, as a dripping, mournful edifice that had been barren of pleasure. In those days it had been his older brother, Gregor, who had brought light and laughter to the old place, but now Gregor was gone. As always, Robert felt the profound ache in his chest that memories of Gregor brought with them. Gregor's death had changed his life and his future. He had been the second son, the spare. Methven should never have been his. His grandfather had told him so, that fierce old man who had made no secret of the fact that Robert was a poor substitute for his brother.

"It is indeed most unfortunate that Miss Brodrie eloped," Mr. Kirkward agreed, his dry, precise tones recalling Robert to the room with its sterile shelves of uncut books and its uncomfortable furniture. "Such volatility in a bride quite ruins one's plans."

"Better before the wedding than afterward," Robert said laconically.

He saw Kirkward's pale gray eyes blink rapidly behind his bottle bottom spectacles. Like Lord Brodrie and the minister before him, the lawyer was evidently thinking him a cold fish.

"Quite so." Mr. Kirkward shuffled the papers he had taken from his document case. Robert noted his discomfort. He had seen it in other men who had been uncertain how to deal with him. His brusque manner, his lack of warmth, intimidated many people. He knew that. It could be useful; he had never seen the need to change. Charm was a concept that was alien to him.

"Any preferences for your next choice, Rob?" Jack asked. He threw Robert a glance laced with malicious amusement. Jack was one man who was most certainly not intimidated by him. But his cousin knew him better than most men.

"I don't *have* the luxury of choice," Robert said

tersely. "As I understand it, there is no one suitable. I have to wed a descendant of the first Earl of Cardross, and sadly his line was not very fecund. Only Miss Brodrie and one other cousin are eligible."

"That would be Lady Annabel Channing," Lady Methven said, nodding. "Pretty girl, but a complete lightskirt. You would never know if your heir was yours or someone else's."

Mr. Kirkward made a choking noise. He took off his glasses and polished them feverishly on a white handkerchief.

Jack laughed. "I wouldn't mind a brazen bride," he said. "That might have its benefits."

Robert did mind, but there was little he could do about it. "My attempts to find a suitable wife have foundered," he said. "I might as well choose an unsuitable one since she is the only eligible woman left."

If only he had not kissed Lucy MacMorlan. One kiss had made him ache to take Lady Lucy to his bed when what he was obliged to do was take another woman as his bride. He did not like Lucy very much. Her meddling had cost him dearly. He certainly did not trust her. But liking had little to do with wanting, and he wanted her badly.

"You will do nothing so unbecoming to the name of Methven as marry a lightskirt, Robert," his grandmother corrected him.

"I'll do what I have to do," Robert said bleakly. "Grandmama, there is no alternative." He would marry an entire brothel of lightskirts if that were the price he had to pay to keep his lands.

"I regret to inform you that Lady Annabel wed last month in London," Mr. Kirkward said primly.

"Then we are in some difficulty," Robert said. He felt a violent fury to be so hamstrung by fate. All his life he had taken control, wrested it to him when he had none, fought for it. To be outmaneuvered by a royal decree three centuries old, to be able to do nothing to secure his estates and the future of his clan was intolerable.

"We simply *cannot* allow ghastly Wilfred Cardross to take Methven land," Lady Methven said. There was a plaintive note in her voice, as though she suspected Robert of backing off from the fight. "He is a horrible man and he will clear the people from the estate and destroy their communities and sell off everything that he can and squander it all on the cards."

"I have no intention of allowing Cardross to take the Methven estates," Robert said. The earl was a hard landlord who Robert knew would force the crofters from their traditional homes and livelihoods. Many of the families of men who had fought for the Methven clan for generations would be turned off, abandoned into poverty, families divided and their strong community spirit extinguished. Those on the far-flung northern islands that were part of his patrimony would simply starve in these hard economic times.

He could never allow it. It was his duty as laird to protect the welfare of his people, and he was not going to fall at this, the very first hurdle. It was his fault that they were in this position in the first place. If he had not turned his back on Methven and on his duty as heir all those years ago, he would not have been in Canada when his grandfather had died and would not have taken so long to claim his inheritance. He realized that his fists were clenched tightly. Tension seeped through every muscle in his body. It was impossible to allow Wilfred Cardross to triumph. Yet how to prevent it…

Mr. Kirkward cleared his throat. "My lord, if I might mention…" He sounded timid. Robert wondered if the lawyer genuinely was afraid of him. Surely his reputation was not *that* bad.

"Of course, Mr. Kirkward," he said.

"There is one other family line we have not previously explored," Kirkward said. He searched through the sheaf of papers in his case with agitated fingers, and Robert saw he was holding a family tree. "We discovered it a number of weeks ago, but as you were already betrothed to Miss Brodrie it seemed irrelevant…." He placed the parchment on the table and smoothed it with his hand. "There is a slight problem, my lord, but perhaps, as you are—forgive me—desperate…"

Robert felt a prickle of irritation. He preferred directness to all this circumlocution.

"Spit it out, Kirkward," he advised.

"You would be obliged to be brother-in-law to the man who stole your bride," Kirkward murmured. "A sacrifice, but a small one perhaps, given that half of the Methven estates is at stake—"

Robert cut him off with a chopping motion. "Kirkward," he said, "I have no idea what you are talking about."

Mr. Kirkward flapped the genealogical list in his hand. "We had been interpreting the terms of the royal decree very strictly by looking for direct descendants of the Cardross earldom in the male line," he said. "However, when we looked in the female line we found another line of descent."

Robert thrust the hair back from his forehead in a quick, impatient gesture. "Would that meet the terms of the original treaty?" he asked swiftly.

Mr. Kirkward sighed with the air of a man at the end of his tether. "All the legal advice I have taken suggests it would meet the terms, my lord."

Robert felt a flash of hope. Then he remembered the lawyer's previous words. "When you said I would be obliged to be brother-in-law to the man who stole my bride…"

"Mr. Kirkward is referring to Lachlan MacMorlan," Lady Methven said. She was squinting upside down at the family tree, head on one side. "The Duke of Forres's daughters are kin to Cardross."

Robert looked up sharply. "I know the Forres are kinsmen," he said, "but I thought it was too distant a connection."

Mr. Kirkward was shaking his head. "Straight down the line from the youngest daughter of the first Earl of Cardross." His eyes darted from Robert's face to Lady Methven to Jack. "There is, however, an impediment."

"Naturally," Robert said ironically. "When was it ever easy?"

"You may not wed any lady over the age of thirty or a widow," Jack murmured, quoting from the original royal treaty. "No lady under the age of seventeen, no foreigners, especially no lady with English blood—"

"I need no reminders," Robert said dryly. He could not quite believe that when he and Jack had first heard the ridiculously tight terms of the royal treaty they had actually *laughed* at it.

"Lady Christina MacMorlan is one and thirty," Lady Methven said. "And Lady Mairi is a widow, so they are both ineligible."

That left only Lady Lucy.

Lady Lucy MacMorlan was his only chance.

Lady Lucy who wrote erotic love letters like a wanton and kissed like an innocent. Lady Lucy who had ruined his betrothal, lied to him, caused scandal after scandal, was deceitful and manipulative and had done it all for the money.

Lady Lucy whom he wanted with a fierce lust that was quite inexplicable.

Jack shifted in his chair. "And suddenly it's your birthday, Rob," he said dryly.

There was an abrupt silence in the room. Everyone looked at Robert.

"Whatever can you mean, Jack?" Lady Methven said.

"Only that Rob likes Lady Lucy MacMorlan rather a lot," Jack said, his grin broadening.

"Thank you, Jack," Robert said dryly. "A helpful intervention, as always." He stood up. "You mistake. I do not *like* Lady Lucy at all and I do not trust her an inch."

Lady Methven looked scandalized. "Robert! She is a sweet girl."

"She is a manipulative little minx," Robert said brutally. He thought about Lucy. He had every right to be angry with her, but he could not deny that he was still attracted to her. He thought about the taste of her and the feel of her in his arms. She might be a deceitful hussy, but there was a spark that burned between them like a flame on dry tinder. That heat and desire were exactly what he would have wanted from the woman in his bed.

If only he could trust her.

Mr. Kirkward cleared his throat. "Lady Lucy is heiress to sixty thousand pounds, which will be paid upon her marriage."

Jack whistled. "A not inconsiderable sum. Not that you need the money, Rob."

Robert did not. He had made a vast fortune of his own in Canada, trading in timber, but to marry an heiress was never a bad thing.

"She is also a most generous donor to charity," Mr. Kirkward continued.

Robert's head snapped up. "With what?"

Mr. Kirkward looked confused. "With the earnings from her writing, my lord. Lady Lucy is a benefactor to both the Foundling Hospital and the Greyfriars Orphanage. She donates anonymously, but it was not difficult to discover."

"Your skills of detection impress me, Kirkward," Robert said. He remembered Lucy claiming that she wrote for the money. The one thing she had not done was to justify her actions by telling him she gave the money away to charity. He wondered about her motives.

"You see!" Lady Methven said triumphantly. "I told you she was a sweet, generous girl." She sighed. "I'll allow that Lady Mairi might have been a better choice of bride, though. She is older, widowed and therefore has no false illusions about the married state—"

"Thank you, Grandmama," Robert said, "for the vote of confidence."

Lady Methven snapped her fingers. "You know what I mean, Robert. Besides, Lady Lucy is very particular. She had two seasons in London and three in Edinburgh and refused every suitor." Lady Methven wrinkled her nose up. "The gossips say Lady Lucy's heart was broken when her fiancé died and she has never met another man to match him, but personally I think that is so much nonsense. Duncan MacGillivray was a dry old stick and no suitable match for a young gel, but whatever the case, she has turned down many proposals of marriage."

"She will not have the chance to turn me down," Robert said smoothly. "I cannot afford a refusal."

He pushed the hair back for his brow. He knew he had no choice other than to marry Lucy. "Do you know whether Lady Lucy returned to Forres or to Ed-

inburgh after the wedding, Grandmama?" he asked
Lady Methven.

Mr. Kirkward cleared his throat delicately. "My lord,
I made discreet inquiries into the whereabouts of the
duke's daughters once I realized they might be eligible…." He flicked through the papers. "Apparently they
belong to a club called the Highland Ladies Bluestocking Society. It is an elite and prestigious society for
Scottish ladies with academic credentials and it meets
regularly in a different castle each month."

"So I have heard," Robert said. The Highland Ladies Bluestocking Society was as famous for its secretive nature as for its scholarly interests. No one who
was not a member could attend the meetings, and no
one quite knew what those meetings entailed. Robert
imagined an esoteric group of ladies sitting around discussing dry-as-dust history and literature all day before
changing for dinner and indulging in more discussions
on intellectual subjects.

"Unfortunately," Mr. Kirkward continued, "I have
been unable to ascertain where they are currently meeting. It is secret information."

"Grandmama?" Robert said. He knew that Lady
Methven was not a member of the society, but she knew
plenty of ladies who were.

Lady Methven smoothed her skirts. "Really, Robert," she said. "The Highland Ladies is a secret society. The clue is in the word *secret*. You cannot expect
me to give away any details."

"Even to save Methven?" Robert queried. "I need

to find Lady Lucy quickly and make her an offer of marriage."

"What unromantic haste!" Lady Methven looked down her nose. "You should be trying to *woo* her, Robert, not dragoon her into marriage!"

"I do not have time to be romantic," Robert said.

"I'd like to see you even try," Jack murmured, sotto voce.

Lady Methven gave an exaggerated sigh. "Oh, very well, but do not let it slip that I told you or I will be drummed out of Edinburgh." When Robert merely raised his eyebrows she said, "They are meeting at Durness Castle."

Robert managed to swallow the instinctive curse that rose to his lips. It would not do to offend his grandmother with his language. She already considered him sadly uncouth. But Durness was remote, in the far north of Scotland; it would take him several days to reach it, longer if the weather turned bad. Worse, Wilfred Cardross owned the estate adjoining Durness. It seemed more than a coincidence. He had seen Cardross paying court to Lucy at Brodrie, and now he wondered what the earl was planning.

"The Highland Ladies like to travel," Lady Methven said. "It broadens the mind."

Robert sighed sharply. Some of his own estates, including the northern Methven stronghold of Golden Isle, lay in the same area. He had not been there since Gregor had died.

The day seemed darker all of a sudden, the gray clouds gathering and thickening into rain.

"It will be good for you to wed a member of the Highland Ladies Bluestocking Society, Robert," his grandmother said thoughtfully. "An educated woman will have a civilizing influence on both your manners and your mind after all those years living in the wilds of Canada. She may instruct you in both the social refinements and any intellectual accomplishments in which you are deficient—literature, mathematics, astronomy, geography, manners and conduct..."

Behind him, Robert heard Jack give a snort of laughter and made a mental note to threaten his cousin that if a word of this conversation ever reach the inns and clubs of Edinburgh, he would be a dead man.

He half expected his grandmother to start issuing him with instructions on how to fulfill the other requirement of the treaty, the need to produce an heir within two years. Her advice on that would be a step too far.

As far as he was concerned, Lucy MacMorlan would give him a far greater gift than that of scholarship: the ability to claim his estates unchallenged by anyone, take them and hold them safe. All he had to do was persuade her to marry him.

Lady Lucy owed him a bride. Now he was going to collect on the debt.

CHAPTER SIX

THE SHEEP'S HEAD Alehouse at the bottom of Candle-maker Row was not the sort of inn frequented by the aristocracy, most of whom had fled the narrow, crowded passageways of Edinburgh's Old Town many years before. It was dark, cramped and smelled strongly of tobacco and stale beer. A man would not recognize his own mother in the gloom, and if he did he would be shocked to find her there. Which was exactly why Wilfred Cardross had chosen it. He had also changed his usual flamboyant style of dress for something a little less obvious. It was one of the reasons he was in a bad mood; he hated not to be the center of attention.

The other reason the earl was tapping his fingers irritably on the battered wooden table was that his guest was late. He disliked being kept waiting. It was not appropriate to a man of his elevated station in life. So when Mr. Stuart Pardew slipped into the seat opposite, he greeted him with an ostentatious checking of his pocket watch and no offer of refreshment.

Mr. Pardew seemed completely oblivious of the earl's ill temper. He shook the rain from his cloak and stretched his legs toward the fire with a contented sigh. He raised a hand to summon the servant and ordered a tankard of ale. He looked thoughtfully at the earl's near-empty glass and then failed to offer him a refill.

As soon as the bartender had gone, Cardross pushed his glass aside and leaned forward, elbows on the table.

"Well?" he demanded.

Mr. Pardew looked at him blandly. He had a round, open face, reminiscent of a friendly dog. It was his greatest asset in a life of crime because he looked so honest that no one ever suspected him.

"Methven means to wed one of the MacMorlan sisters," he said.

Cardross's mouth pinched. "Will that hold up in court?"

Pardew shrugged. "Kirkward thinks it will. Descent is through the female line. He is certain he can make the case." He took a long draw on his pint of ale and smacked his lips appreciatively. Cardross looked pained. Silence fell. Pardew, the earl thought, measured every drop of information for its value. He burrowed in the pocket of his cloak and took out a bag. It clinked softly as it landed on the table. For a moment Pardew's eyes gleamed, revealing the true depth of his cupidity.

"Which sister?" Cardross said softly. He leaned closer.

Pardew took his time. "Lady Lucy," he said. "Neither of the others is eligible under the terms of the treaty."

Cardross sat back. He felt obscurely relieved. "Lucy will never agree," he said. "She is set against marriage." Everyone knew that Lucy MacMorlan had refused endless suitors.

Pardew yawned. "Then Methven will do whatever he has to do to persuade her." He tilted his head slightly and looked thoughtfully at Cardross. "He is ruthless in protecting his inheritance. You know that."

Cardross did know. From the moment that Robert Methven had returned to take up his estates, he had been single-minded in restoring the lands his grandfather had so systematically run down. Cardross cursed him for it. The old marquis had been so neglectful that Cardross's men had easily been able to take some cattle here, annex some land there. They had burned villages and pillaged crops without redress. Then Robert Methven had returned. The very next raid had met with a vicious response that had sent Cardross's clansmen back with their tails between their legs.

"Something must be done." Cardross was thinking aloud. "I cannot rely on fate to remove Methven's bride a second time."

"Too risky," Pardew agreed, his eyes on the bag of money.

"Indeed. But I cannot do anything too obvious." There was a plaintive note in Cardross's voice at the trouble Robert Methven was causing him. "The Duke of Forres is a rich and influential man. I cannot afford to alienate him."

"Perhaps you could marry Lady Lucy yourself." Pardew looked bland again. "If you could manage that."

Cardross looked at him sharply but could detect no sarcasm in Pardew's expression.

"Lady Lucy would never consent," he said. "She hates me."

"That is most unfortunate," Pardew agreed. For a second Cardross could have sworn he saw a spark of mockery in the other man's eyes. "I am afraid, my lord, that you may have to accustom yourself to getting your hands dirty after all. All in aid of the greater good, of course."

Cardross shuddered. Getting his hands dirty literally or metaphorically was simply not his style, but he thought Pardew was probably correct.

"Find some men who can arrange an abduction," he said. "Men experienced in—"

"Violence, my lord?" Pardew said affably.

Cardross shook his head. How Pardew liked to try and provoke him. "Men experienced in kidnapping," he said, "but with sufficient self-control not to damage the goods."

"Ah," Pardew said, the light of understanding breaking in his eyes. "I see." He paused, looking at the bag of money again. "That will cost a great deal, my lord. The kidnapping is easy, the self-control very expensive."

"Of course," Cardross said wearily. He pushed the bag of coins across the table and Pardew pocketed it in one swift move, like a spider gobbling its prey.

"Thank you, my lord," Pardew said with deceptive deference.

"Does Methven show any sign of visiting Golden Isle?" Cardross asked.

Pardew put down his tankard. Suddenly the expression in his eyes was very bright and very sharp.

"No, my lord," he said.

"I need more information for my contact there," Cardross said.

"Ah." Pardew looked resigned. "That will need a little more...financing. The king's officers are, unsurprisingly, very careful in whom they place their trust."

Cardross smothered a curse. More money. It always came down to more money.

Grudgingly he pushed another money bag across the table to Pardew, who turned so that his back was to the room. He loosened the drawstring. Cardross saw the flash of gold.

"It's all there," he said irritably. "Though if you wish to count it like a damned moneylender, pray do so."

"That won't be necessary," Pardew said. He was smiling genially. The second bag disappeared into his pocket, following the first. Cardross heard the chink of coin against the wooden table leg.

"That is very satisfactory, my lord," Pardew said. "I will have some information for you to pass on to your contact very soon." He drained his tankard and stood. "Such a pleasure doing business with Your Lordship."

After Pardew had gone out, Cardross ordered another brandy and stared half-drunk into the fire. A vague sense of self-pity plagued him. It seemed so unfair that he had gambled away his fortune and was now obliged to sell secrets to the French in order to pay his debts. He was not at all clear how he had got into such a difficult situation. It was even more unfair that the lucrative sidelines he had developed in the northern isles, selling island men and boys into the slavery of the navy press-gangs, smuggling, would be put at risk if ever Robert Methven chose to take back his northern territories. Cardross lived in fear of that day.

If he wed Lady Lucy MacMorlan he would not only thwart Methven's latest round of marriage plans, but he would also gain Lucy's sixty thousand pounds. Greed curdled in him at the thought. He needed that money. He deserved it.

He would have to act fast. Fortunately he had been farsighted enough to plant a spy in the Duke of Forres's household a long time before. Now it was time for the woman to earn her money.

"MY DEAR, THERE is nothing remotely inappropriate in it." Lady Kenton rested a reassuring hand on Lucy's arm. "Why, the practice of massage has a long and noble history as a medical and therapeutic treatment. All the ancient civilizations embraced it." She leaned closer and lowered her voice so that the other members of the Highland Ladies Bluestocking Society could not overhear them. They were taking tea in the conservatory at Durness Castle. The chink of china and the babble of conversation rose to the glass roof and filled the air.

"My practitioner, Anton, was trained by a Swedish physician, Dr. Ling," Lady Kenton said. "He is an expert. I recommend him to you." She sat back and took a sip of her tea.

Lucy fidgeted with her teaspoon, avoiding Lady Kenton's eye. Her godmother was a fellow member of the Highland Ladies Bluestocking Society and was the most reassuringly respectable of ladies, but Lucy could not quite eradicate the idea that massage was decidedly improper. The thought of a man's hands on her body, and that man not even her husband, was truly shocking. Except that her shoulder and her back ached badly from too much writing and she was desperate to find a remedy.

"He is medically trained, you say," she repeated cautiously.

Lady Kenton smiled. "Indeed he is. He is practically a doctor himself. And should you have any further qualms, my love, let me tell you that Anton is not a man who..." she paused delicately "...is interested in women, if you take my point. Besides, your maid would be present to preserve the proprieties. I can send him to you this evening, if you wish. He accompanies me everywhere."

"Thank you," Lucy said. "Well, that sounds very helpful." Lady Kenton's traveling entourage was legendary. On every outing of the Highland Ladies Bluestocking Society, Her Ladyship was accompanied by her own pastry chef, her laundry maid, a manicurist, a hairdresser and now a masseur.

Lucy flexed her fingers. "I confess I am in a great

deal of discomfort from holding my quill. My shoulder aches incessantly."

"What are you writing at the moment?" Lady Kenton inquired. She refilled the china cups and passed one to Lucy. "Last time we met you were working on a treatise on Shakespeare's sonnets. How is that progressing?"

"Mr. Walsh has agreed to take it for the winter edition of the *History Review*," Lucy said.

Lady Kenton beamed. "Excellent! He has always been a good friend to us and eager to publish our works."

Lady Kenton herself was a well-known author of stories based on Highland folklore. Many of the members of the Highland Ladies Bluestocking Society were authors or poets and were published in a variety of journals. Lucy was proud to be the youngest of their published authors.

"Have you given any further thought to a betrothal with your cousin Wilfred Cardross?" Lady Kenton inquired. "I am certain that your dear mama would have approved the match."

They were back on her godmother's favorite topic. Lucy had known it would only be a matter of time. Lady Kenton was a woman with a mission.

"I cannot marry Wilfred, ma'am," she said, deciding that bluntness might offend her godmother but it was better than prevarication. "I told you, I don't like him."

Lady Kenton's plump little face took on a dissatisfied expression. "You cling to the ghost of Lord Mac-Gillivray," she said disagreeably. "Your father was a fool to permit such an engagement, promising you to a doddery scholar old enough to be your grandfather!" Her fingers beat an irritable tattoo on the arm of her chair. "Really, Lucy, to throw yourself away on a man with one foot in the grave! I could only be glad that he died *before* the marriage, because the wedding night would most surely have finished him off and that would have been both scandalous and very unpleasant for you."

Lucy could feel the hot color stinging her cheeks. She was not going to tell her godmother that she and Lord MacGillivray had planned to spend their wedding night in animated discussion of James MacPherson's epic poems. She opened her fan and flicked it back and forth to cool her hot cheeks. There was an odd, trapped feeling in her chest, as though her laces were drawn too tight. She felt it whenever anyone addressed the topic of her engagement.

The door of the conservatory opened and Robert Methven strode in. He was about the last person Lucy had expected to see, and she felt her heart leap up into her throat at the sheer shock of his appearance. He looked as though he had ridden hard. Rain had spattered his traveling cloak, and as Lucy watched he swung it from his shoulders to reveal a beautifully cut sporting jacket beneath. He did not look at home indoors. There was something too restless and too physical about him to sit comfortably with the elegant furnishings of the conservatory, the pastel shades of the ladies' gowns, the clink of teacup and the polite chatter of conversation.

"What on earth is *he* doing here?" Lucy exclaimed, too discomposed to phrase the question with her usual courtesy.

Gentlemen were only invited to the meetings of the Highland Ladies Bluestocking Society if they were eminent scholars. She was certain that Robert Methven could not possibly be present in an official capacity. Yet it seemed that he was, for as Lucy watched, Lady Durness sailed forward to greet him, taking his hand warmly in hers. He bent and gallantly pressed a kiss on the back of it. The high-pitched conversation in the room dropped for a moment and then swelled again to an excited babble.

Methven's gaze scoured the room and fixed hard and fast on Lucy. Lucy's heart jolted. Her fan flicked out of her trembling fingers and leaped up in the air, to land on the rug by her feet.

"Ah." Lady Kenton sounded agreeably pleased. "This afternoon's tutor has arrived."

"Tutor!" Lucy was scrabbling to retrieve her fan, grateful that her scarlet face was hidden as she bent down.

"Allow me, Lady Lucy."

Methven had gone down on one knee beside their table, picking up the wayward fan and handing it back to her gravely. Looking up, Lucy saw a fugitive smile in his eyes as he took in her flustered appearance. Damn him.

"Thank you." Lucy knew she sounded ungracious. She took the fan gingerly from him, making sure that their fingers did not touch. He straightened up and bowed. "Perhaps I might join you?" he said.

It was the last thing that Lucy wanted. She felt extremely discomposed.

"It might be better, my lord," she said, staring pointedly at his mud-spattered boots, "if you changed your attire after what must have been an arduous journey. You are hardly dressed for the drawing room."

Methven pulled up a spare chair. "Then it is fortunate we are in the conservatory," he said. "I am persuaded that you will forgive my disorder."

Fizzing with annoyance, Lucy drew her skirts away from the offending boots. Lady Kenton gestured to a footman, who fetched an additional cup and replenished the pot.

"How do you take your tea, Lord Methven?" Lady Kenton inquired.

"Hot and strong," Robert Methven said, looking at Lucy, who was furious to feel herself blushing.

"I hear you are to tutor our meeting this afternoon, Lord Methven," she said. "How singular that will be."

"You do not think me qualified to lecture you, Lady Lucy?" Methven quizzed gently. "Or perhaps you fear my delivery will be lacking?" He stretched and Lucy averted her gaze from the muscles rippling beneath his splashed pantaloons. Until that moment she had not even been aware that she was staring at his thighs. How inappropriate of her.

"You are in good company," Methven added. "My grandmother considers me a complete dullard."

"I could not possibly comment," Lucy said, "until I know your subject. We do, however, have very high standards here at the Highland Ladies Bluestocking Society."

"I am duly warned," Methven said, "and promise not to let the side down."

Lucy waited but he did not enlighten her as to his specialist subject. His silence set the current of irritation coursing through her once again. He knew that she wanted to know, so he was deliberately withholding that information. She supposed her curiosity was vulgar and her implication that he was not qualified to address them was downright rude, but somehow she could not help herself. He ruffled her serenity.

"How did you hear of the Highland Ladies Bluestocking Society, my lord?" she asked.

Methven smiled at her. "So many questions, Lady Lucy. I am flattered by your interest."

"I am not interested in you," Lucy said, "merely in the source of your information."

"Ah." He sounded amused. "Because the Highland Ladies is a secret society?"

"Quite so."

"You may trust my discretion."

Again it was no answer and again Lucy felt annoyed by his deliberate evasion. She watched as he finished his tea and replaced the china cup gently on the table. He stood and bowed to her.

"Excuse me. I must go and prepare for my lecture. I shall hope to see you there, Lady Lucy."

"That depends on the topic," Lucy said.

He laughed. "Are you always so impatient? I had no idea." He put one hand on the back of her chair and bent close so that his lips brushed her ear.

"Sometimes," he said softly, "the anticipation is the best part."

He straightened and strolled away.

"How very provoking that man is!" Lucy burst out. Normally she would not dream of expressing a view of an acquaintance, especially not in public, but Robert Methven had got under her guard. Sensation fluttered in her belly. He was looking back at her now and she felt the awareness like a flame rise and scorch her. It was not unpleasant, but it was disturbing. There was a flicker of excitement in her blood that she had never felt before she had met him.

"I wonder why you dislike him," Lady Kenton said. Her gaze was thoughtful as it rested on Lucy's face.

"The boot is on the other foot," Lucy said shortly. She fidgeted with her teaspoon, avoiding Lady Kenton's gaze. "He does not like me."

"He is direct, perhaps," Lady Kenton conceded. "Not like your Edinburgh beaux. But I saw no sign that he dislikes you. Far from it."

"I am not comfortable with him," Lucy said. It was the closest she had ever come to admitting that there was something about Robert Methven that both fascinated and troubled her. Or, more accurately, something about her reaction to him that troubled her.

"You have lived too much amongst scholars," Lady

Kenton said. "Not that a man of taste and education is a bad thing, but it must be tempered by something a little more earthy, more masculine. Now, Robert Methven is very much a man. Rich, personable and intelligent and I'll wager he is most lusty in the marriage bed. I would think he could give a woman great pleasure."

Lucy closed her eyes and shuddered. Lady Kenton was of a generation that was so much more outspoken in its language, but hearing her godmother's frank assessment of the Marquis of Methven's sexual prowess when she was looking directly at him across a tearoom was more than a little disturbing.

"I did not look for lustiness in my marriage, Aunt Emily," she said. "I wished for a meeting of minds, not bodies. Lord MacGillivray was sober in his conduct and intellectual in his studies."

Lady Kenton stifled a broad yawn. "I am well aware of that, my love," she said, "and thought him a dead bore for it. Why, in my day we wanted so much more than that, a hero fresh from the battlefield with a sword in his hand. The youth of today have let their standards slip, I fear."

A hero fresh from the battlefield...

Lucy paused. Yes, that was it. There was something primitive about Lord Methven; something disturbing that invoked the warriors of the previous century, the wild men of the northern isles who had Viking blood in their veins along with their fierce Scots heritage. A long, slow shiver brushed across her skin. That was not what she wanted. She had never wanted passion. Her life was smooth and ordered, with a calm and perfect surface, which was exactly as it should be, and that was the way it was going to stay.

CHAPTER SEVEN

ROBERT'S LECTURE ON astronomy and navigation, illustrated with anecdotes from his travels, was received rapturously. The Highland Ladies gave him a hearty round of applause and pressed him to stay for dinner. Since all he had waiting for him was a cold supper and a lumpy bed at the Durness Inn, Robert was quick to agree. His courtship of Lady Lucy MacMorlan would progress all the better through proximity.

Robert had thought long and hard about that courtship. And come up with absolutely no plan whatsoever. His preferred course of action would have been the direct one, but to propose directly to Lady Lucy would be to invite an equally direct refusal. He had also considered the idea of abducting her. It held more than a little appeal, especially after those hot stolen moments between them at Brodrie Castle. Abduction was generally frowned upon these days, but he thought he could probably get away with it. The drawback was that it would make Lucy even less inclined to wed him, and forcing a woman to the altar would not, under normal circumstances, be the way he would behave. But these were not normal circumstances.

The ladies had another tutorial between his lecture

and dinner. There was a choice of two classes, but to
these Robert was not invited. He had no idea what they
were and he found his curiosity piqued. As he wandered along Durness Castle's extravagantly furnished
corridors, he could hear strains of music drifting from
within one of the salons. The music was exotic and
Eastern, punctuated by voices and laughter. He wandered toward the sound; immediately a burly footman
barred his way.

"May I help you, my lord?" The man's expression
belied his courteous tone. His firmly folded arms and
aggressive stance made it clear to Robert that he was
not going to find out what was going on behind that
closed door. The activities of the Highland Ladies Bluestocking Society were indeed a closed book. It piqued
Robert's curiosity extremely.

He strolled out onto the terrace. The air was fresh
and cold, threatening snow even though it was now
well into spring. The shutters of the salon were closed
against prying eyes, but behind them Robert could see
light and undulating shadows. He could hear someone
tapping out the beat of the music, sensual music that
wove its spell of temptation and promise. Not wishing
to appear a Peeping Tom, he retreated from the weather
and sought out the library. This door was locked, as
well. A different burly footman materialized and in-
formed him civilly that the ladies were taking an art
class. What there was about such a venture that neces-
sitated the locking of the door was anyone's guess, but
Robert took the hint and retired to his chamber.

In the drawing room prior to dinner, the ladies all appeared to be in very high spirits. Robert was not the only gentleman present; there was a plump and jolly fellow with a luxuriant gray mustache who was introduced as Mr. Florence the art master and two very handsome young men whose precise role was left rather vague. Robert began to suspect that the reason that the Highland Ladies Bluestocking Society proceedings were veiled in secrecy was that some of their activities were considerably more risqué than others. His ideas of them reading dry intellectual tracts before dinner were clearly misplaced.

He found Lady Lucy seated with her sister Lady Mairi MacLeod on one of the silver velvet chaise longues and asked if he might join them. Lucy looked inclined to refuse. Mairi, however, seemed very happy to see him and patted the seat beside her.

"We did so enjoy your lecture, Lord Methven," Mairi said, her blue eyes sparkling. "Lucy was particularly impressed. She said she would not have believed you had it in you to be so interesting."

Robert saw Lucy press her lips together in a very tight line. He smiled at her. "I am always glad to be able to confound your prejudices, Lady Lucy," he said. He glanced toward the two stalwart young men who were surrounded by a positive bevy of eager ladies.

"I do hope," he added, "that you enjoyed the subsequent class as much as my lecture. Life drawing, was it not?"

Lucy's blue gaze flickered up to meet his. "I did

not attend the art class," she said. "I am very poor at drawing."

"All the more reason to practice," Mairi said, "especially with such willing subjects." She popped a sugared almond into her mouth and crunched it. "Don't you agree, Lord Methven?"

"I am sure that the gentlemen concerned displayed to advantage," Robert said, "and that would be sufficient to inspire any lady."

Mairi giggled. Lucy looked unimpressed. "Life drawing is a serious art form," she said. "It is an intellectual pursuit."

"And a lot of fun, as well," Mairi corrected. She gave Robert a comprehensive look. "Should you ever wish to model for us, Lord Methven, we should be delighted."

Mairi MacLeod, Robert thought, was a flirt. She had a widow's confidence around the masculine sex, a confidence no doubt born of experience. Lucy, in contrast, was no flirt, but neither was she a naive debutante. Robert thought of her untutored but wholly inflammatory response to his kiss. Then he wished he had not, as Mairi was looking pointedly at his pantaloons. He shifted uncomfortably.

"I am honored that you should invite me to pose for you all," he said. "However, I fear I might not measure up."

"I doubt you have any fears on that score, Lord Methven," Mairi said, still staring. "You strike me as a very able man in all particulars."

Robert smiled, turning to Lucy. "If you did not attend the art class, Lady Lucy," he said, "I assume you were learning the Eastern dancing?"

Lucy's eyes opened very wide. In that moment she looked every inch the startled debutante.

"How did you know that was what we were doing?" she demanded. "Were you watching?"

"I have not been looking through keyholes," Robert said. "I recognized the type of music and guessed you must have been dancing. Did you enjoy it?"

He was interested to see that she blushed. "It was… different."

"From the formality of the quadrille and the cotillion?"

"Yes, and even from the energy of the Scottish reels. It felt…" Lucy paused. Her blush deepened. "I had always thought that music was mathematical in the skill it requires to write it. Yet this…" Her gaze, bright blue and very hot, met his and then slid away. "This music was strangely sensual."

In that moment Robert wished that Lady Mairi were not there. He wished that he and Lucy were somewhere else entirely, preferably somewhere warm and comfortable and where they would be quite alone to pursue the conversation wherever it might lead. Lucy's cool, crisp intellectual approach to all things passionate was both naive and intriguing. He remembered thinking at Brodrie Castle that she had a rational rather than an emotional approach to life. Now it seemed she had the same view of music: music, which could be stirring, vivid and sensual.

It was high time Lady Lucy MacMorlan was awakened to all the intriguing possibilities that passion offered.

Frustratingly, however, this was not the time. The room was bright and full and buzzing with people. Mairi, perhaps sensing something of his feelings, rose ostentatiously to her feet and murmured something about speaking to Lady Kenton before dinner. Robert saw Lucy put out a hand as though to stop her sister from leaving them together. Her lips parted. She seemed on the verge of objecting. She half rose from her seat, as though about to abandon him too.

"I do hope," Robert said, "that you will not leave me alone at the mercy of so many ladies, Lady Lucy."

"I am sure you would cope quite admirably," Lucy said. "You would be fighting them off with sticks."

"Which is precisely what I do not wish to happen," Robert said. "Only consider how rude that would appear. Offense would be taken."

Lucy almost smiled. After a moment she relaxed back into her seat. "I thought," she said, "that you had no compunction about being very honest indeed, even if it gives offense."

"Even I have to draw the line somewhere," Robert said. "I do believe," he added, "that you are uncomfortable in my company. That is why you seek to escape me."

Her eyes met his. They were completely expressionless. "I assure you I am perfectly comfortable with anyone," Lucy said coolly.

"So there is nothing special about me? How quelling." Robert settled himself back against the cushions and looked at her thoughtfully. "I thought that perhaps after our last encounter—"

Her blush deepened. Her gaze slid from his. All of a sudden the layers of sophistication were stripped away and she looked stricken.

"I really am sorry," she said. "I profoundly regret ruining your betrothal."

She sounded utterly sincere. There was a vulnerable set to her mouth and a defeated slope to her shoulders that sparked a most inappropriate feeling of tenderness in him. Up until that moment Robert would have said it did not matter whether she regretted it or not, or whether he believed her or not. Whether she was sorry for her actions and whether he had forgiven her were irrelevant. But now, seeing her vulnerability, he felt quite differently. He felt protective.

He did not care much for the feeling. It muddied the waters. He had no time for sentiment; all he wanted to do was secure his bride.

"I'm not angry anymore." He spoke abruptly.

Her eyes widened. "You have every right to be."

"Perhaps." He shrugged, keeping his gaze on the shifting crowd of people filling the drawing room. Anything to avoid looking at Lucy again and feeling that strange tug of emotion.

"I thought I could help you." She leaned forward. "Perhaps I could write some letters for you to use to woo another lady…" She stopped. Robert looked at her.

That eager, appealing look was still on her face and it made him feel a scoundrel because he knew exactly how she could help him.

"It would probably be better if you did not," he said.

Her face fell. "I suppose not. Tactless of me." She bit her lip. "Well, if you think of anything…"

"I will be sure to let you know." Robert smiled at her, deliberately changing the subject. "Lord Brodrie was quite annoyed to discover so much of his finest claret had gone missing, by the way." He raised an eyebrow. "I assumed you had consumed it. I apologize if my kisses drove you to drink. Not the outcome I would have desired."

Lucy was pulling threads out of the silver tassels on the cushions. Her fidgeting fingers were all that betrayed her discomfort.

"Must we speak of it?" she asked.

"That bad?" Robert queried.

She looked up and met his eyes. "I drank the claret for the shock," she said.

"Worse and worse," Robert said. "I had no idea that my technique lacked so much finesse."

Lucy flicked a hunted look around the room. "I would ask you not to mention it," she said. "My reputation—"

"Would surely suffer more if it became widely known that you attend lessons in Eastern dancing or life drawing," Robert said. "What an interesting society the Highland Ladies must be! I can quite see why its workings are secret."

Two bright spots of color burned in Lucy's cheeks. She looked charmingly annoyed. "The Highland Ladies wish to learn and broaden our experience," she said. "Our pursuits are entirely educational."

"Well, that is one word for it, I suppose," Robert said.

"You have double standards," Lucy said. "No one reproved Rubens for painting nudes. No one reproaches the gentlemen who frequent the Edinburgh clubs for their pursuits. People are quick to judge."

Robert scrutinized her thoroughly. She looked exquisite this evening in another demure debutante gown of white silk laced with silver thread, her vivid red hair piled up with diamond pins, so elegant, so discreet.

"It is curious," he said slowly, "that you are so determinedly proper on the outside, Lady Lucy, yet you write erotic poetry, you drink claret and you find music and dancing sensual. Is your propriety all for show?"

Now there was no doubt that he had provoked her. He saw a flash of anger in her eyes and something else, something different. Surprise. *Panic?*

"I *am* proper," she said. "A perfect lady. Everyone says so." Her fidgeting fingers were playing with the struts of her fan now. Robert heard them creak in protest.

"Everyone *thinks* you are proper," Robert corrected. "Unless, of course, you are deceiving yourself along with everyone else and you genuinely believe that you have no passion in you." He leaned closer to her. His fingers brushed her bare arm above the edge of her glove and he felt her shiver. He smiled. He suspected that Lady Lucy was in denial of her own passionate desires and he would be very happy to point out to her what it was she truly wanted.

"Tell me," he said, "what it is that you would look for in the man you chose to marry?"

She looked startled. Then her lashes swept down, veiling her expression.

"Why do you ask?" she said.

"I'm curious," Robert said, recognizing evasion when he saw it. "Humor me. You have rejected many suitors. Why?"

There was a strange expression in Lucy's eyes. Suddenly they were a blank blue, as though she had erected a barrier to keep him from reading any emotion there. "It's true that I am considered very particular," she said. "I was betrothed once. Lord MacGillivray was my perfect ideal of a gentleman. I do not expect to wed as I do not expect to meet his equal."

She spoke smoothly, as though she had said the words many times before. Robert wondered why he did not believe her. Something did not ring quite true. It was not that he thought she lied, more that she had become so accustomed to saying the words that she had started to believe them herself.

"A perfect ideal?" he said. He tried and failed to keep the skepticism from his voice. "Forgive me, but I never heard such rubbish in my life. There is no such thing as a perfect ideal."

Lucy stiffened. He saw surprise reflected in her

eyes, and confusion. It was quite clear than no one had ever challenged her on the subject before. "Thank you for sharing your thoughts with me, Lord Methven," she said, after a moment. Her voice was sharp. "I had forgotten how very abrasive you could be."

"Because I am honest?" Robert said.

"Because you are rude and brusque," Lucy corrected. "Your manner is in no way elegant or polished."

Robert was amused. "I imagine, then," he said, "that I in no way fit your *ideal* of the perfect husband."

"Certainly not," Lucy said with crushing politeness. "You are far too frank and unrefined."

"And? Surely I have other faults?" Robert cocked a wicked eyebrow, tempting her to further indiscretion. He waited, watching her struggle between innate good manners and the desire to give him a resounding set-down. She fell for the provocation.

"You are too tall," she said. "And too *wide*."

Robert bit his lip to stifle a smile. "I agree," he said, "that I am both tall and wide, but there is little I can do about those things."

"You are not a scholar," Lucy said. Now that she had started enumerating his drawbacks, it seemed as though she had quite a list. He was interested that she had thought about him in so much detail.

"I could only marry a man of intellectual attributes," Lucy said, "sober, academic, more interested in the cerebral than the physical. You are too forceful."

"You underestimate me," Robert said. "In so many ways. I may not be a scholar but I do read. I have read your love letters." Keeping his gaze on her face, he recited:

"Exquisite beauty beyond imagining, a snare to tempt man to desire…"

He heard Lucy gasp. She shifted, as though his words were making her uncomfortable in some way. Above the neckline of her demure white silk gown, her breasts rose and fell quickly with each sharp breath she took.

Watching her, Robert continued softly. "To steal a kiss, to dare a touch, to taste and stroke and linger over every sweet caress…"

Lucy ran her tongue over her lower lip in a quick, nervous gesture. There was the glitter of heat in her gaze as she lifted it to his face.

"To nip and lick and pluck and take a bite of sweetness to the core." Robert lowered his voice, keeping his eyes fixed on her.

"To dip deep and drink up every drop, to plunder and ravish in sensual excess…"

Lucy made the softest sound in her throat that had his body hardening into instant arousal. He wanted to carry her upstairs, strip that demure gown from her and make love to her.

The dinner gong sounded. Robert saw Lucy jump. The dark, unfocused look in her eyes faded. Her lips were parted and she looked dazed and bemused, which only made him want her all the more.

He could see Lady Durness coming to claim him as her escort for the meal. He stood politely to greet her, hoping that he would be able to move without too much discomfort or embarrassment.

Lady Durness slid her hand into the crook of his elbow. "We are very informal here," she murmured, "but I take it as my privilege as hostess to claim you, dear Lord Methven." She squeezed his arm to emphasize the point. "I hope," she added, turning her pale gray eyes on Lucy, "that Lady Lucy will not mind relinquishing you."

"I shall do my utmost to cope," Lucy said crisply. She had regained her composure very quickly. There was no hint of the emotion Robert had seen in her a moment before. She dropped him the slightest and most dismissive of curtsies. "I hope that you enjoy the meal, Lord Methven."

Over dinner Robert heard plenty more of the activities of the Highland Ladies Bluestocking Society. For a secret society they seemed to possess a number of very indiscreet members. Activities varied from academic lectures on the arts and sciences to the less cerebral and more physical entertainments of riding, hawking and watching naked wrestling, the latter, he was told, solely for the entertainment of the widows and married ladies. Indeed it seemed to Robert that with the life drawing class, as well, a number of the Highland Ladies seemed most anxious to get as many men naked in as many varied and exciting ways as possible. Somehow he suspected that Lady Mairi would be present to cheer on the naked wrestlers, while Lady Lucy, presumably, was barred by her spinster status and her precise ideas of decorum.

Before dinner Robert had paid the butler a discreet sum to ensure that Lucy was seated beside him, but when they came to take their places he was quite amused to find himself outmaneuvered. Evidently Lucy had checked the table and had changed her seat for one at the farthest distance from him. She ate as she did all other things, daintily, precisely and elegantly. She conversed easily with the guests on each side of her, and when she was drawn into conversation with one of the handsome young life models she parried his flirtatious approach with beautifully judged politeness, neither too warm nor too cold. Robert began to see why she had such a reputation for perfection. On the surface she was indeed everything that was well brought up and proper. He wondered if that was why her passions escaped in other ways. Being a pattern card of respectability must be damnably tedious.

She did not glance in Robert's direction once, and Robert was amused to discover that her indifference annoyed him, as did the attentions to her of the handsome young man. He had never given a damn about a woman before, never experienced any sort of jealousy. This woman, though, was different. This woman was his even if she was not yet aware of it, even if she thought him the very least suitable husband in the world.

He had intended to talk to Lucy again after dinner with some vague idea of what his grandmother might have called wooing, but he was beginning to see that his cause was hopeless if he approached it in the conventional sense. Lucy was not indifferent to him; she felt their attraction as fiercely as he did, but she was fighting it for reasons of her own. As far as he could tell, she was averse to marriage with anyone but especially with him. His honor revolted at the thought of forcing any woman into marriage with him, but for the first time in his life he was facing a choice between his honor and the survival of his clan. He knew which he had to choose.

He did not linger over his port and courteously evaded the efforts of the drawing master to extract a portrait commission from him. When the gentlemen joined the ladies in the drawing room, however, Robert saw that Lucy was already leaving. He wondered if she was retiring early for the night, but there was something purposeful about her that aroused his curiosity. He gave her a few moments, then discreetly followed her out of the drawing room. He caught sight of her figure disappearing up the main staircase and along one of the wide upstairs corridors. When he reached the first floor, she had vanished. Then a door opened furtively, farther down. Thoroughly intrigued now, Robert waited. A maid peered out. Her gaze swept the corridor in both directions and, frowning, fixed on him. Without giving him the chance to speak, she jerked her head to indicate that he should enter the room.

"You're early," she snapped. "My lady is not ready yet. Wait in there." Another jerk of the head indicated a door on the right.

Robert felt as though someone had dropped a bucket of ice-cold water down his back. Shock, fierce and wicked, ambushed him. Lucy was expecting a visitor to her rooms, a male visitor. No wonder she had hurried away from dinner with such alacrity. No wonder she had looked furtive. That perfectly proper conversation with the handsome artist's model had evidently been anything but respectable. They must have been making an assignation.

He was startled by the cold anger that possessed him. Not a week ago he had sworn he would marry a lightskirt if it would save Methven; he had simply not imagined that the lightskirt would be Lady Lucy Mac-Morlan. At Brodrie she had sworn to him that she was innocent. His instinct had told him she told the truth.

He closed his eyes for a second. The words of the erotic letters danced on his closed lids, mocking him for a fool. Of course Lady Lucy was not innocent. How could she be? She had tried to play him before, manipulate him with her charm and her wit. Deceit ran in her veins and he was a fool to trust her word in anything. The maid was waiting for him to move, one eyebrow raised in exasperation. "In your own good time," she said.

Moving automatically, Robert stepped into the dressing room and heard the maid shut the door sharply behind him. Immediately he pressed his ear to the panels. Through the wood he could here the sound of voices, muffled as though underwater.

"The gentleman is here, milady." The maid spoke as

though the word *gentleman* was, in this case, a vulgar insult. "I have asked him to wait in the dressing room."

"Thank you." Lucy sounded her usual serene self. She had definitely been expecting this visitor. Robert felt his heartbeat increase.

There was the sound of rustling and then the maid's voice once more. "This isn't right, milady. I know it's not my place to say so, but I have to speak up."

"Nonsense, Sheena." The smoothness in Lucy's tone was slightly ruffled now. She sounded nervous. "It is medicinal. Lady Kenton recommends it and she is most respectable."

Medicinal? Robert had heard lovemaking called many things in his time, but medicinal was not one of them.

"I don't like it," the maid said. "It's downright heathen, that's what it is."

"Oh, Sheena." Lucy sounded indulgent. Her voice was fainter as though she had turned away. "No more of your nonsense. Help me to disrobe, please."

Disrobe? Robert groped for the edge of the dressing table to steady himself. Lady Lucy MacMorlan was disrobing to welcome a male visitor to her chambers. His heart was positively galloping now and so was his imagination. Riotous images of Lucy greeting her lover completely naked hurtled through his mind. So did visions of Lucy, her body pale against the tangled sheets of her bed, her hair released from the diamond pins and spilling over her shoulders and across her breasts. He could see her lover beside her, reaching for her...

He swore, briefly and fiercely, under his breath.

"Ma'am..." The maid was making one last effort, pleading.

"Bring him in now, please," Lucy said crisply.

A moment later that the door opened and the maid's black-gowned figure bustled in. Her cheeks were blazing red and she kept her gaze averted from him.

"Milady says you are to come in," she snapped, making it clear that if it were her choice Robert would be drummed out of the castle and probably the town, as well.

Robert followed her into the chamber. It was a large room with a huge bay window facing the sea. The thick velvet curtains were pulled back, and the evening sunlight drifted through the window in a dazzle of gold. It fell on the woman who was lying on a wide velvet chaise positioned in the center of the bay and burnished her bare skin to rose-gold.

For a moment Robert thought that he had stepped directly into his own fantasy.

Lucy lay on her front with her face turned aside, eyes closed as though she were asleep. There was a blanket covering her demurely from the waist downward, but above it her back was bare. It was curved in the same elegant arch as the bay window. The line of her throat was another pure curve against the velvet cushion, vulnerable and tempting. Robert wanted to trace the tender indentation of her spine and run his lips over the roundness of one shoulder. He wanted to drop his lips to the dip in the hollow of her back and taste the skin there.

His throat dried to sawdust. His mind was a jumble of thoughts and images. The curve of her buttocks and the long line of her legs were visible beneath the silken blanket. Her arms lay slender and pale by her side. She did not open her eyes or address him. He wondered crazily if she was waiting for her lover simply to start making love to her. Then the maid spoke.

"Well?" she said. "Aren't you going to begin the massage? My lady will catch her death lying there like that whilst you waste time."

In that moment Robert caught sight of the phial of oil on a table beside the chaise. The scent of lavender, sweet and faint, caught his nostrils. He saw the towel folded over a small wooden-backed chair.

The relief shattered through him.

He had been mistaken for a masseur. It must be another of the Highland Ladies' extraordinary pastimes.

"Well?" the maid said again.

A gentleman would have explained it was a case of mistaken identity. A gentleman would have stepped back, made his excuses and left.

Robert stepped forward.

CHAPTER EIGHT

LUCY HAD HAD every intention of greeting the masseur coolly and politely, but at the last moment shyness held her completely paralyzed. She heard his soft tread advancing across the thick carpet toward her bed and heard also the disapproving swish of Sheena's skirts as she escorted him. Her maid had been with her ever since she had left the schoolroom. She was extraordinarily protective as well as very conservative. Sheena had thought that Lady Kenton's suggestion of a masseur had been both outrageous and scandalous. Now, when it was too late, Lucy was inclined to agree with her.

Lying on the velvet chaise longue, aware of the cool air caressing her bare shoulders and back and certain that the man was watching her, Lucy felt horribly exposed. Lady Kenton had said that Anton was a professional and, further, that he was not interested in women, but even so this felt awkward and embarrassing. In two seconds she would grab her dressing robe, sit up and dismiss the masseur curtly with no explanation given. *Two seconds, one...*

He touched her. His hands were warm, not cold as she had imagined. They swept in a long glide from her neck, over her shoulders and down across her shoulder blades. She could smell lavender from the oil that Sheena had prepared earlier, but on his skin, or on hers, it had warmed and was scented of other herbs, as well, scents that were sweet and heady. Lucy felt a startled sense of well-being. She began to relax. His hands swept over her again, down her spine to span out across her lower back. Her tight muscles started to ease as he built up a rhythm, stroking over the line of her neck and spine, then spreading out over her ribs and back, down and up again, forward and back as soothing as the tide until she started to lose track of time and lay there conscious of nothing but sensation.

"That feels very good." Lucy kept her eyes closed as his hands moved over her. She was drifting now, her aches dissolving delightfully into pleasure. Her voice sounded a little blurred even to her own ears. She jumped when Sheena shifted sharply, close by. The maid must have heard some note of abandonment in her voice, for she said:

"It's *medicinal,* madam. Remember?" Then, turning to the masseur: "It's my lady's shoulder that troubles her, the left one, from all the writing."

"And my back," Lucy murmured. "It aches."

The masseur changed position and now his fingers were kneading Lucy's shoulder harder and the sensation hung between pleasure and pain and for a moment she was almost tempted to stop him. Yet the persistent throb that had plagued her was already softening, melting beneath his clever hands. She gave a sigh of relief and heard his low laugh.

"Better?" The word was no more than a deep rumble.
"Oh yes. Thank you."

She heard Sheena mutter something disapproving
and did not care. The massage continued, alternating
between the deep kneading of her shoulders that she
moved to meet now with keen pleasure, and a gentler,
softer sweep down the length of her back to the waist.
His hands spanned out, sliding up, brushing the side of
her breasts. It could have been accidental; or it might
not have been. Lucy lay still, breathing suspended. He
did it again. This time Lucy felt her body grasp greedily after the sensation, and when it happened again she
felt a sweet melting warmth swamp her entire body and
it twitched with recognition and desire.

She was depraved. This was supposed to be a purely
therapeutic process. Shockingly she realized that she
wanted to pull the covers away entirely and to experience the masseur's touch over her whole body.
His hands stroked up her sides again and she almost
moaned. Her nipples had hardened against the velvet
of the chaise longue. It felt exquisitely arousing to rub
against the rough material. In fact, her body seemed to
be coming alight now in a curious way she had never
experienced before. Her skin felt as though every inch
was alive. It was acutely sensitive. She had always lived
in her mind before with thoughts and ideas jostling for
space. She had never really been aware of her physical body apart from those occasions when she had hurt
herself: a fall from a horse or this pain in her shoulder.
Now, though, her head was full of how she felt, not of

what she thought. All she was aware of was the way in which his touch rippled over her and how her body rose to his hands, begging for more.

Sheena tweaked the covers higher. Lucy, suddenly aware that she had been wriggling beneath the masseur's hands in a most abandoned manner, tried to school her body into stillness. It was too late. She could not dismiss the sensations. They were pent up tight within her, waiting to burst out in a shower of pleasure.

There was a rap at the door. The masseur's hands checked into stillness for a moment before he resumed the slow sweep and stroke. The loss of his touch more than the sound pulled Lucy from the cocoon of pleasure. She opened her eyes. Sheena had gone to the door. She appeared to be arguing with someone; her head was shaking vigorously. Then she gestured the newcomer to step into the room and came hurrying back to the chaise.

"Madam." Her tone cut straight through Lucy's languor like a cascade of cold water. "There is a gentleman here who says your godmother has sent him. He claims to be the masseur. In which case—" Sheena turned and pointed. "Who is this?"

Lucy sat up, grabbing the blanket and holding it up to her chest, and looked up straight into Robert Methven's eyes.

For a moment she could not believe that he was there. It was impossible; impossible that he was the man who had been touching her so intimately only a second before. Yet since there was no one else in the room, it had to be him.

He picked up the small towel that Sheena had put on the side and wiped his hands on it. He did not look remotely surprised or indeed disturbed to have been caught masquerading as a masseur.

"What the devil are you doing?" Lucy said. Her voice came out as an outraged squeak. She felt at a very distinct disadvantage holding the blanket up to cover her nakedness. Again she was very aware of her body and this time not in a pleasurable way.

"Your maid mistook me," Methven said.

"I had worked that out for myself," Lucy snapped. "The mystery is why you did not correct her."

He smiled wickedly. "I'm not sure that it is much of a mystery, at least not to a gentleman." His gaze swept her from head to foot, making his meaning explicitly clear. She felt more heat build inside her, sliding over her skin.

"I was helping ease the pain in your shoulder and back," he added. "I flatter myself that I was doing rather well. I have a little experience in such matters, having been taught the art of massage on my travels—"

Lucy cut him off with an exasperated chop of the hand and he fell obligingly silent, although his blue eyes still danced with amusement.

"Send Lady Kenton's masseur away, please, Sheena," Lucy said. Her head was starting to ache. She wanted to press her fingers to her temples to ease it, but that would involve dropping the blanket. She turned back

to Methven. "You, sir… You will leave too. Such outrageous behavior—" She stopped when she realized
that her voice was shaking.

"You're upset," Robert Methven said.

"I am not upset," Lucy snapped. "I am angry."

She was lying. She *was* upset, disturbed, shocked,
any number of emotions. What troubled her most was
the memory of his hands on her and the way her body
had sung beneath his touch. Perhaps—no, most definitely—no one should feel such a sense of arousal during a massage. It was medicinal. Everyone had told
her so, but she had forgotten and instead had behaved
in the most abandoned manner. Even now her nerves
still hummed with awareness, her body still ached with
thwarted need and she seemed powerless to dismiss
those feelings.

She waited for Methven to apologize for his appalling behavior. He did not.

She frowned at him.

"What are you waiting for?" she said. "I asked you
to leave. If you please."

She would never, ever be able to face him again. The
kiss in the library at Brodrie had been bad enough, inexplicable, out of character. This was something else
entirely.

He walked over to the window. Strolled. It infuriated her to see it. He was completely in control, while
she was sitting there feeling absurdly embarrassed. It
was quite wrong that their roles should be so reversed

when he had committed such a shocking social solecism. He turned back to face her.

"I would like to oblige you," he murmured, "but I think we should discuss the damage to your reputation that this incident has caused."

"You did not think of the damage to my reputation when you decided to impersonate my godmother's masseur," Lucy said.

There was a curious little silence.

"In point of fact," Methven said, very gently, "I did. Compromising your reputation was exactly what I was thinking about. Fate presented me with an opportunity and I—" He gave a slight shrug. "I took it."

Oh. *Oh.* Lucy felt her heart jolt with shock as though she had missed a step in the dark.

He had intended to compromise her. He had done it on purpose.

A cold feeling of dread crept into Lucy's chest, smothering her breath. She felt shocked, panicked and suddenly desperately afraid.

"I don't understand," she said slowly.

"I think you do," Methven said. She met his eyes and they were so hard and ruthless that she felt a second punch of shock. The panicked sensation in her chest intensified.

"Is this your revenge for the letters?" she said. She tried to keep her voice steady, but a little quiver betrayed her. "Did you do this deliberately to ruin me?"

For a moment he looked taken aback and then his mouth twisted wryly. "Even I," he said, "am not so much of a villain as to do that." He looked down at her. She could not read his expression, and that troubled her all the more. She felt lost, all of a sudden, uncertain.

"Since it requires clarification," Methven said, "I acknowledge that I have compromised your reputation by my scandalous behavior tonight. I therefore deem it a very great honor to offer you my hand in marriage."

Lucy had never previously been naked when receiving one of her fifteen marriage proposals. She had never imagined that she would be. It simply was not possible. She was too proper, too perfect. Yet here she was, clad only in her blanket and her drawers, trapped into marriage by the Marquis of Methven.

She could not marry him. It was out of the question. She could marry no one. She certainly could never give any man an heir.

The idea terrified her.

Nor could she ever explain her reasons, not if she was to keep Alice's secrets, keep the past locked away.

She tried to concentrate, to still her tumbling thoughts.

"I think," she said, "that you may be something of a scoundrel to take such advantage of me."

He bowed. "I think," he said, "that you may be correct."

"A man without honor," Lucy opined hotly.

He looked pained. "That's a little harsh."

"You may be accustomed to marrying people you barely know," Lucy said hotly, "but it is not a habit of mine."

This time he had the audacity to laugh. "Touché," he said. "I did not know Miss Brodrie very well, but you and I..." He gestured to the couch and her partially clothed form. "I thought we were doing rather well in getting to know each other."

The conversation was not going at all as Lucy had intended it. She felt hot and flustered and completely out of her depth.

"I cannot concentrate when I have so few clothes on!" she burst out. She struggled to her feet, wrapping the blanket around her for decency, almost losing her grip on it as her hands shook.

"If you would withdraw," she said, "whilst I dress, then we may talk."

"Of course," Methven said. "You look delightful and I have no complaints, but if you insist. The blanket is slipping," he added helpfully.

With an infuriated squeak Lucy tucked the ends in more securely and scurried off to the dressing room, where Sheena was waiting for her. She half expected the maid to start berating her, to tell her that she had warned her that massage was a dangerous business and that Lucy should have had no truck with it. She was not sure she could bear that Sheena had been proved right.

"I told you—" the maid began.

"I know!" Lucy said, cutting her off.

Sheena's lips set in a firm line. Without another word she held out Lucy's underclothes, first the chemise, then her stays. Lucy shivered as they brushed against her bare skin. She felt cold. Her hands shook slightly as she tried to help Sheena with the buttons on the bodice of her blue gown. She found she needed to dress quickly, to feel more in control. It was odd that having previously worn nothing but her drawers she now felt underdressed in an irreproachably respectable gown.

"I can vouch that nothing untoward occurred, madam," Sheena said.

"I don't think you can," Lucy said bleakly. She knew perfectly well that her maid's testimony would count for nothing in the face of scandal. She was utterly compromised, and the only way to save her reputation would be to marry Robert Methven.

Marriage.

She felt trapped and cold and afraid. The Marquis of Methven had lost one bride and now he wanted another. He had chosen her. He had compromised her.

Lucy shivered. When Alice had died she had locked away all thoughts of love and marriage. Her future had changed with Alice's death. The regret, the shame and bitterness of her sister's loss weighed on her every day. She could never imagine a life with a husband and a family. She did not want it; she was too afraid. She could never lie with a man, never give him an heir, and it would be unfair to wed any man under those circumstances.

There was nothing within her but cold, hollow darkness.

Sheena was fastening her hair with a simple ribbon. "You cannot marry him, ma'am," she said. "It's impossible—"

"I know," Lucy snapped.

There seemed little more to say and nothing that could put off any longer her confrontation with Robert Methven. Already the clock had ticked around a half hour and she suspected that if she did not emerge from the dressing room soon, Methven would come in to make sure that she had not climbed out of the window and run away.

Sheena secured the ribbon. Lucy checked her reflection. She looked the same as she always did, perfectly poised and elegant. There was no indication from her serene image that her stomach churned and she felt chilled and sick.

Methven was standing where she had left him, hands in the pockets of his jacket, staring out of the wide bow window to the stretch of the bay beyond. There was a frown between his eyebrows. He looked intimidating. Cold fear nibbled at Lucy's heart. He was so wrong for her in every way, forceful, physical, determined. The Marquis of Methven, she was certain, would never settle for a platonic marriage of convenience. He would want an heir for those estates he was bent on saving. She had to find a way out of this, though she did not know how she could without leaving her reputation in tatters.

When he saw her he came across and took both her hands in his.

"You look lovely," he said. "Though I had a small preference for the blanket."

Lucy freed herself and moved away from him. His

touch was already confusing her, distracting her from her attempts to order her thoughts logically. His proximity made her feel light-headed and heated. Until Robert Methven had stepped back into her life, she had imagined that she would never feel passion, never experience desire. He could make her feel both, but the fear in her was far stronger.

"Marriage is a business arrangement, Lord Methven," she said, struggling to regain her composure, smoothing her skirts as she sat down. "Let us then discuss business."

His lips twitched. There was a gleam of amusement in his eyes. "How very practical you are, Lady Lucy," he said. "By all means let us do so." He took the chair opposite her, stretching his long legs out in front of him and crossing them at the ankle. He waited politely for her to continue.

"Did you come to Durness specifically with the intention of compromising me?" Lucy demanded.

He inclined his head. "I came to make you an offer of marriage."

"Then why not do so in an honorable manner?" Lucy asked. She took a deep breath and tried to steady herself. It was not easy, not under that perceptive blue gaze that seemed to see right into her soul.

He did not hesitate. "You would have refused me," he said.

He was right; she would have done so. She could not in truth deny it.

When she did not immediately speak, he spread

his hands wide in a gesture of appeal. "Forgive me," he said, "but I had no other option than to force your hand."

"I do not forgive you." Lucy's voice cracked. She was shocked at the depth of her disappointment in him. "It's blackmail. You are completely without honor."

He corrected her, his jaw rigid. "My allegiance, my honor, is to my clan. That has to be my first loyalty."

There was a silence. He made no excuse, no further attempt to justify his actions.

Lucy pressed her fingers to her temples. Her head was aching. She wanted to refuse him here and now, to tell him she would never marry him, that it was out of the question. The problem was that she doubted he would accept a blunt rejection. He would want to know why she was prepared to sacrifice her reputation rather than marry him.

She was trapped. Somehow she had to persuade him to release her instead. She had no idea how she was going to do it, but it was her only hope.

She raised her eyes to his face. He looked so unyielding that she almost lost her nerve there and then, but she dug her nails into her palms and forced herself to calm.

"I understood that your choice of bride was severely limited by the terms of your inheritance, my lord," she said. "In what way has that changed?"

"It has changed only in that you are an eligible bride," Methven said. He smiled, that sudden warm smile that always took her by surprise. "You are familiar with your family tree?"

"Not in any detail," Lucy said. "Do you have a copy of it with you?"

"I'm afraid not," Methven said. "You will just have to take my word for it. I have had the best lawyers in Edinburgh working on the matter."

Of course he had. He would hardly make so fundamental a mistake over something so important. Lucy bit her lip. This, evidently, was not the way out.

"I had no notion that I was on your list of potential wives," she said coldly.

Somewhere near the bottom, if Dulcibella Brodrie was higher up.

The thought popped into her head and irritated her all the more. It was irrelevant. Worse than that, it was foolish. She was not sure why she should care, but for some reason she did. She was too proud to stand in line behind Dulcibella.

Methven's smile broadened as though he had recognized the contrariness of her feelings. "I had no idea either," he said, "or you may be sure that I would have approached you before I offered for Miss Brodrie."

That brought Lucy's gaze up to his with a jerk. He was watching her, the amusement still in his blue eyes, and behind that there was a warmth that caused the blood to beat harder in her veins. She cleared her throat and tried to focus her thoughts. She was going about things quite the wrong way if she intended to refuse him.

"I cannot marry you," she said. It came out rather more baldly than she had intended, but she felt relieved that the truth was out. "You will have to find another lady to wed."

She saw his gaze sharpen on her. There was still amusement there, but there was something harder now too, ruthless, determined.

"You are refusing me," he said. A slow smile curled his lips. "I confess I did not believe you would." He leaned forward and rested his forearms on his thighs. He did not take his gaze from her face. "I had assumed," he said, "that as you were all but naked, allowing me quite shocking intimacies with your body, you would see the necessity of a speedy engagement."

Lucy concentrated hard on blocking out the words *naked, shocking intimacies,* and *body,* especially in conjunction with one another. She was not entirely successful. A tickle of heat curled low in her belly, lighting her blood with fire. She blinked rapidly.

She needed to concentrate, not on her physical response to him, which was wayward and unhelpful, but on her rational argument.

"I do not wish to marry," she said, "and it is wrong of you to try to blackmail me into it."

She had to focus on the one absolute, the only thing that was important, because when she looked into his eyes she tended to forget every last ounce of reason.

"I am aware that blackmail is wrong," Methven said calmly. "However, if we are speaking of wrongdoing, it was wrong of you to write the letters that lost me my bride. This is recompense, a bride for a bride."

He straightened and sat back in the chair, politely awaiting her response.

Lucy was struggling. "I acknowledge that I was in part responsible for Lachlan's elopement with Miss Brodrie," she said, "but I cannot wed you to make good the loss. You will have to find another wife." She drew a breath as she came to the most important point of her refusal. "It would be most ungallant of you to make public the manner in which I was compromised tonight. No gentleman would deliberately ruin a lady's reputation for personal gain. So—" She forced herself to look him straight in the eye. "I can only beg you to accept my refusal of your offer and we shall say no more about it."

There was silence, thick and heavy. Outside, the dusk was falling and twilight was gathering over the sea. The lengthening shadows in the room made it even more difficult than normal to read Robert Methven's expression. Lucy felt edgy and ill at ease, but she forced herself to stay still in her chair and await his response.

He got to his feet abruptly and paced across toward the wide bay window before turning to look at her again, as though she were a puzzle he was trying to unlock. The last of the evening light fell across his face, and now she *could* read his thoughts in his eyes. He was amused by her staunch refusal to succumb to his blackmail. She could see it in the gleam of humor there. He admired her strength. At the same time he was cursing her stubbornness. She could sense frustration in him, as well.

"If I fail to fulfill the terms of the fifteenth-century treaty," he said slowly, "your cousin Wilfred Cardross takes half my estate. You know that." His eyes came back to hers, and Lucy's heart jolted at what she saw there. "Make no mistake," he said, "keeping my ancestral clan lands safe is more important to me than anything, Lady Lucy. What I have, I hold."

A long, slow shiver tickled down Lucy's spine. In the back of her mind echoed Lady Kenton's words:

A hero fresh from the battlefield...

Robert Methven would fight for what he wanted and would fight to keep safe what was his. She had never before seen such single-minded determination in a man. She turned away from the blaze of resolve in his eyes. It felt as though it scorched her.

"You are my only chance," he said simply. "There is no one else I can wed."

Lucy's heart lurched with shock. She had not been expecting that. Her eyes flew to his face. "There must be!" she said. "There has to be! Surely—" she threw out a hand "—if I am eligible, then so must Mairi or Christina be—" Something in his expression stopped her.

"For various reasons they are ineligible." His voice was still soft. "There is only you, Lucy."

It was the first time he had called her by her name. The intimacy of it made her shiver. So did the thought that no one else could help him, because it meant that he would be all the more implacable in claiming her. She rubbed her bare arms to warm herself then reached for the shawl that lay over the side of the sofa. The cool

May evening still required a fire, and there had been no time to light one.

Methven came across to her and leaned down to place his hands on the arms of her chair, caging her there. He studied her face, his blue eyes intent. He did not touch her, but she felt very aware of him, intimidated by his physical presence, almost overwhelmed by the sheer powerful masculinity that emanated from him. It made her heart pound and her entire body stir.

"I cannot let you go, Lucy," he said. "Surely you must see that? But I would far rather persuade you to my cause than force you to the altar by telling everyone of your disgrace."

Lucy stood up. She felt as though she had to in order to regain some sort of control. It was a mistake, though, as it brought her closer to him rather than putting distance between them. At such close quarters he was even more disturbingly masculine and physical.

"Please, Lucy," he said. "Help me."

There was such passion and demand in his eyes. Lucy thought of Wilfred seizing Methven land and turning off the men with no work, the women and children to poverty and starvation. She screwed her eyes up tightly to ward off the images in her mind, but she could not escape them.

"I can't..." she said helplessly. "Truly. I wish I could, but—" Her voice cracked with despair.

Robert was so close. He took another step forward until his body touched hers. Lucy was trembling now, rooted to the spot. She raised her eyes to his face. How stern it was, with shadows darkening the cleft of his chin and the grooves in his lean cheeks and with the hint of evening stubble darkening his hard jaw. She felt a sudden violent urge to raise a hand and run her fingers over the line of his cheek and chin, relishing that roughness against her skin. Her awareness of him hit her again with all the force of a tidal wave. She felt as though she might dissolve under the weight of it. Suddenly her mouth was dry and her pulse pounded in her throat.

"Help me," he said again. His breath feathered across her cheek. His lips were an inch from hers now.

A curious shiver rippled through Lucy. She opened her mouth to tell him she could not, but no words came. He raised a hand and brushed the hair away from her cheek. His lips touched the corner of her mouth. Her knees were trembling now, her toes curling in her slippers.

His lips grazed hers. She thought she would melt if he did not kiss her properly and very likely explode if he did. Then he took her mouth with his and it was her last thought for a very long time.

CHAPTER NINE

ROBERT HAD ACHED to kiss Lucy from the moment he had ended the massage and she had opened her eyes, so cloudy blue with sensual pleasure, and looked at him with such innocent lust and confusion. He had been waiting for this and he had thought the moment would never come and now it had. He would have to be damned careful not to waste it because if he could not persuade Lucy MacMorlan to wed him after this, then there was no hope for him.

Her eyes were closed now, her eyelashes a thick black crescent against the perfect curve of her cheek. He touched his lips to hers again, keeping the kiss gentle, keeping ruthless rein on his desires, because he could tell that this was still new to her, a revelation, and he wanted to show her just how perfect it could be. When he had kissed her in the library at Brodrie Castle, he had wondered if she had ever kissed anyone but him. Her hesitation and inexperience suggested she had not. Her betrothal had evidently been completely passionless and she had had no idea of sensuality.

At Brodie he had give her a taste of passion. Now it was time to awaken it properly, awaken her. His body, already hard, tightened further at the thought, but he ignored the demand of his senses and concentrated on Lucy.

His lips moved over hers with soft persuasion, nudging hers apart so that their breath mingled. Hesitantly she followed his lead, opening to him. His tongue slid across her full lower lip and touched hers and she sighed with pleasure.

"Perhaps I can persuade you," he murmured. "We need not be at odds."

She opened her eyes. They were the color of the Scottish summer sky and midnight, a deep blue, slumberous and soft. She looked dazed, lost in an unfamiliar world. Robert felt so sharp a pull of desire that he almost groaned aloud. Yet it was not merely lust. That was too inadequate a word for what he felt for Lucy. It did not begin to describe his emotions, nor the expression he saw in Lucy's eyes. Her lips parted. He succumbed completely to temptation and kissed her a third time, this time long and deep.

She gasped with shock at the intimacy of it. Yet already she was opening to him, offering her mouth to him, her tongue entangling with his, her body softening against his with instinctive surrender. It was all he could do not to wrench her up into his arms and carry her over to the chaise longue and strip her of the neat debutante's gown to expose her once again to his sight and his touch. Instead he pressed his open mouth to the sensitive hollow beneath her ear. He felt her body shudder. She was so responsive. And she had no idea of the passion locked up inside her. Or perhaps she was beginning to suspect it.

He had no intention of seducing her. To ravish her now, when so much lay unresolved between them, would be a true scoundrel's trick. But he wanted to show her how well suited they were physically. That might persuade her to change her mind about accepting his hand in marriage. He could show her pleasure, unlock her feelings.

Oh yes, and he would enjoy it too. He was not so much of a hypocrite as to pretend this was all for Lucy's benefit.

He dropped his lips to the lacy edging of her bodice. The lace was soft and fine, but her skin was softer. She made a sound in her throat, a sound that called to everything primitive and possessive in him. He raised a hand to skim the underside of her breast. She shivered deliciously, stretching up to meet him, seeking the press of his body. She was all artless desire and willing sweetness, far more than he could ever have imagined. He circled her breast, his thumb brushing her nipple through the thin muslin of the gown, feeling it tighten at each repeated caress. He could sense the tension coiling in her until she made a keening sound, and he kissed her again, harder this time, demanding. She met the demand, tasting him eagerly now, pulling his head down to hers, her tongue tangling with his.

It was too much, too dangerous, without her consent to marriage. Another kiss and he would rip the gown from her shoulders so that he could replace his hands with his mouth at her breasts.

He wrenched himself away from her. Both of them were panting. Her lips were stung deep red from his kisses, shiny, parted. Her nipples jutted beneath the filmy gown. She looked tumbled and wanton and Robert's body hardened to near-intolerable arousal.

"Are you sure I would not make a good husband?" he asked. It had all felt pretty damned perfect to him.

Lucy's eyes were huge and shadowed. She looked bewildered, shock shimmering in her eyes. She took a deep, shaky breath, one hand pressed to her chest as though to steady herself.

"I do not want my husband to kiss me like that," she said. Her voice was soft. "I do not want my husband to kiss me with passion and heat and—" She waved her hands about in jerky little gestures. "With desire."

"You don't want your husband to desire you?" Robert said. There were enough marriages that were colder than the Scottish snows; a dose of lust made an arranged match a great deal more tolerable.

Lucy shook her head in a brief, emphatic gesture. She was regaining her composure, drawing it about her like a protective cloak. High color still burned in her cheeks, but she had recovered a measure of self-control. Robert could feel the distance between them stretch, feel her slipping away from him.

"If I ever wed, it would be a match of intellects, not passions, my lord," she said.

"Why?" Robert said. He took a step closer to her

again, but she moved back, tacitly forbidding him to kiss her again.

"It's what I want," she whispered.

Robert took her by the shoulders and turned her to face the long pier glass on the wall. She still looked deliciously tousled, like a fallen angel, dazed and thoroughly kissed, his for the taking. He lowered his head and ran his tongue along the hollow of her collarbone and felt her shiver in response. It was as easy as that to shatter her serenity and awake the passion in her again. Her composure was wafer thin.

He slid her sleeve down over the curve of her shoulder. The skin there was almost translucently pale, scattered with freckles. He bit down gently on the point of her shoulder and heard her gasp.

"Look at us," he said, raising his head. "Do you deny you want this?"

Their eyes met in the glass. Hers were full of confusion and something else. Fear. It was a fear so harsh and stark that it struck Robert like a punch in the gut. His hands fell to his side and he straightened.

"Lucy?" he said.

"I don't want to feel passion," she whispered. "Never."

Before he could say anything else, she turned from him and ran. The tap of her footsteps increased in pace as she reached the door. It closed behind her with a sharp snap, leaving him alone in the sudden quiet.

His instinctive reaction was to go straight after her and demand an explanation. He was halfway to the door when he stopped. She had run from him because she did not want to speak to him. He had to give her time or very likely he would get nowhere at all.

He flung himself down on the silver chaise where Lucy had lain earlier. The faint bluebell scent of her perfume drifted from the cushions. It sent a tight, instinctive spike of desire through him as he remembered her pale nakedness against the velvet, so he got up again and stalked across to the table, lighting the candle that stood there. The room flooded with golden light. It sparkled from the long mirror, and suddenly Robert could see again Lucy's reflection and the terror in her eyes.

He had frightened her. He felt shocked, horrified, a complete blackguard.

And yet…

And yet the quick heat of her response to him spoke of a desire as strong as his own. For a while she had lost herself in his touch and in his arms. Which made no sense if she was afraid of him.

With an oath he splashed a generous measure of wine into the dusty glass on the side table and drank it down like medicine, then threw his long length down in the fireside chair. The grate was cold and empty and smelled of old ashes. He wondered where Lucy had run. No doubt that fierce little maid would be back soon to berate him for his appalling behavior in frightening her mistress. She could not make him feel more of a scoundrel than he already did.

He wondered if it had been the taste of passion that had frightened Lucy, the fact that he had shown her how it might be between them. She had had no experience of desire until he had kissed her. She had read about it and written about it, but she had never known it. Then, without warning, lust and wanting had become a reality and had overwhelmed all her ideas of perfect gentlemen and platonic matches.

He wondered about MacGillivray too. It seemed that Lucy, fresh from the schoolroom, had idealized the man, so much older than she. He had been a mentor, a father figure, rather than a lover. He had perhaps made her feel safe. And now she had discovered for the first time that physical love was not safe or gentle or scholarly and she was afraid.

It was plausible. Yet for some reason the doubt still hovered in his mind. The depth of terror in Lucy's eyes argued something else. It reflected pain and intolerable memories. He recognized it because he carried with him his own share of unbearable guilt and grief.

She was not afraid of him. She was afraid of something else. Something had happened to her in the past, something so shocking, so terrible, that she could not escape the memory of it. He had seen that fear before in the eyes of men who had been in battle, who had witnessed terrible things and could never forget them.

He released his breath on a long sigh. He needed time, time to uncover Lucy's fears and time to woo her with gentleness. It was the only way forward. Unfortunately with Wilfred Cardross intent on claiming his estates, time was the one commodity he did not have.

"HE SOUNDS PRETTY damned perfect to me," Mairi said. "He's handsome, rich, interesting and attractive." She ticked off Robert Methven's attributes on her fingers. "He's clever. Oh, and according to you, he knows how to kiss. You don't have anyone to compare him with, but you're fairly certain he's very good at it."

"You're so superficial," Lucy said crossly. She was beginning to wish she had not confided in her sister. Mairi simply did not understand her. Only a year separated them, but they had never been very close. She could not talk to Mairi about Alice's death; could not tell her the shock and the horror of it. Mairi's grieving was for the sister she had loved and lost. Lucy's was for a beloved twin who had died tragically in her arms, a sister she felt she had failed. The gulf of shame and regret separated her from Mairi and seemed to push them further apart rather than bring them together.

Lucy still had nightmares, and memories so vivid they transported her back to that shuttered room and Alice's cold hand in hers. She heard the thin wail of the baby. She was haunted. She did not understand why she felt so, but there was an empty space where Alice had been, a void that sometimes left Lucy so grief-stricken and guilty she could barely breathe.

"I always was superficial, darling," Mairi was saying cheerfully, placing her delicate crystal wineglass on the table. "It's my defining characteristic." She shrugged her shoulders beneath the fine silk of her gown. "Well, don't expect me to marry Lord Methven just to save his inheritance. Tempting as he is—and trust me, he is a very tempting man—I like being a widow. There are lots of benefits."

"I don't want you to marry him," Lucy said, even more crossly. "And anyway, you can't. You are ineligible."

And I know he is a tempting man.

She shivered a little, wondering if she would always feel this jumble of emotion when she thought of Robert Methven. He could awaken her desires at a touch, but he could not eradicate her fear and her grief and her guilt.

"No." The look Mairi gave her was shrewd. "You refused him, but you don't want anyone else to have him. You're like a dog in a manger."

Lucy turned her face away. "You don't understand," she said. There was an ache in her chest. She wanted to cry because it was true; her heart did ache whenever she thought of Robert Methven marrying someone else.

"I never did understand," Mairi said. She yawned. "You've rejected every eligible peer in the country because you think they don't measure up to Duncan Mac-Gillivray." She fixed her sister with her wide blue eyes. "You need help, Lucy. MacGillivray was all very well, but he was scarcely a perfect ideal. He was just a man, and a dull old one at that."

Lucy dug her nails into the palms of her hands. She remembered Lady Kenton saying much the same thing. She remembered Robert Methven's brusque dismissal of the idea that there could be a man who was her perfect match. She felt battered and upset. There had been something so appealing, so *safe,* about Lord MacGil-livray. That was all she wanted, to feel safe.

"Take Robert Methven instead," Mairi was saying. "At least he would make love to you nicely."

Lucy shuddered. That was certainly true. She thought of Methven reciting her poetry to her before dinner, his trace of a rough Scots brogue plucking at her nerves. That quiet voice with its undertone of velvet had abraded her senses. She thought of his kisses. She had been completely undone by the power of his touch. It had felt gentle, so very different from how she thought of him. He was ruthless, a hard man, yet his kiss had been very tender. Suddenly she felt hot all over again. The warmth rippled over her skin, flooding her with sensation so that she tingled.

She had never felt like this before, never felt such a conflict between her mind and her senses.

She shivered convulsively in the warm night air.

Mairi had not noticed. She was yawning ostentatiously and checking the little porcelain clock on the mantel. "It's late," she said.

Lucy slid off the bed. "Are you expecting company?" she asked, a little tartly. Mairi could not have made it plainer that she wanted to hurry her sister from her room.

For a moment Mairi looked taken aback, but then she smiled easily. "Not tonight. Lady Durness has taken both those luscious artist's models to her chamber. She is said to be insatiable. She would have preferred Methven, but he is only interested in you."

"Both of them," Lucy said, blushing at the thought and the memory of such drawings in her grandfather's folio. "Gracious."

Mairi was laughing at her, her blue eyes gently mocking. Lucy felt thoroughly naive. "I am astonished she has not fallen pregnant with a brood of miscellaneous children by now," she said.

"There are ways to make sure it doesn't happen," Mairi said vaguely. "Devices, potions…ways to make sure you are safe." She looked at Lucy. "Things no respectable virgin heiress should know."

"Things no respectable widow should discuss either," Lucy said.

She met no one as she hurried back along Durness's long corridors. Torches hung in the wall sconces, but their light could not penetrate the shadows that wreathed the high walls. She hesitated before she pushed open the door of her chamber. It was not that she imagined that Robert Methven would still be there—she was sure he was long gone to the Durness Inn—but the memory of him was potent enough to make her stop and catch her breath.

The room was warm, lit by fire and candlelight. Sheena was dozing in the little armchair before the fire. Lucy's nightgown was stretched out to warm over the iron fireguard. She let out a breath, feeling safe again for the first time that night. Perhaps she would be able to sleep after all.

But she did not know what she would say to Robert Methven in the morning.

After Sheena had helped her out of her gown and had retired to the adjoining room, Lucy walked over to the polished wooden chest of drawers, splashing some water from the jug into the bowl and washing her face. It cooled her skin, but the feverish hum in her blood still made rest an impossibility. She tried to summon up the memory of Duncan MacGillivray with his gentle kindness and his old-fashioned courtesy. He had demanded nothing from her but intellectual companionship. She had liked that. It had made her feel secure.

Yet Lord MacGillivray's image seemed fainter now, fragile, as though he were a wraith fading before her eyes. She could no longer visualize their time of pleasant scholarly camaraderie. Instead it was Robert Methven's face she saw before her eyes, strong, harsh and determined.

She slid into bed and blew out the candle. The unexpected heat of the day had faded completely now and it was raining, hard drops beating on the roof of the castle, the water gurgling in the gutter and spattering on the terrace below. She had her window open, and the sound filled her ears. It was soothing, washing away her troubles and lulling her to sleep at last. The castle was quiet with all the guests asleep. It creaked a little as it settled its bones for the night.

Lucy was sound asleep when something disturbed her, dragging her back from the darkness of sleep without dreams. She opened her eyes. The room was shadowed. She could see nothing. Her mind was still struggling with the dregs of sleep, but her ears caught again the scrape of footsteps, the creak of a floorboard. Then the darkness shifted and something—someone— moved beside the bed. She shot upright and drew breath to scream, but she was too late. She was wrapped in suffocating folds of material, blinded, choked and unable to breathe. She fought the heat and the dark, thrashing out at whoever was near her, but her hands were caught and pinioned and her struggles rendered useless. She heard a man swear under his breath and aimed a kick at whatever part of him she could make contact with. He swore again and picked her up. She was feeling lightheaded now. There was no air to breathe. The thick smothering darkness grew. She held on to consciousness by a thread. Then something hit her, hard, on the back of the head, and the last of the light went out.

CHAPTER TEN

THE FIRST THING that Lucy saw when she opened her eyes was a lantern. It was swinging back and forth in the most sickening rhythm and it kept pace with the pounding in her head and the heaving of her stomach. She rolled over and was violently sick. Fortunately someone had had the intelligence to anticipate this, for there was a bowl beside her bed. Lucy felt profoundly grateful and only a little less profoundly ill. She lay back with a groan and closed her eyes and after a moment she felt the cool press of a cloth against the hot skin of her forehead. She had absolutely no curiosity about where she was or what was happening to her. Her entire consciousness was caught up in feeling so very ill. She closed her eyes and let sleep take her.

The second time she awoke she felt different. The room had steadied. It no longer tipped and spun about her like a carousel. She opened her eyes and saw the same lantern on the wall above her head, scattering shadows across the room. There was nobody there and she felt a huge rush of relief.

She sat up and swung her legs over the side of the bed. Immediately her head swam and she felt nauseated; touching the back of her head, she felt a lump

almost the size of a small egg. It was extremely painful. Her limbs ached too, protesting the bruises and
bumps. Simultaneously she realized that she was in her
nightgown and that it was more than a little tattered
and stained now. Her feet were bare. Memory came
rushing in. She recalled the room at the castle and the
clutch of fear she had felt on realizing there had been
someone there in the dark. She remembered the futil-
ity of her struggle against her kidnappers, the cruel
blow to the head, then the endless darkness, sometimes
rent with a brief flash of light that brought with it terror and sickness.

No one had molested her, though. She knew that at
once and felt so relieved she almost cried. Then she felt
so angry she wanted to break something, wave upon
wave of fury that beat at her and left her shaking. She
sat down on the edge of the bed until it had passed
and her body calmed its shivering and she was able to
think again.

She looked about her. The chamber was small with
the one candle in a lantern on the wall showing battered
wooden furniture, the bed she had been lying on, all
tumbled sheets and sagging mattress, an old chest with
a chipped china bowl on top and a matching ewer with
faded roses painted on it. She padded across the floor
to it and tipped some water into the dish. It was warm
and smelled a little stale, but it was good enough to
wash her face, washing away the cobwebs in her mind
at the same time. After that she crossed to the window
and drew back the broken shutters. There was twilight

outside, the soft blue haze of a Scottish summer night that never turned completely dark. She guessed it must be late, ten o'clock, eleven? Yet that made no sense because the men who had taken her had come for her in the middle of the night. A suspicion, a fear, tickled its way down her spine.

This could not be the same night.

She leaned out into the night. She could see the whitewashed walls of the inn glowing pale in the moonlight, a clear sky with pale stars and the inn sign swinging in a strong breeze. The courtyard below was empty. Leaving the window, she tiptoed across to the door, wincing when the old bare boards creaked under her feet. She did not want to alert anyone to the fact that she was awake.

She turned the knob. The door remained obstinately stuck. She was not surprised, but her heart gave a giddy little swoop down to her toes. She had been hoping it would be open, hoping she could run off in no more than her nightclothes to beg for help. It was probably foolish to plunge from one danger into the next, but she was desperate. She was not going to stay here at the mercy of whoever had taken her.

There was the rattle of a key in the lock, and Lucy shot back across the room just as the door opened and Robert Methven came in. She felt a clutch of shock so strong her knees gave way and she sat down abruptly on the edge of the bed.

"You're awake," Methven said. "How are you feeling?"

"You?" Lucy said. Disappointment slammed into her so sharp it stole her breath.

Robert Methven had kidnapped her.

Robert Methven had hit her over the head and carried her off.

She had refused his proposal of marriage; she had refused to be compromised by him, so he had taken what she had denied him. He had hurt her and frightened her and stolen her away.

It was the casual cruelty of that blow to the head that infuriated her the most.

"You!" she said again. Anger and disillusionment flooded her. Her rage flared. She flung herself at him, beating her fists against his chest.

"You abducted me! You low, scheming, underhand, conniving—" She drew a breath. The anger was in her blood and for a brief moment it felt glorious, wiping out the pain in her head and the ache in her heart that he was not the man she had thought him.

"Devious, sly, calculating—" She pummeled him again with her small fists.

"Clearly there are benefits to being a bluestocking," Methven said. "You are not short of a descriptive word." He caught her arms in a negligent grip and held her. His touch was gentle and that made her angrier still, that he could be so tender now when he had been so violent before.

"I thought better of you!" she finished bitterly.

"Thank you," Methven said. "I am honored by your good opinion."

Lucy fought a battle against a treacherous urge to cry. It was the sickness and the blow to the head, she told herself. It was not because she had been so disappointed in him. He meant nothing to her. His betrayal meant nothing. Inside her the fury still boiled, but she knew that physical violence was pointless against a man as strong as Methven. She would need wit and guile to escape him—or a pistol if she could find one.

Her head ached suddenly with a vicious spike of pain and she swayed. Methven steadied her and suddenly she could not bear his gentleness. "Don't touch me!" She wrenched herself from his grip. "You hit me—"

There was too much anguish in her tone. She could hear it. She did not want him to know she cared.

"You're mistaken." His voice was rough now. "I'd never hurt you."

Their eyes met and Lucy's heart felt as though it turned over in her chest. There was such a wealth of protective fury in his eyes. She could feel it in every tense line of his body, wound tight. Then he turned away. "It was your cousin Wilfred who had you kidnapped," he said, over his shoulder. "He hired men to carry you off."

He offered no proof, made no further attempt to persuade her he told the truth. It was as though in that moment when they eyes had met Lucy had known he did not lie.

"Wilfred?" she said. "Why would he do that?" She felt astounded. It was true that Wilfred had paid her extravagant attention that night at Brodrie Castle, but he had scarcely been serious in his addresses to her. Unless he truly was so deep in hock to the moneylenders and all the rumors that he needed to marry a fortune were true.

"I imagine he planned to force you to wed him," Methven said. "Or possibly to prevent me from marrying you so that he could claim my lands. He knows I have to wed one of his kinswomen, and if he got wind that I had chosen you…" He let the sentence hang.

Lucy raised a hand to the bump on the back of her head. "They knocked me out," she said.

"Aye." That rough tone was back in his voice again. "That was why you were unconscious for so long."

"I was sick." Lucy was remembering the bowl and the cool press of the cloth against her forehead. Had it been Robert Methven who had sat with her while she was so ill? She looked at him, but his face was impassive.

"I'm sorry for that," he said. "They were rough with you, but they said they had not hurt you. They had been well paid not to."

"Oh." The heat flamed into her face. She knew what he meant: the hurts she might have taken. "You…asked them?"

"At the point of my sword." There was grim humor in his voice. "I'm glad it's true. They would probably have sworn red was blue to escape me."

Lucy could imagine, imagine his anger and the men's fear. It made her shiver.

"What of Wilfred himself?" she asked. "Where is

he now?" She felt cold that her cousin could treat her with such cruelty. They had never cared much for each other, but this was outrageous, shameful. She sat down on the bed again and drew the lumpy eiderdown around her, seeking comfort from its folds.

"I have no idea where he is," Methven said. He sounded indifferent, but Lucy caught the hot thread of anger buried deep beneath his words. She was almost afraid for Wilfred now. "I caught up with them here," he said. "Cardross was taking you to his castle at Cairn Rock, along the coast. I sped him on his way there, on foot, naked, in the rain." He shrugged. "Lucky for him the rain has stopped now, though he may already have caught his death."

Lucy's gaze snapped up to his. "You took his *clothes?*"

"He was lucky I didn't send him to the bottom of the loch," Methven said. "If he had touched you I would have killed him."

Lucy stared at him for a long time. "You mean that," she said, frowning a little.

"I do." A muscle twitched in his jaw. "He was waiting here for you, all lordly, pleased with himself and his plans, not a little drunk, which made him all the more full of his own importance…" His shoulders moved as though shaking off a distasteful memory. "He's a grotesque apology for a man, to try to use a woman against me."

"Thank you for coming after me," Lucy said. "I was less than grateful earlier. I apologize."

A faint smile lightened the grimness in Methven's eyes. He looked across at her. "I'll always come for you," he said. His tone was fierce. "I'll always protect you."

It was a promise. It sounded as though he was claiming her. Silence fell between them, sharp with awareness.

Lucy broke it, wrenching her gaze away, looking around, taking in the slovenly room, the sagging mattress.

"Where is this place?" she said.

"An inn near Thurso." Methven looked around too and gave a grimace of distaste. "I apologize. It's a little Spartan in its comforts for the daughter of a duke, but if you are hungry they might be able to rustle up some bread and cheese."

Lucy shook her head. She was not hungry. What she really wanted was a bath, but she doubted the inn ran to such a luxury, especially not in the middle of the night.

"It will do until tomorrow," she said. "When you take me back to Durness."

He did not answer her. She looked up and saw the quizzical expression in his eyes as he watched her, and suddenly her stomach dropped and she felt as though she could not breathe. She understood his earlier words then. He *was* claiming her.

"You are not taking me back to Durness," she said slowly. She felt chilled all of a sudden.

"There would be no point." Methven sounded blunt, unsentimental, making her face the truth. "It's too late.

It was already too late when I found you. You have been missing for a day and a night, Lady Lucy. If I take you back unwed you will be ruined." He smiled. "You really will this time."

Silence again, broken only by the sigh of the wind against the shutters and the hiss of the logs as they settled deeper in the grate. Lucy swallowed hard. She could hear her blood beating loud in her ears.

Marriage. Or ruin.

Her perfect reputation, her perfect life was in tatters. This time there really was no escape.

She looked at Robert Methven.

"So as I am already ruined you are taking me for yourself," she said. She was starting to feel afraid. She could feel the chill of it seeping through her blood. This was impossible. There had to be a way out.

He shrugged. "If you wish to put it like that. If you were feeling particularly grateful to me, you could say I am saving your reputation."

"Grateful!" Fear and disbelief blocked Lucy's throat. "I refused to be compromised by you! You cannot simply take what is denied you—" She broke off because of course he could take what was denied him. She was here, in his power. She did not believe he was a man to take by force, but suddenly she was sure of nothing, alone here with him, frightened, in pain.

She felt the sagging mattress sag farther as he sat down on the end of the bed. He did not answer her immediately, and in some way his quietness was more frightening than the implications of his actions. It meant that he had already thought through everything that needed to be considered. He had decided what he was going to do. He was determined and she would never be able to change his mind.

"Lady Lucy," he said, "I am offering you the protection of my name. It is all I can do to help you now."

"How fortunate for you that this is precisely the outcome you wished," Lucy said coldly. She looked around the shabby chamber. "If it comes to that, how do I know that the story you told me about my cousin is true? Maybe you were my abductor all along!"

Methven's expression hardened into stone, colder, more remote than the rock of the mountain. "You may believe that if you wish," he said. "All I can say is that I told you the truth and I would be honored if you would accept my offer of marriage this time."

"And if I refuse?" Lucy said. "Or shall we drop the pretense and agree that I have no choice?"

"There is always a choice," Methven said.

"Not if I wish to keep my reputation," Lucy said.

He smiled. "That is the choice."

Lucy rubbed her forehead where there was a vicious ache.

Marriage. Or ruin. The words echoed in her head. She knew how it would be if she did not wed. Her name would become a byword for scandal, the abducted heiress who returned home with a tarnished reputation. No longer would she be the perfect debutante, the perfect *anything.* She would be damaged, dishonored, spoken of in scandalized whispers. Her father would be mortified, the whole family disgraced.

Accepting Robert Methven's proposal was the only way to save herself. Yet Methven would want a marriage in every sense. He would want an heir. Darkness raked through her heart. She could not marry him. She could not give him an heir. The thought terrified her. She saw Alice's tearstained, terrified face and felt the cold clutch of her fingers. So much blood, so much pain... She gulped back the sob that caught in her throat.

Intolerable choices.

Her head ached suddenly, viciously, and she closed her eyes.

"You need to rest." Methven's voice was soft. "We'll talk more tomorrow."

"I won't do it," Lucy said. She could feel panic clogging her chest. "I won't marry you. I can't."

He was watching her steadily, and the gentleness in his eyes made her want to cry.

"Don't think about it now," he said. "You've been through an ordeal. You'll feel better in the morning."

She would not feel better. Nothing could fix this, not this time. She turned her face away and squeezed her eyes tight shut against the burn of the tears. She was not going to show any weakness now.

"I need you to give me your word that you won't try and run away," Methven said.

Lucy opened her eyes and glared at him. "It would give me the greatest pleasure to run away."

He raised his eyebrows. "In that case," he said, "I am going to have to restrain you for your own safety."

Lucy shot bolt upright with outrage. "Restrain me? Don't be absurd!"

He smiled, implacable. "Then give me your word."

It would have been by far the most sensible thing to do, but Lucy was sick and tired of being told what to do. It felt like a small rebellion to thwart him, no matter how childish she secretly knew it to be. Besides, she was certain he would not go through with it.

She turned a shoulder. "I don't promise anything," she said sulkily.

He shrugged, as though her attempt at mutiny was of no consequence. "Then I must tie you up. I did warn you."

"You won't," Lucy said. "You can't."

"I can," Methven said, over his shoulder. He had gone across to the dresser and was rifling through the contents of the top drawer. Lucy could see that it was full of gaudy clothes: skirts, blouses, barmaid's attire perhaps. He was removing something that looked like garish silk scarves.

He meant it.

For a second the shock held her still, and then she darted across the room toward the unlocked door. He was too quick for her. He caught her just as she was reaching for the handle, his hand closing about her wrist. "Please do not make a fuss, Lady Lucy," he said, in her ear. "I have no intention of hurting you."

It was the warmth of his body and the sudden intimacy of his touch that held her motionless. He scooped her up and dropped her back on the bed. Lucy was thrown off balance for one crucial second, and in that moment he rested one knee on the bed and leaned in to loop the silk tie around the bedpost, twining it expertly about her wrist. Lucy pulled on it and only succeeded in tightening it to a tourniquet.

"Release me," she said, through shut teeth. She could not believe that he was doing this. This was a different side to Robert Methven she was seeing, a man stripped of formality, a man, she suddenly realized with a flash of insight, who had been ruthless enough to make his own way in the wilds of Canada when his family had cast him out. She had seen flashes of this resolve in him already. Now it was undisguised.

He was laughing down at her. "Are you going to beg me?" he asked.

Lucy glared at him. "I'm a duke's daughter. I don't beg."

"You're stubborn." He was tying her right wrist now. "I like that."

"It's of no consequence to me whether you like it or not," Lucy said, kicking her legs impotently. "Let me go."

"No." He spoke calmly. "I don't trust you not to run away. Not only would you put me to the trouble of fetching you back, but you would put yourself in danger."

"You are an oaf," Lucy said. "A complete boor."

"You're very polite in your insults," Methven said. "Such a lady." He tilted his head to one side. "And yet not so much of a lady sometimes. You didn't kiss me like a lady would." He smiled, that wicked smile that made her shiver. "I liked that too."

He stood back to admire his handiwork. Her arms were spread wide now, tied to the bed head, not so rigidly that she could complain of discomfort but not so loosely that she could slip free either. She lay flushed and furious, completely outraged that he had followed through on his threat.

"So this is your idea of wooing," Lucy snapped. "I should have guessed after your scoundrelly attempts to compromise me earlier. Do you intend to keep me tied up until I consent to be your wife?"

"I don't think that *scoundrelly* is a proper word." His hands checked on the knots, sure and methodical. "I had not thought to keep you restrained," he added with the same slow smile, "but the idea has some appeal."

Oh.

For some reason the thought and the look in his eyes made Lucy feel hot all over. She saw his gaze fall to her night rail, transparent in the pale light. Looking down, she could see what he saw, see the shadow of her nipples beneath the fine cotton, their peaks brushing the thin material. With her arms so widespread she could do nothing to cover herself. She felt hopelessly exposed and vulnerable and yet hot and excited at the same time. She shifted restlessly against the bed, and Methven's gaze sharpened hungrily on her, dropping lower to the junction of her thighs before he raised it, deep blue and glittering, to her face again.

Lucy's heart turned over. Their eyes held. A furnace built in the pit of her stomach. Her lips parted.

"I won't take what isn't yet mine," he said.

He pulled the covers up over her and turned away abruptly, snapping the taut thread that pulled between them, leaving Lucy feeling shaken.

"Try to get some sleep," he said roughly.

"Like this?" Lucy asked.

He threw her another dark glance. "You'll manage."

He locked the door and put the key in his pocket. Lucy felt her spirits sink a little lower. Tied up and locked in with him. He really did mean to marry her this time.

Light was still penetrating the broken spars of the shutters. Here in the far north the daylight simmered down to a deep blue haze but never quite turned dark. Lucy could still make out the shape of the furniture, the wooden chair Robert Methven had thrown himself down on, which looked far too hard to allow for sleep.

"Is there really no one else who can help you save your inheritance?" she said after a moment.

He flicked her the slightest of glances. "You won't sleep if you keep talking."

"I'm not tired," Lucy said.

He grunted. "Well, I am. Damnably tired. I rode all day to find you and scant thanks I get for it."

She could see he did not want to talk, but she persisted anyway. It might be the only chance she had to persuade him to let her go. If he did she would manage to cover the scandal somehow. Her family would help.

They had done it before, when Alice had died. They could do it again. Hope bubbled up in her, the sort of hope that was probably completely pointless but she had to believe in it anyway.

"If we could find another branch of the family," she ventured, "there might be someone you could wed—"

"Save your breath."

He sounded grumpy, as though the prospect of marrying anyone was repugnant to him in this moment. Perhaps it was. Lucy realized that she had never really considered his feelings about the arrangement, obliged to marry, given scant choice.

"You have certainly dropped the formality," she said, "now that you do not think you have to woo me anymore."

"Forgive me, but I did not think we were in a formal situation." She could hear the amusement in his voice.

"You are absolutely certain that I am the only woman who will do?" she persisted.

This time she saw his eyebrows lift as though he was surprised by her question. Perhaps he had recognized the vanity beneath it. A small smile lifted one corner of his mouth and drove a crease down his cheek.

"I am absolutely certain." The wooden chair creaked as he shifted. "It is ironic, since you have no desire to wed me that you are everything I want in a wife."

That pleased her. It pleased her a lot, although she knew it should not. She also knew she should not ask the next question.

"Why?" she said.

He looked at her for longer this time, and this time he did not smile. "I want you," he said.

There was silence in the shadowed room, hot and alive, for five long heartbeats, and then he shifted on the chair again and turned away so she could not see his face. "I said try to get some sleep." His voice was rough. "We have a long ride ahead of us tomorrow."

"How do you know that I can ride?" Lucy said.

"I'm sure you can," Methven said. "The alternative would be to ride with me, and you would hate that more."

"Instead of which I'll be tied to the saddle?"

"Aye." He was smiling a little grimly. "I'll be leading you too. In case you make a break for it."

Lucy tried to wriggle into a more comfortable position. On the lumpy mattress it was no easy matter. She was furious to be so restrained, but now that her first wave of fury had simmered down she had to admit that she had been less than mature in telling him she would run away. It would be the height of stupidity to do so, alone, unarmed and in a state of undress. There were plenty of masterless men roaming the wild glens, and she had no desire to plunge straight into further danger. On the other hand, she had seen clothes in the chest of drawers that had held the scarves that tied her. There might be something there she could change into. And if she were able to arm herself, as well, escape was not impossible. She could return to Durness and from there she could take a carriage home. Since Methven would not help her she would have to do it for herself.

She thought about it for a long time, planning, calculating and desperately hoping.

Methven shifted again, giving a long sigh of discomfort.

"Are you not intending to sleep?" Lucy inquired innocently. The sooner he fell asleep, the sooner she could start trying to slip her bonds.

"I could sleep if you would be quiet for long enough." He sounded even grumpier now, as though sleep would be impossible on such an uncomfortable piece of furniture. Well, it served him right.

The mattress smelled musty, of damp and mouse droppings. Lucy wrinkled up her nose and tried not to inhale too much of it. She wished she could have had a bath. She probably smelled as bad as the bedclothes.

In the cracks of light that came through the shuttered window and in the dying glow of the fire, she saw Methven's sword belt lying across the back of the chair, discarded for the night. A prickle of excitement crept along her skin. He would be certain to carry a pistol, as well.

Stealthily she tested the ties again. The silk was slippery. That gave her hope.

She settled down to wait for Robert Methven to fall asleep.

CHAPTER ELEVEN

THE WOODEN CHAIR was abominably hard.

Robert's body ached in places he did not even recognize. It had been a punishing two days. Lady Mairi MacLeod had woken him in his bed at the Durness Inn during the early hours of the previous morning with some panicked story of how her sister had been carried off. He had not slept since, searching for Lucy along all the roads from Durness, following the trail of the abductors until he had finally caught up with them in this godforsaken place. He had dispatched the hired thugs and sent Wilfred packing. He had tended to Lucy while she was sick and all the thanks he got for his efforts was a repeated refusal of his offer of marriage and the threat that she would run off.

She was stubborn, Lady Lucy MacMorlan, and spoiled, and a great deal of trouble and yet he still wanted her.

And now she was tied to the bed, and that made the wanting all the more acute. He might be exhausted but not so much that he could not make very thorough love to her. Robert thought about the slippery silk ties and about Lucy restrained. He thought about the delicate curves and hollows of her body beneath the thin night shift. He thought about the scent of her skin and the sensation of it beneath his hands. All the thinking and no doing was playing havoc with his senses, making him so hard he could burst, making him want to part her sweet thighs and plunge into her.

Madness. He ran a hand over his hair, rubbing his forehead to try and banish the images of lust. He cursed his vivid imagination as he grew an even more monstrous erection.

He shifted for the hundredth time on the chair.

"You are still awake." She did not sound pleased.

"So are you."

"I am uncomfortable."

"So am I," Robert said, with feeling. "Why don't you invite me to join you on the bed?" he added. "It would be more pleasant for both of us."

It could do no harm to make love to her now, now that she was to be his bride. He ached to have her. The desire pounded in his blood.

"I don't think so." She sounded prim, but underneath the formality ran a thread of anxiety. He was forcibly reminded that she was a virgin. She needed careful wooing, not ravishment. She certainly should not be seduced on a frowsty mattress in a mouse-infested inn.

Damnation.

"Then we are both destined to endure an uncomfortable few hours," he said.

Nevertheless he did sleep, after what felt like several eternities. He was troubled by visions of Lucy slipping wraithlike through his dreams—at one point he even imagined her hands on him—and he stirred but did not fully wake. The exhaustion of the past two days, the relief that she was safe and the promise of the future all lulled him.

He awoke several hours past dawn. The room was cold and full of pale gray light. The shutters were open, rattling in the breeze. It took him no more than a split second to come completely awake, instinct warning him that something was wrong. He leaped from the chair with an oath. All his muscles screamed a protest.

Two strides took him to the bed. It was empty, the bonds hanging limp on the wooden rail like a mocking taunt. They had not been cut, which could only mean that Lucy had managed to wriggle out of them somehow. He frowned. That must have hurt. As a sign of how determined she was to escape marriage to him, it was speaking loud and clear.

The window was wide. He ran across to it and leaned out. There was a low roof beneath, sloping down to within six feet of the ground. Spinning around, he took a swift inventory of the room. The drawer in the dresser was half-open, spilling clothing onto the floor. Lucy's nightgown lay abandoned in a pile of tumbled white.

His sword belt had gone from the chest. His pistols had been taken, as well—along with his money. This time he swore even harder. At least he still had his dirk. Grabbing his coat, he unlocked the door and headed down the stairs, taking them three at a time. There was a rusty old claymore adorning the lath-and-plaster wall of the hallway; he took that, as well.

His horse was missing. By now he was not in the least surprised. He had underestimated Lady Lucy MacMorlan before. This time his mistake had been spectacular. He had thought that as long as the door was locked and he held the key, as long as she was physically restrained, he could let down his guard. It was an amateur mistake. Lady Lucy might be the oh-so-proper daughter of a duke, but she was the descendant of Malcolm MacMorlan, the Red Fox of Forres. She was from warrior stock through and through. Scratch the surface and the trappings of nineteenth-century civilization were thin in all of them.

He smiled grimly. Lady Lucy was magnificent. She was indeed everything he wanted in his wife and the mother of his children.

The only other horse in the stable was a mangy nag that looked as though it was going to keel over if ridden too hard. It would have to do. Ignoring the angry shouts of the landlord, who had lost a blunt claymore and had been cheated of both the price of the room and the hire of the nag, Robert headed off down the road toward Thurso at the fastest trot the horse could raise.

LUCY HAD BEEN traveling for several hours. She was not at all sure she had been going in the right direction. Navigation was not one of her strong points. Nor had she seen anyone to ask. The countryside of high crags and bare rock was golden with bracken and hazy purple-gray with heather. The sun was already bright and hot. Nothing and no one moved in the landscape. Only an eagle circled lazily above in the pale blue.

It felt unnaturally quiet and Lucy felt a prickle of unease. The horse felt it too. His ears were pricked and Lucy could feel tension in him.

She liked Robert Methven's horse. He was a rich chestnut with bright, intelligent eyes. He was fast, brave and clever. He reminded her of his master, but that she did not really want to think about, for she had treated Methven shamefully, stealing his horse, his pistols, his sword and his money. It had been quite easy in the end. He had been sleeping deeply and barely stirred when she had lifted the sword belt from the chair and swung the saddlebags with the pistols in them over her shoulder. Lucy had judged searching his pockets for the key to the door to be too risky, so she had clambered out of the window and taken the low drop to the stable yard instead. She and Alice had spent years climbing in and out of windows at Forres Castle. Or at least Alice had. Lucy had watched, so she knew how to do it.

The only thing she was not entirely happy about was her outfit. She had not had long to rummage through the chest of drawers and so had emerged with a motley collection of clothes. There was a low white blouse, which she wore with a bright scarf to conceal her décolletage, there was a pair of boy's breeches that were a passable fit, a jacket that was too small and tight and some stockings with holes in them. Footwear had been a problem until she had reached the stables and had been able to steal a pair of well-worn boots from one of the grooms. They were slightly too big and would give her blisters if she tried to walk far in them. Her hair was loose and unbrushed. All in all she knew she looked ragged and unkempt.

The lane wound slowly downward toward a loch that gleamed in the sun, reflecting the soft blue of the sky. There was a scattering of crofts by the side of the track, barely enough to be thought a village, with a few chickens scratching in the dust and some washing flapping on a line. The walls were falling down, the earth so poor it could barely support the neat rows of cabbage and beans that had been sown. Farther out, Lucy could see houses that had been abandoned, the roofs fallen, grass growing through the cracks in the walls. Some had been burned and the charred and blackened remains of fallen spars gleamed malevolently in the sun. There was a strange atmosphere about the place, part fear, part despair. Lucy felt it with a trickle of apprehension down her back.

As she drew level with the first croft, a man came out of the gate, laying aside his hoe and dusting soil from the palms of his hands. He was young, no more than three or four and twenty, but his face was lined with tiredness and he moved slowly.

"Good morning…mistress." He raised a hand to shade his eyes as he looked up at Lucy, clearly unsure what to make of her. She could read his thoughts; the horse was highly bred, she was wearing a man's sword on a belt that was far too big for her, the saddlebags bulged and her clothes were cheap. She suspected he thought her a thief, though he spoke politely enough.

"Where do you travel?" he asked.

"To Durness," Lucy said. "Am I on the right road?"

"You need to turn northwest," the man said. His eyes had widened at her cut-glass accent and he stood up a little straighter. "The road forks past the knot of pines." He pointed. "You can water your horse by the loch there."

"My thanks," Lucy said. She turned back on a thought. "Who is the laird here?" she said.

The man's face darkened. "Cardross," he said, and spat in the dust.

Cardross.

So these people were Wilfred's tenants, so poor they could barely scrape a living from the neglected land. Lucy felt chilled although the sun was hot. It had not occurred to her that she might have wandered back onto Cardross land. She was going to have to be very careful.

She felt the man's eyes on her back as she rode down to the loch, but when she turned to look back he had gone. She wished she had some food. She could have asked back in the village, but she suspected they would have none to spare. She rode a little way along the strand, allowing the horse to drink its fill. She did not dare stop longer now that she knew she was on Wilfred's land. Robert Methven might have sent Wilfred and his men away with their tails between their legs yesterday, but they would surely be back and they would want revenge.

There was a shout behind her and she wheeled around. To her horror, three men on horseback were coming out of the knot of pine trees directly toward her. One, on a prancing gray, she recognized immediately as her cousin Wilfred Cardross. He had found some clothes and evidently he was planning on getting his hands dirty this time.

Lucy yelled an alarm. She had no idea if anyone could hear her and still less if anyone would come to her aid, but it was worth a try. It also had the benefit of unsettling Wilfred's highly bred gray, which reared up and almost unseated him.

She grabbed one of the pistols, her fingers slipping on the buckles of the saddlebags in her haste, and aimed it at the man to the right who was hurtling toward her. Her hand was shaking and the shot went wide. She had never been much of a marksman. Alice had always bested her at the archery butts. The man reached her a few seconds later and grabbed her, toppling her from the saddle. She tumbled painfully to the ground, winded, the pistol spinning from her grasp. Instinct prompted her to scramble up, to try and run, but her assailant caught her by the arm and spun her about. She could feel the ground vibrating under the hooves of the other approaching horses.

The man hit her hard across the face. She stumbled, falling over on her back, the rock jarring her. Stones scored her palms. Shock and pain intermingled. No one had ever raised a hand to her before in her life. Suddenly her situation was very real; real and terrifying.

She heard Wilfred's querulous voice:

"I told you not to hurt her!"

The man swore in reply.

Lucy rolled over. She was not going to lie here at Wilfred's feet like a helpless offering. Sheer determination and a refusal to be beaten had brought her this far. She could not lose her nerve now.

Something hard dug into her hip: the hilt of Robert Methven's sword. For a moment she was absolutely still. Then hot, fierce fighting spirit swept through her and she grabbed the pommel and leaped up, spinning around, holding the weapon in both hands, taking her assailant completely by surprise with a long, slicing cut to his arm. He howled in pain, staggering back, and with an oath the other man threw himself from the saddle, drawing his own sword as he ran toward her.

It was two against one. Lucy set her teeth and set to work.

ROBERT HEARD LUCY'S shout, a sound that for a brief second froze his blood. He abandoned the nag on the edge of the woodland and burst through the trees, the claymore in his hand. He thought he would never forget the sight that met his eyes.

Lucy was standing facing him, holding his sword in both hands. One of her assailants was already down, bleeding copiously, his sword arm hanging useless at his side. The other thug was circling Lucy warily while Wilfred Cardross was advancing on her from the left.

Wilfred was speaking.

"Lucy, my dear," he was saying, "this is foolish. Put up the sword and let us talk. We are kin—"

Lucy did not spare him a single glance. "Do be quiet, Wilfred," she said, never taking her eyes off the man in front of her. "You are putting me off my stroke."

With a yell Robert hurled himself on the first man, who spun around to face him, his face a mask of shock and terror. The claymore might have been old, but it was sound. The fight was short, sharp and bloody. Robert fought dirty. He had no time to do otherwise. He crowded in on his opponent, giving him no space to use his weapon properly, throwing him off balance. The man stumbled and Robert followed up ruthlessly, knocking the sword from his hand, his blade slicing through the man's thigh. With a scream of pain the man fell, scrabbling back, abject terror in his eyes, as Robert raised his sword to his throat.

"Robert! Watch out!"

At Lucy's shout Robert spun around. Wilfred's other clansman had grabbed the second pistol from the saddlebag and was aiming it at him from his prone position on the ground. Robert kicked the gun from the man's hand and the shot went wide, hissing past his shoulder with an inch to spare. The man staggered to his feet and made after his colleague toward the horses, limping and swearing. Robert let him go. They were cowards all, Wilfred Cardross's men.

As for Wilfred himself, Lucy was running rings around him and looking as though she was enjoying it. Her blade came up so fast at one point she almost skewered Cardross's Adam's apple. Wilfred brought his sword up just in time to parry the attack. Robert checked himself on the point of intervening. He had thought Cardross's superior height and reach would give him the immediate advantage, but Lucy was like quicksilver, faster and more agile. Cardross was fighting in earnest now, but his cousin was too good for him, cool, ruthless, classical in her style. Robert, who had once had the fastest reactions of any man and a skill honed through living dangerously, acknowledged that he was not sure he would be able to beat her in a fair fight.

She was smiling. Robert had never seen her like this. It seemed impossible that Lady Lucy MacMorlan could turn into this wild creature with the demonic light of battle in her eyes. He was surprised to find it intensely arousing.

He stood back to enjoy the show. Lucy's blade swept in a low arc, dangerously close to Wilfred's groin. Robert laughed. That would be the end of Wilfred's plans for future generations.

Wilfred had had enough. He ducked under Lucy's sword and ran for his horse.

"Go, then, you craven coward!" Lucy yelled after him as Wilfred and his men hurled themselves onto the horses and galloped off, the stones scattering from their hooves.

Robert went up to her. She was panting, her breasts rising and falling rapidly with a combination of anger and exertion. Her red-gold hair fell about her face.

Her eyes still shot sparks. They met his, bright blue with passion. The need to kiss her, the desire for her, punched him like a blow to the solar plexus.

He was a second away from pulling her into his arms when he saw the marks on her face, and fury and shock sliced through him in equal measure.

He fell back a step, raising a hand, and touched her cheek. "They did this to you?"

The fierce expression in her eyes changed, as though she had only just remembered what had happened. She touched the tips of her fingers gently to her cheekbone and winced.

The anger in Robert was like a live thing. He had never felt such protective fury in his life before. He turned to pursue Cardross and his men into the woods, but Lucy caught his arm and clung on.

"Let them go," she said. "It doesn't matter."

"It matters," Robert said.

"No, it does not. Not now. Please, my lord."

He heard the vulnerability beneath the words. She was looking cold and pale now as reaction set in. He covered her hand with his and felt her tremble.

"You called me Robert before," he reminded her.

She smiled faintly. "It was not a moment for formality."

"And I thank you for the warning," Robert said. Cardross and his men were almost out of sight now. All that was left was the dust from the horses' hooves hanging in the air.

"You could have let him shoot me and saved yourself the trouble of refusing my offer for a third time," he said.

Lucy frowned. "Don't jest," she said.

"I'm not," Robert said. "Why did you help me?"

She turned to look up at him. Her gaze, clear and full of candor, searched his face. "We were on the same side," she said.

"Were we?" He felt encouraged that she thought so. Last night, in the room at the inn, they had been locked in opposition. She had run away into danger rather than wed him. Yet it seemed she did not think of him as her enemy.

He felt her shiver again. The breeze was cold down here by the water.

"Come along," he said. "We must get you to shelter and get off Cardross's land. Next time he'll be back with more than a couple of men."

Lucy unbuckled his sword belt from about her waist and handed it to him carefully. Now that the heat of battle had gone from his blood, he noticed her attire for the first time. Gone was the elegant duke's daughter in her debutante pastel colors and modestly cut gowns. She was wearing a motley collection of clothes, chiefly a striped red, white and blue cotton scarf, a pair of boy's breeches that fit her very snugly and a white blouse cut low enough across her breasts to affect both his concentration and his anatomy. It was fortunate he had not noticed earlier.

She started to fiddle with the scarf at her neck, straightening it and tucking it into the neck of the blouse. Robert, torn between admiring the blouse and the breeches, realized that he was staring. Lucy had noticed the direction of his gaze, as well.

"What?" She held the scarf tightly together, obliterating his view.

Her blue eyes fizzed with annoyance.

Robert cleared his throat. "Very patriotic," he said. Then, as she raised a haughty eyebrow: "The red, white and blue scarf."

She frowned. "This was all there was in that godforsaken inn." She turned a shoulder. "There was a mirror. I did see what I look like."

"And what do you think you look like?"

He had no complaints at all.

"Blowsy." She tucked the ends of the scarf more closely into the top of the blouse. "Like a tavern wench."

"I wouldn't do that," Robert said. "It only draws attention to your breasts."

"They got in the way when I was fighting." She looked down in disgust at her cleavage. "I was afraid they would fall out of the blouse."

"That would most certainly have stopped your cousin's clansmen in their tracks," Robert said.

"I'm not accustomed to showing so much." Suddenly she looked vulnerable. "Debutantes don't."

"I've seen more of you than that."

She flashed him another sharp look. "It doesn't help to know that, thank you."

The scarf fluttered in the breeze like a ragged flag.

It's gaudy silk reminded Robert of the bindings he had used to tie her.

"How did you escape?" he asked. "I thought I had tied you firmly."

"I wriggled," Lucy said succinctly.

That did nothing to calm Robert's inflamed imagination. He could visualize her, her body restrained by the silk scarves, writhing on the bed. He picked up one of her wrists. Faint red marks showed on her white skin. He felt a complete cad.

He dropped her wrist and she rubbed the place he had held.

"You jumped from the window," he said, remembering.

"I climbed down from the roof," Lucy corrected.

"Why did you not simply take the key?"

She gave him a look as though he were mad. "And risk waking you by searching your pockets?"

"Generally I sleep like the dead, even on a wooden chair."

"Thank you," Lucy said. "I'll remember that for future reference." She looked about them. "I thought you wished to go. Are we instead to stand here waiting for Wilfred to return with an army?"

Shaking off the wayward visions of Lucy in bondage that still plagued him, Robert scooped up his sword belt, stowed the pistols, mounted Falcon and gave Lucy a hand to pull her up to sit in front of him. For once she did not argue.

"What were you doing here?" Robert looked around

at the waters of the loch reflecting the cool blue of the sky.

"I wanted a bath," Lucy said shortly.

"It will be freezing in there," Robert said.

"I swam in the sea every summer when I was a child," Lucy said.

So swimming was another of her accomplishments. Robert was not surprised. Nothing Lucy could do, he thought, was likely to surprise him ever again.

As Falcon started to pick up the pace toward the road he felt her soften in his arms, as though she had at last started to relax. Some of the prickly tension seeped from her. She sighed, leaning her head back against his chest. He found it very pleasant. Her body fit into the curve of his. Her hair smelled of fresh air and apple sweetness. Some strange sensation that was not lust, but equally was not something he recognized, shifted and settled inside him and he drew her a little closer into the shield of his arms.

"What happened to the second pistol?" he asked. His lips were close to her ear. Her hair tickled them. "Did you fire it?"

"I missed." She sounded disgruntled. "Shooting has never been a skill of mine."

Robert tried not to laugh at her tone. "Well," he said, "you might not be able to shoot, but you fight extraordinarily well."

"So do you," she said, glancing at him over her shoulder, "though you don't fight by the rules."

"Where I have been, there was no such thing as a

fair fight." He drew her back against him, closer still, so that their bodies touched. "I fight to win."

"I might have guessed." She smiled. For a second her cheek brushed his. "Was it very lawless, out there is the wilds of Canada?"

"Entirely," Robert said. Then, surprising himself: "I'll tell you all about it one day."

"I'd like that." She settled against him. "It must have been very hard for you to be sent away from everything you knew."

It had been intolerable. In the beginning he had not known how he would survive, mourning his brother's death, cut adrift from everything he knew, everything he loved. The chill wreathed his heart again. He had been a hotheaded young fool to challenge his grandfather's plans for him. The irony was that the old laird had been grieving too, mourning the loss of his grandson and heir. Robert could see that now. His grandfather had taken out on him all his grief and disappointment, but Robert had been too young and his feelings too raw to be able to deal with it. He had told his grandfather that he would prove his mettle elsewhere, away from Methven, and then he had boarded the first ship he had found.

He wanted to change the subject back to Lucy. He was not comfortable talking about himself. It was not something he ever did.

"I suppose your father had his daughters trained in swordplay as well as his sons?" he said. He had heard of many Highland lairds doing so, especially if their sons were as stodgy as Angus or as lazy as Lachlan.

He felt her laugh, a soft tremor against his chest. "Of course my father did not teach us how to fight," she said. "He is a scholar, not a warrior. I learned from books." She favored him with another smile. "That is why I fight by the book instead of like you, like a…a brigand."

"No one could learn to fight as well as that from books," Robert said.

Her eyelashes flickered down. "Well, we did have some practical lessons at the Highland Ladies Bluestocking Society. We hired the best swordsman in Edinburgh to teach us."

"Of course," Robert said. "Of course you did. I suppose you had lessons in between the Eastern dancing and the massage."

"A lady should always be able to defend herself," Lucy said serenely.

"What else did you learn under the Society's auspices?" Robert asked. "Just so I am prepared."

"Archery and falconry," Lucy said. "Fencing, pistol shooting. But as I said, I am not a good shot."

"Bad luck," Robert said. "Actually it is good to know there is something you do not excel at. You enjoyed the sword fight, didn't you?" he added.

He felt her surprise in the sudden jerk of her body.

"No." She sounded startled. "Fighting is not something to be enjoyed." She frowned. "It's uncivilized."

"That's what you would like to believe," Robert said,

"but sword fighting can be primitive and wild and exciting. It calls to something in the blood."

He could tell that his words had disturbed her from the way that she stiffened. She sat up a little straighter, moving out of the shelter of his arms.

It was curious to Robert that she was so utterly devoid of understanding of herself. She had all the wildness of a Highlander. She simply hid it well. Her passion escaped in so many ways, though: in the sensual writings of the love letters, in the undeniable pleasure she took in the physical. Robert was willing to bet any money that she would be equally passionate making love. If her kisses were anything to go by, she would burn him down.

He shifted in the saddle. He had to stop thinking like this or the journey, already long and arduous, was going to be very uncomfortable indeed.

CHAPTER TWELVE

By four in the afternoon they had reached Findon, a small town on the coast. Lucy was swaying with exhaustion, aching in every limb and starving hungry, but she had tried her best to hide it from Robert. She felt nervous and on edge and very aware of him. She told herself it was simply their physical proximity, manifest in the brush of his body against hers as he rode Falcon with strength and easy grace, the hard muscle of his thighs, the protective clasp of his arms about her. Yet what she felt was more than simple awareness. She felt vulnerable, as though she had been unable to defend herself against him. Robert had seen all these things about her that she had not even suspected herself. She did not know how it was possible for him to understand her so well when no one else did.

She had never previously thought herself in the least bit wild. Alice had been the wild one, forever tumbling into trouble. Lucy had been the sensible twin, and after Alice's death that propriety had become suffocating. She had failed Alice the one time it had really mattered and to atone she had tried to turn herself into even more of a model of perfection. But the wildness that must always have been buried deep in her had still escaped.

It had escaped in the writing of those shocking letters. It had escaped in the primitive fury she had felt when Wilfred had attacked her. It had escaped when she was in Robert Methven's arms.

He held her now, reins in one hand, the other clasped possessively about her waist. It felt strange and disturbing but also treacherously good.

She distracted herself by looking about at the neat, respectable houses, the streets swept clean and the smartly painted shop fronts. The place looked a great deal better cared for than the Cardross estates. There was a stone jetty where boats bobbed at anchor and the fishing nets were drying in the sun. The air was sharp and keen and scented with the tang of fish and salt.

"This is very pretty," Lucy said. "Who owns the land hereabouts?"

"I do," Robert said. "I own this sweep of the coast and out there—" He gestured to the hazy blue of the sea. "I own Golden Isle."

He reined in and for a moment sat staring at the scatter of dark islands on the horizon. There was something in his eyes: pride, yes, but something else Lucy could not read or understand, something darker. She thought for a moment that he might say something else, but instead he turned the horse abruptly down a cobbled side street, where the afternoon shadows cooled the air, and clattered through an arched gateway and into an inn yard.

Their arrival caused a degree of flurry. The landlord, a fair florid man in his mid-fifties, immediately came running, wiping his hands on the large striped apron about his waist.

"My lord!"

"McLain." Robert swung down from the saddle and held out his hand. "How is business?"

"Business is good, my lord," the man stuttered, "but I had no idea you were to visit… You sent no word—"

"Rest easy." Robert reassured him with a quick clap on the shoulder. "It was a sudden change of plan."

He lifted Lucy down from the saddle and set her on her feet. "May I introduce my betrothed, Lady Lucy MacMorlan?" he said. His voice was suddenly cool and formal, the warmth of greeting drained from it. "We have had a difficult journey and require a couple of rooms and some hot water to wash and food, of course…"

The landlord's mouth fell open. He stared at Lucy, realized he was staring, shut his mouth with a snap and bowed deeply. "Welcome, my lady!" He shot Robert another glance. "Betrothed, you say, my lord?"

Lucy tried not to laugh. She could imagine how she must look, travel sore and dusty, dressed in boy's trews and a harlot's blouse. Small blame to the landlord if he thought the laird had brought his mistress to visit rather than his future wife.

"A sudden engagement," Robert said smoothly with a quick look at Lucy that warned her not to contradict him. "You are the first to know."

The landlord turned to the gaping scullions. "Fetch

my wife to conduct Lady Lucy to a room!" He clapped his hands sharply. "Now! Run!"

He led them inside. Lucy was so tired and saddle sore that she could feel her legs trembling, but she forced herself to walk steadily and smile at the staring servants. There was the most delicious smell of roasting meat, and her stomach rumbled longingly. She wanted to dash down the passage to the kitchens and fall on it, no matter how unbecoming that might be to the daughter of a duke. That really would convince the landlord that she was a slattern.

McLain bowed them into the dark-paneled parlor and murmured something about fetching refreshments. As soon as the door had closed behind him, Robert turned to her.

"You'll understand," he said formally, "that I had no choice other than to introduce you as my betrothed. Not if I did not wish to show you dishonor in front of my people."

Lucy did understand, but she did not see why she should let him get away with such high-handed behavior.

"I see," she said coolly.

Immediately the formality dropped from him and he grinned. "No need to take that frozen tone with me, my lady. I had no intention of accepting a third refusal."

"I am aware of that too," Lucy said. This would be no convenient betrothal, made to save face and broken off when it had served its purpose. It was far too late for that now. She would be wedded—and bedded. She felt the smothering panic rising in her throat and forced it back down again.

Robert's eyes searched her face for a moment. She could feel his gaze on her for all that she kept her eyes stubbornly averted from his, and then he took her by surprise, leaning forward to give her a brief, hard kiss she felt all the way down to the tips of her toes.

"We'll talk about it over dinner," he said.

"Shall we?" Lucy said, refusing to yield.

His smile widened. "Aye, we shall. And until then—" he was pulling the engraved signet ring from his finger "—you should have a betrothal ring, I think."

The ring was warm from his body and felt heavy and solid as he slid it onto Lucy's finger. It was far too big and she instinctively closed her fingers about it to hold it in place.

"I'll buy you something prettier." His voice was soft.

"I like it very well." She cleared her throat. She felt odd, as though he had finally claimed her, as though his protection enveloped her. "It feels strong and unyielding, like you."

"Ah, lass—" He moved so quickly she gasped and then she was in his arms and he was kissing her properly this time, with heat and passion and possession. For a long moment she yielded to the demand of his mouth before she remembered that nothing between them was settled and she could not wed him; that she had run and stolen and fought and lied in order to avoid marrying him. She wanted to draw back then, but it was too late because a stronger part of her wanted to be seduced, so she was struggling against her own desires as well as his.

"Don't fight me." His whisper echoed her thoughts. "We are on the same side. You said so yourself."

He did not understand. He could not, of course. The fear beat against the sweetness of the kiss and she made a small sound of distress. Robert let her go at once.

"Lucy—" he said, and her heart bounded because she knew he was going to ask her the cause of her distress and she did not know if she could answer truthfully. She had locked the truth away so tight and deep eight years ago and never permitted the light to expose it again.

He opened his mouth to speak but closed it again, as there were voices in the passage directly outside the parlor door.

"That will be Isobel," he said. "Before I turn you over to her, can I get you anything else?"

"I'd like some new clothes," Lucy said. She glanced down at the filthy striped scarf. "Something a little more becoming."

"I'll send out for something for you," Robert said.

"That makes me feel more like a mistress than a wife," Lucy said tartly.

The sudden heat in his eyes scorched her. "I can make you feel more like my mistress if you wish."

Lucy's blush stung her cheeks. She could only be glad of the knock at the parlor door, snapping her out of the moment.

"My lord?" A diminutive woman was standing there,

much younger and altogether different from how Lucy would have imagined the landlady to be. Behind her bobbed a dark-haired, bright-eyed girl of no more than fourteen who was trying to peer around her mother to see what Lucy looked like.

Robert enveloped the woman in a bear hug. "How are you, Isobel?"

He stepped back, took both her hands and planted a kiss on her cheek. "You look well. And how is my goddaughter?"

The girl gave a little squeal of excitement. For a moment Lucy thought she was going to throw herself into Robert's arms, but somehow she managed to restrain herself although she was almost jumping out of her skin with the effort. Robert took her hand and, a twinkle in his eye, bent his head to place a kiss on the back of it. The girl giggled.

"Don't put ideas in her head please, my lord," Isobel said briskly, not one whit overawed by her guest. "She already thinks you are some sort of hero."

Robert glanced at Lucy, who was biting her lip in an effort not to smile. "Far be it from me to disabuse her of the idea," he said. "Lady Lucy—" he drew Lucy forward "—may I present Mrs. Isobel McLain and her daughter Elizabeth?"

"Bessie," the girl said, dropping Lucy a deep curtsy. "My lady." She raised frankly curious eyes to Lucy's face. "You're very pretty," she said. "But what happened to your face?"

Lucy saw Isobel stiffen. "Bessie! Hush." She turned

to Robert. "I'll look after your lady well, my lord." She gestured to Lucy. "If you would care to come with me, my lady."

"No need for me to act as lady's maid, then," Robert said lazily.

"I am sure you rate that amongst your many talents, my lord," Isobel McLain said tartly, "but Her Ladyship and I shall manage very well without you."

Lucy's weariness returned as she struggled up the stairs in the landlady's wake. Bessie skipped along lightly behind. Lucy could feel the girl's eyes on her in frank appraisal, feel too the questions jostling on Bessie's lips and the struggle she was having to keep them in.

There was already a bath in the room; the air was scented with lavender and other herbs Lucy tried to identify. There was lemon balm and another fragrance, sweet and enticing.

"Chamomile," Isobel said, smiling. "For relaxation. There is a woman who lives out on the Thurso Road who makes herbal remedies."

"How wonderful," Lucy said, heartfelt. "Just what I need."

As she slipped into the hot water and Isobel drew the screen around the bath, she was afraid she might fall asleep with the sheer pleasure of it. The water was deliciously soothing after the hard ride. Her aching muscles eased and she slid deeper to wash her hair, as well.

Behind the scene she could hear Bessie whispering to Isobel, and Isobel hushing her irrepressible daughter.

"You will not ask Lady Lucy any questions," Isobel was saying severely. "It is very bad manners."

"I don't mind," Lucy said, opening her eyes. She squeezed the water from her hair. It felt soft and smelled gloriously sweet. She wrapped the bath sheet about her and padded over to the dressing table. The smooth worn boards of the floor felt warm beneath her bare feet.

"We are still waiting for the clothes Lord Methven has sent out for, my lady," Isobel said. "There's only one dressmaker in Findon, and Lord knows if she has anything suitable." She was eyeing Lucy carefully. "I wondered if I might lend you something in the meantime—we are of a height, I'm thinking—and my Sunday best would do." She blushed. "But if you prefer not—"

"That is very generous of you," Lucy said, appreciating the offer and quick to put Isobel at her ease. "I'd be very happy for the loan of a gown."

Isobel beamed. "I did not think you would wish to keep those things," she said, nodding toward the pile of dirty linen in the corner, "but if you do I can wash them—"

"Good gracious, no, thank you," Lucy said. "I can't wait to see the back of them."

Bessie giggled. "We thought Lord Methven had brought home a circus performer as wife, my lady," she volunteered.

"I'm not surprised," Lucy said. She looked at her reflection in the glass. Her hair spilled softly about her bare shoulders. It would take some combing to remove

all the tangles. She looked tired and pale. Her gaze
went to the livid bruise that was starting to form on her
cheekbone. It looked an angry red, a reminder of Wilfred's casual violence, his disregard for family loyalty,
and the ruthlessness she had not even imagined was in
him. She touched it gently. She would never forget and
never forgive him. Nor would she forget the fury and
protectiveness in Robert's eyes as he had looked at her.
There would be reckoning with Wilfred soon enough.

"I have tincture of arnica for your bruises, my lady,"
Isobel said. There was a shadow of something in her
eyes and suddenly Lucy understood. She put her hand
on the other woman's arm.

"You mustn't think—" She stopped. "This was not
Lord Methven's doing. My cousin, the Earl of Cardross,
and some of his clansmen attacked us on the road."

The jar fell from Isobel's hand to clatter on the floor
and roll away. "Lord save us, you are the earl's cousin?"
She had gone a shade paler. Bessie was staring now,
her mouth open, a mixture of shock and fright in her
wide eyes.

"I'm afraid so," Lucy said. "Well, second cousin.
But I am nothing like him. Really I am not." Wilfred's
name was probably enough to give children nightmares
in these parts. Looking from Isobel's set face to Bessie's scared one, she felt shocked. She had never liked
Wilfred, but the face he had shown to his family was
vastly different from the one she was seeing now.

"Mercy me," Isobel said. "We are safe from Cardross
now because Lord Methven protects us, but a few years

back, in the old laird's day, there were many incursions into the land. They burned the town once and drove off all the livestock."

"He burns his own lands," Bessie said, "when the people anger him."

Lucy felt chilled. "The law—" she started to say, but Isobel shook her head.

"Cardross was the law in these parts," she said simply. "The old laird left us to fend for ourselves, but then he died and Lord Methven came back."

"He fought for us," Bessie said. Her eyes were shining. "Like a hero from the old stories."

Lucy smiled, but beneath it she felt a sharp pang of shame. She realized that she had been so wrapped up in her books at Forres and in Edinburgh that she had had no idea of what life had been like for people such as these. She had lived in a gilded bubble, remote from the villagers she had met that morning, who scratched a living so close to poverty and starvation, or Isobel and her family who worked hard to make their business successful. Suddenly she could see why Robert fought so hard for the welfare and future of his clan and why he had been prepared to do anything to secure that future. These people mattered to him. Their livelihood mattered to him. And Wilfred's violence and cruelty could not be permitted to triumph.

Isobel sat down on the edge of the bed. "We heard rumors the laird had to wed a kinswoman of Cardross in order to fulfill the terms of his inheritance," she said.

"We thought it a great sacrifice to make for our future, begging your pardon, my lady."

Lucy laughed. "I think it probably is."

Isobel shook her head again, her eyes alight with amusement this time. "I think it is probably not, judging by the way he looks at you, my lady." Then, as Lucy blushed, she added slyly, "No sacrifice at all, I'm thinking."

"Was it a sudden engagement?" Bessie was all that was inquisitive. Her gaze had gone to Lucy's hand, where she turned and turned the heavy gold band. Lucy half expected Isobel McLain to reprove her daughter, but when she looked at her, Isobel had an identical expression of curiosity on her face. Lucy laughed at the mirror image.

"Not really," she said. "Lord Methven has asked me three times to wed him."

"He's a determined man," Isobel said dryly. "When he believes in something."

Lucy felt a lump in her throat. Robert Methven certainly believed in protecting those he cared for. "Yes," she said slowly. "Yes, he is."

"And such a handsome one," Bessie piped up, making Lucy laugh.

"I won't argue with that," she said.

"He likes you, my lady," Bessie said. "He likes you very much."

Isobel reached for the comb. "I'll dress your hair, my lady," she said, "and Bessie can run along and fetch my blue muslin."

"Please, there's no need to wait on me," Lucy said hastily. "I can do it myself and you must have so much work to do about the inn."

Isobel's eyes warmed. "Bless you, my lady, that's kind, but there is no more important task than looking after Lord Methven's lady." She started gently to untangle the knots in Lucy's hair. "Once this is done you can join Lord Methven for dinner. You'll be hungry, I don't doubt."

"Yes," Lucy said. "I haven't eaten all day." She remembered Robert saying that they would discuss their betrothal over dinner. Suddenly her appetite was gone, for what could she say, what could she do? All choices were made, all chance of escape was lost.

She was still staring blankly at the mirror long after Isobel had finished her hair.

THE METHVEN ARMS was buzzing that night, but Isobel led Lucy down to a private parlor—evidently the best parlor—that had been put aside for their sole use. It was an intimate little space, warm, paneled in oak and lit by a merry fire and several stands of candles. Robert was waiting for her. He too had had time to bathe and shave and find fresh clothes. He stood up as Lucy went into the parlor, tossed aside his newspaper as though it no longer held any interest for him and held a chair for her at the little circular table.

"You look lovely," he said quietly.

Lucy smoothed her skirts, suddenly self-conscious. For a moment she felt so shy she could not look at him but concentrated instead on the deep red wine he was pouring into the crystal glasses for them. At least her appetite had returned. The table was positively groaning beneath the weight of food: a pot of steaming stew, delicious fresh rolls that smelled sweet, slices of beef and ham and crowdie cheese that looked rich and creamy. Lucy wondered if it would look too greedy to fall upon it immediately.

"The landlord keeps a good table," she said.

"Iain McLain used to be coachman at Methven until he was injured in a carriage accident," Robert said. "My grandfather set him up here and he has made a great success of it."

He raised his glass and touched it to hers. *"Slainthe mhath,"* he said. "A toast to my very beautiful and very talented comrade in arms."

His eyes were deep blue as they dwelt on her face. His expression made Lucy feel very hot.

"I've told Isobel we will serve ourselves," Robert said, "so that we shall not be disturbed."

Lucy reached for a bread roll, smothering it in butter. There was a vast pot of beef stew; she ladled some eagerly onto her plate.

"What was your grandfather like?" she asked. "He was laird before you, wasn't he?"

Robert paused. He did not smile and Lucy felt a ripple of disquiet, sensing something amiss but not quite sure what it might be. She knew so little about him. She wore his ring and she was going to wed him, but of the man himself she knew almost nothing. He gave so little away.

"My grandfather was fierce and proud and steeped in the old ways," Robert said, after a moment. He took the ladle from her, helping himself to the stew. His expression was clear. If it had not been for that momentary hesitation, she would have thought there was nothing amiss. "He remembered the rebellion of forty-five," he said. "He hated the English and their kings and could not understand how the world had changed."

"Did you like him?" Lucy asked.

Again she felt that flicker of hesitation in him before he answered, "No, I did not like him. There were many matters on which we disagreed. He neglected his estates shamefully in his later years, which allowed your cousin Cardross to stake a claim here. Since I returned I've worked damned hard to put matters right." He tilted his wineglass to his lips, took a deep swallow. "I am sure he is spinning in his grave to see my methods. He disapproved of me badly and did not wish me to succeed him, but there was nothing he could do to prevent it."

"And your grandmother?" Lucy asked. "She is fierce too."

This time Robert did smile. "Oh, Grandmama has a soft heart for all her sharpness." His voice had changed, softened. "She was the only one—" He stopped. Lucy waited. When he resumed, his voice was smooth again and had no expression. "Methven was never meant to be mine," he said. "I had an elder brother. Gregor. He was to be the next laird."

Lucy laid down her fork. "He died," she said, remembering, feeling quick sympathy. "I am sorry." She, with her painful memories of losing Alice, was immediately alive to wondering how he had felt to lose his brother, the heir. It could not have been anything other than terrible.

"Thank you." She could see that her words had not reached him. He did not meet her eyes. "It was a long time ago."

"You quarreled with your family and went abroad after your brother's death, didn't you?" It was all coming back to Lucy now. In those dark days after Alice had died, she had been scarcely aware of anything else happening at all, but she could remember her father mentioning that there had been a terrible tragedy and that Robert Methven had left the country and gone to Canada.

"Why did you go?" she asked.

Robert looked at her. His blue eyes were blank. "My grandfather considered me unworthy to succeed him." His voice was cool. Only the white of his knuckles on the fork betrayed him. "We quarreled badly over his plans for me. I decided to try and prove myself elsewhere."

"But to go so far from home?" Lucy stared. "After your brother died you were heir to the Methven estates! Surely—"

"I was young and foolish," Robert said, interrupting her, cutting her off. He picked up the wine bottle. "Would you care for more?"

It was so clear a warning to drop the subject that Lucy almost flinched. He was not prepared to give her an insight into his emotions. She felt chilled by the rebuff.

She ran her fingers over the engraved initials of the signet ring on her hand. It felt warm and heavy, but the comfort of it was illusory. It did not bind them closer because it seemed Robert did not want that intimacy.

"Thank you," she said, as coolly as he, and filled the silence between them by drinking half of it even though she was not sure she should take any more.

"I have sent a letter to your sister Mairi to tell her that you are safe," Robert said, after a long pause. "Also your father. I have asked for your hand in marriage." He gave her a lopsided smile. "Actually I have told him we are to wed tomorrow."

Lucy jumped, spilling some drops of her wine on the shiny wooden surface of the table.

"Tomorrow!" she said.

"Aye." His blue gaze challenged her. He nodded toward her hand. "You wear my ring. I was under the impression that you had accepted my proposal."

Lucy touched the golden band lightly. "You offered it to me to protect my reputation here in public."

"I offered it to you because I want to marry you," Robert said. His gaze was dark now, opaque. She could not tell what he was thinking. "You have seen for yourself now how Wilfred Cardross works," he said harshly, lifting his gaze to hers. "Would you be prepared to let this land fall into his hands?"

"That's not fair," Lucy said. She pushed her plate away, appetite gone. Even so, she was thinking of Isobel and Bessie and the horror and fear in their eyes. She thought of the bare plot of land at the croft where she had stopped to ask for directions. She thought of Wilfred's guile and cruelty, of men's livelihoods stolen and their homes gone, their families dispersed. She raised a hand to touch her cheek and felt the throb of the bruise.

"He cannot be allowed to win," Robert said.

"No," Lucy whispered.

"Those who are strong have a responsibility to protect others." He covered her hand with his. "You are strong, Lucy."

"You believe that?" Lucy's fingers trembled on the stem of the wineglass. She had never thought herself strong. She had despised herself for her weakness in failing Alice and Alice's child.

"You can help my people." Robert's tone was steady and the look in his eyes deep and intent.

"Yes," Lucy whispered. She had known there was no going back. Robert would agree to nothing less than marriage now, and even if he let her go, there was no possible way to save her reputation. She could never step back into her old life as though nothing had happened. Already it felt distant, lost to her.

"You need a wife to fulfill the terms of the treaty," she said, moistening her lips. Her throat felt sore and rough. She took another mouthful of wine and could not taste it.

"No," Robert said. His fingers tightened over hers. "I need you."

CHAPTER THIRTEEN

LUCY LOOKED INTO ROBERT's eyes and saw the certainty and the determination there.

"You would want a wife in your bed and an heir for Methven," she said.

She saw the leap of heat in his eyes. "I would," he said. "I require an heir."

"Then I can't marry you," Lucy said in a rush. "I can't sleep with you. I can't give you an heir. It's impossible."

She was not sure what she had expected him to say to that. She had not thought that far ahead. She had seen no further than blurting out the truth. Now, to her surprise, he said nothing at all. He demanded no explanations; he did not contradict her or ride roughshod over her words. Instead his gaze swept over her thoughtfully and she felt the trembling inside her ease and the tight knot of panic in her chest loosen a little.

"I suspected as much," he said. A faint smile tugged the corner of his mouth. "Tell me more about that."

Startled, she stared at him. "You don't *mind?*"

He shrugged, the tiniest hint of tension in the line of his shoulders. "Lucy," he said, "you went to a hell of a lot of trouble to run away from me. At every point you have refused my offer of marriage even at the cost of your reputation. What sort of fool would I be if I had not realized that there must be some…" He paused. "Some very important reason why you felt that you could not wed me?"

He looked up suddenly and her heart jumped at the expression in his eyes. "I flatter myself that you do not object to me personally, but if I am mistaken, perhaps this would be the moment to tell me."

Unbelievably she felt a flutter of laughter in her chest. "Robert," she said. "No, I…I do like you—" It was only then she realized quite how much she did like him, and felt alongside the leap of excitement in her blood a sickening lurch of misery that she was so damaged that what they might have had together could never be.

Robert got up and came across to her, sitting on the edge of the table, one booted leg swinging. "I am encouraged to hear it," he said. "So tell me, Lucy, if we cannot wed, what reason could possibly be strong enough? After all—" His tone had hardened a little. "You were prepared to marry MacGillivray." His voice was dry. "He was your perfect ideal."

"There is no such thing as a perfect ideal," Lucy said. It felt good to be so honest after so many years of pretense. It felt as though something had opened inside her, spilling out the truth at last. "Lord MacGillivray was a good man," she said, "but he was ideal only in the sense that he was safe."

"He did not want to bed you," Robert said softly.

A flame burned deep in the blue of his eyes. "You chose MacGillivray because he did not desire you." His hand was beneath her chin forcing it up so that she was obliged to meet his eyes. "You are afraid of intimacy," he said. His fingers were cool against her hot cheek. His eyes searched her face, all humor gone now.

"No," Lucy said. "I am afraid of the consequence of intimacy, not intimacy itself. I am afraid of pregnancy and childbirth…" Her voice cracked.

"Why are you scared, Lucy?" Robert said. "What happened? Tell me." His voice was very quiet, steady and soothing, and he took her hand in his, drawing her to her feet and over to the fireside, where there was a cushioned settle. He pulled her down to sit beside him. "You can tell me anything," he said.

"My sister Alice," Lucy said. "She was my twin. She died in childbirth." Suddenly the pain of memory caught her. It felt as though it was ripping her in half. She put an arm across her stomach to keep it in, but it was too huge, too violent. She gasped aloud with it.

"Help me, Lucy! I am so afraid!" The words, like a cry in the dark, echoed through Lucy's mind.

She put her hands over her face, then let them fall. Her eyes were dry, the tears locked up inside. She had never once cried over Alice's death because she was afraid that once she started, it would be impossible to stop.

"It started the night you came to Forres," Lucy said. "Alice was watching the gentlemen on the terrace that night. She saw Hamish Purnell and fell in love with him at first sight. Well," she corrected herself, "she fell in love with the idea of being in love with him. It was a schoolgirl crush at first, but it became so much more. Only at the time I did not realize."

She screwed her eyes up tightly. She had never talked about this and now she could feel the panic growing in her, locking her muscles, making her heart pound. Her chest felt tight.

Robert took her hand again. His was warm and comforting. He rubbed his thumb gently over the back of it, soothing, back and forth. It gave her the strength to go on.

"Purnell was married," Lucy said, "but still he started an *affaire* with Alice. She would slip away to meet him in the woods. She thought it was all impossibly romantic. I warned her to be careful, but she would not listen to me. Alice had a great ability only to hear what she wanted to hear."

Suddenly she was angry with Alice, her anger as fresh and vivid as though her twin's folly had happened only yesterday. "I knew what she was doing was wrong. I told her—" She stopped, caught out by a sob that tore at her lungs.

"What happened?" Robert's voice was very quiet.

"It ended," Lucy said. "Or so I thought." The words tasted bitter in her mouth. She had been very naive and she hated herself for it. She stared at Robert, not really seeing him, seeing instead Alice's face. "After a while I realized that there was something wrong. Alice was always bright and impulsive, laughing where I was seri-

ous, frivolous where I was staid. But then she changed."
She looked down at her hands, at her fingers interlinked
with Robert's, hers pale, his tanned and strong. "She
became thin and quiet and withdrawn. It was as though
all the color had drained out of her."

"She was pregnant," Robert said.

Lucy nodded. "I was terribly hurt that she had not
told me. I felt as though I had failed her in some way,
that she did not want to confide in me." It still hurt
now, the thought that Alice had not trusted her. They
had always told each other everything. Except this time
was different.

"Did you tell anyone else?" Robert asked.

Lucy shook her head. "Alice made me swear to tell
no one, made me promise on our mother's grave."

Of course she had agreed. They had kept each other's secrets always. And even though Alice had kept
this from her for so long, even though it was the biggest and most frightening secret in the world, too big
to hold alone, Lucy had tried. She had tried so hard.

"Such a huge secret to carry on your own," Robert
said, his words echoing her thoughts. "I am sorry you
had to do that."

"Alice planned to have the baby in secret and give
it away and that way no one would know," Lucy said.
"She was so afraid of getting into trouble." She stared
into the red heart of the fire. "I had never realized,
because Alice always seemed so brave, but beneath it
all she was just a frightened child herself. And I was
no better."

"You were very young," Robert said, "and no doubt you were terrified too."

"I was sixteen," Lucy said. It felt like a lifetime ago, as though it had happened to a different girl. Yet it was as fresh and painful as a new wound.

"Alice went into labor prematurely at seven months," she said. "I was with her when it happened. Neither of us knew what to do. It was terrifying."

The cold, the bitter chill she always felt when she remembered, was lapping at her now. She wanted to push the memories away, to run and hide as she had always done, yet something stronger, something at last more powerful, was helping her on. She felt it in the strength and reassurance of Robert's touch and saw it in his eyes.

"I knew that something was going wrong," Lucy said, "but Alice begged me not to leave her. Even at the end she was so scared of getting into trouble, so I left too late and when I finally ran for help…" She stopped. "I could have saved her," she whispered. "I could have saved the child. If only I had gone sooner. But I did not."

She stopped. Her teeth were chattering. She felt exhausted, cold to her bones.

"Lucy," Robert said, and there was so much gentleness in his tone that she shook to hear it. She wanted to put her hands over her ears, to block out his tenderness, because she was so close to the edge of control now that she could not bear it and she knew another word from him would bring her down.

"It was not your fault Alice and the baby died,"

Robert said. "Don't punish yourself. You did what you thought was best. You were *sixteen,* Lucy. You have to forgive yourself."

"I can't," Lucy said. The tears were very close now and it terrified her because she had never cried for Alice and the baby, she had never dared to cry, afraid that if she started she would never stop. But now she felt the huge rush of desolation like an unstoppable tide and it was too late, it was on her and over her and she cried and cried and Robert held her shaking body against his until she had soaked him with her tears, as well.

"Sweetheart…" Robert's grip on her tightened and he held her closer still. She was shocked by how good it felt to be held like this. A part of her, the old fear, wanted to draw back, but Robert's arms were unyielding about her and after a moment she accepted him and the comfort she craved.

"I'm sorry," she whispered. "So very sorry."

He raised her face to his at that and brushed the hair away from her hot wet cheeks and kissed her. "You have nothing to be sorry for." He sounded fierce. "You did nothing wrong, Lucy. It was not your fault that they died. You do not know that your sister would have lived, nor a seventh-month child." His voice had dropped. "You were very brave. Unbelievably brave and honorable."

His words only seemed to make her cry all the harder. She felt helplessly unable to stop, sobbing, gulping and wondering as finally the tears started to fade whether she looked as dreadful as she thought she must.

"How much you have suffered," Robert said softly, stroking the hair back from her damp cheeks. "Unbearable to have to carry it all alone." He held her a little way away from him. There was a smile in his eyes as he looked at her.

"I know," Lucy said defensively. "I look awful."

"The question is whether you feel any better now that you have spoken of it," Robert said. "You never told anyone, did you?"

Lucy shook her head. "I couldn't talk about it. I felt so guilty and sick to even think of it. I have nightmares. Waking ones too. I see it all again in my mind's eye, over and over. It's as though I cannot escape."

Robert kissed her very gently. There was no demand in the kiss, only comfort and sweetness.

"You do not turn away from me," he said, as their lips parted. "I am glad of that. It is no wonder you do not believe you could ever lie with a man and bear his child." His lips brushed her hair, pressing soft kisses. "After all you have been through, it would be no wonder if you believed all men were self-serving bastards like Hamish Purnell."

"I trust you," Lucy said. "I know you are not like that." She dropped her gaze, fixing it on one of the mother-of-pearl buttons on his jacket, rubbing her fingers over their smoothness. "And yes," she added, "I do feel a little better. I feel…" She stopped. It was as though a crack had opened in the darkness, shedding a sliver of light into the emptiness of her heart. It was hard to believe after eight barren years, but it was true.

Yet it was not enough.

She looked up and saw that Robert was watching her. From the look in his eyes he already knew what she was going to say. Her heart lurched.

"It makes no difference," she whispered. "It can make no difference to us. Don't you see that, Robert?" Her gaze implored him. "I'm still too damaged, too afraid—" She saw the instinctive repudiation in his face and pressed her fingers to his lips to silence him. It felt impossible to make sense of the warring demands of her mind and her body, of the sweet seduction of Robert's kisses and at the same time the cold fear that numbed her mind and her heart when she thought of the marriage bed and of bearing a child. She thought of the tiny frail burden that had been Alice's son and she shuddered. She had failed a child who had depended on her. She could not trust herself. Not even now, when the truth was revealed at last.

"I can't offer you anything," she said, with painful honesty. "It is not fair to you."

Robert took her hand in his and kissed the fingers gently. He head was bent and the firelight burnished his hair to rich chestnut.

"If you marry me I will settle for whatever you can give," he said roughly. "If you marry me I swear not to force you into an intimacy you do not want."

Lucy's eyes widened with shock. "But you cannot make a match on those grounds," she stammered. "You need an heir."

Robert's smile was wicked all of a sudden. "In time

I will have my heir," he said. He kissed her again, long, slow and languorous so that when he released her she was flushed and panting.

"I do not believe it impossible," he murmured, "with time and trust."

"The difficulty is not in kissing you," Lucy said.

"So I had observed," Robert said.

Lucy smiled a little, but beneath it she felt an edge of sadness. She trusted him not to ask more of her than she was prepared to give. Still, she was not sure she would ever be brave enough to give him the heir he desired. The thought was enormous and terrifying and it made her shrink inside. It took her back to the shuttered room and the scent of death and the fear in Alice's eyes.

Yet Robert's gaze was steady on her and his touch felt warm and solid and comforting.

"Marry me," he said softly. "Have faith that together we can make all well."

Lucy thought about Wilfred Cardross laying claim to Methven land and his men burning and pillaging the villages and Isobel's tired face and the terror in Bessie's eyes. She thought about the clansmen who had given their loyalty and their lives to the laird for hundreds of years, losing their lands and their livelihood. She thought of the poverty and the misery and the starvation that were the price of her freedom. She remembered the barren village she had ridden through and the dirt and squalor of the crofts. She felt the burn of old hatreds and the echo of that enmity in the blood.

She thought about never seeing Robert Methven again.

She thought about the faith he had shown in her, his belief that together they could overcome her fear.

She thought about being his only hope.

He was watching her. There was tension in the line of his jaw and a coolness in his eyes as though he had taken the biggest gamble of his life and was convinced he was about to lose his stake.

"Yes, I'll marry you," she said slowly, and felt the fear grip her by the throat so fast she almost contradicted herself immediately.

But her promise was given and she saw the flare of triumph and satisfaction in his eyes. "Thank you," he said.

"But not tomorrow," Lucy said quickly. "In a few days…" She fell silent as he shook his head.

"Tomorrow," he said.

She understood his insistence. It was the ultimate test of her trust in him. She met his eyes and knew she could not fail, could not fall now, at the very first challenge. If she was going to try to overcome her fears and be a true wife to him, if she was going to give him the heir he needed, she had to have belief in him equal to the faith he had in her.

"Very well," she said. "We wed tomorrow."

CHAPTER FOURTEEN

ROBERT STOOD ON the jetty staring out to sea. It was late. The ocean had fallen into darkness and only the roar and hiss of the waves hinted at its endless ebb and flow. Somewhere out on the northern horizon floated Golden Isle, the one part of his patrimony he had shamefully neglected since his brother had died. Since inheriting the Methven marquisate, Robert had diligently visited every one of his estates and spoken to as many of his people as he could. He had poured endless time, money and effort into tending to their welfare. He had defended these northern lands against Wilfred Cardross's incursions, but Golden Isle was the one place he had never set foot. It was the one place he never wanted to see again. It held too many memories; memories of Gregor's death, memories of his quarrel with his grandfather and his estrangement from all he had held dear.

He had a factor, an estate manager who undertook all the business of the islands. As far as he was concerned, that was good enough. It had to be because he was not prepared to do more. He never asked McTavish for a report on Golden Isle, and the man never offered any. It was as though the place did not exist.

Tomorrow he would leave Findon with his bride and travel south and never think about Golden Isle again.

He shifted as guilt scored him like a knife.

That is not good enough.

It was Lucy's face he could see, Lucy's words he could hear, as clearly as if she had spoken them to his face. Over dinner she had tried to draw him out on the subject of his brother's death and that painful quarrel and estrangement from his grandfather. He had rejected her attempts because he was ashamed of the stubborn boy he had been, sacrificing so much for his pride. He had not wanted her to see his weakness. He had not wanted her to know he had been so rash and reckless, so determined to prove to his grandfather that he cared nothing for Methven, that he was prepared to go thousands of miles away and hurt those he loved in the process. He did not want her to know that it was his fault that Wilfred Cardross had the means to claim Methven land because he had been abroad and thereby given his enemy the advantage.

Lucy was gallant and strong and brave. Now, having heard her story, he was astounded by her courage. Lucy, he knew, would not approve of him neglecting even one acre of his estate. She was prepared to risk all on marrying him to thwart Wilfred's greed and cruelty. If she had the faith to do that, he should have the courage to lay his own ghosts to rest and visit Golden Isle again.

Cursing softly under his breath, he bent and picked up a pebble and shied it into the water, listening to the splash it made and the hiss and the pull of the waves on the beach. As a boy he had loved Golden Isle. He and Gregor had spent so much time there.

There were no lights showing out at sea tonight. In times of war the islanders used a chain of beacons to warn of danger and summon help, but now all was calm and quiet.

Suddenly restless, he turned his back on the sea and set off back toward the inn. The cobbled streets were wet with rain. The warm candlelight showing behind the inn's diamond panes drew him, but the window of Lucy's chamber was dark. He wondered if she was asleep or if, like him, she felt restless tonight. He felt a sudden rush of possessive pride that on the morrow she was to marry him. Lucy MacMorlan was everything he wanted in a wife, but he could see how profoundly terrified she had been by the experience of her sister's pregnancy and death in childbirth. It was little wonder if she was petrified to face the same perils as Alice had when she had gone through such an ordeal at the age of only sixteen. It made sense of the perfection she had striven to achieve. In trying to atone for what she saw as her failure in causing her sister's death, she had forced herself into a pattern-card existence that no one could maintain, so her passion had escaped in other ways. And now she was lost and confused because she felt such a strong attraction to him—he knew she did—yet she was too afraid of the consequences to give herself up to it, to give herself to him.

He drove his clenched fists into the pockets of his coat. It was fortunate that Hamish Purnell was already dead or he would have hunted the man down and killed him for the way that he had ruined Lucy's future as well as betrayed her sister.

With a sigh Robert lifted the latch and went inside. He wanted to see Lucy. He was taken aback by how strong was the desire to hammer on her door and demand she let him in. He needed her, and not simply to fulfill the terms of his inheritance. He needed Lucy in ways far more profound and disturbing. He scowled. Such vulnerability was alien to him and he did not care for it.

There was only one solution. He pushed open the door of the taproom and went in search of the brandy bottle in lieu of his bride.

LUCY WAS DREAMING. She was running down dark corridors with no ending and no way out, desperately seeking something she could not find, her heart racing, dread snapping at her heels like a hunting dog.

She woke panting and drenched in sweat, tears wet on her cheeks. The blood was pounding in her ears, the bedclothes tangled about her limbs like shackles. Gradually the terrified flutter of her heart steadied and she started to breathe more easily, but the rags of the nightmare clung to her senses.

Alice.

She was swamped by an enormous sense of loss and grief. She felt sick and frightened.

Blinking, she could see the gray light of morning edging its way around the bed curtains. The shreds of the nightmare faded. It was her wedding day. Immediately the nausea and fear swamped her again. It was her wedding day and all she could think was that she felt terrified: terrified that Robert would not keep his word and that he would insist on consummating the marriage and that she would suffer, as Alice had, and lose her life and fail her child.

Her heart was starting to pound again. She could feel the familiar panic welling in her chest, threatening to smother her. She lay still and breathed deeply. She tried to tell herself that she trusted Robert and that he was a good man, but the words of reassurance were like a bat squeak in the dark compared to her fear. She felt trapped and panicked. She had to find a way out.

And then she remembered Mairi's words: *"There are ways to be safe...."*

She stilled, thinking. Isobel McLain had said that there was a wise woman in the village, out on the Thurso Road, a woman who treated the ills of the townspeople with tinctures and medications. Perhaps that same woman also brewed medicines that were sovereign against pregnancy. Perhaps that was the way to ensure that she would be safe.

She slid from the bed, shivering in the cold morning air. The servant had not yet been in to light the fire, and the room felt chilled. Her bare feet winced at the cold of the floor.

She pulled on her clothes haphazardly, opened the door of her chamber and trod quietly down the stair. The inn was awakening slowly. There were clatters and crashes from the kitchen and the sound of voices. She knew she would have to be quick.

She let herself out of the main door, giving silent thanks for the fact that the hinges were well oiled and the door did not creak. The morning air was fresh and cold. A sea mist had blown in and it clung around the houses like a shroud, muffling all sound. Damp tendrils of mist soon soaked Lucy's pelisse. The light was strange, pale gray and eerie. No birds sang in the silence. It felt extraordinarily lonely.

Before long the press of houses and shops thinned out and the road snaked away into the mist toward Thurso. There were only a couple of crofts here, still and quiet. A few lights glowed behind the shutters, but they were all barred against the weather. Lucy trudged up the track toward the last cottage. A chicken was scratching in the pen. The ducks ran quacking ahead of her, the noise suddenly loud in the silence.

She knocked at the wooden door and waited. There was no answer. Nervousness rose in her and she was about to turn and run when the door swung open. A woman stood there, younger than Lucy had imagined, her face serene, her smile warm. She showed absolutely no surprise to be disturbed so early on such an inclement day. She did not curtsy but she inclined her head.

"My lady."

She knows who I am.... That alone was almost enough to make Lucy turn and run, but the woman had drawn back and Lucy found herself stepping over the threshold after her.

Inside, the croft was warm and dark, lit by a peat fire smoldering in the grate and with one lamp burning on the dresser. There were leaves drying in baskets before the fire. The woman gestured her toward one of the high-backed chairs made from woven rushes. They were filled with brightly colored cushions. The whole croft was neat and cosy and such a contrast to the cold misery that filled Lucy that it felt quite incongruous.

She did not want to sit. She felt too on edge. She pressed her gloved hands together.

"Some tea, my lady?" The woman nodded toward the kettle that was humming softly on the hob.

"Oh," Lucy said, "no, thank you. I—" The words stuck in her throat. Now that the moment had come she had absolutely no idea how to ask for what she needed.

"There'll be something you're wanting," the woman said. She had her head on one side like a curious bird. Her eyes were suddenly very bright. "How can I help you?"

Lucy met her gaze and had the disturbing feeling she already knew exactly what she wanted.

"I am a little anxious for my health," she said rapidly. "I understand that there are medications that you make…"

The woman nodded slowly, the secretive look still in her eyes.

"I have been a little fragile these last few months," Lucy continued, "and my doctor warned me—" She swallowed hard, the lie so difficult to force out.

"I need to wait a little before I have children," she

said, the words coming in a sudden rush now. "Wait and build up my strength. So I am anxious to avoid… That is, I should try not to conceive…"

The woman nodded again. "You and the laird will be finding another way around the inheritance, then."

"That's right," Lucy said, smothered in guilt. "We have already discussed it. The courts will rule in Lord Methven's favor—" The lies dried up in her throat, but the woman was already nodding again, turning away toward a little wooden cabinet on the wall as though the workings of the king's courts were of absolutely no interest to her.

"There is a tincture of herbs that might help you," she said. "Rue and pennyroyal."

Lucy's relief was so great that she felt her knees weaken. She grabbed the back of the chair for support. "It works?" she whispered.

"It works well." The woman smiled. "There is more than one woman in the town can attest to that." She opened the cupboard with one of the little keys that hung on the chain at her waist. "I'll get you a jar."

Lucy put several sovereigns down on the table. She saw the woman's gaze rest on them; then she scooped them up and they disappeared into the deep pocket of her gown. She placed the jar softly on the table. "Take it every day," she said. "That way you will be safe."

Lucy's hand was shaking as she grabbed the pot and shoved it into the pocket of her cloak.

"Thank you," she said. Her voice was shaking too. The wisewoman nodded one final time, the same incurious blank gaze back in her eyes now, and then Lucy was out of the cottage, gulping in the cold air and stumbling down the path.

Outside, the fog was as dense as before. It seemed to wrap Lucy about with sorrow as she hurried up the road, past the kirk where she was to be married that afternoon, back toward the inn. The hard shape of the jar bumped against her leg as she walked, reminding her at each step of her betrayal. Instead of relief now, she felt guilt and unhappiness and shame at what she had done.

"To keep you safe..." Mairi's words echoed in her head and she told herself that the tincture was no more than a safeguard and a way of protecting herself if Robert did not keep his word.

Nevertheless she felt miserable. Robert had been honest about his need for an heir and had told her that with time and trust he believed she would feel safe enough to consummate the marriage. Lucy hoped so too; she desperately wanted it to be true and she was desperately afraid that it would not be, that the damage the past had done could never be undone.

She had not expected to feel so unhappy to be deceiving Robert. He was too good a man to blame her for her failure to conceive. He would go to the courts and argue his case, and with luck and a good lawyer he would win and keep his northern estates. And he would never know that she had deceived him.

Lucy was shivering as she lifted the latch and hurried back into the warmth of the Methven Arms. She met Isobel coming down the corridor toward her. The landlady's anxious expression dissolved into relief when she saw her.

"Thank goodness!" she said. "We thought you had run off!"

Lucy's teeth were chattering with cold and reaction. "I needed some fresh air," she said.

Isobel's eyebrows shot up. "You are soaked and chilled to the bone! Come inside and get warm. It's almost time to start getting ready."

While the landlady hurried away to commandeer hot water and hot food, Lucy went upstairs. There was a fire burning in her chamber now and the room felt warm and cheerful. She spread her cloak over the back of a chair and heard the pot in the pocket bump against the wooden frame. Quickly she grabbed it and pushed it to the bottom of the Armada chest.

She could hear Isobel's step on the stair and Bessie's excited voice. It was time to dress for her wedding.

THE FOG HAD lifted by the time that Lucy was ready to go to the church and a pale sun was peeking through the clouds. Iain McLain was taking the role of her father and giving the bride away and he, Bessie and Isobel walked beside Lucy through the town to the kirk. It was very quiet. There were no crowds lining the streets or people hanging from windows to see her pass. The silence was so deep it almost felt funereal. Lucy felt her spirits sink still further at the silence.

"Oh dear," she said. "I knew no one would want to

celebrate the marriage of the laird to a relative of Wilfred Cardross, and who can blame them?"

Robert was waiting for her at the door of the kirk, as was traditional. He looked shockingly handsome, the breeze ruffling his dark hair. When he saw her his expression relaxed almost as though he had truly been afraid that she had run out on him. Lucy remembered Dulcibella leaving him standing at the altar and felt a sudden and fierce pride that she would be the one standing beside him today. Her feelings shook her. They were so unexpected when she had been prey to such nightmares and dark fears. But Robert was here now and he looked so strong and so steady and protective that Lucy's world steadied too.

As she walked up the path toward him, there was the clatter of hooves on the road behind and she swung around to see two riders galloping toward them, cloaks flying. One of them Lucy recognized as Robert's handsome cousin and groomsman from the ill-fated marriage to Dulcibella. The other...

"Mairi!" Lucy's voice wobbled as her sister flung herself from the saddle and ran toward her, grabbing Lucy into the tightest hug.

"Tell me we're not too late for the wedding," Mairi said. "We've ridden all day and all night."

For a moment Lucy could not speak, she was so overcome with emotion. "Don't cry," Mairi said, seeing her brimming eyes. "It is not a good look for a bride."

"They're happy tears," Lucy said. She rubbed her palms against her wet cheeks.

"I couldn't resist standing as your groomsman a second time," Lucy heard Jack Rutherford saying as he clapped Robert on the back.

"I'm not sure I should allow it," Robert said. "The first time was a disaster." But he was grinning as he shook Jack's hand.

"It depends on how you look at it," Jack said, bowing to Lucy and giving her a wicked smile. "Lady Lucy, your servant. I'd say Rob had a lucky escape last time around if it means he can marry you. Thank you for your sacrifice in taking him on."

"Well, at least he did not have to marry me," Mairi said.

"That would have been a sacrifice too far," Jack said with feeling, and they glared at each other through a very taut silence.

"Tell me," Lucy said quickly, looking from her sister's flushed, angry face to Jack's tight one, "how you got here in time. Lord Methven only proposed to me last night."

"Robert always was confident," Jack said. "He sent word from Durness four days ago."

"And Jack always was tactless," Robert said, into the heavy silence. "I took nothing for granted."

"Arrogant," Lucy heard Mairi murmur, "just like his cousin."

It was turning into the most awkward wedding day on record and they had not even reached the altar yet. Once again Lucy threw herself into the breach.

"Well," she said, "we must not keep the minister

waiting." She grabbed Mairi's hands, drawing her along the path toward the door. "You may be my matron of honor. Bessie is my bridesmaid."

"I'm scarcely dressed for it," Mairi said, looking down at the splashes of mud on her hem, "but I would be delighted." She smiled at Bessie, who dimpled and dropped a curtsy.

"...a complete nightmare," Lucy heard Jack say in a stage whisper to Robert as they made their way in at the door. "Almost strangled her several times on the journey. I hope for your sake that the sister is different. I had a letter from Forres, by the way, sent by special envoy. The duke sends his best wishes to you both and thanks for the brandy."

"Brandy?" Lucy said, turning.

Robert smiled at her. "It is an old island tradition when asking for the hand in marriage of a man's daughter. You present him with a bottle of your best brandy."

"Bribe him more like," Mairi said tartly, "to overlook the scandal."

"Don't mind me," Lucy said.

"Sorry." Two bright spots of color still burned in Mairi's cheeks as her gaze rested on Jack. "I'm sorry, Lucy. I didn't mean to imply anything."

"Well," Lucy said, "I am a scandalous bride, no question. I should be grateful to Lord Methven for rescuing my reputation after the tarnish applied to it by cousin Wilfred."

"Lord Methven is lucky to be getting you," Mairi said, glaring at Robert as though he had committed some heinous crime. "You are doing *him* a favor. As for his questionable relatives—" She looked down her nose at Jack, who grinned back at her, unabashed. "One must hope you are not obliged to spend too much time in their company."

"Perhaps we should have asked both of you to leave your weapons at the door," Robert said, looking from Mairi to Jack and back again. He drew Lucy's hand through his arm. "Are you ready, my love?"

My love...

There was a lump in Lucy's throat. She most certainly was not that, but the words were a sweet gloss over a marriage that was born of necessity. She nodded, slipping her hand into the crook of his elbow and drawing closer to his side.

Together they stepped into the cool shadowed interior of the kirk.

Lucy stopped dead. The church was packed, every pew taken with the people from the town dressed in their Sunday best, carrying flowers, smiling.

Her breath caught in her throat. "This is for you," she whispered to Robert.

"And for you," he said, and Lucy felt the tears prick the back of her eyes again.

The service seemed very short. Isobel and Iain McLain were witnesses. Jack and Mairi studiously ignored each other throughout. Lucy remembered little of what was said, though she remembered making her vows and Robert making his, his voice strong and steady, his hand holding hers.

Afterward it seemed that the entire town escorted them back to the inn, the children running along beside them throwing flowers beneath their feet, the pipes playing, the crowds cheering, the streets alive and loud. Robert's people were in the mood to make merry. They had brought food to celebrate at the wedding feast, chicken, eggs, potatoes, cheeses and delicious bannocks with rich butter. Lucy and Robert were escorted to the high table. The press of guests was so great that the two of them were squashed together on the long settle. Lucy could feel the hard length of Robert's thigh pressed against hers; oddly it seemed impossible to ignore it. She took a gulp of wine to steady herself and felt instead the heat bloom in her cheeks.

"That's better," Mairi said approvingly. She was seated a little way down the table next to Jack Rutherford, whom she was ignoring with great deliberation. "You looked as pale as a corpse before."

It was hardly a felicitous description for a bride, Lucy thought, but it was fairly accurate. Despite the mildness of the day and the huge open fire that blazed in the grate, her hands were frozen and she felt cold and scared. She looked at him. Robert. Her husband. Her mind simply could not accept the fact. Too much had happened, too fast, for her to be able to understand it. The change between her life a mere week before and her life now was huge, a chasm she did not know how to bridge.

Robert was talking to Iain McLain, and as she watched he emptied his tankard of ale and one of the potboys ran to refill it. Sensing her gaze, Robert turned to smile at her and leaned closer so that his words were for her alone.

"You've nothing to fear," he said softly, and Lucy blushed that he had read her doubts of him in her eyes. He touched her cheek briefly, a comforting gesture, before pulling her plate toward her. There was roast chicken and it smelled delicious, but when she had tried a mouthful it had tasted like ashes. "Eat," he said. "It tastes good and you have barely touched it."

She tried. It still stuck in her throat, but another glass of wine helped. Gradually she could feel her tense muscles unlocking. She started to relax. She drank more wine, nibbled on the food and chatted to Mairi and to Isobel. The tables were pushed back and the fiddlers struck up, first a slow, evocative piece that sounded almost like a lament and then suddenly shifting into a dance that was fast and furious, with whoops and wild shouts of glee. The hall came alive with whirling figures. Lucy joined Robert in a country dance. She was spun down the line from hand to hand until, panting and flushed, her hair tumbling about her face, she came back to the start and into Robert's arms again. He kissed her there and then in front of everyone, and the crowd roared its approval. The music shifted into a dance called the Bride's Reel and Lucy danced until she was breathless.

A few dances later the door of the hall burst open and the guizers came in, outlandish figures in straw suits, pointed hats and masks that hid their faces. Immediately the guests burst into rowdy applause and the music spun louder and wilder.

"I do hope that isn't cousin Wilfred lurking under one of those fetching straw bales," Lucy murmured.

One of the guizers was bowing to her, holding out a hand for her to join him in the dance. Everyone laughed and applauded when she got up to join him. She had no idea of the steps, but by now it scarcely seemed to matter. Seven of the Findon men performed a sword dance and then Lucy danced with Robert again and then with Jack and soon she was spinning through an endless succession of dances as the pipes and the fiddles beat out the rhythm and her head rang with music and laughter.

Then, suddenly, the door crashed open. A man stood there, travel-stained in the torchlight, his face set in lines of great weariness. He staggered into the room.

"My lord!"

The fiddle music faded and spluttered to a halt. The chatter and laughter died. Someone pushed the newcomer down onto the settle and he sank down gratefully. Another man pressed a tankard into his hand and he drank it down in one gulp. Lucy could feel a strange atmosphere in the room now, watchful and tense. Conversation bubbled softly like a kettle coming to the boil. Everyone was waiting.

"My lord." The man wiped his mouth on his sleeve. "I am Stuart McCall. I come from Golden Isle."

Lucy felt Robert stiffen beside her and she glanced sharply at him. He was very still now, his eyes cold, unsmiling. She could feel the emotion in him, dark and turbulent. There was anger there and something else, something that felt like pain. She looked at his tight, set face and it was like looking at a stranger. She did not understand, but she felt the Robert Methven she had thought she was starting to know slip away.

"You have come to wish me joy on my wedding, I hope," Robert said. He drained his tankard. Lucy saw his throat move as he swallowed; saw the deliberate way he placed the empty glass on the table and raised his eyes to meet those of the newcomer. It was intimidating, but the man did not flinch.

"Aye, my lord," McCall said. "And to ask for your help."

There was something terrifying in Robert's stillness. "My help?" he said softly.

"Aye, my lord," McCall said again. "The people of Golden Isle are starving, my lord, and no laird has taken the trouble to visit us for ten years, since—"

Robert's palm slapped down on the table, making Lucy jump. "You have a factor to take care of your needs," he said, his voice hard and angry.

"Neil McTavish cares nothing for the isle," McCall said steadily. "He has done nothing to help us whilst the crops fail and the ships no longer call to trade with us. He has failed to protect us from Wilfred Cardross."

There was a hiss of indrawn breath around the room as Cardross's name hung on the air. McCall looked up and looked Robert directly in the eye.

"You are the laird. It is your duty to help us."

There was another rumble of debate around the

room, quickly hushed as Robert looked around, his expression fierce.

"Are you accusing me of failing in my duty as laird?" he said, very softly.

This time the silence was deadly. Lucy, watching, feeling the tension in every cell of her body, could see the way that no man would meet his fellow's eyes. Oh, they respected Robert as laird well enough here in Findon. She had learned that in only a few short days. They trusted him, believed in him and knew him to be a strong man who would protect them. But it seemed Golden Isle was his weakness. It seemed he had washed his hands of the place.

McCall straightened up. His words echoed Lucy's thoughts. "I hear you are a just and fair laird," he said. "But you have cut Golden Isle loose from your protection. You have failed in your duty."

Robert was on his feet, eyes blazing, his hand going to the hilt of his sword.

Jack Rutherford put out a quick hand to him. "Let's step aside and talk about this, Rob," he said quietly.

"Not on my wedding day," Robert growled. He sat down and gestured for his cup to be filled. There was an ugly set to his mouth. The atmosphere in the room simmered on the edge of violence. Lucy could sense all the complicated emotions in Robert; there was anger, but it was shaded by shame and, she was certain, pain.

She could feel Jack's gaze on her. He was pleading with her silently to intervene. Either he overestimated her influence or he was desperate, probably the latter.

Lucy could feel the tension in the air, feel everyone looking at her now.

She put her hand gently on Robert's wrist. "My lord," she said. "I know better than most the danger posed by my cousin of Cardross and know as well that you would never let a single one of your clansmen come to hurt. I am ready to retire. Why do you not speak with these gentlemen and then come and join me?"

She saw the tension in Robert's eyes ease slightly. She could still feel the reluctance in him. After a moment he took her hand in his, kissed her fingers and gave her a faint smile.

"As you wish, my lady."

It felt as though the entire room released the breath it had been holding. Everyone stood as Lucy and Mairi left the room. There were a few smiles, a few nods to her and there was respect in every man's eyes.

Isobel McLain led them up to the chamber Lucy had left only that morning on the way to the wedding. It had been tidied, and rose petals and herbs sprinkled over the bed, scenting the air with the sweetest of fragrances.

"What was wrong with Lord Methven tonight?" Mairi said as she helped Lucy into the nightgown that Isobel had left warming by the fire.

"I don't know," Lucy said shortly. She was tired and apprehensive, aching from the tension and strain of the day. "I don't know him well enough to know what was wrong." She wished she had asked Isobel what was going on, but at the same time she did not want the landlady to realize how little she knew. It felt humiliating.

"It was the mention of Golden Isle that changed him," Mairi was saying. She appeared not to have heard Lucy or noticed the note of apprehension in her voice. "He was perfectly at ease before that, but it was clear that he did not wish to go there—"

"Why do you not ask Mr. Rutherford?" Lucy interrupted. "He will know."

That got Mairi's attention. "I'd not give Jack Rutherford the time of day," she said sharply.

"What on earth can he have done to upset you?" Lucy said, eyeing her sister's face. "He seems very charming and he is as handsome as sin—"

"He's too handsome for his own good," Mairi said. She was folding Lucy's gown with such sharp jerky gestures that Lucy was afraid the delicate muslin might tear. "He certainly knows it. Arrogant pig!"

"Oh dear," Lucy said, trying to stifle a smile. "You really do not like him."

"I loathe him," Mairi snapped. "I'll be glad to see the back of him tomorrow. I'm going back to Edinburgh. I assume you'll be going to Methven?"

"I don't know," Lucy said. Her stomach felt suddenly hollow with longing for her old life. "I don't know where we are going," she said slowly, "or even if we will have a wedding tour. It has all happened so quickly."

Mairi sat down on the end of the bed. "I suppose this is the moment when I should give you some maternal advice," she said.

"Maternal— Oh!" Lucy could feel herself blushing. "Please don't feel you have to advise me," she said awkwardly.

Mairi's expression cleared. "Oh, well, if you have already done it—"

"We haven't," Lucy said shortly. "That is I… We… It's a marriage in name only."

Mairi's eyebrows shot up into her hair. "You are teasing me."

Lucy frowned. "Why would I do that?"

"Because…" Mairi stopped, took a deep breath. "Because Methven looks at you as though he cannot wait to bed you," she said bluntly. "That's why."

Lucy's blush spread downward. She felt very hot. She did not want to have to explain the details to Mairi.

"We don't know each other well," she said instead.

Mairi covered her hand with her own. "I understand," she said, although clearly she did not. "But in time… Well, he will want an heir…."

Lucy nodded. "In time." Now, though, with the vast expanse of the empty bed beckoning to her, she could not imagine a time when she would feel ready for that.

"If he's gentle with you it will not be so bad the first time," Mairi said. "It may hurt a little and you might not like it much, but if it gets too bad try to think about something else—Scottish country dancing, or the bagpipes, or what color wall hangings you would like when you refurnish Methven Castle—"

"You're not helping," Lucy said, interrupting her.

Mairi frowned. "I'm *trying* to help. I was going to

say that it is certain to get better and by then you will be pregnant anyway...."

Lucy shivered, crossing her arms over her chest. Mairi went over to the window and pulled it closed.

"There is a chill in the air tonight," she said. "Get into bed. Everything will be fine."

Mairi tucked her in, kissed her cheek and then stood back, looking suddenly uncertain. "Would you like me to wait with you?"

"No, thank you," Lucy said hastily. Then as she saw Mairi's face fall she realized that she had been a bit abrupt and caught her sister's hand. "I am so grateful you came to the wedding," she said softly, hoping her sincerity could bridge the gap with her sister. "It made all the difference to me."

Mairi's expression lit with a smile. She squeezed Lucy's hand. "I expect you were missing Alice today," she said. "I know I'm not the same, that we have never been as close—"

Lucy shook her head quickly, silencing her. "I'm lucky to have you," she said.

Mairi gave her a quick hug and went out and Lucy sat there in the sudden quiet. The party had resumed down in the hall. She could hear the music and the roar of voices. She had no idea how long Robert would be. She supposed he would have to visit her room for appearances' sake even if he had no intention of staying with her tonight.

Suddenly she felt restless and lonely and so unsure. She went across to the Armada chest and rummaged among the petticoats and bodices, her fingers closing around the hard cold shape of the pot of pennyroyal tincture. She should take it, just to be sure, just to be safe.

Yet Robert had said that she had nothing to fear and some instinct, deeper and more stubborn than the fear, made her want to trust him.

She knelt there until her legs were cold and aching and then slowly she put the pot back in its hiding place in the chest and straightening up, closed the lid.

CHAPTER FIFTEEN

ROBERT WAS IN a vile mood. Once he had agreed to speak
with Stuart McCall, no fewer than five more men from
Golden Isle had appeared to join the meeting. Robert
was surprised he had not seen it coming. McCall could
scarcely have rowed himself over from the island on his
own. The others must have been waiting outside for the
opportunity to come in and petition their laird. Simply
seeing them made Robert feel guilty for the years of
neglect. He did not like being in the wrong, but ever
since the previous night he had been plague to guilt
and doubt. It was a new sensation for him.

The islanders packed Iain McLain's little office, a
motley crowd, fair and weather-beaten, their blond hair
and vivid blue eyes speaking of their Norse ancestors.
They had refused the offer to sit, all except the oldest
man present, one of the island elders so ancient Robert
thought he could barely stand. The men looked uncomfortable and hemmed in, as though their natural place
was in the open air or on the high seas and enclosed
spaces constrained them.

Robert had introduced Jack as his cousin and right-
hand man and the islanders had all nodded politely, but
it was clear from their reserve and the watchful gaze

of their blue eyes that Robert had a long way to go if he was to regain—and keep—their respect. He could scarcely blame them for that.

The men waited silently while McCall told Robert of the desperate plight of his people on Golden Isle. The war against France had evidently taken a heavy toll on the islanders in terms of lost trade. Harvests had been poor and now the population was on the verge of starvation. The press-gang had taken almost all the young men for the navy with no compensation or consideration of how their families would manage when they were gone. McCall said that boys as young as twelve had been taken. Robert felt furious and even more guilty. He had left Golden Isle in the hands of his factor; he had not wanted to know.

McCall blamed the factor. He leveled serious allegations against McTavish, not only that he had neglected the welfare of the islanders, that he had failed to import the food that was needed and failed to sell their produce at a fair price, but also that he was in the pay of Wilfred Cardross. As soon as Cardross's name was mentioned, the atmosphere in the room chilled and hardened. The men shifted, muttering among themselves. There was a pause. Robert could feel something in the air, a moment of hesitation. The men were looking sideways at McCall, waiting. McCall took a deep breath.

"Cardross is a traitor," he said. "He has been using Golden Isle secretly as a rendezvous with enemy French ships."

Robert saw Jack straighten and come alive, his gaze

narrowing with sharp interest. Up until that point he had been listening politely, but Robert had known his cousin's attention was elsewhere. Now, though, his interest was acute. There was nothing Jack liked more than a challenge.

"You are accusing Wilfred Cardross of treason," Robert said. "You need to be very sure of your facts."

All the men looked back at him, certainty in their eyes.

"No mistaking it," one of them said. He looked as though he wanted to spit on the floor at the mention of Cardross's name but thought better of it in the laird's presence. "I've seen with my own eyes that totie wee craft he calls a ship. All scarlet and gold and sails as poorly as a tin tub, out there in the bay meeting with the French privateers."

"He takes their brandy and lace," another man said, "and gives them information in return."

"What sort of information?" Robert questioned sharply.

"Defenses, troop numbers, maneuvers," McCall said quietly. "Details of the garrison on Zetland." The others nodded.

"One of Cardross's crew was Frazer's wee boy from Orkney," one of the elders said. "He gave the game away when Cardross betrayed his brother to the press-gang."

"Double-dealing traitor."

"Turncoat."

"He stole *our* free trading rights," someone said,

sounding outraged that the islanders' own illegal smuggling trade had been curtailed by Wilfred Cardross's actions.

"Bastard." The word was hissed with a great deal of venom. Robert felt the ripple of violence and hatred around the room, growing now like a living thing.

"The problem was that no one believed Frazer's wee lad." The eldest of the elders, whom Robert had believed to be asleep, now spoke up from the depths of his chair. "But they would trust you, laird. They would believe you."

"Aye." Again the word rumbled around the room, this time accompanied by a number of fervent nods. All eyes were on Robert.

Robert took time to reply. He knew that if he accused Wilfred Cardross of treason without proof, no one would believe him either. The earl would merely claim that he was using wild claims to undermine his case in the lawsuit. He would argue it was spite that motivated Robert's accusations, not fact. And if Robert could not make good the charge, then he would be the one in trouble.

He looked at Jack. His cousin knew what he was thinking; if they were going to catch Cardross, they would have to set him a trap. That suited Robert fine. Ever since he had seen the damage Cardross's men had done to Lucy's face, he had wanted to hunt him down and kill him.

"You had better leave the matter with me," Robert said.

The islanders regarded him with unblinking eyes. "But you will take it up with the authorities?" the eldest elder prompted.

"I swear it," Robert said. It was his neglect that had allowed this to happen. It was his responsibility to put the matter right.

"I'll be sailing for Golden Isle on the afternoon tide the day after tomorrow," he said, getting to his feet.

He saw them awaken then. Light and hope sparked in their eyes. They turned to look at each other; nodded their approval. Robert offered McCall his hand, then shook hands with all the other men in turn. "Go and join the wedding feast," he said. "I need to talk with my cousin."

"We wish you joy on your marriage, Laird," the eldest elder said, tipping his cap to Robert. "Even if it is to a relative of the Cardross."

Jack was idly tracing the outline of a sailing ship on the back of one of McLain's account sheets. He looked up as the door closed behind the last of the islanders. His green gaze was bright.

"What are we going to do, Rob?"

"I thought that you would be traveling back south with Lady Mairi MacLeod," Robert said.

Jack's expression closed. "I'd rather help you out here," he said. He pushed back from the desk. "I like these northern isles. They remind me of when we were in the wilds of Canada, a long way from the reach of the law." He drove his hands into his jacket pockets.

"Besides, I like a challenge. I get damnably bored otherwise."

"I thought Lady Mairi was a challenge," Robert said.

Jack scowled. "Mind your own damned business," he said, "or I'll call you out on your wedding night. We were talking about Cardross."

Robert smiled and accepted the change of subject. "Do you believe him a traitor?"

"Without a doubt," Jack said unhesitatingly. "It all fits. His pockets are to let, he's in hock to the moneylenders and in the pay of the French and then you come back and not only is he in danger of losing his claim to Golden Isle, but his treasonable activities are also going to be exposed." He grinned. "He'll be terrified."

"Good," Robert said. "I need you to go to Methven, choose thirty of the best men and bring them back here to Findon. Do it discreetly. I don't want Cardross to hear."

Jack nodded. A smile still played about his lips. "You want everything already to be in place when he comes after you," he said.

"I do," Robert said. "I will use McTavish to draw Cardross out. I'll plant some ideas in McTavish's mind. If he truly is in Cardross's pay, he will send word to him straightaway. And when Cardross comes, we will be waiting for him."

"Do you mean to take Lady Methven with you to Golden Isle?" Jack asked.

Robert frowned. "What has our grandmother to do with this?"

"I mean your wife, you fool," Jack said. "It would be safer to send Lady Lucy to Methven until her cousin is taken."

"Lucy stays with me," Robert said. He felt a blaze of pure protective possession. He did not want Wilfred Cardross anywhere near her, and the safest way to ensure that was to keep her by his side and safe with his sword. He remembered the way he had felt when he saw Lucy fighting Cardross's clansmen on the shore of the loch. Terror had flared through him in a way he had never experienced before. He had tried to tell himself that he only felt that way because Lucy was the key to saving his clan lands, but that did neither of them justice. What he felt for Lucy was a complex mixture of emotions. It had been that way from the start. As a rule he did not like complexity of emotion. It clouded the judgment and made a man weak. He was beginning to see, however, that when it came to Lucy he had very little choice about how he felt.

He looked up to see Jack watching him speculatively and wondered if he had given away more of his feelings than he had intended.

His cousin said nothing, however, merely raising his glass of brandy in a toast. "Well, then," he said. "Don't waste any more time." He nodded toward the door. "You need to get an heir before Cardross kills you."

You need to get an heir...

Robert was not sure what expression was showing on his face, but whatever it was, Jack lowered the glass slowly, his eyes narrowing.

"Sorry," he said. "Sensitive subject? Is Lady Lucy already—"

"No," Robert snapped, feeling a sudden urge to punch his cousin.

"Oh," Jack said. "Then—"

"It's a marriage in name only," Robert said, wondering why he was confiding at all, and in Jack, of all people. Maybe he had had too much brandy.

Jack choked on his drink. Robert had to slap him on the back, which he did with considerable satisfaction.

"You're joking," Jack said, coughing, eyes streaming, "or possibly you're mad."

"It's called patience," Robert said, through his teeth. "Not a virtue you are very familiar with."

"I resent that," Jack said. "What on earth were you thinking, though, to make a marriage in name only when you have wanted her from the moment you saw her?"

"Mind your own damned business," Robert said, "or *I'll* call *you* out on my wedding night."

Jack sighed, draining his glass. "I have to believe that you know what you are doing, for the sake of Methven."

"I do," Robert said.

"Good," Jack said. He jerked his head toward the door. "Now go and play chess with your new wife or whatever it is that people do when they are married in name only."

They went out together, Jack back to the wedding party, Robert into the inn and up the darkened stairs. He rubbed a hand over his hair. He felt tired and his head ached as though he had had too much ale. He went into his chamber, which was all in darkness, and splashed water on his face, then stood in the window embrasure, leaning his palms on the stone, staring out to sea.

He knew he had to keep his word and return to Golden Isle, but tonight he did not want to think about it anymore. He wanted Lucy. He needed her.

He opened the door of his chamber. A light still showed beneath the door of Lucy's room opposite. He knocked and then pushed open the door.

Much to his surprise, Lucy was still awake. She was sitting up in bed prim and neat in a white nightgown that he saw with amusement was fastened up to her throat. She was reading a slim leather-bound volume.

Robert grinned. She looked exactly as he would have expected, very proper and respectable in a manner that should have forbidden him to touch her. Unfortunately the very laced-up neatness of her made him want to unlace her at once and tumble her on the bed. Except that he had promised he would not and he was a gentleman of his word.

She looked up from the book, pushing the hair back from her face. It rippled like autumn leaves in the pale light and he itched to touch it, to bury his face in its silken softness, as he had from the first moment he had seen her.

"I thought you would be asleep," he said gruffly. "It's been a long day and you looked tired throughout it."

He saw Lucy bite her lip and wished the words unsaid. They were not a particularly tactful compliment to his bride, whom he had thought looked beautiful and gracious—and strained. Nor had he made matters easy for her at the wedding feast. He was painfully aware of that. Being reminded of Golden Isle and the way he had failed in his obligation to the people there had set him in a dour mood, and everyone had felt the ill effects of that.

He wished he had not agreed to her terms. He wanted to take her now and lose himself in the taking, savoring her sweetness, letting it wash the darkness from his soul. He did not want to think about the past. But even more he did not want to dwell on what he could not have. He needed to woo his bride with tenderness, to overcome her fears, not tumble her with no care for her feelings. His headache gripped his temples more tightly.

"You were all that was charming," he hastened to add, knowing he had sounded like a gauche boy. "I merely meant—"

"I was nervous." Lucy laid the book aside and spoke simply. Her eyes, when they met his, were clear blue with candor. He understood then and felt a rush of protectiveness.

"I promised I'd not hurt you," he said. The words came out more roughly than he had intended.

Her eyes widened. "I know that." Now, suddenly, she sounded every inch a duke's daughter. "I trust your word. But there is more to marriage than what happens in our bedchamber." Her gaze fell. She plucked at the edge of the blanket. "I am not sure I know how to be a wife," she said. "I have had so little time to prepare."

Robert sat down on the edge of the bed and took her hands in his. "You know as much as I," he said. "I have no more experience of being a husband than you do of being a wife."

A tiny smile touched her lips. "I suppose not," she said.

"I was concentrating so hard on finding my bride I never thought about what happened after the wedding," Robert said. He was not quite sure why he was being so honest with her. Such a baring of his soul was hardly natural to him and yet her frankness deserved equal honesty.

Her smile grew. "I had not imagined you would be nervous, as well."

"I'm terrified," Robert said promptly.

"Dear me," Lucy said. She sounded demure. "You will forgive me if I find that hard to believe. I cannot see that you frighten easily."

"I have thought of a way you might help me, however," Robert said.

"Indeed?" Her eyebrows arched.

"I want to stay here with you tonight," Robert said softly.

Wariness flared instantly in her eyes, quenching that flame of amusement. "But you said—"

He pressed a finger to her lips and she fell silent. "It's all right," he said. "You have nothing to fear. I only want to be with you." He was shocked to find himself within an ace of begging her. He knew he did not want to be alone. He knew he needed her.

"Please," he said.

Lucy did not look entirely convinced. Robert leaned forward and kissed her very gently. Her lips felt impossibly soft and plush, yielding to his. His body hardened with arousal.

She did not recoil from the kiss, but nor did she respond. He could feel the uncertainty in her and the fear. She trusted him, but that trust was on a knife edge and he could not betray it no matter how, in this moment, he was cursing his sense of honor. There were, however, other ways to deepen the intimacy between them until she was ready to consummate their marriage. She would never overcome her fears if they maintained a proper distance. Instead they would drift further and further apart until they became isolated strangers. He was not going to allow that to happen.

He pulled off his boots and tossed them aside. She was watching him, her blue eyes troubled. He shrugged himself out of his jacket and pulled the shirt over his head. Now her eyes were as huge as dinner plates as her gaze rested on his bare torso.

"You've got brothers," Robert said, to lighten the tension. "Surely you must have seen a man in a state of undress."

"When we were young," Lucy said. "But they didn't look like you." Her voice sounded slightly husky. "Lachlan is skinny and Angus is lumpen. They don't have…uh…muscles." She pulled her gaze away from his chest, blinking as though she had stepped into sudden daylight. Robert liked her surprise. It made him feel like a god.

The breeches, though, would have to stay for now. He had no intention of taking her beyond surprise and into shock.

He blew out the candle and slid into the bed beside her. He felt her shift a few decorous inches away from him and bit his lip to smother a grin.

"There is plenty of room for both of us," he said. It was not actually true. The bed was small. The cotton sleeve of her nightshirt brushed his bare arm. Farther down, her hip was wedged against his and her bare thigh was warm against the material of his breeches. He gritted his teeth.

They lay like effigies for minutes. He could hear her breathing, quick and shallow. She was as rigid as a statue.

She shifted a few inches farther and he grabbed her arm to prevent her rolling off the high mattress completely. He braced himself on one elbow above her and gently smoothed the hair away from her face. Her skin was like silk, so soft, so tempting. Oh, he should not do this. He had intended only for her to become accustomed to sharing a bed with him, nothing more, but desire drove him hard.

"If I promise to take it no further," he said, "will you kiss me?" He hoped she could not tell from his voice how much he wanted her to agree. He was sure she could.

Her breath fluttered. Her breasts rose, brushing the side of his chest. She made a little sound of assent in her throat that made his cock harden further in an instant. Best that she did not know that or very likely she would leap from the bed, never mind roll out of it.

Robert touched his lips to hers again. This time, after the initial hesitation, they warmed beneath his, moved and parted. Hot lust rolled through him like the tide. He reined it in with iron control and instead of kissing her to within an inch of her life, he drew back.

She was looking at him as though he were some sort of complex puzzle she could not quite decipher. She raised a hand to his cheek and rubbed her fingers experimentally against the roughness of his skin. Robert closed his eyes and tried not to groan.

This time she was the one who tentatively kissed him, stealing a hand about the nape of his neck and bringing his lips down to hers. She was a little clumsy and unpracticed, but he let her explore, feeling the curiosity behind her anxiety, willing her to let it free. Her tongue slid between his lips, tasted him and discovered him. Such innocent exploration was so arousing he thought he might explode, but somehow he managed not.

"All right?" he murmured as their lips parted.

She blinked. Her eyes were a sleepy blue.

"Kissing you is nice," she whispered. "That is what worries me."

"Don't worry," Robert said. "Don't worry at all."

A faint shadow came into her eyes. "I think you are trying to seduce me," she said.

"Not yet," Robert said, hoping it was true. He smiled. "You have my word."

She nodded. He saw her relax. The third kiss was so good it almost undid all his honorable intentions once and for all, sweet, exciting, hot, full of endless promise. He drew back, watching her, the rise and fall of her breasts beneath the fine lawn of the nightgown, the hot color of arousal in her cheeks. This time she did not open her eyes.

The room was sinking into twilight. Downstairs the wedding feast was rolling on, the guests roaring out songs now, the thunder of feet beating on the floor as they danced.

Robert put out a hand and pulled the ribbon at the neck of the nightgown. The smooth silk slipped between his shaking fingers. He bent his lips to the exposed hollow of her throat and curled his tongue against the warm saltiness of her skin. Lucy made a little sound but kept quite still. Robert felt strung out like a wire, wound tighter than he had ever believed possible. Very slowly and carefully he edged the linen from her shoulders and kissed the shadows above her collarbone, the curve of her neck, the little dip beneath her ear, before returning to the base of her throat where the pulse hammered against his lips.

Her lashes fluttered. Her eyes opened.

"That's nice," she whispered. "Thank you."

She sounded so polite. It made him smile. It also

made him want to ravish her, ruthlessly and impolitely. Once again he held back.

"It can be nicer," he said. "But we will wait for that."

He wondered if he had imagined the flicker of disappointment in her eyes. She had said that she was not afraid of intimacy itself, and he could see that was true. It was the consequences of passion that frightened her.

He kissed her again. Again she responded with trust and openness and a sweet eagerness that almost drove him over the edge.

Just a little more...

He drew the nightgown down a little farther so that he could press his lips to the hollow between her breasts. It was deliciously warm and soft, and her skin smelled of lavender and roses. He could see her nipples taut against the thin cover of the silk night rail. The lust roared through him and he drew back abruptly.

"Enough," he said, "unless I am to perjure myself already."

Her eyes opened. She looked puzzled for a moment; then understanding dawned and she blushed.

"Do you wish to go back to your own chamber?" she asked.

"No," Robert said, praying for self-control. "I want to stay here with you."

She nodded and closed her eyes. She released her breath on a little sigh, then curled herself into the curve of his shoulder and protecting arm. Her body pressed softly, sweetly, against his.

Dear God. Robert knew he should be glad she had

such unquestioning trust in him, but he wondered, half despairing, if every night he spent with Lucy would be passed in this state of helpless arousal. With a sigh that was a great deal more frustrated than hers had been, he closed his eyes and tried to sleep.

He was still hovering on the edge of wakefulness a couple of hours later when Lucy's scream pulled him wide-awake. His hand was halfway to his dirk before he realized that it was no intruder but a nightmare that had disturbed her. He rolled over to look at her. She was lying on her back, panting hard, her eyes wide. Her skin was sheened with sweat and when he touched her she felt feverish, her face burning, her hands ice cold. He tried to draw her toward him, but for a moment she fought him, resisting his comfort.

"It's all right." He spoke softly to her, as to a child, soothing her. "It was a bad dream, nothing more. You're safe with me."

Her gaze flickered to his face. He saw despair in her eyes.

"Alice," she said.

He had guessed as much. She had said that she experienced nightmares. He could not expect them to be banished so quickly. He repressed the quick pang of anger and despondency he felt that her fears had resurfaced so soon. It was a sign that she was afraid of her marriage, terrified at the prospect of needing to provide an heir. But he could not let the despair take him too. He was certainly not going to give up now, when they had barely begun.

Gently, carefully, he drew her back into the shelter of his arms. He could feel her shivering and used his body to warm hers. Gradually the shaking ceased, she relaxed and her body grew soft next to his again.

"Thank you," she whispered. He caught the glint of tears on her cheek and brushed them away with the pad of his thumb.

"Go back to sleep," he whispered.

He held her until she did.

IT WAS STRANGE waking up with a man in her bed. It felt unfamiliar and awkward. Lucy woke as pale early-morning light was sliding beneath the shutters and pooling in the room. The nightmare had fled, driven out by Robert's gentleness and the warmth of his body. She remembered drifting off to sleep in his arms. She felt oddly peaceful inside.

For a moment she lay still, absorbing the strangeness of the situation and then she rolled over to look at her husband. He was asleep, the covers low on his hips, one bronzed arm resting across her body possessively. In the gray light she could see the perfection of his musculature, like one of the marble statues in the library at Forres. Except that Robert was warm and living and strong, and she wanted very much to touch him, not with the detached interest she had felt for those cold sculptures but with curiosity and greed.

She felt sensation stir inside her and in that moment remembered Robert's kisses and caresses of the previous night. She had been tired and nervous and wound as tightly as a spindle, but she had trusted him and he had not broken his word. She shivered a little as she remembered his lips drifting across her skin. She raised a hand to her throat and traced the path they had taken. Last night she had been almost too exhausted and afraid to be aroused. Almost. The desire had still stirred in her, though. And this morning it was sharper, keener. She felt awake and wanting in some way she did not understand.

Following an impulse she did not want to resist, she placed the palm of her hand on Robert's chest, over his heart. His skin felt warm and firm. She wanted to press her lips against him and see what he tasted like. The thought was a shocking one. It made her jump inside. She leaned closer, studying his face, the fan of tiny lines at the corners of his eyes, the long thick lashes, the hard slash of his cheekbone. There was stubble darkening his cheek and jaw. It looked rough. She was fascinated. She had never been so close to a man before, not like this.

His hand came up, trapping hers against his chest. His lashes flickered open, his eyes a deep dark blue. He smiled, a sleepy smile that made something quicken and tumble in Lucy's chest.

"Good morning," he said softly.

His hand tangled in her hair, drawing her down to kiss him. "It is too early to get up," he whispered against her lips. "Everyone is still asleep."

It was true that the inn was still quiet. Lucy found herself whispering too.

"What shall we do, then?"

Robert smiled. He drew her down into the warmth of the bed and started to kiss her again as he had the previous night, long, slow kisses that felt sweet and languorous and filled her body with a heavy heat. It felt different to be doing this in the light of morning, more wicked, more sensual still. Lucy's senses were flooded with the taste of him and the scent of his skin. It mingled with the faded lavender of the bedclothes and made her head spin with longing and need. He kissed her for a long time; she lost track of time and place and everything except for him, the heat of his body, the touch of his hands and mouth on her, the essence of him. When she finally broke away, dizzy and racked with desire, she found that her nightgown had slid from her shoulders above and was wrapped about her thighs below and it felt too tight, heavy and imprisoning and she wanted to be free of it.

There was a great deal that she wanted.

"Are you all right, sweetheart?" Robert was stroking her cheek. His fingers felt cool, whilst she felt as though she was burning up.

"No," she said crossly. "I want…"

He laughed. "We can't do that."

How provoking. The hot, heavy weight of demand inside her almost made her drive her clenched fists into the mattress in frustration. Why did her body have to torment her when her mind would not let her be free? For a moment she seesawed between longing and fear; for a moment it seemed the sweet need might actually win, but then the scales tipped and the familiar fear swept back, like a steel trap, tightening, draining away all the pleasure until she was left desolate and empty again.

She bit her lip hard. She would *not* cry.

With a sudden burst of energy, she threw back the covers and stood up. Anything rather than lie here and feel that dark tide sweep in to claim her.

"I am getting up," she said.

"Come back to bed." Robert's voice had deepened. Lucy shivered again, this time not entirely from cold or fear. "No really, I—"

"We need to talk." He was propped on one elbow now, deliciously rumpled. She felt a little pang of longing. He looked so handsome and so ruffled. Her heart seemed to squeeze tight with happiness and pain, inextricably linked. She edged toward the door, then remembered that they were in her chamber and realized she had nowhere to run.

"I don't think—"

"You're frightened." He spoke flatly, denying her the chance to pretend. "I understand. But all will be well now, Lucy." There was gentleness in his eyes. It made her want to cry. "I'll look after you." She wanted to believe him. She wanted it so much. And when she could not she felt her heart shrivel with despair.

"Lucy." Robert was holding out a hand to her. "Come here."

She could not. For a moment she was absolutely frozen with fear and misery.

Suddenly she knew she had to escape, from the

intimacy of the room and the look in Robert's eyes, from the panic that filled her chest and stole her breath. Memories pressed too close, frightening her. Her defenses felt so fragile now. Something was changing, but she was not quite sure what it was.

"I have things to do," she said desperately. "Shopping... I need to pack a bag... Mairi can help me."

"I doubt you will find the Findon shops occupy you for more than an hour," Robert said. He sighed, pushing back the covers, standing up.

"My reputation will never survive the knowledge that my bride was out of bed so early the morning after the wedding," he said dryly as he bent to retrieve his shirt from the floor and pulled it over his head. He came across to her and kissed her again, thoroughly, unhurriedly, so that she could feel the desire beating beneath the gentleness.

"We can't go back, Lucy," he said fiercely, against her lips. "I won't let us." He dropped his hands from her shoulders and strode from the room.

CHAPTER SIXTEEN

"YOU ARE UP EARLY." Jack strolled into the breakfast parlor, where Robert had just finished his meal, and glanced ostentatiously at the clock. "Well, you did tell me it was a match of convenience, I suppose." He slid into a seat and reached for the coffeepot. "You look rough," he added, with mock sympathy. "Uncomfortable night?"

Robert glared at him. "I'm up early because there is much to do before we are ready to sail for Golden Isle."

Jack grinned, unabashed. "Of course. And all of it more important than seducing your wife."

Robert threw down his paper with a bad-tempered slap. "I told you last night to mind your own damned business," he growled. He stood up. "You'll find me at the harbor. When you have stopped wasting time."

He went out. The May morning was bitterly chill, but he welcomed the cold. It helped to clear his head and subdue other parts of his body. He liked the early morning when the light was still rising and the air was fresh. It was a time he had always relished.

It was a time that now gave him the chance to think about Lucy. As he strode through the quiet streets of the awakening town, he thought of the way she had responded to his kisses, the way she had kissed him back, and touched him with innocent curiosity and delight. She had been half-seduced, until her memories had turned her cold and driven her from the bed. He had seen how it had happened, watched her withdraw into herself and reerect all the barriers she had used to protect herself in the past. Well, he was going to tear down those walls. He could not allow the tragedy of the past to destroy their future.

As he turned the corner down to the quayside, the wind buffeted him fiercely. It had chased all the clouds away, and out to sea he could see Golden Isle floating on the horizon. He squared his shoulders. He had married Lucy to save his inheritance, and the isle was a part of that. The previous night he had been brought hard and fast to see his responsibilities. He would not shirk them now.

He spent all day at the quayside loading provisions for the voyage, talking further to McCall about conditions on Golden Isle and discussing with Jack the plan to lure Wilfred Cardross into a trap.

Eventually, when the cold sun had sunk behind the mountains to the west, he walked back to the inn with Jack, aware of exhaustion in his limbs, conscious that he had pushed himself to the extreme of physical exertion in order to block out all else.

One look at Lucy was sufficient to bring back every one of those frustrations.

She was sitting in the firelit parlor, talking in a low voice to her sister as they finished their evening meal together. They had evidently been shopping, for Lucy was wearing a new gown. Even Robert, not precisely versed in the ways of fashion, could see that it became her tremendously. It was a rich, deep brown, threaded with gold, with a low neckline that framed in pretty white lace the upper curve of her breasts. Her red hair was piled up on her head, but tendrils escaped to curl against her neck. It looked as though she had been painted in autumn colors, vivid and bright. Unlike the previous day, when she had been pale and strained in her wedding gown, now she glowed, her eyes a deep sapphire blue in the shadows.

Beside him, he heard Jack give a low whistle of appreciation. Lady Mairi, Robert thought, looked as though she welcomed that as little as he did. He gave Jack a glare while Mairi stood up in a rustle of silk.

"You are back at last," she said, her tone making it clear that she thought Robert had shamefully neglected his bride. "You must forgive us for taking dinner without you. We were hungry."

She slipped past them, taking care to keep as much distance from Jack as she could, even, Robert was amused to see, moving her skirts carefully out of the way so that they did not brush against him. A moment later Jack seemed to pull himself together with a jerk and walked off after her. Robert closed the door behind them.

Lucy had got to her feet too. For all her elegance, the expression in her eyes was uncertain. Robert remembered the previous night, when she had told him she did not know how to be a wife, and felt a pang of tenderness.

"There is plenty of the beef left," she offered. "If you are hungry."

Robert was starving, but there was something he preferred to do first. He crossed the room to her, caught her in his arms and kissed her. He sensed the surprise in her and the slightest hint of resistance. Then she made a startled sound in the back of her throat and he felt that resistance melt and she kissed him back.

It was almost enough to make him forswear his dinner in the need to take her upstairs and make love to her. With an effort he hauled himself back from the brink and released her. Hell, if he gave in to his desires, he would terrify her anew and the small amount of progress they had made would be completely undone.

"I should wash too," he said gruffly, "and eat."

She nodded. Her cheeks were rosy red, her eyes bright as stars. She chewed her bottom lip between her teeth, watching him. Robert smothered a groan as he felt his body tighten to near intolerable tension. He groped for the doorknob, needing to put distance between them.

"I'll just…" He waved a hand vaguely, reversing from the room, almost colliding with Isobel, who was coming the other way with a tray of food. He apologized, cursing himself for a clumsy fool. One way and another, his wife was tying him in knots.

He could see Lucy looking at him, a tiny frown

between her eyebrows, as though she was worried about him.

"Are you feeling quite all right?" She took a step toward him, reaching out. He jerked back from her.

"Nothing that some hot food will not remedy."

Her hand fell to her side. "Of course." She smiled at Isobel, dropped him a flawless curtsy and went out.

Robert ran a hand through his hair, cursing himself anew. He would far rather Lucy had stayed to talk to him even if there had been a danger he would have fallen on her rather than on his meal. Now he had upset her, confused her perhaps. Truth was, he was feeling so very on edge himself that he was doing nothing to reassure her.

He threw himself down into his seat and attacked the beef bad-temperedly. Who knew that this marriage business would be so damned difficult?

LUCY PACED HER bedchamber. Mairi had helped her to change for bed—in the absence of a maid they helped each other—and now she was wishing she had asked her sister to stay. Any company would have been welcome. She had picked up her book and tried to read again, but the words seemed to make no sense. She could not concentrate. All she could think was that she had no idea why Robert had kissed her so deliciously and then backed away from her as quickly.

That morning he had sworn he would not allow her to place barriers between the two of them, and although she was trembling inside, she had been willing enough to try to make a leap of faith. For the sake of her marriage and the future of the Methven estates, she knew they could not live locked into separate, barren existences. She could feel a tiny part of her heart opening each day, shedding a hint of light. She trusted Robert not to hurt her. That was a start. So she had been prepared for him to come to her tonight and to take things a little further than they had done before. And then he had flinched from her as though she were a plague carrier.

Men. She had absolutely no understanding of them, and at the current rate of progress she would never have any.

She heard steps on the stair and jumped to her feet. The floorboards creaked on the landing; she heard the low exchange of words as Robert bid good-night to his cousin. She waited. She realized she was holding her breath.

The door of the room opposite closed, the latch dropping with a decisive click. There was silence. Lucy sat down again in the armchair. She could hear nothing but the ticking of the clock on the chest and the crackle of the fire, loud in her ears. Her fingers dug into the velvet of the arms as she waited, as the tension ratcheted up inside her. Time passed. Her bare feet grew chilled. He was not going to come to her. He was not even going to bid her good-night.

Quickly, before she could think, before she allowed herself to be afraid, she banked down the fire and grabbed the candle from the stand. She opened the door and stepped out onto the landing. Chill draughts wreathed about her ankles and set her shivering. She tiptoed across the landing and knocked lightly on the door of Robert's chamber and, without waiting for a summons, walked in.

He was sprawled in the chair before the fire, a glass of brandy at his elbow. He looked up at her and he did not smile. Decidedly he was not pleased to see her.

This was a mistake.

The frightened kick of her heart almost sent her straight back through the open door, but some imp of stubbornness drove her on instead.

"You did not come to bid me good-night," she said. She shut the door, placed the candle carefully on the dresser. "Only this morning you said you would fight for a future for us, yet now you shun me."

There was a silence so long that for a moment she thought he was not going to answer her. Then his gaze lifted to hers. It was a very bright, glittering blue. She wondered if he was drunk, and her heart skipped a whole beat.

"I am trying," he growled, "to respect your wishes and not ravish you to within an inch of your life." His gaze swept over her, insolent, appraising, and she became acutely aware of her bare feet and the tendrils of hair escaping from her long, thick plait.

"It is difficult, however," he continued, in an even tone, "when you appear in my bedchamber in no more than a transparent nightgown."

"Oh." The color burned her cheeks. She felt like a naive fool. "I see."

"Yes," he mocked. "And I apologize for finding you so entirely irresistible. It is making my life hell." He stood up. Lucy took an instinctive step back. That checked him. One dark eyebrow rose. She realized he was not drunk, and the relief swept through her leaving her weak.

"I'm sorry," she said. "I'll go now." But she did not move.

He waited, giving her plenty of time to decide while her heart pounded so hard she was sure he could hear it. And still she did not move. She could not take her gaze from his face, the expression so hard, carved from granite. It did not frighten her now. She knew that behind that strength lay a tenderness that made her heart ache.

It took him only two strides to cross the space between them and take her in his arms, and when he did she gave a gasp of relief as she pressed closer to him, her arms going around him and straining him closer still.

"Why are you staying?" He spoke softly, against her hair.

"Because we promised to try…" She was shaking. "Because I want to be with you. Because I trust you."

He held her a little away from him. His eyes were gentle. "I won't make love to you, Lucy," he said. "It's too soon. You are not ready."

She knew that he was right. She wanted him, but it was not enough to banish the memories that hovered like dark wings about her mind. It was not enough to eradicate the fear. Not yet.

"I know," she said. A part of her wanted nothing more than for him to ravish her completely, but she did not want to regret it later. "But last night…" She stopped, remembering what he had said about finding her irresistible. She was asking too much of him, testing his control beyond anything that was fair. She might know little of men, but she did know that.

"I'm sorry," she said again. "It isn't fair to you. I didn't realize."

He scooped her up then and laid her down on the bed, coming down beside her, pulling her into his arms.

"Damn it all," he said, his breath tickling her ear, "I'd still rather you stayed with me, fair or not."

So HE WAS a fool. Robert looked down at his wife lying on the bed beside him and knew he was in for another night of frustration and discomfort. Yet it was a small price to pay. Lucy had reached out to him. For the first time she had come to him freely. The realization that she was prepared to entrust herself to him made his heart bound. If it meant that eventually he could drive out the darkness inside her and replace it with light and hope, it had been worth it—even if he expired of thwarted desire in the process. There were no guarantees in life; he knew that better than anyone, but he was determined that Lucy's life would not be blighted by fear.

He reached out and took the ribbon that tied her plait

between his finger and thumb, tugging on the end of it, loosening the bow. He started to unravel the plait, working with concentrated intent, running his fingers through her hair as he had always longed to do. It was as soft and silky as he had imagined, rippling through his hands like burnished fire. The color, the texture, fascinated him.

Lucy lay still, her eyes dark and wide as she watched him. Eventually he consciously gave in to the impulse to lower his head and kiss her, and she shifted on the bed and made a noise of surrender in her throat, as though she had been waiting only for this moment. The touch of her mouth was sweet and hot, branding him. He was already hard, but he held his control in an iron grip and grimly told himself that it was good to discover reserves of restraint he had no idea he possessed.

Leaving her briefly, he divested himself of his jacket, shirt and boots as he had done the previous night. This time when he came back to her, she reached eagerly for him, running her hands over his bare shoulders, his arms and back, exploring him. Robert gritted his teeth and allowed her free rein. Her touch was full of an innocent curiosity that was as tempting as it was beguiling.

"So smooth. So hot." Her voice was a whisper. Her hand slid across his stomach, just above the band of his trousers, and his cock jumped. He caught her wrist in a tight grip.

"Enough," he said. "Unless you want to test my honor too far and prove me a liar."

She blinked, her eyes opening wide. "Oh." She ran

her tongue over her bottom lip and he almost groaned aloud. Instead he kissed her again, sliding his tongue into her mouth, exploring her deeply, until she was shifting restlessly against the sheets, her hands moving over him in urgent, restless caresses.

He drew back. The shutters were not closed and in the blue of half-light she looked tumbled and tempting and ripe for ravishment. Her eyes were slumberous with passion, her lips parted, her breasts rising and falling rapidly beneath the shimmering white of her night rail. Robert took a deep, hard breath to steady himself. These were dangerous games.

He touched her cheek. "How are you, sweetheart?"

She smiled at him and raised a hand to rest it against his bare chest. "I am very well, thank you," she whispered. "I feel…quite safe."

God help him. He felt very far from safe. If he felt any more tender and protective toward her, he would be completely undone. He pressed a kiss against the curve of the throat, felt the heat of her skin, tasted the salty sweetness and felt his body surge.

"Do you wish me to stop?" He barely recognized his own voice, it was so rough with repressed desire.

"No." Her lips curved. "Not if it pleases you to continue." There was a glint of challenge in her eyes and no fear at all. She was all feminine triumph for his weakness.

"It pleases me," he ground out. "You please me very much."

He put a hand to the ribbon that tied her nightgown

and pulled it. The neckline gaped. He glimpsed her body beneath, all secret shadows and curves. He ached for it. Slowly, carefully, he traced a line from beneath her chin, dipping into the hollow of her throat and dropping lower and lower to the valley between her breasts. He heard her catch her breath. Her nipples hardened beneath the thin linen of the nightgown. He bent his head, taking one tight peak in his mouth, feeling the material against his teeth as he bit down very gently on her nipple. Lucy's gasp of shocked pleasure was all the reward he needed; once again he felt like a god. She arched up from the bed, her body open to him, begging for more.

"Oh…" She sounded shaken. "Oh please…don't stop."

Robert pulled down the nightgown so that she was bare to the waist. The candle was burning down now and the shadows had sunk deep and the room was gray and black. Lucy looked pale and ethereal in the half-light. Robert wanted to see her, but he did not dare break the mood to relight the candle. Instead he stroked her shoulders lightly, reverently, his caresses leading back by slow degrees to the voluptuous swell of her breasts. He stroked upward from her ribs, following the underside of her breasts to their tip, his touch feathering the nipple. She groaned, her breath coming in quick pants. He repeated the caress, again and again, feeling her tighten beneath the tips of his fingers, gentle yet certain, driving her to fulfill a need she had not yet recognized.

When his lips traced the same pattern over her ribs to the tips of her breasts, she once again cried out, rising from the bed, her body silently begging for more. He gave it to her, little nips and sucks and bites that had her squirming, forgetful of her fears, lost beneath his touch. She tasted of hot skin and roses and sweet arousal, and he was so hard he wanted to bury himself in her. But he did not forget this was only the beginning. It would take only the slightest misstep to awaken her to her fears again.

Her fingers dug into the sheet as his lips dropped from her breasts to stroke the curve of her stomach and his tongue flicked wickedly into her belly button. The nightgown was wrapped about her thighs, knotted from the frantic writhing of her body. He wondered if she was aware that she had parted her thighs in instinctive invitation. She lay panting on the tangled sheets, her eyes tight shut and a small frown furrowing her brow.

"I want…" Her voice was slurred as though she were drunk, as though what she wanted eluded any words she knew.

Robert slid one hand over her leg, his palm firm against the soft skin of her inner thigh. She shook uncontrollably, raising her hips in mute plea.

He leaned forward, kissing the hot damp skin of her neck where the tendrils of hair clung. His lips brushed the curve of her ear.

"You want surcease." Between them there was not going to be any false modesty or inhibition. If she were to trust him, it would have to be openly and honestly, with no pretense, admitting to her needs and pleasures. He could not lay the ghosts of the past to rest any other way.

She opened her eyes at the words, but in the same moment he parted her, finding the swollen nub at the very core of her. He watched; her expression changed, her eyes widening, her lips opening as she felt his touch on her. Something hot shimmered in her eyes, hot and disbelieving, almost accusatory as though she could not believe how he made her feel.

He flicked her tight little nub once, twice, in a smooth stroke, and she came immediately, helplessly, on a scream, her body jolting with the force of it. He stroked her again and saw the pleasure catch her a second time, more fiercely than the first. The shock and disbelief in her eyes dissolved into sheer sensual delight and her body slumped, her eyes closing, and she lay boneless and gasping, sheened in sweat.

After a moment he lit the candle, then pulled the remnants of the innocent-looking white nightgown from her and cast them aside, drawing her into his arms, where she lay without protest. Her breasts still rose and fell rapidly against his chest, which was a particular torment, but one he felt he could bear if the result was witnessing such pleasure in her. For there was no doubt he had taken her to the very edge of bliss and he had taken such enjoyment in watching her learn what it felt like. He had had no idea that simply giving her pleasure would make him feel so frightfully pleased with himself. It was a startling discovery.

"What on earth did you do to me?" She sounded exhausted but recognizably like Lucy again. Her eyelids fluttered open. Her eyes were like dark stars, heavy with satiation.

"I showed you how good your body can make you feel," Robert said. He suspected that Lucy associated the physical body only with pain and danger. Her experience had colored everything for her and now it was his turn to show her that the physical, the sensual, could bring pleasure beyond belief.

A slow smile curved the corner of her mouth. "So you did. I had no notion."

Robert kissed her. Her response was different this time, open and accepting, weighted by the knowledge of pleasure. He plunged his tongue deep in her mouth, allowing his desires full rein, mimicking the movement he wanted for his body by plundering her mouth instead. She groaned deep in her throat and opened wider to him and suddenly he was within an ace of spilling his seed in his breeches, which he had not done since he was sixteen years old.

He rolled away, cursing his lack of control. They had only been married for two nights and there was not a chance in hell that he would risk frightening Lucy by exposing her to his needs. That would have to wait. She might look like a wanton angel, but she would turn back into a frightened virgin swiftly enough if he rushed his fences.

She was still lying sprawled on the bed in slumberous abandon, her hair ruffled, her eyes half-open, watching him. The candlelight gilded her skin, picking out the freckles scattered over her shoulders. She looked delectable, soft, rounded, ravished. The hunger in him was like a ravening beast howling for satisfaction. Never had he set himself so hard a task as keeping his hands from her.

"What are you thinking?" she asked.

There was not a chance in hell that he was going to tell her that he was thinking of making love to her, that he wanted to spread her and take her and seal their bargain by making her his.

"I'm thinking," he said, "that nothing would give me greater pleasure than to make you cry out your pleasure again."

She looked shocked by his bluntness, and for a moment he thought he had gone too far. Her trust was so fragile, always balanced against the fear of memory. Yet she also possessed a healthy intellectual curiosity. And she was passionate through and through, and had just started to understand where that passion might take her.

He waited.

Her gaze flickered up to meet his, a little shyly. "Is that possible?" She sounded detached, rational. "I mean, is it possible to experience the same degree of pleasure over and over again—"

"Why don't we find out?" Robert said politely. He did not move. This was for her to choose, to decide how far she wanted to go.

She stared at him. He could see the pulse beating

hard in her throat. Her voice was husky. "You mean you are asking me—"

"If you would like to find out. Yes."

She bit her lip, looked down. He knew it was hard for her; reality was creeping back now here in the light, as sensual bliss receded. Which was all the more reason to conjure it again. The night was still young. Downstairs the inn taproom was turning rowdy.

"Trust me a little further," he said. "Indulge your desire to learn."

She smiled at that. "I confess I have always been keen to learn new things."

He smiled too. *Good.* Because if he could not indulge his own pleasure tonight, then driving Lucy to the extremes of carnal lust seemed like a very fair revenge.

Lucy saw Robert's smile and wondered why on earth she had agreed. The first time she had had an excuse; she had wanted to build on the intimacy they had already established and show that she was committed to their future. She had wanted to demonstrate her trust in him. That trust had led to such sensual bliss she could not have imagined. Even now, as the tide of it lingered in her body, she was still disbelieving it could have been so good.

And now he was offering to do it all again. Differently. Which would be simple self-indulgence, but oh she wanted to indulge herself. She wanted it quite desperately. And it would be safe because he had promised that tonight was all about her pleasure. She did not have to worry about him bedding her or the dangers of consummation. She could release herself from the hold of the past and live only in the present. Robert had asked her to put herself in his hands, and really it would be an insult to refuse. Oh, she could convince herself that black was white, that silver was gold, tonight.

Yet even so she was anxious. Her heart was battering her ribs, and her tension was growing with each beat.

"Here." He had strolled across to the table by the window, struck a light for another candle and poured two glasses of wine. He brought them back and handed one to her, clinking his glass softly against hers. "Drink."

"This requires wine?" Lucy said.

He laughed. "Perhaps. You seem a little tense. The key is to have just enough wine to relax you but not too much to make you insensible."

"I'll remember," Lucy said. She took a gulp, then another, almost emptying her glass. It was a fine wine, smooth as it slipped down her throat. Robert took the glass from her hand and placed it on the dresser. A moment later she tasted wine again on his lips as he kissed her. He was right; her head spun now, deliciously, sensually, and she was not sure if it was the claret or the kiss that made her feel so faint. Warmth tingled down her spine and along her skin.

"Lie down." His soft instruction had her heart racing. She lay back on the bed, suddenly shy, wanting to shield herself from his gaze, but he spread her arms wide and sat back on his heels looking at her. Now, in the light, there was no hiding. It felt too intimate, but regardless of her old fears she made herself lie still and face it. After a moment the trapped feeling faded away.

"You are beautiful." He touched her shoulders lightly, slid his hands down her arms, stroked her breasts again with the same gentle gliding caresses he had used earlier. Lucy was starting to recognize the responses of her body now. She had been so satiated that she had thought she could not be reawakened, yet each sly drift of Robert's hands over her seemed to tighten a cord within her. She remembered how good the massage had felt and how it had made her body beg for more. He could command her response so easily.

Was there anything wrong in that? The little voice at the back of her mind reminded her that he was her husband and that tonight she did not need to be fearful. She did not need to think. She could leave that for another day.

With a sigh of surrender she allowed her body to soften and open, flagrantly exposed to him. She watched him through half-closed lids as he studied her nakedness and was surprised how fiercely she enjoyed that look of acute longing on his face. It made her feel feminine and powerful.

He lifted her, his hands strong on her waist, and kissed her so deeply her head spun. Then he dropped his lips to her breasts and the dark tight spiral of desire quickened in her. Her head fell back. She arched. She could feel his hands spread against the bare skin of her back holding her securely as his mouth plundered her with tugs and licks and kisses. Her dizziness grew, the wicked delicious pulses in her belly beating a demand of their own.

He laid her down gently on the bed and slid his palms down her thighs and she quivered. Her skin felt hot and feverish. Her whole body was alight. She felt his hands drawing her legs wider apart and the brush of his hair against the soft skin of her inner thigh. She was sufficiently shocked to half waken from her sensual haze; she rose on her elbows, but Robert placed a palm on her stomach just above her pubic bone and pressed gently down. Immediately her belly fluttered with longing and she fell back on the bed with a groan.

He held her apart. A slick lap of his tongue over her nub again had her flying, her body twisting and beating through such acute delight that she called his name in shock. The sensation built and built again as he touched his tongue to her core. She felt herself hang helpless on the edge of pleasure, waiting, desperate to fall, each stroke taking her closer and yet spinning out the feeling until she was mindless with the driving need. It was different from the feeling she had experienced earlier, sharper and crystal clear, almost too extreme to bear. She chased the sensation, wanting surcease, desperate for it, and found that the more she grasped after it the more elusive it became. She knew she was begging. She could hear her own broken words, feel too the curve of Robert's smile against the skin of her thigh.

Finally, when she was sure she could take no more, when she was twisting and writhing beneath his hands and his tongue, she felt herself gather and fall apart at last, the force of it leaving her spent and breathless.

Hot darkness pressed on her lids. Her body still twitched and jolted. It did not seem able to stop. She felt overwhelmed and yet in some odd way still aroused and wanting. It was unbearable, as though she had taken all she could and yet still snatched after more. And then she felt Robert's tongue again, pressing down on her where she still pulsed, driving her straight to the peak again. It was shocking, fast and inescapable and she came a second time, crying out, the feeling ripping through her as sharp as claws this time, painful in its intensity.

This time when she came down, the sweet sensual arousal did not fade but lingered, throbbing in every cell of her body. She felt it from the top of her head to the tips of her toes and deep inside her, where the pulse of it still beat. Robert was lying beside her now and his mouth was on her breasts, nipping and tugging at her, and each lick and slide of his tongue echoed through her down to her belly, where there was a tight knot of need. It felt indescribable, hot, tormenting, unendurable. She could not believe that he could keep her body singing like this, hanging on the edge of pleasure, replete and yet not fully satisfied, until she writhed with frustration, desperation. There was no room in her mind for thought now. No space for anything other than sensation.

He spread her thighs wider apart. Cool air kissed

her core. She was so sensitive now that even that soft touch had her body jerking and shuddering.

"No more. I can't..." It was too much. It was lovely. It was intolerable. She wanted to beg him to stop. She wanted to beg for final oblivion. "I can't do it again."

"I think you can." Such a wicked whisper in her ear. "Once more. Trust me."

Trust me.

He moved. The candle wavered in the cold night air. Ripples of chill covered her body. She lay, scarcely breathing, with pleasure suspended on the tightest thread, her body screaming for release.

She felt him slide his fingers over her. She was so slick now, hot and wet. It took no more than the lightest, most gentle touch and she came for the past time in a blinding rush of light that plunged her body into abject and total surrender.

She was not sure how long it was before she opened her eyes. She felt exhausted, drained, her body aching in ways she had never known. In the mirror tilted over the dresser she saw her reflection, hair tumbled, eyes glittering, a wicked wanton sprawled on the bed in complete abandonment, limbs spread, body ravished by Robert's touch, his kisses. She felt shocked; she had not known she could look that way. She reached for the sheet to cover herself, but Robert held it out of her reach. His gaze was all over her, hot, intimate, from the pink flush of her breasts to the spread of her thighs.

"Too late for modesty," he said. His eyes glittered with possessiveness and pride.

Back in her right mind, she was horrified at her abandoned behavior, at the way she had begged for release, begged for pleasure. Robert saw her appalled expression and laughed, tumbling her into his arms, drawing her close. She allowed her hot cheek to rest against his bare shoulder and breathed in the scent of his skin, starting to feel drowsy, overcome by the sheer physical satiation of the experience.

"You're pleased," she whispered, and felt him turn his head toward her. "Pleased you could do that to me."

It had not all been entirely for her pleasure, she thought. Self-denial must have been an enormous frustration to him. Pushing her to her limits, demonstrating his mastery of her body, making her submit utterly was some small recompense.

His lips brushed her hair. She could hear the smile in his voice. "It pleased me a very great deal," he said.

"I liked it very much too."

He kissed her for the whispered confession, but already she was slipping toward sleep, exhausted, the darkness washing into her mind. And for once no nightmares stalked her dreams.

CHAPTER SEVENTEEN

LUCY AWOKE FEELING different, her body ripe and fulfilled and yet hungry in some way. She rolled over and
reached for Robert, but the bed beside her was empty.
Blinking, she saw the room was full of daylight.

She rolled onto her back and watched through half-
closed lids the play of the sun and shadows across the
ceiling. Such pleasure. She could scarcely believe it.
Such intimacies. She was shocked, if truth be told. She
was shocked by the desires of her body, desires she had
never remotely guessed at. She could see now that she
had kept those needs locked down, she had intellec-
tualized them so that they were cold and passionless
and were no danger to her. And now Robert had cut
through all that, awakening the desire that was in her.

Yet he had not taken advantage to push matters beyond what she had been comfortable with. And she
had given him nothing in return for the most blissful
night she had ever experienced, which seemed rather
unfair, on reflection.

She remembered that in the throes of her passion she
had promised to trust Robert, to allow him to do anything to help her overcome her fears of intimacy. She
had not understood then that this meant surrendering

everything to him. She shivered again. Already she wondered where that promise would take her; already her perfidious body was wanting so much more. But now that she was awake she could feel the darkness nibbling at the edge of her mind again, reminding her that eventually he would want her to be his wife in more than name, that he needed an heir from her body.

She gave a little shiver, pushing the dark thoughts from her mind. The breeze from the open window was cold on her naked body. She was about to pull up the covers, but then she stopped, looking curiously at her nakedness. She had never scrutinized her body before. She had turned away from physicality because she had seen Alice die, seen her racked with pain. Now, for the first time, she thought about her body as a means of pleasure. She ran a thoughtful hand down over her breasts. They were so round and ripe, the nipples stung pink from Robert's attentions the previous night. They felt sensitive, but pleasurably so, and her skin felt curiously alive.

Her hand dropped to her belly. A hot ache was flowering there at those secret memories of pleasure. Her belly was rounded too; she was not thin like Mairi or Lachlan, but curvy. Really she was rounded all over, for her buttocks were plump, albeit tight and high from the riding, and her thighs were quite sturdy. She was no lithe and slender creature and yet she felt very desirable this morning.

Again the shard of doubt and fear snagged at her heart. This, then, was how Alice must have felt. Seduced by passion, helplessly in love, she had given everything of herself and as a consequence had lost everything. Passion was so deceptive, so dangerous. It could make someone forget all sense. It could make someone forget everything.

For the first time, though, she stopped the thought in its tracks before the cold fear could take hold of her. Alice had loved and Alice had died and that had been a tragedy, but that did not mean that the same thing would happen to her. The sliver of light in her heart strengthened a little.

There was a knock at the door and Isobel bustled in with a tray. Lucy hastily pulled the covers up to hide herself, but the landlady's smile was knowing. Lucy could see her discarded nightgown lying on the floor by the bed, see too the rumpled bedclothes that told their own story. She remembered how she had cried out when Robert had driven her to orgasm and wondered suddenly whether anyone had heard her. She had had no thought of it at the time, had not cared, and no doubt no one would think of it as anything other than proof of their laird's prowess. But still she blushed.

"Lord Methven thought you might need to rest." Isobel sounded brisk. She placed the tray on the bottom of the bed and helped Lucy into the lacy peignoir that lay over the high back of the chair. "He says to remind you that you sail for Golden Isle on the afternoon's tide, so you have a little time."

Some of Lucy's pleasure ebbed at the thought that Robert was not here to tell her his plans in person. It was like the day before, when he had vanished for the entire day, leaving her to her own devices. She remembered the wedding feast and the change that had come over him when Golden Isle was mentioned.

"Isobel—" She was raising the cup of scented hot chocolate to her lips but paused. "I know that Golden Isle is part of Lord Methven's estates, but why does he…" She stopped, chose her words with care. "Why does he dislike the mention of it?"

Isobel's expression was guarded. She started to fidget, picking up Lucy's nightgown, smoothing it between her fingers, and laying it down again. "Lord Methven has not told you?" she said.

Something in her tone caught Lucy's attention. "Not a word."

We do not know each other well….

For all the intimacies of the previous night, Lucy was suddenly all too sharply aware that there was so much she neither knew nor understood about Robert. Another shard of loneliness pierced her.

Isobel laid the nightgown over the end of the bed. Then she looked up and met Lucy's eyes.

"It was where Gregor Methven died," she said. "They say Lord Methven hates the place. He quarreled so badly with his grandfather in the aftermath of his brother's death that he took the first boat from the harbor and never set foot there again."

LUCY'S FIRST VIEW of Golden Isle was through a fog of rain and hail. It looked gray, not golden, and for the first

time she had some sympathy with Robert not wishing
to go there. Huge cliffs rose straight out of a boiling sea.
Seabirds whirled and called like banshees. The cliffs
were gray, the sea was gray and the sky was gray. It
felt like the end of the world.

They had been sailing for six hours and Lucy was
cold, wet, sick and miserable. All day she had been
waiting for Robert to speak to her, to tell her his plans,
to confide in her about Golden Isle and his feelings
on returning there. But Robert was busy, preoccupied
with the preparations for the voyage. When she went
down to the quay to find him, he greeted her absent-
mindedly before going back to supervising the loading of provisions. Lucy felt excluded, with no role and
nothing to do.

She had said goodbye to Mairi there on the quay at
Findon, and it was only through exerting the greatest
self-control that she had not broken down and begged
her sister to come with them. She could imagine Mairi's
reaction to her begging for company on her wedding
trip; her sister would be concerned that the wedding
night had been a complete disaster and would no doubt
ask her all about it, loudly, tactlessly and at considerable length. So she hugged Mairi tightly instead and
sent her on her way back to Edinburgh with a letter for
their father and a promise that she would invite them
all to Methven as soon as she returned. She watched
Mairi ride off with Jack Rutherford. Naturally they
were quarreling already.

At first the voyage had been smooth. A pale sun

shone through milky-white clouds as the little yacht slipped out of Findon Harbor. Lucy sat in the cabin and watched Robert as he worked with the crew. He was dressed the same as they, barefoot, in rough linen breeches, open-necked shirt and leather jerkin. It was clear he had done this many times before, since he was a child perhaps. He was surefooted on the spray-dampened deck and completely at ease with the men. Once again Lucy felt lonely, very much the aristocratic lady, sitting alone in the cabin with nothing to do.

Gradually as the coastline faded from view, the wind freshened and pewter clouds started to mass on the horizon. The yacht began to buck and roll, and soon Lucy started to feel very ill indeed. She had never been to sea before and had only once set foot on a boat when they had visited Wilfred Cardross at Greenock and he had proudly shown them over his yacht. It was considerably larger than this little vessel, and the saloon had been furnished in red velvet with gold braid with the arms of Cardross prominently displayed. Lucy had thought it garish and vulgar. Now, though, she would have given much for a comfortable berth in which to lie down as the boat lurched through the waves and her stomach lurched with it.

The door of the cabin opened abruptly and Robert came in. He had been carrying a tray on which there appeared to be two bowls of broth. Just the smell of it made Lucy want to retch. He took one look at her face, placed the tray down with a bang and, grabbing her arm, dragged her out into the corridor, bundling her up the steps and out onto the deck so swiftly she almost tripped over her skirts.

"What on earth are you doing to me?" Lucy hissed. "I feel vile. Leave me alone!"

The fresh air was like a slap in the face after the staleness of the cabin below. Almost immediately her head stopped spinning and her stomach settled as she gratefully breathed in the cold, salty air. The spray was cool against her skin. She clung to the deck rail and let it settle on her like rain.

"If you watch the horizon you will not feel as sick."

Robert was beside her, his arm about her waist as he steered her to a seat in the lee of the main mast. She sat down on a coil of rope and fixed her gaze on the distant horizon where the sea rose and plunged like a dizzying ride on an unbroken horse. It was cold out here and already her gown and cloak were soaked through, but it was far preferable to being inside.

"Would you like some soup?" He was smiling at her. She wanted to slap him for being so at ease when she felt quite the reverse.

"No, thank you." Food would be a step too far.

"Then if you wish to stay here I shall fetch you a blanket to keep you warm."

"You are all consideration."

His smiled widened to a grin at her frosty tone, but he returned with two thick ship's blankets that smelled fishy but were blessedly warm.

"This part of the crossing is called the roost," he

said. "It's where several currents meet. That's why it is so rough and takes so long."

Lucy did not much care as long as it stopped, but instead it got progressively worse, the rain falling like a shroud over the sea, the sails cracking overhead, the boat creaking alarmingly, battered by each wave.

Eventually, with the clock creeping around to eight in the evening, the cliffs of Golden Isle reared out of the fog and the little boat slipped into the harbor. Robert helped Lucy as she climbed stiffly ashore. There was no one to greet them. McCall, the man who had come to Findon the previous night, muttered something about letting everyone in the village know that they had arrived and disappeared into the mist. The harbormaster provided a trap, pulled by a small horse that appeared to be in a bad temper.

"It is three miles to the village," Robert said, handing Lucy up into the trap and settling her on the hard wooden seat. He had turned dour again. His face was set in harsh lines and Lucy could feel the tension in him. After so many years, to return to this godforsaken place and be greeted by nothing but the blanketing mist and the gray moors... Her heart shivered to think how he must feel.

There was silence between them for the first mile. The track was rough and the pony was singularly uncooperative, stopping frequently for no particular reason. Lucy, cold and soaked through to the skin now, huddled down on the seat as a brisk little wind whirled down from the hills. She watched Robert's hands on the reins and his set face, and thought he looked like a hard-faced stranger.

"Isobel said you had not been back to Golden Isle for many years," she ventured.

"No, I have not." His face was stubbornly uncommunicative. His tone warned her to ask nothing further. He turned up the collar of his coat, perhaps to shield himself from the rain, perhaps to hide his expression from her.

"You care so much for your estates and your people. It seems surprising to me…" Lucy faltered. She could hear the nervousness in her own voice. "It's so beautiful here," she added, hoping he could not tell that she was lying and thought it the most godforsaken place on earth.

"Aye, it is." He was staring moodily at the road as it unrolled before them. It was clear he was not going to answer any other part of her comment. She began to feel annoyed. Damn men and their inability to communicate. Or rather damn Robert's deliberate attempts to keep her out. He must know that Isobel had told her about Gregor and the quarrel with his grandfather.

But perhaps the events of the past were too painful for him to broach. She understood that. She had felt that too, after Alice had died. She had folded the pain away deep inside. And grief had no time limits.

She put out a hand and touched his sleeve. She was scared, but she wanted to be brave enough to broach this with him. She wanted him to know she was here by his side in whatever it was he had to face. She felt lonely and alone. She could do with *his* support in her new role as his wife, but one of them had to make the first move. He had been so gentle and patient with her when she had voiced her deepest fears to him. It was hard to understand the change that Golden Isle had brought about in him and to see him become this stern and uncommunicative stranger.

"Sometimes it is hard to go back to a place that holds so many memories," she said carefully. "It helped me to talk to you about Alice. Perhaps if you talked to me—"

"The cases are not the same," Robert said. His tone was as hard as flint. "I do not want to talk about it, madam. Have I not made that plain?"

With an abrupt jerk of the hand, he stopped the cart and jumped down. His gaze, dark blue and brooding, rested on her. "As you have so many talents, I am sure you can drive the trap down the road to the house."

Without another word he leaped over the stone dyke and headed off across the fields and left her sitting there, outraged and utterly infuriated. She was so angry she thought she might just explode like a kettle left boiling too long on the hob.

She was even more bedraggled and furious by the time she had coaxed the recalcitrant pony to start moving again. Clearly it knew where it was going, which was far more than she did. The little trap rolled past a series of crofts by the side of the road. Lucy kept her chin up and nodded and smiled at everyone she saw. They passed a kirk and a school, and the clouds lifted sufficiently for her to see the southern end of the island spread out ahead of her—more high cliffs and rocky buttresses with a lighthouse standing tall. Finally the trap clattered through a gate and into a yard, and a groom ran out to the horse's head. Lucy waited. No one came to help her dismount. By this time if she had had the chance to turn around and head back to the mainland, she would have taken it and damn Robert Methven and his inheritance.

The house was a substantial size, L-shaped and built of stone. It was painted white with the prettiest stepped gables she had ever seen. And now the door had opened and someone was hurrying toward her, a housekeeper, as warm and welcoming as the light that spilled out onto the cobbles behind her. Lucy felt her knees almost buckle with relief.

"Mrs. Stewart," the woman said, curtseying. "Please to come in, my lady, and welcome to the Auld Haa and to Golden Isle. I hear the master has gone over to the village to see the factor."

The master, Lucy realized, was Robert. It seemed everyone knew where he was except her.

But at last she did not care, for the house was warm and dry and there was hot food and a bath and a soft bed beckoning to her. Mrs. Stewart offered to act as maid, but Lucy wanted to be on her own for a little. Mairi had promised to send Sheena to her, but until the maid arrived she would manage. For now she wanted some peace and quiet in a room that did not move up and down and she wanted some time to think.

As she washed away the smell of fish and the weariness of the voyage, she reflected that she had learned plenty about her husband today. She had learned that he could be infinitely tender and patient with her and yet not prepared to expose his own feelings and emotions in the same way. She wondered if he ever would.

She was sitting before her mirror, brushing her hair before she retired to bed, when she heard the front door bang and Robert's voice greeting Mrs. Stewart and then his footsteps on the stairs. Her heart bumped against her ribs. He knocked at the door and came in without waiting for her invitation. Once inside, though, he hesitated, resting his broad shoulders against the frame.

Lucy put the brush down. Otherwise there was a danger she might throw it at him.

"You managed to get the horse to move," he said, with the ghost of a smile.

"By tomorrow I will have trained it to jump and gallop," Lucy said, "and next time you walk away from me like that I will run you down."

His smile grew. "Aye, I do believe you would." He came across to the table. His eyes met hers in the mirror.

"I'm sorry," he said. "I behaved badly. I apologize."

It was a start. And she had already learned there was a time to pursue certain issues, and this was not it. If she tried to get him to talk about Gregor's death and his breach with his family, matters might end badly again. Even so, she was still angry with him and was not prepared to let him off easily. She looked at him straight.

"Thank you." She intended to sound cold and she did. His smile turned rueful.

She dropped her gaze from his—let him take that as a dismissal—and picked up the brush again. But instead of leaving, he took it from her and started to draw it in long, slow strokes through her hair. It felt delicious. She wanted to tell him to stop out of sheer annoyance with him, but the sensation was too good to resist. She fought the urge to close her eyes and revel in the feeling.

Robert's lips brushed the side of her neck. Her eyes flew open and she fixed him with another hard stare. He smiled again and resumed his brushing.

"I hope your chambers are comfortable," Lucy said coolly above the hot beat of her blood.

"I have no idea," Robert said. "I am staying here with you again tonight."

"You are too presumptuous," Lucy said, looking down her nose at him. "I have not invited you to stay with me."

She saw a flicker of amusement in Robert's eyes. "So you want to punish me," he said.

"You deserve it."

"I apologized—"

"Which was good, but not sufficient."

The flare of amusement and heat in his eyes grew brilliant. "What else do you want of me?"

"I have not yet decided," Lucy said.

"Perhaps you could devise something to make me suffer."

Lucy tried to repress the leap in her blood, but it was

too late; he had seen her reaction reflected in her eyes. In a moment he had thrown aside the brush, pulled her to her feet and was kissing her, deep kisses that stole her breath, demanding kisses that made her ache with desire and remembered pleasure.

He tossed her onto the bed and followed her down. It was very soft and yielding and it almost swallowed her up.

"I am still very angry with you," Lucy said, holding him off, her palms against his chest.

"I know." Lust flared in his eyes. "So now you have learned that like wine, anger can give lovemaking an edge that is entirely pleasurable."

He kissed her again and she rolled over so that she was on top of him and he promptly tumbled her beneath him again. Infuriated, she struggled against his dominance and succeeded in climbing on top of him again. Again he tumbled her beneath him. She gave a little squeak of anger and frustration. He kissed her. She bit him. He pinned both her hands above her head and ravaged her mouth.

This time they both shed their clothes urgently, hands bumping. She was trembling inside, eager yet afraid.

"I can't—"

"I know." His voice, his hands, both soothed her, stroking. "Don't be afraid. Don't even think about it."

Despite their quarrel she found it was easy to trust him, in this at least, to give herself up entirely to his touch, his hands and his mouth on her. This time she explored him too, the broad muscles of his back, the slope of his shoulders, the fascinating planes of his stomach and the roughness of his thighs, until he groaned and took her hands from his, pressing her back down on the bed and holding her still while he drove her to impossible heights. Once again she trembled on the edge, then fell so quickly and easily into the dark vortex where nothing existed but the sensations of pleasure and desire. She felt dazzled, almost despairing that he could demand so much from her and she was powerless to resist, yet hungry for the bliss he gave her. He took her limp body and kissed her and she felt herself stir and quicken again for him and she cried out as she came.

Afterward they lay facing each other in the darkness. She was panting.

"That was entirely delightful for me, but for you?"

"It gave me pleasure," Robert said.

She hesitated. "And yet it seemed a little…unfair?"

His laughter was shaken, as though he was in some discomfort. His voice was a harsh whisper. "I admit that I am so hard it would be the work of seconds to please me too."

"Then it seems cruel to deny you." She felt strange, as though she had moved beyond herself, had become someone extraordinarily voluptuous and sensual. Yet she knew now that she had always been this way until fear had locked down her erotic desires and transformed them into something cold and intellectual. Now that wildness, so long repressed, had been released. She realized it was because she felt safe with him. Here in this hot darkness she could indulge any fantasy she chose, knowing he would never force her to take the step to final consummation unless she chose that too.

"I don't want to shock you." His tone was a warning.

"I shock myself." She reached for him, slid her fingers along his length. She had seen plenty of drawings, of course, in those books in her grandfather's collection. None could have prepared her for how hot he felt, or how smooth, like the finest silk, or how hard.

She stroked. He groaned. She closed her hand around him.

"Like this?" She was suddenly afraid of hurting him.

"Too gentle." His voice was strained. His hand closed about hers, showing her. "Harder."

She tried. It felt alien, frightening and yet wonderful to have so much power. Then, remembering the pictures, she wriggled down the bed and took him in her mouth. His muffled curse, the way his body leaped to the touch of her lips and tongue, made her feel even more wickedly wanton and sensual. Now it was no longer a case of him pleasing her. Now she had seen the extent to which she could please him.

He tangled his hand in her hair and gently drew her up to kiss her, hot openmouthed kisses that were fierce and demanding. She reached for him again, stroking, and felt his body convulse and then he fell back still and spent.

It was a while before he spoke. His eyes were closed and his chest rose and fell with his harsh breaths. She hoped she had not damaged him. Inexperience and eagerness might be a fatal combination.

"Where did you learn…" He sounded exhausted.

"My grandfather's collection of French pornography."

He opened his eyes and looked at her. "Of course." A smile twitched his lips. "I forgot. All research and no practical application."

She wriggled down to lie beside him. "Not anymore," she said.

CHAPTER EIGHTEEN

THE CHAIR AT Robert's desk rocked back as he stood up. He strode across the bare wooden floor of the estate office and stood looking out across the rough pasture to the sea. This had been the factor's office from time immemorial, and when he had stepped into it a week before, it felt as though he had never left: the same battered desk, the same view of the south harbor, the same windows coated in salt carried inland on the sea spray, the same smell of damp books and damper boots. The familiarity was comforting, but it disturbed him, as well. He and Gregor had stored their fishing rods in a corner of the office. They had sat together in the window, bored and restless when the weather was bad; they had run out with high spirits down to the beach when the rain had cleared. He could almost hear Gregor's voice carried on the wind:

"Come on, Rob! We'll miss the tide!"

Pulling the little boat into the water and taking the oars together, lying in the springy grass to watch the peregrine falcons hunting above the cliffs, slipping away secretly to join the free traders on their smuggling expeditions… For a moment his chest hurt and he caught his breath. There were ghosts here on Golden Isle and he was still not comfortable with them.

He knew that he had bitten Lucy's head off the previous week when she tried to get him to talk about how he felt. He was ashamed of it. The truth was he had lost the two things most precious to him on Golden Isle, the brother who was his best friend, and the only life he had known. He had rebuilt his life, but he could never replace the brother he had lost, and being on Golden Isle only exacerbated the ache of loss. It constantly reminded him of the past. He wanted to emulate his younger self and take the first boat leaving the harbor, but this time he had to stay and do his duty. So he buried himself in his work day after day to drive away the memories, and the one thing he certainly was not going to do was to rake over old feelings by talking about how he felt.

Robert's factor was watching him, his pale eyes keen in his narrow face. The factor was a man perpetually on edge with nervous tension; he had almost fainted when Robert arrived unannounced at his house on his first night on Golden Isle. McTavish had muttered something about tidying the place up for the laird and had kept Robert standing on the doorstep while he hurried off like a frightened rabbit. Following him in uninvited, Robert had seen him putting various papers on the fire, apparently because he had no kindling.

Mindful of McCall's accusations that the factor was in Cardross's pay, Robert had taken him page by page through the accounts for the last seven years. They made grim reading. As Robert had suspected, the crops had suffered from successive poor summers so that the island could no longer produce sufficient food to support the population, let alone sell the surplus to passing ships. The war had affected trade badly and the press-gangs had taken almost all the able-bodied men. There was hardly anyone but the women and the children left to work in the fields. It was a dire situation.

Robert was well aware that he had neglected Golden Isle shamefully, but the more he scoured the accounts, the less he could see McTavish doing any useful work to protect the estate even though he was being paid good money to do so. In fact, the reverse was true. McTavish had repeatedly sold island produce at less than its market value. He had failed to import vital raw materials. He had, in fact, allowed the islanders' condition to deteriorate slowly but inevitably. It made Robert question where his factor's interests really lay. It seemed that McCall and the other elders' suspicions of him were indeed correct.

"My lord?" the factor said, clearing his throat nervously.

"I will be taking some of the men and repairing the beacons this afternoon," Robert said. He turned back to the room in time to see an expression of alarm crossing McTavish's face.

"The beacons, my lord?" the factor repeated faintly.

"Yes," Robert snapped. "The beacons that are supposed to be used as a warning of danger in times of war. The beacons that you have allowed to fall into disrepair."

The factor paled. "There is no one to do the work, my lord—"

"There is me," Robert said, "and the handful of men whom the press-gang have not yet taken. We will also restore the watchtower on the headland." He reached for quill and ink and drew a sheet of paper toward him. "I am writing to my cousin to send more men from Methven—"

"M-Methven men, my lord?" McTavish's voice was shaking now. "There is surely no need."

"There is every need," Robert said. He sat back and fixed the factor with a narrow gaze. "You have just said yourself that we are short of hands here. If I bring in Methven men we will soon have the island defenses back in place."

He could see that the idea did not appeal to McTavish, and the reason was not far to seek. The factor did not wish the island to be defended, quite the reverse, in fact. His attitude reeked of guilt.

"I have heard reports of a French privateer that has been sighted in the waters near here," Robert continued. "I suspect a raid and in these times of war we need to be vigilant. I am summoning half my clansmen so that we may trap and capture the pirate." He wrote swiftly, his pen scratching across the paper, dusted the letter with sand, folded it and handed it to the factor. "Take this to the mainland, McTavish, and from there arrange for its safe delivery to Methven."

He watched, smiling grimly, as McTavish hurried out of the estate office and down the path to the south harbor, the tails of his coat flapping in the wind. He was certain that the factor would either arrange for the letter to be taken directly to Wilfred Cardross or read it and send Cardross word of the contents. It would take the best part of a week for Cardross to hear the news, longer if he had moved south to Edinburgh, but when he did find out, he would come to Golden Isle as fast as a cat with its tail on fire. Cardross could not afford for his French ally to be captured because the pirate would surely sing like a canary to save his own skin and in the process give away Cardross's treason.

He returned to the desk and wrote a second letter, this one addressed to Jack at Findon.

Start sending the men over as soon as you receive this. I have poked the hornet's nest and want us to be ready and waiting. He added a few more lines, signed and sealed it. Stuart McCall could take it to the mainland once McTavish was on his way.

Robert threw himself down in his chair. All they had to do now was wait.

"EVERYONE SAYS THAT Lord Methven hates Golden Isle," Sheena commented the following morning, as she helped Lucy to dress. "After his brother's death he never set foot here again and neither did his grandsire. Everyone says that they left the place to rot. It is as though he blames the island for his brother's death and the people suffer for it."

Lucy sighed. Sheena had only been on Golden Isle for a week and already she was gathering gossip like a magpie gathering shiny dross. Each morning she repeated to Lucy what she had learned the previous day, and each morning Lucy struggled not to feel cast down by her maid's words. It was clear to her that Sheena was right. Yet she knew Robert was hurting. She could feel it in him, but he was not willing to share his feelings in order to lessen the pain.

She could not fault Robert's devotion to the estate since their arrival. He spent the best part of each day with McTavish going over the accounts and discussing payment for this year's yield of crops, fish and feathers, or walking the island to talk to all the crofters, from the peat cutters on the northern hills to the men who worked the mills on the burn, to the fishermen in the south harbor. Over breakfast he would discuss with Lucy his plans for the day, but he never invited her to join him. Over dinner he would tell her about his work on the estate. Afterward they would sit in the parlor and share a malt whisky, and Lucy would play on the ancient piano. It was pleasant and domesticated, but at the same time Lucy felt excluded.

In contrast the nights were so different, bright with intimacy and hot, wicked addictive pleasure. Step by delicious step Robert was leading her to the ultimate consummation, and a part of her longed for it. Yet at the same time Lucy was finding the gulf between the days and the nights increasingly difficult to deal with, as though she were wed to two very different men, the one silent and withdrawn and the other a man she trusted with her body and would trust with her life.

"Mrs. Stewart is quite a talker," Sheena said. "She tells me everything. She's lonely, poor lady. She used to be housekeeper at Methven but fell out with the old laird and he sent her here. I'd run mad being marooned on a place like this." She looked toward the window, where the mist pressed close as a shroud. "Golden Isle? Gloomy Isle is more fitting."

"I've seen the sun," Lucy said. "It came out once last week and the island looked beautiful. I think the mist will lift today."

Sheena snorted in disbelief. She finished threading the ribbon through Lucy's hair and stood back to admire her work. "There. That looks pretty. Let's hope Lord Methven notices. He does not strike me as a noticing man, not where it matters."

Lucy looked sharply at her maid's reflection in the mirror, but Sheena's face was averted and she was busying herself picking up the spare pins and tidying the top of the dressing table. Lucy wondered suddenly if the maid deliberately set out to hurt her. These little barbs, planting doubt and sowing unhappiness, were becoming more frequent. Yet it seemed an absurd idea; Sheena had cared for her since she was a child. She had been a servant at Forres forever and was utterly loyal.

"What will you do today, madam?" the maid said.

"I don't know," Lucy said. Suddenly she felt lonely. "I have no idea."

The Auld Haa was too small a house to require much

in the way of running, and what was needed Mrs. Stewart did anyway. Lucy was hardly going to make the poor woman's situation more miserable by taking over her duties. Nor was she going to sit at home waiting for visitors, or going out to pay house calls. Society on the island was very limited; the wives of the two lighthouse keepers had called the previous day, one, Mrs. Hall, very genteel and reserved, the other, Mrs. Campion, very opinionated with a loud laugh, both united in disparaging the islanders as barbarians. Mrs. Campion had coyly suggested hosting a dinner for Robert and Lucy and inviting the schoolmaster and the parson. These, she implied, were the only islanders of sufficient social standing to be worthy of an invitation. The merchants who owned the booths down by the harbor were very poor and beneath her notice. Besides, they were foreigners, Norwegians, whom she considered beyond the pale. Lucy found her snobbery unbearable. She had not invited the ladies back.

She could take up her writing, of course, but suddenly the *Lady's Guide to Finding the Perfect Gentleman* seemed both uninspiring and downright irrelevant. Perhaps, though, she could make some inquiries into the history of the Golden Isle. She felt a faint stirring of interest. She had heard some stories from Mrs. Stewart, who was indeed as talkative as Sheena said, tales of gold from an Armada shipwreck as well as stories of the Vikings who had been the ancestors of the islanders. Their warning beacon still stood on the hill behind the Auld Haa, and the south harbor still held the cuts where their longboats had rested.

"Will you go out with Lord Methven today?" Sheena persisted.

"I doubt it," Lucy said shortly, and thought she saw a faint smile on her maid's lips before she turned away to fold the nightclothes into the drawers.

"May I come with you today?" she asked Robert spontaneously as they sat in the breakfast parlor with the scent of fresh coffee in the air and the bright sunshine breaking through the mist to pattern the wainscot. "It is a beautiful day and I should like to see more of the island."

Robert put down his cup with a sharp clatter. "I shall be working on rebuilding the beacons today," he said. He got up and went out, leaving Lucy feeling hurt at the rebuff.

She had had enough. She saddled up one of the sturdy little ponies from the paddock and went out riding. There were no sidesaddles and she was obliged to ride astride, which meant she had to borrow some breeches from Mrs. Stewart's nephew. She soon discovered the pony was a feisty little creature with a mind of its own, bigger than a Shetland pony but twice as bad tempered. They had a short sharp battle over which of them was in control and then the pony settled down as docile as Lucy could have asked.

In the following few days she rode all over the island, exploring from the heather-strewn cliffs of the north to the softer green fields of the south. The crofters waved as she passed by; on the second day one of them offered her a drink of milk to refresh her on such a hot afternoon. On the third day she was invited into one of the croft houses and offered griddled oatcakes as well as milk. After four days the island women decided it was time to try and teach her to spin. She was hopeless at it and just listened to their chatter as they spun, learning about life on the island. At first the women had been reticent in front of her, looking at her sideways, wary and unsure what to make of her. Lucy understood their reticence and perhaps they began to understand that she was lonely because after they had all laughed over her woeful efforts at knitting, they sat down to tea and all differences of background were forgotten.

"I hear you have been out riding," Robert said over dinner one night. He had come in late and walked straight into the paneled dining room in his mud-splashed boots, his shirtsleeves rolled up to the elbow.

"That's right," Lucy said. "Would you care to join me one day?"

"I have too much work to do."

Something snapped within Lucy. She pushed away her bowl of vegetable broth and stood up.

"You are behaving like a spoiled child," she said. His rejection stung; inside she felt shriveled with dismay that she was trying to reach him and he kept pushing her away.

He fixed her with his hard, direct blue gaze. It was intimidating, but she was determined not to allow it to silence her.

"I know you do not like it here," she said precisely. "I understand that it is painful for you because of Gregor's death and your quarrel with your grandfather—"

Something so vivid and elemental flashed in his eyes then that she stopped instinctively. There had been grief there; she had felt it like the burn of a flame. Yet Robert did not speak and with a sinking heart she saw him lock down his emotions even harder, the frown pulling down his brow, his jaw tightening like a steel trap.

"I know you do not want to talk about it." She plowed doggedly on. She had started this—again, and against her better judgment—and this time she would have her say.

"No, I do not want to talk about it." The quietness in his tone was terrifying, as was the controlled stillness that hung about him like a cloak.

"But I am only trying to help you."

"I do not require your help." Each word was bitten off.

"And I do not wish to be married to so miserable and dour a husband." She flung down the napkin that she was still holding. It landed with a slap, trailing in the broth. She stalked to the door, hoping that he would call her back, apologize, say something, anything. But he said nothing.

"Don't come to my bed tonight," Lucy said, over her shoulder. "I am your wife, not your mistress, and I won't be ignored during the daytime and only found use for at night."

Up in her bedroom, she curled up on the window

seat and looked out over the fields to the sea. Tonight the moon was full and bright and it bathed the island in a golden light, rippling over the water and gilding the land. For once the island looked peaceful and lived up to its name.

The candle flame was burning down and she was cold. She had not heard Robert come upstairs. She was not sure what she would do if he did come to her. She felt bruised and disappointed that he rejected every attempt she made to reach him. He had shown her such tenderness; it was the hardest lesson to learn that his gentleness with her did not mean that he wanted to share an emotional as well as a physical closeness.

She heard a sound below, the scrape of leather on stone, the creak of the gate. The moon cast the long shadow of a man across the wall. She could see from the way he moved that it was Robert.

She was curious. By now she had heard so many stories about Golden Isle, the legends, the shipwrecks, the free trading. On a night like this it was easy to believe in ghosts and myths. She slid from the seat, grabbing her little half boots, sliding her feet into them. Her cloak was warm and it was, fortunately, not a cold night. The stair creaked as she tiptoed down, but no one came. Mrs. Stewart and the other servants had rooms in the west wing. She opened the door and felt the cool breeze nip at her skin. She could just see Robert's figure heading away across the field toward the cliffs. She followed.

CHAPTER NINETEEN

WILFRED CARDROSS WAS drunk when the messenger came into the hall, dusty and mud spattered, two letters clutched in his hand.

"Urgent messages from Golden Isle, my lord," he said, and backed out quickly before Cardross's boot could speed him on his way.

Cardross tipped the blowsy serving wench off his lap—she was someone from the kitchens, he had no idea whom, and she had been rather inexpertly trying to arouse his lust, but he was too bored and too drunk to be interested. He reached for his wineglass first, spattering drops over the letters, tilted it to his lips and drank greedily.

"Fetch me more," he said to the indignant girl, slamming his glass down on the table with a force that made the crystal shiver.

"Hope it chokes you," the wench said viciously, under her breath as she headed off back to the kitchens.

Cardross ignored her. He opened the first of the letters, tearing it a little in his careless haste. As expected, it was covered in McTavish's writing. Cardross read a few words and threw the letter down on the table in disgust. McTavish was as nervous as an old woman, rambling about warning beacons and Methven's suspicions of a French raid. The French pirate, Le Boucanier, would never show himself if there was any chance of capture. And while Le Boucanier was free, Cardross knew his own secrets were safe.

Yet even as he tried to reassure himself, a sliver of doubt wedged itself in the earl's gut and started to gnaw at him. Supposing, just supposing, Methven was clever enough to trap the French privateer. Le Boucanier would very likely trade his own freedom in return for information on the Scottish nobleman who was treasonably selling his country's secrets to the enemy. Cardross glowered into his wineglass. Could he take the risk?

Then another line in the letter caught his eye.

"Methven is sending for half his clansmen from his western estates to mend the beacons and defend the isle..."

Cardross paused. How entertaining it would be, he thought suddenly, if the press-gang should take all those Methven men and impress them into the Royal Navy. Then not only would the marquis lose half his clansmen and plunge his other estates into hardship and ruin, but Cardross could also claim the reward for leading the recruiting officers to such a rich prize. The more he thought about it, the more he liked the idea, and the more he liked the idea, the more he wanted to be there to see Methven's anger and despair on losing those clansmen he had tried so hard to protect.

Cardross laughed, slopping the last of the wine into

his mouth. Some of it splashed onto the table and he cursed aloud. He shouted for his steward to bring him pen and ink. He would write immediately to Wilson and Scott, the northern recruiting officers, and have them sail to Golden Isle to take the Methven men. Greed, like a canker, ate into him, and it felt sharp. He would sail too; Wilson in particular was a brutal and corrupt individual who would cheat him of his blood money if given half a chance. And once the Methven men were taken and Robert Methven had retreated south to lick his wounds, he would be able to take up once again the lucrative business of free trading and of passing information to the French. He could not lose.

The earl was so taken with his idea that he almost forgot the second letter lying unopened on the table. Snatching it up, he unfolded it and scanned the few lines, first with impatience, then with a quickening interest. When he had finished he paused, tapping the paper against the table edge, a smile on his lips. His spy in Lady Methven's household had come through with a ripe piece of news. His smile grew as he thought about it.

Robert Methven would not meet the terms of his inheritance. There would be no heir.

Now he would most certainly go to Golden Isle to witness the downfall of his rival. In fact, he would go so that he could inform the marquis in person of his wife's betrayal and enjoy Methven's shock upon receipt of the news.

His steward had not appeared. Neither had the girl

with his wine. Cursing them both, Cardross staggered to his feet and set off to make preparations for his voyage north.

IT WAS THE ghosts that had finally driven Robert out of the house. He had sat for a long time after Lucy had gone, eating nothing, aware of nothing but the frustration that was locked tight inside him. Eventually he had gone down to the sea, to the bay where he and Gregor had gone so many times as children. He had loved Golden Isle then. It had been special, Gregor's kingdom. He had never once thought that would change.

Then Gregor had died and he had hated Golden Isle for taking his brother from him, hated it as much as he had loved it before. He realized that he and Lucy shared that common thread. They had both lost a sibling who had been so dear to them that the loss haunted them still.

The night air was soft and gentle, as was the hush of the tide on the sand. Robert sat on one of the rocks that commanded the shore and felt the cold granite rough against his palms. On the high cliffs above was the Devil's Bridge, where Gregor had fallen. No one could explain it. Gregor and he had both been as sure-footed as mountain goats; the cliffs held no fear for them. Yet on that day, Gregor had gone over the Devil's Bridge to try to save one of the boys who had got into difficulties climbing down the cliff face for the gannets' eggs. The lad had survived, but in trying to help him Gregor had fallen from the bridge and had died.

Robert sighed. He knew he had to go back to the Auld Haa and find Lucy. He had to apologize—again—for his dourness. He had to stop running. Lucy had been much braver than he; she had trusted him with her fears while he had withheld his from her.

He stood up. Tonight was such a calm night. The moon patterned the shifting sea with silver. It felt peaceful.

Then he saw Lucy. She was standing on the other side of the Devil's Bridge. At first he thought she was a ghost conjured by his memories. Then, with a clutch of fear that nailed him to the spot, he realized she was not. It really was Lucy and as he looked she started to walk across the narrow arch of the cliff toward him.

He heard the rattle and tumble of stones as they fell from the arch into the chasm below.

Pure cold fear pierced him and held him still.

She is going to fall.

He was running, stumbling over the tussocks of grass toward her, half falling, swearing, until he collided with her and clutched her to him, snatching her away from the edge of the cliff and those dark, dangerous rocks, feeling her warm and real in his arms, even as he panted with exertion and dread.

"Robert?" She did not even sound out of breath. "I came to find you. I was worried—"

"You little idiot! You stupid, foolish, crazy—" He realized that he wanted to shake her. The violence in him was vast, spawned by utter terror. He was trembling. He could not speak. Then the relief swamped everything and he held her cruelly tightly, his face against her neck, feeling her warmth and hearing her breath.

"Oh," she said, and there was a revelation in her tone. Then more quietly: "Oh."

"I thought I was going to lose you," Robert said. He could feel himself shaking. He had to make a huge effort to loosen his grip on her. "I love you so much and I thought Golden Isle was going to take you from me too."

He did not know where the words had come from. He only knew that they were true. His complex emotions had turned out to be fairly simple after all. He had named them lust, tenderness, admiration, anything other than love.

Lucy cupped his cheek in her palm and held him as fiercely as he held her, and he felt the emotion crash through him as powerful as the tide and as irresistible. He pulled her down onto the soft, springy turf, a deliciously comfortable bed, and she came easily into his arms and he pushed the cloak from her shoulders and found beneath it just her nightgown, shredded by the sharp rocks where she must have scaled a couple of the field walls. He ripped the remaining shreds from her and felt her shiver. The little half boots he found ridiculously erotic and did not remove. Her naked body was pale and golden in the moonlight and when he kissed her she kissed him back, hungrily, fiercely, sliding her hands over his back, pulling him closer. There was no hesitation in her and no doubt, and he knew the waiting was over. He was hit by such a wave of possessive desire that for a moment he could not breathe.

He cupped her face in his hands, feeling her hair silken soft against his palms.

"I don't want to hurt you." He was afraid of the force of his need for her.

"You won't." She strained up to kiss him, her breasts brushing his chest. "Please, Robert. I want this. I love you too."

His hands were shaking as he loosened his pantaloons. He parted her thighs and slid into her, trying to be careful of her even in the midst of his raging need for her, and felt her jerk with the discomfort of his entry. He heard her breath catch. Her eyes opened. She looked bemused, on the edge of losing that lovely sensual pleasure.

"I'm sorry," he whispered. "In a moment it will ease."

She nodded. "Don't stop," she whispered. "Please don't stop now."

Robert held himself still against the need to plunge into her, claim her wholly, and kissed her again, putting all his love and longing into that kiss. He felt her body start to soften again and open to him, and he started to move, a gentle slide, holding himself under absolute control even as the hot, slick clasp of her threatened every thread of restraint he possessed. He heard her sigh and she reached for him, pulling him deeper within her, and it was glorious, and she tilted her hips up to meet his thrusts and he was lost. He felt himself tip over the edge and fall, hard and fast. The physical release was astonishing, blinding in its brilliance, sharp enough to make him groan. Beneath that pleasure was another sensation, a need fulfilled, a claiming, a coming home.

He wrapped Lucy in the red cloak and carried her back to the house and took her up to his bed. He wanted to make love to her again, but he knew she would be sore after this first time, so he contented himself with holding her and it was frighteningly good, the possessive desire submerged now in other emotions so powerful and deep that he was shaken. It gave him a deep peace to hold her. It reminded him how much he loved and needed her, but with that love came the edge of fear. Somehow he was going to have to learn to live with that fear because if he had his way he would never let her out of his sight again, and that, he could see, would be most inconvenient.

"Robert?"

She was awake. She reached out a hand to him and touched his cheek as she had done earlier, and once again he felt a shockingly strong pang of tenderness and need.

"I'm sorry I didn't talk to you before," he said. He felt humbled, different. He moved his head against the pillow and instead of the restless frustration that had driven him before he felt peace. "I was trying to ignore how much I hated being on Golden Isle by burying myself in the work and refusing to discuss it."

Lucy was lying beside him, her head supported on

one hand as she watched him, her hair falling over her bare shoulders.

"It is no wonder you hate it here," she said softly. "Your brother died, Robert. It is where a part of your life ended."

Robert put out and hand and drew her down to rest against his chest. "And now it is where another part of my life begins," he said. "My future with you."

LUCY WOKE SLOWLY, in the dawn. She lay still for a moment. She was warm and there was a hum in her blood that felt like contentment. Something nagged at the corner of her mind, like a thought, like a shadow. Then she remembered.

Tonight there had been no nightmares.

She thought about what had happened. She had given herself to Robert with no thought of refusal, no thought of anything other than meeting his need with her own. He had reached out to her completely and she had wanted him too, loved him too.

She felt a tiny stirring of fear. It whispered across her mind, then faded away. She waited for it to return and to grow into the monster that always stalked her. She waited for the darkness to come. Instead there was nothing. The bed was warm and deep; she felt serene and content. She yawned.

She could be pregnant. Deliberately now she tested her feelings. She forced herself to face the harshest fear. Again she felt a faint stirring of disquiet, but it smoothed away like the sea washing away footprints in the sand. She thought that perhaps she would always feel the fear a little—it was foolish to imagine that it would ever go away completely—but that somehow it had lost its power.

Rolling over, she looked at Robert. He was still asleep. He looked very peaceful, the harsh lines smoothed from his face. The stubble darkened his chin and his cheek. Lucy paused. Behind the man she could see the shadow of the boy he had been when tragedy struck so hard. She hoped that his hatred of Golden Isle had gone now.

She had known that he loved her. She had seen it in his eyes and felt it in his touch when he had held her with such ferocity and gentleness out on the cliffs. She had known that his fury could have sprung from no other cause. And she loved him too, for his strength and determination to do his best for his clan, for his loyalty, for his patience and his tenderness with her.

"Lucy."

He was smiling at her. He reached out and traced the line of her shoulder and arm, taking her wrist and turning it over to press a kiss against her palm.

"How are you, sweetheart?"

She could see the shadow of doubt in his eyes. He was afraid that she would be regretting what had happened, that the night had plunged her back into the darkness of her fear.

"I am very well," she said honestly.

"You are certain?" His gaze was very keen on her face.

There seemed only one way to reassure him. She leaned down and kissed him. When she drew back, the light in his eyes had sharpened from tender to something a great deal more heated and intense. She looked at him as the blue morning light illuminated every strong plane of his face, the hard, exciting line of his mouth, his jaw, his cheek. He was watching her, and his gaze was very intent and very blue. She knew he was waiting for her to decide what she wanted. Last night had been impulsive, in the heat of the moment. Now he wanted her to choose.

Her heart crashed against her ribs. She felt excitement hollow in the pit of her stomach and steal her breath. She knew what she wanted.

They looked at each other for another long, long moment and then Robert tumbled her beneath him. It felt impossibly urgent and desperate and yet at the same time so pure and intense. Robert's mouth was hot as a brand on Lucy's throat. She reached for him, careless of anything but sensation and need. His hand came up to her breast, teasing, toying with her, stroking up the underside in a way that made her shiver. She had already learned the vast, generous capacity of her body to enjoy its pleasure, and now she wanted to let go completely. It was the first time that she had felt utterly free of shadow.

She tilted her head back and Robert tangled one hand in her hair, arching her breasts up to his mouth, and when he took her nipple in his mouth she sighed and felt the melting heat take her, softening her and making her eager for him all over again. His hand stroked between her legs, his mouth tugged at her breast, she felt deliciously wanton as he played her body and slowly, inexorably, drove her toward mindless pleasure. It was delicious, well nigh irresistible, and yet a corner of her mind rebelled. He was not to have it all his own way.

Quick as a flash she slid from beneath him. The shifting of weight on the mattress threw him off balance and he rolled over. Lucy shifted, moving to sit astride him, her hands spread wide and grasping the high wooden bed head, sinking down so that he impaled her. He was as hard as a rock.

His gasp of shock and pleasure was a reward in itself. She started to move, easing herself up and back down, the sleek friction, the sense of control, giving her a rush of triumphant power. She could feel every muscle in his body clenched so tense with the frustration of not being in command. She leaned forward and kissed him softly, tasting him, then drawing back. She brushed her breasts against his chest. She enjoyed his moan.

"Lucy…" His voice was a harsh whisper.

"Yes?" She paused and he threw his head back, the line of his neck taut.

"Don't stop."

She gripped him tightly. "Do you like it like this?" She raised herself on him, then slid down deep. "Or like this?"

"Minx." The word was wrenched from him.

One final slide and he gave a groan and caught her around the waist, tumbling her beneath him. The mattress dipped and groaned as he plunged into her. Lucy arched to meet each thrust. The hot pleasure gripped her, irresistibly sharp, irresistibly sweet. She came at once, tumbling over the edge, the clasp of her body quickening Robert's as he emptied himself into her with a shout. They lay in a hot, tangled knot of pleasure and release.

"Damn it," Robert said, when his breathing had settled sufficiently that he could speak. "I wanted it to be slow and gentle this time."

"Maybe next time," Lucy said.

Robert threw the bedclothes over them both and drew her close into the crook of his arm, but Lucy felt too restless and awake to settle. She felt drunk with the sheer physical pleasure of sex, the relief, the release. She wriggled out of his arms and went across to the window, kneeling on the tapestry seat and staring out over the garden to the sea.

"How beautiful it looks so early in the morning," she said. "So peaceful."

"Come back to bed," Robert said. He was propped up on one elbow, watching her, darkness and shadows and lust in his eyes. It sent an answering spike of lust through her. Wickedness gripped her, the sort of wicked she had never allowed herself to be before. It unfurled in her like the purest temptation. For so many years she had denied her physical needs. Now she felt an almost desperate hunger to make up for lost time.

"No," she said. She let the curtain fall open so that

the pale daylight illuminated her naked body. "If you want me, come and get me."

She saw his eyes widen. He did not need to be invited twice. With a roar he leaped from the bed, reaching for her, but Lucy was too quick for him. She flung open the bedroom door and was away down the stair, her bare feet pattering on the wood. She could feel him close behind her. She dashed into the dining room, ran around the table, making the china clatter, and out again, then into the parlor, where Robert caught her from behind. His arm was across her bare stomach and his body was hot at her back. He was panting. She could feel he had the most monstrous erection again. She rubbed herself against it and felt him give a growl low in his throat.

"Damn it, woman," he said. "You're insatiable."

Lucy giggled, feeling deliciously wanton. "Can you not deal with me, my lord?" she murmured provocatively. "Too old? Too tired?"

In response he pushed her forward so that she was leaning over the rickety old piano, her breasts pressed against the cold shiny wood, palms flat on the top. She felt his fingers at her slick opening, then his cock.

"I have always said that you are so talented with this instrument." He slid into her and she gasped at the invasion. He felt so big and this was so new and different, the sensations deeper and fiercer, the need in her all the wilder for it. She pushed back against him, feeling the cold slide of the wood against her breasts, back and forth, and the push of him deeper still as he drove into her. He held her hips and took her in hard thrusts that had her gasping. The piano strings quivered and resonated to each jerk of her body, a cacophony of tumbling sound that built and built. Robert's thrusts were inexorable, pushing her deep into ecstasy. She came in a blind spiral of rushing darkness, wanting to take him with her, but he drew back.

"I can wait," he murmured.

She thought he would release her then, but he was relentless. He took up the rhythm again, catching her around the waist, holding her body still for his plunder. It was sublime, glorious. She clung to the smooth wood, bracing herself as he rocked deeply inside her, meeting each thrust as he drove her closer again, lifted her higher. She loved the sheer carnality of it, the way her breasts jolted with each plunge of him inside her, the stretch and clench of her belly, the utter wanton physicality of it. It was another revelation, pure lust, blazing and flagrant in its demand.

Her orgasm caught her sharply, raking through her, making her shake. She heard Robert shout and felt him spill himself deep inside her, the final lunge of his body catching her again and sending her spinning into bliss beyond ecstasy. She slumped into his arms, the echo of that same ecstasy still resonating through her.

She was shaking, her legs unsteady, and he picked her up and carried her across to one of the armchairs, where he sat down with her on his lap and started to kiss her again, sweet and gentle, the corner of her mouth, the line of her jaw, the hollow of her collarbone. She snuggled close and breathed in the scent of his skin, the heat and the sweat and the faint sandalwood soap smell that made her head spin in slow circles.

"The Highland Ladies Bluestocking Society did not teach us to use a piano thus," she said, pressing kisses against his chest. Her palm was splayed over his heart and she felt the rumble of his laugh deep in his chest.

"I'm exhausted," she murmured.

"It serves you right." Robert brushed the tangled hair away from her face and kissed her gently, his lips lingering on hers now with tenderness.

"You're cold." His touch was warm on her chilled skin as he picked her up and carried her back up the stairs to their bedroom. "Let me warm you."

He laid her on the bed and slid in beside her, drawing the covers over them both. Lucy could feel the aching tiredness in her body that was the aftermath of sheer pleasure.

"I love you." She kissed him.

She did not awaken again until the room was bathed in high sunlight. Robert was dragging on his shirt and cursing that he was going to be late for a meeting with the harbormaster. As he came back to the bed to kiss Lucy with lingering passion, she saw Sheena slip into the room with her breakfast tray. She felt almost too decadently exhausted to eat and drink.

Sheena was picking up her nightgown and indicating by silence and delicately raised eyebrows that she had noted the tumbled state of the bedclothes and Lucy's air of dishevelment. The maid placed the tray on the nightstand and walked over to the Armada chest, rummaging around in its depths.

"You'll be wanting this," she said. "I noticed you hadn't been taking it. That's foolhardy and dangerous, if you'll pardon me, madam. You must have known this would happen."

Lucy looked up from her cup of hot chocolate. Sheena was holding in her hand a little pot. At first Lucy did not recognize it, but then she remembered with a queer jump of the heart the tincture of penny-royal.

She remembered that frightened girl, haunted by the past, and felt a huge pang of compassion for her.

"Actually," she said, "I don't want it. I don't need it. I'm not afraid anymore." And she felt a surge of excitement and happiness wash through her.

Sheena's eyes had opened very wide. "But, madam," she said, "you can't take such a risk! You must have it!" There was a note of panic in her voice as she held the pot out to Lucy. "I'll get you another tincture," she said rapidly. "In case you are already enceinte. No one would know." Then, pleadingly, "It wouldn't be safe for you to have a child, madam. Think of what happened to your sister! Please listen to me—"

"No," Lucy said firmly. She got up and took Sheena by the arm, drawing her over to sit down on the bed. The maid's face was crumpled as though she was about to cry. She was shaking. Lucy felt shocked; she had had no idea that Sheena too had been plagued by the fear that she might lose her mistress, but the maid had been nurse to both herself and Alice. It made perfect sense.

"Sheena," Lucy said gently. "I understand that you want to protect me. You've done so since I was a baby. But there is nothing to fear. I promise you."

It was clear to her that Sheena did not want to talk about it anymore. The maid's expression was stony, her lips set in a tight line.

"Very well, madam," she said. "We'll speak of it no more." She grabbed the tray and started to tidy away Lucy's chocolate cup despite the fact that the drink was only half-finished. Lucy grabbed a piece of toast before Sheena whisked herself and the tray around the door.

Later, when she was dressed, Lucy picked up the little pot of pennyroyal and slipped it into the pocket of her cloak. She walked down to the cliffs, feeling the tug of the breeze on her cloak and the first warmth of the sun. She stood on the edge and threw the pot over. She hurled it as far and with as much force as she could, and heard it bounce off the rocks below, before the wash of the sea swept in to take it away.

It felt good.

The sun was strengthening in a blaze of gold. Lucy stood with her face upturned to it. For a moment on the breeze she thought she could hear Alice's voice and Alice's laughter. The sound no longer haunted her through the dark. There were no more waking night-mares, only the memory of Alice dancing in the sunlight. She could feel Alice's presence beside her still but it was a gentle ghost now.

Lucy opened her heart and let her memories of her sister fly free.

CHAPTER TWENTY

LUCY WANDERED ALONG the beach, taking off her shoes and stockings and feeling the sand cool and damp between her toes. It was odd how she felt every tiny physical sensation these days; she was aware of scents as never before and noticed every taste and touch as though it were new. It was such a change from her previous life where she had lived in books and in her rational mind. Now she still loved her reading and her writing, but her life had the dimension of the senses, as well. She felt as though she had come alive.

The previous week had been perfect. The sun had shone and Golden Isle had lived up to its name. Robert had been persuaded to take some time away from his work rebuilding the estate and had joined her for a picnic at Golden Water, the tiny loch that gave the island its name. They had ridden together over the high hills and bathed in the sea. Even now, as summer was coming to these northern islands, the seawater was so cold it was shocking, but there was one protected cove where the pools were warmed by the sun. Lucy smiled now as she remembered pulling off her clothes and plunging into the green depths of the water completely naked. It had been a memorable afternoon.

And they had talked. As they lay in bed one night Robert had told her how his grandmother had been the only member of his family who had continued to write to him, in defiance of her husband, during his years in Canada.

"She will like you very much," he predicted, as he pressed kisses against the soft skin of Lucy's throat and down to the hollow between her breasts. "When my work is done here I shall be proud to take you to Methven."

Lucy had wondered then about that work. She had seen the boats to Findon coming and going increasingly frequently, bringing men and materials to Golden Isle. McTavish had been dismissed and Jack Rutherford had come from Methven to deal with the accounts, so Robert said. Lucy was certain that something else was going on, but when she asked Robert he told her that he was merely strengthening the defenses against the French privateers that had been seen in northern waters. Jack, urbane and charming, said the same. Yet still Lucy wondered.

The wind was cool on her face. Evening was falling and the shadows were lengthening. She wrapped her shawl more tightly about her shoulders and walked a little more quickly back toward the harbor. Ahead of her she could see a group of the island women and children scavenging over the rocks, collecting driftwood. So few trees grew on Golden Isle that timber was always very highly prized.

The tide was coming in, sucking at Lucy's bare feet,

the chill sting of the water making her shiver a little. The water splashed her dress and petticoat, splashed too on the rocks where the children were playing in and out of the pools. Their calls and cries reached Lucy on the stiff breeze. It felt peaceful and yet for some reason she also felt a premonition she could not shake. Something was wrong.

As she reached the quay she saw that Robert was there, and Jack. She felt the little lift of her heart that she always felt now on seeing her husband. She hurried her steps toward the harbor, but she had no time to call out a greeting. A strange hush had fallen over the crowd on the quay and they had turned out to sea where the sun was dropping into the water in a big ball of fire. In front of it, black against the fiery red, was a ship.

"The navy," someone murmured, and then the whisper ran around like wind through corn. "The press-gang...the gangers are here."

In the same moment someone turned and pointed away to the south where on the headland a beacon was flaring into life. "Attack! The village is under attack!"

Lucy felt the ripple of something go through Robert like lightning. "Cardross," he said. "He's come and he has brought the press-gang with him."

Lucy could feel the terror and the hatred in the crowd like a living thing. They had seen this before, witnessed the destruction of their lives. Robert grabbed her hands. "Get to the Auld Haa," he said. "Lock yourself in and come out for no man." He kissed her. "I'll come to you as soon as I can."

"No," Lucy said. Her repudiation was immediate. "I want to help, Robert." She turned and waved a hand toward the women and children in a ragged huddle on the quay. "Let me look after them. If Wilfred comes, then I can take care of myself. I'll cut him down with a broadsword."

A flicker of a smile lit Robert's tense face. "I know you could do that," he said, "but I can't let you. It's too dangerous." He pulled her to him and she felt the thunder of his heart against hers and the quick, impatient need in him to be away to defend his island. "You cannot risk your life, Lucy," he said. "This isn't just for me, though God knows I would do everything in my power to keep you safe. It's for Methven."

Lucy understood then. He was talking about the future, the promise of the heir she could even now be carrying. She felt terribly torn, wanting desperately to help, hating the thought of waiting helplessly for events to unfold, yet understanding how important it was to Robert, to the entire Methven clan, that she should be safe.

"Damn Wilfred," she said unsteadily. "You must go, Robert. Stop him." She threw a glance over her shoulder to where the gangers' longboat was making its steady way ashore. "I know you won't let them take any more men," she said, "but be careful. The gangers answer to no laws and respect no man."

Robert gave her another hard kiss that for all its brevity shook her to her soul.

"Come back to me," she whispered. "It takes two

of us to make an heir for Methven." She drew back a little. "Besides, I love you and have no desire to be a widow quite yet."

"I love you too," Robert said. He kissed her again, longer, deeper, before releasing her and turning away to where the men waited for him.

Lucy walked slowly up the road to the Auld Haa in the gathering twilight. When she reached the gate, though, she hesitated. Ahead of her the road wound uphill toward the northern beacon. It had not been lit, which meant that no one had warned the crofters to the north of the island that they were in danger of attack. Again the sense of premonition tickled down Lucy's neck. Wilfred had set fire to the crofts in the south. The press-gang were sweeping in from the west. But what if there was another attack here, on the vulnerable, unprotected crofts to the north? Golden Isle was riven with inlets and coves. Men could come ashore in any number of places and spring an attack before anyone had guessed.

Grabbing the smoldering torch that lit the entrance to the Auld Haa, Lucy hurried up the track toward the beacon a few hundred yards ahead. The stony track slipped beneath the soles of her shoes. Away to her left, Golden Water shimmered in the last of the setting sun. The cold wind breathed gooseflesh down her spine. She felt as though someone was watching her. She thrust the torch into the heart of the kindling and turned back to the road, relief in her heart.

"Not so fast, cousin."

Wilfred Cardross was standing directly in front of her, no more than a black shadow against the cobalt blue of the night dark sea. Behind him were five of his clansmen. Lucy could hear the beacon fire hiss and spit as it roared higher. At least it was too late for Wilfred to douse it now, and soon it would be seen from the crofts. They would know to rally their defenses.

Wilfred was walking slowly toward her. She could see his face now in the livid light of the flames. He was dressed in all his finery, foppish laces and bows, but the expression in his eyes was feral, a contrast to the refined elegance of his attire. Lucy's heart thumped. She raised her chin defiantly and met his eyes.

"Wilfred," she said. "I see you have brought more men this time. How wise of you."

"Cousin Lucy," Wilfred swept her a bow. "How charming to find you here. I do thank you for saving me the trouble of coming to look for you."

He gestured with his head and the clansmen moved forward. Their expressions were hungry. Lucy felt the fear claw at her throat and beat it back.

"How neglectful of Methven to leave you to fend for yourself," Wilfred said contentedly. "He should have been more careful in protecting his property."

"My husband," Lucy said, "is protecting his clan, a concept I believe you are unfamiliar with, Wilfred. You steal from yours, don't you? Rob them and steal their cattle and burn their houses?"

Cardross laughed. He was looking to the south where a line of fire now marked the devastation his men were wreaking on the island. "There is precious little left to protect here," he said. "The press-gang will take the remaining islanders and all the Methven men, as well." His gaze came back to fasten on her. "And when I take you, that will be the end."

He came a step closer. Lucy could see his face in the firelight. He was smiling. He was enjoying this. She backed against the rough stone of the beacon wall, groping for the handle of the torch she had brought with her. Her fingers grazed the stone, felt the lick of the heat. At all costs she had to keep Wilfred from guessing what she was about. He thought she was not armed; she did not want to give away the element of surprise.

"What's the matter?" she said contemptuously. "Are you afraid I will push you over if you come too close, Wilfred?"

Wilfred raised his sword point and touched her beneath the chin. Lucy felt the prick of the blade against her throat.

"I'm not afraid of you," Wilfred said. "Nor of your laird." He raised his head, listening. "Here he comes."

There was the scrape of hooves on stone in the road, one horseman, alone. Lucy turned her head sharply and felt the sword bite deeper. A trickle of blood ran down her neck.

"Methven!" Wilfred had raised his voice. "I am so glad you got my message. I have your woman."

"No—" Lucy began, but Wilfred moved the sword over her breast, to rest against her heart.

Robert walked forward into the circle of the firelight.

He was alone. Immediately four of Wilfred's clansmen surrounded him.

"Ah, Methven," Wilfred said courteously. "Throw down your sword, there's a good fellow." When Robert did not immediately comply, he pressed a little harder against Lucy's breast. Lucy bit her lip hard between her teeth to smother her gasp.

Robert threw down the sword. His gaze never left Lucy's face.

"Good," Wilfred said. He shifted, the sword moving over Lucy's breast like a caress. "There is something you should know, Methven," he said. "Your lovely wife has been betraying you." His sword flicked Lucy's bodice, tearing a gaping rent in it and leaving a long scratch on the white skin of her breast. Lucy caught her breath at the sting.

"Betrayal," Wilfred repeated, smiling a little as he admired his handiwork. "It is so ugly, is it not?"

Lucy's heart was starting to race. She felt sick nausea rise in her throat. She knew Wilfred was reveling in this. When she had bested him by the loch he had been humiliated. This was his revenge.

"I fear," Wilfred said silkily, "that you will get no heirs from your wife's body." Again the sword flicked. There was another tear in the gown now, crossing the first, so that Lucy's bodice fell farther apart and the slivers of material floated to the ground like falling leaves. Looking down, she saw another cut from his sword on her breast. The pain followed a second later. It was sharp and the blood showed red in the firelight.

Wilfred smiled. He gave another flick of the wrist and now her bodice was in tatters, shredded, the gleaming skin of her breasts exposed in the firelight. Robert made an instinctive movement and immediately Wilfred's men pressed closer to hold him back. Lucy raised a hand to cover herself, but Wilfred raised the point of his sword to her throat again.

"Keep still, coz," Wilfred said.

Someone laughed. Lucy saw a pulse beat in Robert's jaw. His muscles were locked with tension. And still he did not speak.

Wilfred's attention had come back to her. "Speaking of betrayals, cousin Lucy," he said softly, "your maid will do anything for a handful of gold. She was the one who sold your secrets to me."

Lucy felt the nausea rise in her throat. She thought of Sheena standing in the bedchamber at the Auld Haa with the pot of pennyroyal in her hand. She felt dizzy with shock and disbelief. Wilfred raised his voice. "Your deceitful wife, Methven, visited the wisewoman to purchase a brew to ensure that she never conceived a child. All the time you were plowing her—" the sword skipped down between Lucy's breasts to point lewdly to the junction of her thighs "—she was ensuring that she would not fall pregnant. Whilst you waited for the good news of an heir, she knew it would never be. She has betrayed you as surely as if she handed your estates to me."

"It wasn't like that." Lucy found her voice. It was

raw from the smoke, pleading. "It was never like that! Robert, I swear—"

Robert ignored her words. He was looking only at Wilfred.

"Let her go, Cardross," he said.

Wilfred laughed. "Lady Lucy comes with me," he said. "I've waited a long time for my sport with her. When I've done I'm sure my men will want their share too." He had taken Lucy's arm now, his fingers biting into the flesh above the elbow. One of his men had come forward to her other side. Lucy reached back a little farther and felt the end of the torch slide into her grasp. The flames scorched her palm, but she gritted her teeth against the pain.

"Come along, coz," Wilfred said. "You won't be so dainty with me by the time I have finished with you." As he jerked Lucy forward, Robert let out a roar. He spun around on the closest of Wilfred's clansmen, knocking him off balance, leaping aside as the other three men piled in on him. He grabbed the fallen man's sword and turned to face his assailants, laying one of them out with the flat of his sword and making short work of a second. In the same moment Lucy brought her arm around in an arc, bringing the flaming torch swinging in to Wilfred's body. Wilfred screamed as the fire caught at his lacy sleeves and burned. He let go of her and ran. She heard the splash as he leaped into Golden Water.

Lucy swung the torch back toward the other man who had been standing foolishly gaping at her, mouth open in shock. He backed off with a yelp and ran, Robert hastening him on his way with a wicked slashing of his blade. Some of the Methven men were coming running now, encircling the pond where Wilfred still splashed and swore, two of them running up to engage Wilfred's remaining clansmen.

Lucy dropped the torch back into the fire. She was shaking so much she could barely stand. Robert had reached her side in two strides. For a brief moment his hands rested on her shoulders as he surveyed Wilfred's handiwork, the slashed bodice, the angry-looking crisscross of cuts on her breast. His expression was flat with murderous fury.

"If you had not set fire to him," Robert said, "I would have killed him myself for what he did to you."

"It's only a scratch," Lucy said. Her teeth were chattering. "It was for show, to humiliate and frighten me."

Robert's hands fell to his side. "You must get back to the house and have it tended," he said.

For a long moment he looked at her, but there was no gentleness or warmth in his gaze. Then he said, very quietly. "I know what Cardross said was true. I saw it in your eyes."

He turned and walked back to where his horse was tethered. Lucy ran after him. Her heart was cracking.

"Robert, wait!" she called. "Please let me explain—"

Robert half turned toward her. He made a sharp gesture and she stopped.

"*Was* it true?" he said. "About the tincture?"

"Yes," Lucy said, "But—"

"And when did you procure it?" His voice was cold, but beneath the anger Lucy could feel pain. She could see it in his eyes too, the searing hurt of betrayal.

"When, Lucy?" His voice was very steady.

"On the morning of our wedding," Lucy said. Her voice was thin, shaking. "But I didn't take it! Please believe me! I never took it!"

Robert shook his head. He looked weary, heart sore. "I thought you trusted me," he said. "I told you that you could. Yet it seems you never believed me."

"It wasn't like that!" Lucy said. "Yes, I trusted you, but—"

She stopped. That one small, betraying word was all it needed because it showed just how little faith she had placed in his word.

"You know how it was for me," she whispered. "I was terrified. I needed to feel safe."

"You were safe," Robert said. "You were always safe with me. The pity of it is that you never trusted me." His voice changed and she knew it was the end. He would accept no justification, no further explanation. Maybe in time he would be prepared to listen, but the lovely, bright and infinitely precious future they had only just started to build lay smashed in pieces at her feet. Lucy was stubborn and determined, but she could not find the words; her throat felt raw and tears smarted in her eyes.

"You must be cold," Robert said. "You have done much for Golden Isle tonight and I am grateful." His chilling politeness felt like another blow. "I will take you back to the Auld Haa and then I must get to the village to help my men."

"Of course," Lucy said stiffly. Her heart cracked a little more. "Do not trouble to take me back—"

"I insist."

He held out a hand to help her mount before him. She could not help a tiny wince of pain as her burned hand touched his. He turned it over so that the palm was cradled in his.

"You're burned," he said.

"It's nothing," Lucy said. "No more than a few blisters."

Robert let her go and she missed the warmth of his touch so badly it pained her more than the burns. They rode in silence down the track and he left her at the gate of the Auld Haa without another word.

CHAPTER TWENTY-ONE

ROBERT WORKED THROUGH the night alongside his men to damp down the fires and make sure that all his people were safe. He did not rest. He did not want to think, did not want to feel. Cardross had been captured and all his men taken. In an even greater feat the privateer Le Boucanier had been captured too, drawn out by Jack, who had used Cardross's yacht to lure him to a rendezvous. The press-gang had swept in and taken the pirate as their prize. It was a rough justice that worked in the islands, so far from the rule of the king's law, but Robert was satisfied with it. Cardross would be tried for treason and Robert's lands were safe.

Eventually, as dawn was breaking over the eastern sea, Jack came up to him, filthy and smelling of smoke, looking, Robert thought, very much as he must look himself. Jack handed him the leather drinking bottle and he gulped down the liquid gratefully, feeling it ease his rough throat.

"You need to rest, Rob," Jack said.

"There's more to do," Robert said tersely.

"And time to do it all," Jack said. "Go. Sleep. Talk to Lucy—"

Robert made an uncontrollable movement and Jack paused, his green eyes steady on his cousin's face.

"Lucy was trying to save Methven for you," Jack said. "You fool, don't you see? Lucy needed to feel safe in order to wed you. She had been through a terrible ordeal when she was too young to be able to deal with it. She was trying to protect herself against anything like that ever happening again. The potion gave her the courage to marry you and help you save Methven from Cardross."

"She should have trusted me," Robert growled.

Jack sighed. He ran his hands through his hair, smearing soot all over his face. "Yes, she should have trusted you," he said, "but at that stage she could not." He looked up. "She could have refused you again, Rob," he said simply. "But she did not. She believed in you and she wanted to save Methven."

Robert glared at his cousin. "You have an interesting way with an argument," he said. "You should have been a lawyer."

Jack grinned. "You know I'm right."

"What I don't know," Robert said, "is how you know all this."

"That deceitful bitch of a maid told me," Jack said. "I think she thought it might help save her miserable hide." His gaze narrowed. "Everyone on Golden Isle loves Lucy for her courage tonight." He sighed. "You love her too. Don't let Cardross ruin it, Rob. Don't let him win."

"You're a brave man," Robert said. "To dare to say this to me."

"Someone had to," Jack said.

Robert rested his forearms on the top of the gate and watched the ripples of dawn light the sea. He was exhausted, bone tired, but deeper than that he felt sick at heart. Jack was right. He loved Lucy so much that to know of her betrayal hurt like a physical blow. It hurt all the more because he had heard his people talking of her courage and the way she had helped them, when all the time she had been prepared to deny them the one thing that they needed to be safe from Cardross, his heir.

He had thought that Lucy trusted him completely and although he understood deep down that this was not about him but all about her terror and her past, he felt cheated and betrayed. All the lovely warm intimacy that had filled the past week was lost, cheapened because all the time she had been deceiving him, knowing that there would be no child. He felt heartsick.

But Jack was right about something else too. If he turned from Lucy now, Cardross would have won in every way that counted. Not only would he have tried to steal Robert's estates, but he would have destroyed his joy and his hope and his love. He would have stolen his future.

Robert straightened and thrust the water bottle back into his cousin's hands. "I don't know why it matters to you," he said.

"Because I would see you happy, you fool," Jack

said, clapping him on the shoulder. "Now get back to the house and find her."

"There's something I have to do first," Robert said.

He crossed the field and walked up the rough path to the estate office. Mercifully it had been untouched by the fire that had swept through the village. In the pale morning light he rummaged through his desk drawer and found the sheets of paper he had secreted there. He read what was written on them. He shook his head ruefully.

Then he set off across the fields to the Auld Haa to find his wife.

LUCY HAD NOT slept. As the first light of dawn slipped through the window, she got up stiffly, pulled out her portmanteaus and started to pack. She did not want to wait for Robert to tell her to leave. She wanted to be ready. Even so, when she heard his step on the stair and saw his tall figure duck beneath the lintel of the bed-chamber, her heart started to race because she had not quite prepared the words she was going to say.

One look at him undermined her completely. He had washed off the worst of the smoke and dirt and sweat, but he still looked rumpled and so tired she wanted to take him in her arms and soothe him to rest. She doubted that such an intervention would be welcome, though. She would do better to sit on her hands than touch him.

He had a battered leather knapsack over one shoulder. He let it slide down and onto the bed. His gaze took in the portmanteaus, the crumpled clothes, her own disheveled appearance.

"Where are you going?" he said.

"Away," Lucy said. There was a big lump in her throat. She was not sure she could say anything else at all.

"Where?" Robert was looking puzzled. She ached to touch him, to reach out to him, to throw herself into his arms.

"To the mainland." How husky her voice sounded. "I don't know. Away. Home. Somewhere."

Now he was looking even more confused. She would have laughed had she not felt so damned miserable. "Why?" he said.

"It's better that I should." Lucy threw the last of the crumpled petticoats into her portmanteaus. "It's best that I go away."

"Best for whom?" Robert said. There was a new note in his voice now, more authoritative, less confused.

"For you," Lucy said. "Of course."

"How very thoughtful of you," Robert said. Then: "I assure you, I should not be the least better off were you to leave me."

Lucy's heart started to slam hard. She looked at him. There was mockery and tenderness in his eyes. It made her heart pound all the harder to see it there.

"Lucy," he said.

She trembled. "I went to the cliff," she said. She spoke quickly, the words tumbling over each other. "I was trying to find the pot of pennyroyal I threw away so that I could prove to you I had not opened it."

His gaze was steady on her. "Did you find it?"

"No," Lucy said. A sob caught in her throat, startling her. "I think it must have fallen into the sea. I am better at throwing than I thought."

She remembered numbly that she had wanted to explain, to tell him that she had never really intended to take it. She had thought that her greatest fear would be if she fell pregnant. Now she realized that her greatest fear had been eclipsed. What she feared most was living without Robert. She could do it, of course. Very likely she was going to have to do it now. But the color and the joy would be gone from her life because she had learned too late that what really mattered was not to live in the shadow of fear but to embrace life. In life there were no certainties, but while there was hope and love and the strength to build something good, that was what mattered.

"I expect they taught you how to throw at the Highland Ladies Bluestocking Society," Robert said. He strode over to the dresser, turned and looked at her. "You don't have to explain, Lucy," he said.

Lucy's heart broke then. He did not want to know. Her intention had been to cheat him of the heir he needed, and even if she had not done it the intent to betray was sufficient.

She could not blame him. He had told her from the first that she could trust him, but she had been unable to believe him.

She sat down on the bed—her legs were trembling too much to stand—and tried to resist the urge to bury her face in one of the shifts and simply cry.

"You have nothing to prove to me." Robert's voice was soft. "If you tell me you did not take the medicine, then I believe you. I trust you. And even if you did, I understand. You were terrified, haunted by the past. I cannot blame you for that." He rubbed his eyes. He looked so weary that her heart ached for him.

"I was angry at first," he said. "I did feel betrayed. It was a shock. But I know that you trust me now, and that is what matters. I know I love you and that you love me too."

For one long, long moment Lucy was quite still and then she threw herself into his arms. They closed about her hard and sure, holding her against his heart.

"You do understand," she said. A button scored her cheek. She could taste her own hot tears.

Robert was stroking her hair in a long tender caress and she reveled in the gentleness of it. "Hush," he said. "It's all right." He picked her up and carried her over to the bed, sitting down with her on his knee. He brushed the hair away from her hot, wet face and kissed her soothingly, as though she were a small child in need of comfort. Gradually her shaking ceased and the fierce dread inside her eased.

"I have something to tell you, Lucy," Robert said. He looked around at the open chest, the piles of clothes and the battered portmanteaus. His blue gaze touched her like a caress. The heat trapped in his eyes was enough to burn her down.

"You always said I was no poet," he said. "That I was too blunt and unscholarly to be poetic. Well, hear this. If you leave me I will be in pieces. Shattered. You are my perfect ideal, Lucy. Once upon a time I was foolish enough to think no such thing existed. Well, I have learned better now."

Despite herself Lucy gave a snort of laughter. "Perhaps I was wrong," she said. "Perhaps you do have the makings of a poet after all."

Robert did not smile in response. Instead he reached for the knapsack and opened the battered leather flap, tipping the contents out onto the bedcover. "Is this romantic enough for you?" he asked. "If not I shall go away and try again."

Lucy stared at the crumpled piles of paper. Each one looked as though it had been screwed up into a ball by a bad-tempered hand. "What on earth—" she began.

"Look at them," Robert said.

She unfolded the first sheet and smoothed it out. It contained a couple of lines of writing, disjointed words, some underscored, others crossed out. The second sheet was the same, and the third. Lines scribbled, repeated, crossed through, then finally discarded.

"Robert." She put the paper down slowly. "You wrote this yourself? For me?"

He looked part proud, part shamefaced, like a schoolboy. "It's not very good, I'm afraid."

It was not.

THE LADY AND THE LAIRD

"My love is like a cloud of rain that lightly falls upon the plain..." She spluttered with laughter and tried to turn it into a cough.

"My love for you is tender and true..."

"You copied that one from somewhere else," Lucy said. "I have heard it before." She was trying to stop the smile that was tilting her lips, but it burst out, defiant. "But you *tried*," she said. "That is what counts." She could feel tears roughening her throat again. "Oh, Robert!" She looked at him through eyes made brilliant with unshed tears. "You really do love me if you are prepared to do this for me."

He took her hands. "I'd do far more than write poetry to prove how much I love you, Lucy." He gave her fingers a tiny squeeze. "You do understand?"

She did. She could imagine him swearing at the ink stains on his fingers; she could see him sitting at his desk in the estate office this past week with his head in his hands after discarding the tenth sheet of paper.

"I love you too," she said. "So very much."

He drew her back into his arms and kissed her hair. "If it's too soon," he said, his voice a little rough, "if you still feel afraid to have a child, we can wait. I am prepared to go to the courts and argue my case—"

Lucy pressed her fingers to his lips. "I'm ready," she whispered. "I don't want to go back. And who knows..." She smiled, hope radiant and bright in her heart. "I may already be carrying your child."

With one movement Robert pushed the portmanteau off the bed. It fell with a crash, spilling its contents

across the rush mat. As Lucy opened her mouth to protest, he kissed her deeply, bearing her back against the
yielding pillows. His fingers strayed to the buttons of
her bodice. One popped open, then a second.

"Just in case you are not," he said, "shall we try
again?"

EPILOGUE

Methven Castle, September 21, 1813

LUCY WROTE THE DATE at the top of the page and paused in thought, tapping her pen against her lips. A letter such as this was going to be difficult to phrase correctly. It required a great deal of thought.

Her gaze slid to the window. It was too beautiful a day to be indoors. The glen dozed in a misty golden glow and the high mountains were etched against a sky of perfect blue.

On the terrace below, Lucy could see the Dowager Marchioness of Methven sitting surrounded by dogs, looking out across the topiary garden to the mountains beyond. Lucy suspected that she was asleep, although Lady Methven would most certainly deny that she was any such thing. As Robert had predicted, his grandmother most heartily approved of his wife. He had told her so only the other day.

"Grandmama is a frightfully high stickler," he had said. "It is very hard to earn her approval."

Lucy had not contradicted him, but she had not agreed. In her opinion it was very easy to please the dowager, who had taken one look at her, realized that she was utterly in love with Robert and had therefore taken her to her heart. It was a very soft heart underneath that starchy exterior.

The dogs set up an excited barking and Lucy saw that Robert was walking along the terrace toward his grandmother, carrying in his arms the four-month-old heir to Methven. James Gregor Methven was blissfully and silently asleep. Lucy watched with amusement as Robert handed the small bundle to the dowager with care and concentration. As though aware of her scrutiny, he looked up at the window and raised a hand. A moment later she heard his step on the stair and he came into her study. He smelled of sunshine and fresh air and he rested a hand on the back of her chair and bent down to kiss her with satisfactory thoroughness.

"How does your writing progress?" he asked.

"I can't find the words," Lucy said.

Robert smiled at her, a wicked smile that made her blush. "Do you need any help with your research?"

"It's not that sort of letter," Lucy said, reproving. She laid down her quill with a little sigh. "I am writing to Lachlan to congratulate him on Dulcibella's inheritance of the Cardross estates."

Robert threw himself down in the little armchair beside her desk. The noise he made sounded like a cross between a growl and an humph. Lucy bit her lip, trying not to smile at his grumpy expression.

When Wilfred Cardross had been found guilty of

treason the month before, the king had graciously seen fit to award his estates to Dulcibella, Wilfred's closest living relative. Lachlan and his runaway bride were now richly rewarded. Fortunately at the same time the king had equally graciously canceled the fifteenth-century treaty allowing the lairds of Cardross to claim back Methven land. And since Robert now had an heir anyway, he really had very little to complain about. Even so, Lucy was tempted to tease him.

"What a pity you did not wed Dulcibella in the first place," she said innocently. "If only you had, the Cardross and the Methven land would all be yours now."

Robert's glittering blue gaze came up and fixed on her. There was a light in it that made her heart start to race.

"And whose fault was that, madam?" he demanded.

"I believe it was mine," Lucy admitted. She looked at him under her lashes. "I have said I am sorry."

"Not good enough." With one sudden movement Robert came to his feet and grabbed her, sending the chair toppling backward and the blank sheet of paper sailing to the floor. He picked her up in his arms and strode through the door to the bedroom beyond, tossing her down on the bed.

"You owe me," he murmured, his lips brushing her ear. "You owe me a very great deal."

"Robert!" Lucy squeaked as her husband started to ruthlessly relieve her of her clothes. "You cannot do this. It is broad daylight and your grandmother is downstairs and—" She stopped as Robert kissed her, a very long, very sweet kiss.

"You were saying?" he murmured as he nibbled wickedly at her throat.

I forget," Lucy said. The room was full of sunshine and her mind was full of light and she felt him move over her and into her with such infinite gentleness. She nipped his shoulder with her teeth to encourage him. He had been treating her like spun glass since he had come back to her bed, but in the past week or so she had tired of such delicate handling.

She smiled secretly to herself. When she had found she was pregnant with James she had been understandably anxious. Robert had broken with convention and scandalized society into the bargain by staying with her throughout the entire labour in order to reassure her. If she had loved him before it was nothing to how much she loved him now.

She pulled him closer, wrapping her legs around him and tilting her hips up and heard him groan as the gentleness took on a most satisfying edge of urgency. The pleasure caught them both and they lay entangled, the sun patterning their bodies, the only sound in the world their breathing and the faint voices of the dowager and little James's nursemaid floating up from the terrace below.

"So," Lucy said, turning her head to look at her husband, "do you think you can forgive me?"

Robert smiled. "On reflection," he said, "I think I do prefer matters as they are. I have no need of the

Cardross estates. I have Methven and I have James and I have you." He kissed her. "I have all that I want in the world."

* * * * *